Ivory White

HOUSE OF MISFITS

CAMBRIA HEBERT

Published by Cambria Hebert
http://www.cambriahebert.com

Interior design and typesetting by Classic Interior Design
Cover design by Cover Me Darling
Edited by Cassie McCown

Once upon a time...

There is a girl with skin as fair as ivory and hair as black as night.
She was the apple of her father's eye, but now that he has died,
someone wants to dip that apple into poison.
Advised to flee, Ivory escapes her elite world in New York City
and stumbles into a place she didn't know existed.
A modern-day princess, afraid and lost on the dark streets, running for her life.
Ivory White has no one to call, nowhere to turn.
All she has is a random number scrawled on a torn napkin.
She calls. He answers.
Ivory is thrust into a house filled with misfits—
a band of completely untrustworthy men.
But can this group of men keep her safe?

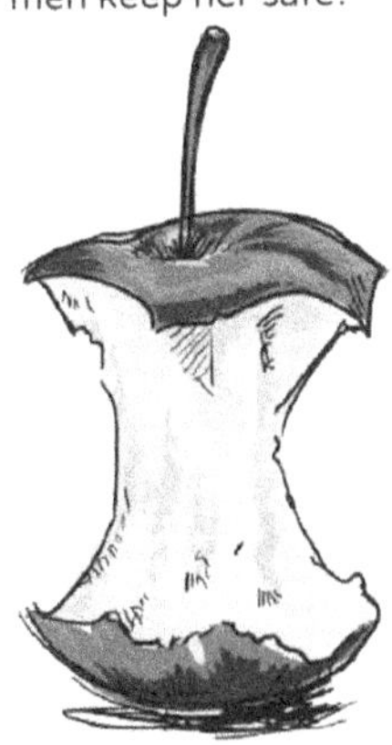

Ivory White

HOUSE OF MISFITS

CAMBRIA HEBERT

Once upon a time…

a baby is born, so pure and privileged she could only be named Ivory White.

Everything is perfect… until all hell breaks loose.

Prologue

HUNTSMAN

"I WANT IT DONE. QUIETLY. QUICKLY. NOW." THE VOICE ON the line was smooth and calculating. Malice saturated every calm syllable.

These were the most dangerous people. The ones who ordered murder like they did takeout.

Greed was an affliction, and it seemed people who already had too much were cursed with it. It was never enough. Some people always wanted more.

That's why they came to me.

I got my hands dirty so they didn't have to. Blood washed off just as easily as anything else.

"Do you hear me?" The voice spoke again, the whiplike tongue lashing out because I took too long to reply.

From across the street, I watched my target, the one whose death was being ordered like a pizza.

I made a sound into the line.

"I'll be waiting." The line clicked off, and I continued to hold the phone to my ear even though no one was there.

I stared a bit longer before finally lowering the cell.

This was a simple job. Easy money.

Yet for the first time in my entire career, I hesitated.

One

Ivory

I BEGAN EVERY MORNING HERE IN THE FOREST THAT GREW within the city. Trees twisted and tangled up toward the sky. The avocado-colored grass and large rock formations were a perfect contrast to the high-rise buildings crowding the space just across the street.

My feet were light on the path, barely making a sound as I jogged my way along the familiar route. There were other people out jogging and enjoying the quiet before the city awoke entirely.

I ignored them.

I was here for me and me alone. This was my time. The only time I truly ever got for myself. As soon as I slid back into the black car waiting for me on the other side of the park, my day would be gobbled up by everything and everyone.

Nearby, a squirrel ran across the path and leaped onto the side of a wide tree. Wind that could almost be considered cold kicked up, blowing the designer jacket I wore against my frame.

Suddenly, the sun, which had only just risen, was swallowed by a large, dark cloud, shrouding the park in shadows. Gazing up, I noted the moon still hovering. Only half of it was visible. It seemed ominous, as if the reason the sun suddenly disappeared was that the moon didn't want to give up the sky.

A cold feeling crawled up my spine despite the warmth of my body from exercise. With the sun hidden and the moon staring, my sacred alone time suddenly felt more like the beginning of some creepy movie.

Up ahead, the tunnel under the bridge I always jogged through seemed menacing. A small light flickered on within and glowed orange, making the space seem haunted.

Wow.

My imagination was severely out to play this morning. Perhaps this was a sign that I would have a good day at work. Hopefully, the creativity kept flowing. Hopefully, it would be less… chilling.

I almost veered around the jack-o'-lantern-like tunnel this morning but stopped myself. Why should I deviate from what I liked to do? I had run here daily for years. Nothing bad was going to happen. No one would dare—

Oomph.

A heavy, violent hand slammed down on my back, making me trip and stumble midstride.

Panic clawed at my throat, and a shrill sound escaped me, causing even more pain in my neck. Trying to right myself, I failed because I was lifted off my feet completely, my body hefted into someone solid and much larger.

I started to kick and scream, and at that very moment, a sweaty palm slapped over the lower half of my face and the kicks I launched were successfully evaded.

The hammering of my heart was so fierce that pain pierced my chest, threatening to split my ribcage in two. Above the hand, my nostrils flared, and I tried to scream even though it was muffled.

My body hit the concrete wall like a rag doll, my cheek

bouncing off the rough, cold side before my body rebounded like it hit rubber and not something unforgiving.

The body shoved in, slamming me back against the wall, pinning me there ruthlessly so I couldn't move or run away.

My lips parted, and a scream unlike anything ever released before formed inside me. The flash of a silver blade caused pain, not because it cut through my delicate flesh, but because it effectively stopped the forceful yell in my throat.

"I don't have any money," I croaked, my normally cool, even voice unrecognizable. "But if you let me go, I'll get it and give it all to you."

He shoved me even harder into the wall, and the same sore spot on my cheek that hit earlier scraped again. "I'm not here for your money," a low, foreign voice intoned.

I tried and failed to crane my head around. *Where the hell is my bodyguard?* He always ran a little ways behind me so I didn't feel crowded, but he should have been here by now. He should have been doing something about this!

"Wh-what do you want?" I wheezed.

"Your life."

I caught a barely there glimpse of myself in the shining blade the man brandished. My skin, which was usually white as snow, was now translucent. A blue vein ran down my forehead and across my cheek like some sick scar. My lips were also colorless, my eyes wide with fright.

Like a living corpse. Like this man had indeed already started sucking the life out of me.

"No," I begged, the plea falling from my lips without thought. I'd never begged for anything in my entire life.

But I would now.

The flickering orange faded out, and darkness converged. The only light was from the ends of the tunnel, and it was dim at best.

"Please," I whimpered, somehow managing to get my arm

free from between myself and the wall. When my icy fingers closed around the thick, warm wrist that wielded the knife, I was shocked.

He didn't even seem threatened by me. In fact, the beating of his heart was even against my back. His breathing wasn't heavy. He was utterly calm. So in control that me grabbing the hand holding his murder weapon didn't even shake him.

The power in his body, in his wrist alone, outweighed mine tenfold.

My fingers shook and fought for the strength he already had.

I was going to die.

Here, just blocks from my impressive apartment, in the middle of a peaceful forest that had suddenly turned menacing.

I had only one thought. One single thought as the knife lifted, promising pain. My life was filled with so much, but in death, only one thing remained.

"Daddy," I whispered.

The sound of the blade cutting through the air, so sharp it practically whistled, made me cower against the cold wall, anticipating pain. Violently, my head was forced back, my scalp screaming as my eyes watered, blinking up at the darkness overhead.

Swipe. It was a sound, not a feeling, and suddenly, my head was released, making me stumble sideways.

"Get out of here. Run away and don't come back."

"Wh-wh—" I started to turn toward my attacker but was roughly shoved again.

"Agh," I cried, falling sideways. My hand caught the brunt of my fall, and pain exploded up my arm instantly. "*Ah!*" I gasped, falling onto my side, cradling my hand.

Squinting down, I noted that my perfectly manicured,

nails were scuffed, one of them broken and barely hanging on.

"My nails!" I gasped, suddenly indignant. "What the hell?"

Out of nowhere, anger rose up, pushing away the worst of my fear. I started to lunge toward the man.

Slam.

I cried out when I was pinned to the ground, his heavy body like an anvil in the center of my back. My throbbing hand pounded on the ground beside me as I struggled to get up.

Strands of hair rubbed over my cheek and neck, making me pause.

"Don't push me," the man growled. "I'm giving you this one chance. Take it and go, or die right here."

I sucked in a breath.

"I'll go."

"Don't come back. Trust no one."

"But I—"

Snap!

I screamed in agony, and he cursed, standing up off my body. The pain was actually blinding for a moment. At first, I thought he'd stabbed me after all, but as I writhed, I realized all he'd done was rip the fingernail off my hand.

Blood dripped down my finger, spreading across my palm.

Scrambling up, I staggered away, feeling his presence but too afraid to turn back.

Cradling my hand, I lunged toward the other end of the tunnel, toward the light. Toward people who could help me.

Hair brushed my neck again. Panicked, I reached up… grabbing a handful of air. I reached again.

It was gone… I stopped dead in my tracks. Forgetting my painful digit, I felt all around.

"My hair!" I gasped. "What did you do to my hair?"

"Proof," came the voice from the darkness.

"Proof," I repeated, my voice like a ghost.

"You no longer exist, Ivory White."

He knows my name. That knowledge brought on a whole new level of panic. This wasn't just a mugging. This wasn't just some weird random act of violence.

He really did come here for my life.

He was letting me go.

"Why?" I asked, my voice oddly calm. "Why are you letting me go?" It was dangerous, but I had to ask.

"Consider it a debt I owed your father."

"Daddy," I whispered again.

"But if I ever see you again, you won't walk away."

Gasping, I spun. The newly choppy, uneven strands of my hair flew out around me as I moved.

He was gone.

Light suddenly filled the tunnel, reaching toward my sneakers and filling the park with brightness once more.

Shaken, confused, and radiating with pain, I limped out of the tunnel, stepping into the sun. I felt my eyes squint and blink as if I hadn't seen daylight in years rather than moments.

Up ahead, someone jogged down the path, and I raised my arms to signal for help.

Nearby, a branch snapped, acting as a sharp warning. Alarmed, I folded in on myself.

The sensation of being watched wrapped around me like wild vines reaching up from the ground to hold me in place. Shuddering, I whirled and saw no one…

But I knew he was still there.

Watching.

Waiting.

If I made a mistake, he would slay me.

At the very edge of my vision, a man concealed by all black slithered behind some trees.

Trust no one.

Frightened and confused, with his words echoing in the back of my scattered mind, I fled.

Two

Ivory

So many people are going to get fired for this! I promised myself as I rushed down yet another dark, unknown street.

The sun had long since set, the moon once again taking over the sky. I was still out here, and the more time that passed, the more confused I became. Cold seeped through the clothes I wore—clothes that were so inappropriate for what I was doing.

Were there even clothes appropriate for running for your life?

I snorted softly. Of course there were. There was an outfit for every occasion.

A sudden sound from behind caused me to shriek and whirl. Black hair whipped around, slapping me in the cheek, making me whimper. Earlier, I'd caught a glimpse of myself in the reflection of a building. It was not good. Not good at all. All my glorious locks were destroyed. Hacked and uneven. Torn roughly from my head by a blade not meant at all for hair.

Tears sprang to my eyes, and I dashed them away. Heart pounding and teeth chattering, I took in the area around me, expecting to see the hunter appear.

There wasn't much to see, though, because it was dark

and none of the streetlights seemed to work here. "What the hell do I pay taxes for?" I muttered, still scanning the area around me but finding nothing.

Seeing nothing didn't make me feel better. In fact, it only made my anxiety grow. Just because I couldn't see a creeper creeping didn't mean he wasn't there. I was being followed. Watched.

Hunted.

I might not see it... but I could *feel* it.

A bitter wind kicked up from the side, pushing all my hair into my face and tangling the now-short strands like unruly vines.

I nearly tripped over my untied shoelace as I hustled farther down the sidewalk, but I didn't stop to fix the issue. You didn't bother turning on the alarm when the house was already on fire.

Tugging my hand into my chest a little farther, I adjusted the makeshift bandage I had wrapped around my bloody hand. My nail-less finger still ached and stung, but the bleeding had stopped awhile ago. Probably because the sock I was using as a bandage had clotted up, dried, and was now stuck to the torn flesh.

It seemed nearly impossible that this was happening right now. I had never in all my twenty-three years experienced anything even close to this. Attacked. Nearly murdered. Hair chopped off, fingernail ripped away. Threatened. Forced to use my sock—my freaking sock!—as a bandage. I had no money, no cell, no identification, and my feet had blisters from running around the city all day. So many times, I almost gave up and called someone to come get me. All I would have to do was snap my fingers and it would be done.

But I didn't.

I was too scared. Confused. I needed to think.

How could I think when I was stumbling around, lost in the dark, without any safety at all?

At the end of the block, lights illuminated the sidewalk and music spilled out from a building. Even though the music was terrible, it was still a welcome sound. It meant I wasn't alone. It meant maybe there was a safe haven within reach.

I was in a part of the city I'd never even known existed. Everything was foreign here, as if I'd fled to another country instead of to the other side of the place where I'd always lived. I always knew there was a difference from one end of town to the other, but this? I could barely process it all.

Something shifted in the alley I rushed past, making me squeal and run a little faster. Again, I almost tripped and fell, but this time, I caught myself on the side of the building I'd been trying to reach.

The already loud music grew louder when the door to the place shoved open and a few people stumbled out. They were laughing and unkempt.

When they turned to glance at me, my body froze. I felt as if a spotlight had been shone on me and any minute they would yell, *Ivory White, is that you?*

That didn't happen. Instead, the people turned back to their laughter and good times and went in the opposite direction.

Still, the uncomfortable feeling of being seen sent me reeling.

Trust no one.

Reaching up, lifting the hood on my jacket, I tucked it around me, concealing my badly chopped hair and tired, pale face. Since the sun had gone down, I hadn't bothered with the hood. My black hair blended in with the night anyway. But if I was going inside, this hood would offer the only protection I had right now.

Pushing off the brick wall—I *really* wished I had some hand sanitizer—I moved past the long row of wide windows lined on the inside with colorful string lights that probably stayed up year round. It was a bar. And it was packed.

The perfect place to hide.

Without a second thought, I slipped inside, glancing behind me because it was a compulsive urge I couldn't deny. My nose wrinkled at the putrid odor of beer and sweat as I tucked my injured, sock-covered hand into my pocket and pushed on, weaving through the people crowding around tables and standing in places they probably weren't even supposed to stand. A long bar ran along the back wall, and I headed in that direction.

I could borrow their phone. No. I couldn't. I didn't know who to call. Who to trust.

Suddenly, I was overwhelmed by this predicament. This had never happened to me before. I'd never not known what to do. It was so confusing my head nearly swam with despair.

The song changed over to something even louder and more horrible than the last. Swaying on my feet, I reached out to steady myself.

A hand closed over my shoulder, and I jolted. "Get your hand off of me!" My voice was cool and steady, the complete opposite of how I actually felt.

"You first."

Personally affronted, I glanced down to where a very large and dirty hand cupped my shoulder. My eyes followed the hand to the wrist and trailed up the arm, which was covered in plaid.

It was not an attractive plaid.

My eyes spoke when my voice did not. *What did you just say to me?*

A set of bottom-heavy lips tilted up in one corner, and as they moved, they pulled along a five-o'clock shadowed jawline with it. This unshaven, plaid-wearing person who was man-handling me didn't speak either. Instead, his very dark eyes pointedly looked down at his shoulder.

I gasped and nearly fell over when I jerked away from him. *Oh my God, I was touching him!*

The hand that had been clasped around my shoulder curled around my waist, its presence the only reason I didn't fall completely.

His touch was warm and felt so wide at the small of my back. The heat from his palm seeped through the thin fabric of my top, and the skin at my waist tingled.

"Let go!" I snapped, straightening away. "What part of don't touch me do you not understand?"

A dark, fluffy brow arched. "You touched me first."

His eyes were incredibly dark. Not deep brown. Onyx. Like a night sky without stars. Still, though, the sky in his eyes glittered.

Right now, they glittered with humor.

Was he laughing at me?

Snapping up to my full height, I delivered a disdainful look. "I nearly slipped on this… this filthy floor, and you got in the way of me reaching for the counter."

Sweeping his gaze down to the floor, he stared as if trying to see the filth I pointed out. "Looks to me like you nearly tripped on your own shoelaces." His eyes flicked back to my face.

The entrance to the bar opened, a cold wind blew in, and the bell I hadn't even noticed before rang, signaling someone's arrival. Forgetting about the man trying to argue with me, I spun to see who had come in. If it was the man who was after me…

Would I even know him if I saw him?

A couple smiled and waved to another couple already seated at a nearby table.

Sagging in relief, I nearly fell over again.

"Whoa." That same warm hand caught me around the waist again.

"I said don't touch me," I hissed.

I expected him to remove his hands immediately. He didn't.

"Stop falling over, and I wouldn't have to."

I gasped as he directed me to a nearby barstool. Once I was seated, he pulled his hand away, plopping down on the seat adjacent to mine.

"Can I buy you a drink?"

"I didn't come here to drink,"

"Why else would you come to a bar?"

I ignored him.

It was a blissful two seconds until two intrusive fingers curled around the edge of my hood and tugged slightly.

Jolting away, I knocked into the person sitting on the other side of me, but I didn't apologize. How could I? I was too busy defending myself against this plaid-wearing pirate.

Did I mention he totally looked like a pirate? Dark and smooth with eyes that held secrets.

"Stop that," I scolded, smacking his hand away.

"Why are you wearing that?" he asked as though he didn't even notice how much I wanted him to get away from me. Leaning back in, he said, "Are you hiding?"

I stiffened, and my injured hand curled into a tight fist in my pocket.

"Are you meeting someone?"

This time, it was me who peeled back the edge of the hood so he could feel the full weight of my sidelong glance.

He held up his hands in surrender.

The bell over the door jingled again, and I disregarded him completely. A couple of men walked in, one of them in a dark coat, and the hairs on my arms lifted. Forcing my outward appearance to remain unruffled and calm, from beneath the hood, I watched him covertly while my insides pretty much cartwheeled around inside me.

My fingers were shaking so much I tucked them under the backs of my thighs, sitting on them to keep them still. The pressure made my injured fingertip sting with renewed pain, but I didn't pull back. I embraced the pain to remind myself I had to be on the lookout.

The men joined a table across the room, and then the shady-looking one's eyes glanced in my direction.

Stiffening, I spun on the stool, putting my back to him as I slinked deeper into the hood.

Staring at the rows of liquor lining the wall, I also noted the neon signs all over the place. On all the walls, there was wild, colorful paint without any kind of order or design. It reminded me of something... something I couldn't quite place. It was hard to think right now.

One of the signs was on the fritz, and it was buzzing and blinking like it was waiting for the perfect moment to go out. I wished it would. The bright strobing was making me dizzy.

A brown bottle plunked down in front of me, and I blinked.

"Since you aren't meeting anyone else, you can have a drink with me," the persistent pirate declared.

I gestured to the bottle. "This is your idea of a drink?"

"You want something else?"

The bartender moved past, and I called out, "Excuse me. Can I please have a bottle of Perrier?"

"Perry what?" the man asked, glowering at me.

"Perrier," I pronounced. "Sparkling water..." I said as if it were obvious.

"I don't serve water at my bar."

"That's bad customer service," I informed him. "You should always have what a customer might request."

Both his hands slapped onto the bar top, making me jump. As he leaned closer, I got a hearty look at his Asian features and hair that hadn't been combed for probably a week. Shame. He might have been good-looking if he didn't appear to be constipated and in need of moisturizer. "You haven't bought anything, so you aren't a customer."

"Well, I tried to buy some water." I reminded him.

"No one buys water at The Rotten Apple."

"Ew." I pursed my lips. "With a name like that, I'm surprised anyone buys anything at all."

A growl vibrated the back of the bartender's throat, and he leaned even closer. Normally, I wouldn't have budged an inch. Men didn't scare me. No one did.

Until now. Until earlier today.

Do not show your fear! a voice inside me insisted.

Instead of shifting back, I held still and lifted my chin, meeting his challenging gaze.

"Back off, E," the guy beside me said, shoving the bartender back to his side of the bar.

"Water," *E* barked, offended. "Fancy water."

"I'm dehydrated," I said, realizing I hadn't had anything to eat or drink all day.

No wonder I was dizzy.

"Just get her a water, huh?" The man beside me cajoled. He had a nice voice, and I couldn't help but look at him. He saw me looking and smiled. There was a dimple in his cheek. "That's just his personality."

"They have medicines for that," I informed.

A glass of water was roughly slammed down in front of me. The liquid splashed over the top, splattering the bar top and discarded peanut shells littering the area.

The glass had a smudge on the side.

There was no ice.

I was pretty sure he'd just gotten that out of the tap. And

by out of the tap, I mean from the spigot in the sink under the bar.

My stomach heaved.

"Earth!" someone yelled from down the bar.

The bartender gave me a look he probably thought would scare me.

I smiled sweetly.

When he was gone, I glanced around the room again, focusing on the door.

"Everything okay?"

My eyes went back to the man beside me. "Fine."

"I haven't seen you in here before."

"Nor will you ever again."

"Guess I wouldn't want to go back to the place where I was stood up either," he quipped, tilting a bottle to his lips.

I gasped. "I've never been stood up in all my life!"

"First time's the worst."

I gasped again. "I was not stood up!"

The bell rang out, and I stiffened, swiveling toward the rush of winter air that came in with the patrons.

"Seems to me like you're waiting."

It was a couple. Young. In love. Her scarf didn't match her outfit.

I turned back to the brown bottle and smudged glass of swill sitting before me.

"What's your name?"

I slid a glance out of the corner of my eye. "I'm not telling you."

"I'm Neo," he answered as though I hadn't just rejected him.

I sighed. I'd never met anyone so dense before. "What's it going to take to get you to leave me alone?"

He went silent, and frankly, that made me worry. Curious, I peeked around the hood to see him scrawling something on a scrap of paper. Finishing his writing far quicker than I anticipated, he glanced up, his dark stare colliding with mine.

The smirk that glittered in his eyes made my back teeth slam together. If we were anywhere else, under any other circumstances, I would eat this man for breakfast. He would rue the day we met.

But we were sitting inside a rotten apple. He was the worm living there...

"Here," he said, holding out the wrinkled scrap he'd just scrawled on.

I stared at it dubiously. "What is that?"

"My number. That way when you regret rejecting me later, you can call."

I scoffed. "I can assure you I won't call."

"You might. I'm pretty irresistible."

My eyes flashed up at the smooth humor I heard in his voice. He was smiling. His eyes were amused, and the dimples in his cheeks were both on full display.

A funny feeling wriggled around inside me, and I pressed my hand to my midsection.

"Everything okay?" he asked, his brows coming together.

"Fine. I just haven't eaten in a while."

"Want to get some—"

"No." I cut him off and snatched the number out of his hand, hoping he would now leave me alone.

"Next time," he said.

He must be a professional at getting rejected. He acted like it didn't even bother him.

My head was pounding, and the world was turning slightly blurry. Inside my pocket, my finger started to throb more than ever.

"Better put that away before you lose it." He gestured to the paper I still held. Actually, it wasn't a paper. It was a ripped piece of napkin, and I passed it into my pocket with my injured, sock-covered finger.

"Now leave me alone," I announced like our deal was complete.

Someone jostled into me from behind, slamming into my back hard enough that the stool I was perched on pitched forward. My hands flung out and a strangled sound ripped from my throat, but there was nothing to catch myself on. The sound of the wood clattering against the floor made me wince, and I waited for the pain to radiate through my already fatigued limbs.

No pain came.

There was only warmth.

Warmth and a weird sensation of safety… something I hadn't felt at all the entire day.

Instinctively, I curled my hands around that feeling and tried to pull it closer. What I got was a handful of red and black plaid.

When I jolted in shock, the hands holding my back were forced to tighten, and my body was tugged farther into his lap.

"What are you doing!" I shrieked, slapping at his very wide shoulders.

"Keeping you from hitting the floor. A place you seem to keep wanting to go."

"Put me down!" I demanded, smacking him again.

He smelled good. Actually, no. He was probably smelly, just less smelly than the rest of this place.

Brr-bring!

Over Neo's shoulder, I caught the flash of black the second the bell rang. I went still, slinking down a little to use his body to hide mine.

It was a man with shady vibes, dressed head to toe in black with a black ball cap pulled low over his face. Even though his eyes were shadowed, I could tell he searched the room for something, for someone.

If I ever see you again, you won't walk away. The chilling words of the hunter in the forest haunted me.

My stomach tightened, and my breath caught. He was looking for me. He was here for me…

"Change your mind?"

The rumbly voice was so close to my ear, my head popped up. Neo had to tilt his face back to look down at me.

Our eyes met, and there were a few beats of absolute silence between us before I whispered, "What?"

"I thought you wanted me to put you down."

Following his gaze, I realized what he was alluding to and almost died. The urge to leap away from him was strong. But the urge to stay hidden against him was stronger.

My fingers gripped the front of his shirt so tight I knew when I let go, the fabric would be wrinkled. My body hunched into his, and my head ducked against his shoulder so close the fabric of his shirt brushed my cheek.

The fabric was soft, much more pleasant than it appeared.

"One minute, please," I requested, peeking over his shoulder again to look for the stalker.

He was gone.

Confused, I sat up, glancing all around the bar.

Had he left? Had he not seen me and moved on?

Relief so strong washed through me. With a sigh, I collapsed. I was exhausted. My feet hurt. I was cold, my face needed to be washed, my hair needed help, and my fingernail… Well, I didn't know what to do about that. And also, I really, really wanted a decent glass of water.

Fatigue seemed to be the most pressing of all my problems because my eyes drifted closed for long moments.

"I was going to say I was sorry… but it looks like I don't need to."

The new voice intruded on the relief I'd so badly needed. Reality came crashing back. My eyes popped open, head snapped up.

Two sets of eyes stared at me.

I looked first at the set I'd never seen before and then quickly at the pair belonging to the man whose lap I was still sitting in.

Oh my God, I was still sitting in his lap!

Scrambling up, I stood with the bar at my back and the two men watching me as though they'd never seen a woman before.

"You," I said, jabbing a finger at the newcomer. "You pushed over my chair?"

His already round eyes went rounder, and his head bobbed. His cheeks were slightly chubby even though he was on the small side. The brown hair on his head was unruly, too long, and needed some serious conditioner.

He bounced from one foot to the other, and suddenly, all I could think was that he looked like a giant puppy. "It was an accident."

"I could have been seriously hurt!"

"Good thing Neo was there to catch you." He smiled, and it made him look dopey and goofy.

"It was fate." Neo grinned, spreading his hands wide as if he'd just won the lottery.

An entire day's worth of pain, fear, and exhaustion seemed to explode out of me all at once. "As if someone like you would ever be my fate!" I hissed coldly. "Just being in the same room with you, breathing the same air, is toxic to me."

"Whoa," the little one said.

Saying nothing, Neo leaned toward me, and yes, I admit I flinched. But he didn't touch me. Instead, he snagged the beer bottle he'd set in front of me and lifted it to his lips, silently staring with those endlessly dark eyes while his throat worked to swallow that swill.

The label on the bottle peeked out from between his fingers. *Rotten Apple: Poisoning Guaranteed.*

I recoiled.

His lips were slick when he finally pulled the bottle away. The tip of his tongue slipped out to grab some of the glistening moisture on his lower lip.

"Door's over there," he said, pointing somewhere behind me, but his eyes never left mine.

A pang of guilt assailed me. I had better manners than this.

Now wasn't the time for manners.

I broke our eye contact first, rotating to find the door he pointed at. It was a side door and probably led out into some seedy alley.

I started toward it, wondering for the millionth time tonight what I was going to do, and fresh, hot tears pricked the backs of my eyes.

I should just go home. There was nowhere else to go. To hide.

"Hey!" a deep voice shouted from behind, and for the second time that day, a large, heavy hand slammed down on my shoulder.

Three

Neo

She looked like someone who'd just stepped out of a storybook. Nothing about her belonged here in my world.

Even though her clothes were casual, they were far too upscale for this place. The fabric was delicate and soft just like her limbs and the way she walked. Her round blue eyes scoured every inch of the place as though she had never been anywhere like this before.

And the hood. The royal-blue hood pulled up over her head was like a cloak, shrouding her in mystery and concealing so much more than just her features.

When I finally got a glimpse of her creamy white skin, I had to force myself not to react. She didn't look like anyone from my world either. Not her heart-shaped face, perfectly formed chin, or red-rose lips formed in a bow. A few strands of hair so dark lay against her cheek, and I could only think of black velvet.

That mouth, though. The standoffish, almost haughty way she looked at me, it didn't really match. Like the storybook she stepped out of had a beautiful cover and artwork, but the interior words were aggressive and messy.

She's scared.

It became more and more apparent the longer I sat beside

her. She felt backed into a corner, into this bar, which was clearly out of her comfort zone. I understood that. I could even make allowances for her aloof, unfriendly behavior.

I was interested. Definitely intrigued.

Intrigued as I was, though, I wouldn't be insulted.

"Door's over there." I directed, watching every nuance in her expression. She was the kind of book you had to read between the lines. You had to infer what the words didn't say to really understand.

An inkling of regret shone behind her eyes. For a split second, I thought those bow-shaped lips would part and an apology might spill out. Instead, her gaze pulled away, and even though weariness clung to her more heavily than that hood draped over her head, she straightened and turned.

With her hand tucked into her pocket, she started toward the door. The set of her shoulders bothered me. They were proud and straight, but they also seemed to strain to remain that way. As if they were struggling under the weight of whatever stress she carried.

Whatever I might have done was interrupted immediately by a man rising off his barstool. He moved so quickly it fell back, cracking off the floor with a sharp bang.

"Hey!" he roared, clapping his hand down on the narrow shoulder of the retreating girl.

Her body sagged, then jackknifed up. A shriek peeled out of her throat as she jolted away, spinning with wide, fearful eyes.

I stood immediately, abandoning the beer I'd been leisurely chugging.

"Give it back!" the man spat, his words slightly slurred.

"What?" she asked, gazing at him nervously.

The hand still stuffed in her pocket shook under the fabric.

"You took my wallet, and I want it back!"

"I would never!" She gasped, horror overtaking the fear on her face.

"Listen here, you little liar." The man took a menacing step toward her.

She shifted back, but the voice that emanated out of the hood was cool and authoritative. "How dare you imply that I am lying? Lying is beneath me."

Amusement made my lips purse.

"But stealing isn't."

"This is ridiculous," she muttered and turned to go.

His hand was seemingly very large when it wrapped around her upper arm to jerk her back. She cried out, and the hand that had been hidden in her pocket flung out. She had some sort of bandage wrapped around her fingers.

"Let go! Please!" Her voice was strained.

I took a step forward.

"What's going on here?" A new voice entered the mix.

Fig.

Just great.

Officer Paul Fig, of course, would be here. And of course he would see it as his duty to "keep the peace" even while he was off duty.

"This wench just stole my wallet right out of my pocket!" The drunken man accused.

She gasped again.

Fig looked between the two and pursed his lips. "Ma'am, did you take this man's wallet?"

"No!"

"Check her pockets, then!"

"My word should be enough," she declared.

Everyone within earshot laughed. She definitely wasn't from around here.

Fig stepped closer. "Empty your pockets, ma'am."

She was utterly still for long moments as if she couldn't believe he actually wanted to check her pockets.

The drunk man was impatient and lunged like he would do it for her. She leaped back, knocking into a nearby table and lifting her arms to protect herself from whatever he was about to do.

I frowned.

"I'll handle this," Fig said, inserting himself between the girl and the drunkard.

"Your pockets," the officer said again.

Straightening, she let out a wobbly sigh and reached into her pocket. "There's nothing," she declared.

Fig gestured to the other one.

The hand without the weird wrapping slipped in. Everything about her changed. Her body nearly screamed with tension like she was a live wire about to explode.

"Ma'am." Fig pressed.

Slowly, her hand withdrew. The flash of a money clip caught my eye.

"Ah-ha!" the drunk man wailed. "I knew it! That wench is nothing but a thief!"

Her head was bowed, totally concealed by the hood she wore. Any facial expression was hidden by the shadow of the cloak. Everything about her screamed out in heavy confusion as she stared down at the clip lying against her very pale, very delicate-looking palm.

"But I didn't take this," she said, astonishment pitching her voice higher.

"I want her arrested. I'm pressing charges!"

She gasped, and her chin flew up. Some of her deathly white skin flashed. "No! Here!" She tossed the clip back like it was infected with an incurable disease and turned to flee.

The money clip slapped against the floor, and the drunk man bellowed in protest. "Get her!"

Fig lunged, capturing her arms from behind and towing her back. "You really want to press charges?"

"Abso-fuckin-lutely."

Beside me, Fletch shifted from foot to foot. Nervous energy spilled off him. I glanced his way, then back at the unfolding drama.

"I didn't do it!"

"It was in your pocket, ma'am. We all witnessed it," Fig said as though he were a true professional.

He wasn't.

"Then someone else put it there!" she cried.

"We can sort this out at the station."

"The station?" she questioned, looking over her shoulder.

Fig produced a pair of handcuffs from his jacket. Of course he would carry them even when he was off duty. "You're under arrest for theft—"

A strangled sound erupted from her, and she spun, dislodging one of her wrists from his hold. "You can't arrest me! I didn't do anything."

"Anything you say can and—"

"This is ridiculous. I told you I didn't take that… that wallet. Who did this?" In a whirlwind of fluster, she shoved the hood back from her head to stare around the room.

A collective beat of silence passed.

She was even more beautiful than I'd thought. Definitely a storybook beauty. Unreal almost.

Black hair, perfect white skin, red lips, and eyes as blue as the summer sky. Her cheekbones were well defined, her chin graceful, and her straight nose dainty.

If I didn't know any better, I'd swear I was staring at a walking, breathing princess.

"Who did this?" she demanded again, breaking the spell she'd cast over us all.

Fletch hopped from one foot to the other and sidled closer to me.

Oh shit.

"You!" The princess accused, pointing at my friend. "Did you steal that and frame me? Did you put that in my pocket when you knocked into me?"

Fletcher made a sound and shook his head adamantly. "No. No way."

"Fletcher," Fig intoned.

Fletch slinked into my side a little more.

"Leave the kid alone, Fig. He's just been sitting here with me."

Blue eyes burned into my face for long seconds, accusing me of being a traitor. How I could be a traitor to someone I didn't even know was beyond me. But damn, if I didn't feel a peck of guilt.

"It was him!" she declared, turning back to Fig. "I didn't do it. He did."

"Yeah? Well, my shit was in your pocket. I'm pressing charges," the drunk man swore.

"We can work out the rest at the station." Fig grabbed her other wrist, twisted her arm behind her, and slapped the cuffs on without a second thought.

"You can't arrest me!" she cried.

Fig started in on reciting her rights, and the bell over the door rang.

The fussing princess stilled and looked across the room.

A large man in a brown jacket with the collar turned up stood in the doorway, his face shadowed by a hat and his hands stuffed into his pockets.

He glanced in our direction, and energy crackled through the air.

She slumped, and all the fight left her. "Fine. Take me to jail."

Fig led her toward the side door, practically dragging her tiny, fatigued body.

"Fig!" I called out, feeling several sets of eyes settle on me. "Is this really necessary?"

"Should I take Fletch down to the station instead?"

I said nothing and he made a gruff sound, punctuating my silence. "Stay out of this, Neo. The last thing you need is me looking at you longer than I should."

Fuck.

And just like that, the woman who didn't belong in my world, the woman whose looks only existed in storybooks, was hauled out of sight.

Four

Ivory

I'd fallen into a nightmare and couldn't wake up.

It was the only explanation for this. Taking in a deep, soothing breath, I told myself that soon, I would wake up in my cushy, precisely decorated high-rise and look out over Central Park with an expertly brewed latte against my perfectly manicured fingertips as the city came alive.

I could skip my run this morning. I could lounge in my Dior sleep set and soak in a hot bath before having my driver and bodyguard escort me to the company.

Calmness washed over me with the internal affirmations, and a smile filled the lower half of my face. Slowly, my eyes blinked open, the nightmare I'd been having giving way to—

Screech!

I blinked.

I blinked again.

I'd been dreaming. I was awake now. So why was I sitting in a jail cell?

A low whimper vibrated the back of my throat as I gazed around. This wasn't a nightmare. It was reality.

Ivory White in the slammer. Imagine that splashed across the headlines.

Wearily, I rubbed my temples, trying to massage away the tension.

Stepmother would need a week at the spa to recover after hearing about this. The entire company was probably up in arms, wondering where I was. Poor Charles. He would have no direction at all without me.

This place was beyond wretched. The floors were dirty old tile that was cracked in some places. None of the walls were soundproof, so I'd been listening to all the officers out front tease each other and complain about the coffee since I'd been left here to rot. The man in the cell on the other side of mine smelled like urine, and he kept singing the same song over and over and over again.

It was a god-awful song, and he only knew three lines.

Down the short hallway, someone else kept running their hands along the bars. I didn't know if they hoped the sound was annoying to the officers or if they just didn't have anything better to do.

I sat with my knees curled into my chest on what I was sure was considered a cot. Frankly, I thought the floor would be more comfortable, but there were bugs on the floor. I'd counted three so far.

Ever since I'd been deposited here, I'd waited for them to come back and get me. I'd waited for the chance to sort out this misunderstanding. I was beginning to think they'd forgotten about me.

I would have made a fuss, but the truth was I had nowhere else to go.

The second I'd seen that intimidating lumberjack-size man in the door of the bar, everything came crashing back. I was on the run. I was alone. Afraid.

Jail seemed like the safe option.

At least when I was standing in that bar. Now that I was sitting here?

I wondered if I would ever feel safe again.

"You ready to make that call yet?" A voice floated through the bars I was caged behind. A female officer stood there, staring like she was bored.

Apparently, when you got arrested, you got one phone call for help. Normally, I wouldn't even need a phone call because my team of lawyers would have descended like a murder of angry crows.

But not today. Today, I was supposed to not exist. Today, I was told not to trust anyone. My bodyguard had basically turned a blind eye to my attempted murder, and no one had even found me yet.

The longer I sat there, the more scarily clear this all became. Someone close to me was responsible for this.

Someone wanted me dead.

Who? Why?

"Miss," the woman spat. "I said it's time to make your call."

I knew a lot of people. But there was no one to call because I was unsure of them all.

"You don't want to make a call? You can sit in here the entire night until the public defender arrives in the morning."

"Public defender?"

The woman made a face. "Yeah, the lawyer that takes cases for free for people like you who can't afford anyone." After a pause, she said, "You will have to tell him your name. He'll need it for court."

"But he's a stranger!" I insisted. How could I just tell all my personal information to someone I didn't even know?

They might be more trustworthy than the people you do *know.*

"Not my problem,"

The man in the cell over started to cry. It was a low keening sound.

"See ya in the morning." The woman turned to walk away, the keys hanging off her belt jingling.

Panic assailed me. "Wait!" I said, unfolding from the cot so fast that the world around me spun. "I want to make that call."

Five

Neo

THE SOUND OF A FAMILIAR RINGTONE FLOATED TO WHERE I worked.

"Yo! Neo!" A voice competed with it. "Phone!"

Dropping the can I was holding, I swiped my palms down the front of my jeans as I went to snatch it off the table. The number was unknown. I almost didn't answer, but something I couldn't identify made my color-splattered finger swipe to accept the call. "Yeah?"

Silence.

"Hello?" I said again.

The only thing I could hear was muffled background noise and the sound of someone crying.

My pulse kicked up. "Virginia?"

Still nothing.

I pulled the phone away from my ear to stare at the screen. The phone was still connected. The call hadn't dropped.

Impatience and worry made me angry, and a rude sound erupted out of my throat. Just as I was about to hang up, a light sniffle floated down my ear canal.

One finger quickly plugged my opposite ear, and I turned away from my friends. "Hello?"

"I-is this Neo?"

I frowned. "Who is this?"

"Um, you gave me your number earlier tonight," she replied.

A vision of her velvety hair and rosy lips swam in the back of my mind. "I thought you said you would never call,"

"I'm desperate."

At least she was honest.

"So you aren't calling for a date?"

"I was h-hoping you could come and get me."

"Where?"

"Jail."

Surprise made me straighten. "You're seriously still in jail?"

I thought I heard a catch in her voice and a quick intake of breath. "They said I had to spend the night until a stranger came tomorrow..."

"Why don't you call a friend? A relative?"

"Your number was in my pocket."

"Hurry up!" someone snapped irritably in the background. The distant wailing seemed to grow louder.

My stomach churned uncomfortably at the thought of a storybook girl sitting in a grim cell.

"Can you come?" Her voice was vulnerable and small. I pictured her red lips pouting and her creamy skin stained with tears.

This woman intrigued me. Insulted me. And now she needed me.

"I thought I was toxic to someone like you," I practically snarled.

"I apologize for what I said. It's been a very trying day."

Words. She probably didn't even mean them. She just wanted something. I wasn't about to get involved with someone like her... the devil dressed like heaven.

"Please, Neo." The whispered plea tumbled to the very bottom of the beating organ in my chest.

Irritated, I snarled into the line even though she couldn't see me. I wasn't about to fall for that. My lips parted to tell her that very thing. But instead, something completely contrary came out. "I'm on my way."

THE SLAMMER TO SLUMS, AS EVERYONE IN THIS DISTRICT LIKED to refer to the local jail, was really no better than any other rundown building in this part of the city. Except this place had better security and a bigger supply of donuts.

The place really wasn't much cleaner either, but it could be argued it was because it was a revolving door to the street rats that ran around here on the daily.

By streets rats, I mean of the human *and* rodent variety.

Every cell in my body actually revolted against me when I stepped over the threshold, willingly walking into a place that often offered to lock me up. They never did, though, as much as they might want to.

Still, it was basically against my religion to roll right in and wave a red flag signaling war.

My religion = anything that offered self-preservation.

Here I was, though, breaking my self-made rules for a woman whose name I didn't even know. For a woman who insulted me.

"Well, well, well, look what the cat dragged in," one of the boys in blue drawled, standing up from behind his desk to shake his head at me.

I grinned lazily. I definitely might not want to be here, but I would damn sure act like this was the best place in the world while I was.

"Officer Friendly," I boasted, calling him that because I didn't know his name. *Friendly my ass.*

"You here to turn yourself in, Neo?" The man chuckled and turned a chair around from his desk, offering it to me. "Have a seat."

I spread my hands. "You know I'm as clean as a bottle of bleach."

"If you're clean, then I'm the next queen of England," Fig announced, stepping into the room from the hallway.

"I look forward to seeing you in a diamond tiara," I quipped.

Fig slapped the folder he was carrying onto the counter. "You here about Fletcher? Worried your little protégé is about to be hauled in?"

"I don't need to be worried about Fletch because he didn't do anything wrong." I lied.

"I might have to believe you this time because I got the culprit the first time around."

"Why haven't you released her yet?"

"Now you know I can't discuss details of an ongoing case with civilians."

I suppressed an eye roll and smiled instead. "If I was a civilian, y'all wouldn't know me by name."

"That's not anything to be proud of." Reba, one of the female officers strolled by.

"You are looking better than ever, Ms. Reba," I drawled. "Is that a new hairstyle?" I held up both my hands to give her a ten out of ten.

She giggled. "You come by anytime, Neo."

I winked at her.

Turning my attention back to Fig, I said, "So? What's the deal?"

A stubborn glint flashed in his eyes. "I said—"

I cut him off. "She called me to come bail her out."

Fig's eyes widened. "You know her?"

I didn't say anything.

Fig and a few other officers shuffled closer. I watched them carefully but didn't move back.

"So, ah..." Officer friendly leaned in. "What's her name?"

Fig pulled out a pen and poised it above a notepad as he listened.

"You arrested her hours ago, and you mean to tell me you haven't gotten her name yet?"

"Won't give it up," Fig said, brusque.

"And her ID?"

"Doesn't have one."

"Thought about doing a strip search. That is one fine-looking piece—" Officer Friendly's words cut off with a strangled choke when I set my full dark stare on him.

He was no longer Officer Friendly. Now he was Officer Scallywag.

Fig smacked his partner in the chest. "He's just kidding, Neo. That isn't how we operate..."

"How much?" I said, my cajoling, charming tone no longer in use.

Fig straightened, sensing the change in me. "You really know her?"

"Pretty sure I don't have to answer that."

He made a sour face. "You're going to play this game."

"You know damn well I don't play games. You also know I don't give out information I don't have to."

"I could arrest you too." He threatened, gauging my reaction.

"You're really pressing charges?"

"That's the victim's right."

Folding my arms over my chest, I relaxed into the conversation. "You know damn well when that fool wakes up tomorrow, he won't remember jack shit about this, and his wallet is already back in his pocket. So why waste everyone's time?"

"Guess we'll have to wait and see tomorrow..."

"Or you could just let this go tonight," I suggested.

"You telling me how to do my job?"

"Seems like someone needs to."

Fig got up in my face, and I held my ground. He was nothing but a man on a power trip. I sniffed the air, leaned closer to the man, and sniffed again. "You smell like a brewery, Fig." I spoke loudly.

His eyes widened and then narrowed.

"You arrested that woman while you were intoxicated, even after she insisted she was innocent."

"She was not innocent! You were standing right there. You saw the wallet in her pocket!"

I pursed my lips. "You know... I was drinking too. And I sure can't remember too clearly what I saw except for some drunken slob yelling about someone taking his wallet, which he found lying at his feet a few minutes later."

A few officers stopped what they were doing and looked up.

"You know that ain't what happened," Fig argued.

"I know you were off duty and drinking when all this happened. I could call up Earth and see what his version of the story is."

Fig's tongue ran across his front teeth. "Isn't Earth a friend of yours?"

"He's the man who owns the establishment where the alleged crime was committed. He's also a witness."

"You been drinking, Fig?" Officer Scallywag said, reentering the conversation. "You know the boss won't like that if he hears."

"I know what I saw, Barron. Beer or no beer."

I gave Officer Scallywag a look reminding him that I hadn't forgotten about his remarks about his newest inmate.

He cleared his throat. "Why don't we just let this one go? No one was hurt, and everyone had been drinking."

Fig's eyes flared, incredulous.

"The amount of paperwork and digging to find her name is going to be a pain the ass," Scallywag whined, trying to convince him.

Fig stared at his partner for long moments and then relented. "Reba!" he bellowed. "Go get the girl."

"You're gonna release her?" she yelled back.

I glanced at Fig. He glanced at me, then at the men standing around. His face was sour, but he nodded once. "Seems it was a big misunderstanding."

"Good choice," I said, lifting a hand to slap him on the back. He gave me a withering stare. I dropped my hand. "I'll wait outside," I announced, knowing when not to push my luck.

"I better not see you or her in here again, Neo!" Fig called after me. "Next time, I won't let it go!"

I suppressed a laugh.

Next time? There would never be a next time.

Six

Ivory

Could it really be considered freedom if you didn't have anywhere to go?

As I glanced around the dingy, depressing, and somewhat frightening police station, there was not one face I knew. No one to offer assistance or even just a friendly smile.

I thought after I had some time to think, I'd be able to formulate a plan. But after hours of sitting in a silent cell alone, I only felt more confused.

Walking on wobbling legs, I pushed through the glass doors leading out onto the dark sidewalk. Heavy, persistent raindrops poured from the sky, pounding everything beyond the tiny awning over the precinct doors.

I didn't know what I'd done to deserve such bad karma, but I was ready for it to stop.

Looking right and then left, I saw nothing but strange darkness and nothing at all to guide me.

"I'm innocent!" a man roared as a scuffle erupted right beside me. "Innocent!" His flailing body knocked into me, and I stumbled.

Drawing back, a uniformed officer gave me a sympathetic smile as he hauled a rough-looking man dressed all in leather into the building I'd just vacated.

A shiver shook my body, and I realized I'd been knocked into the rain and it was drenching my thin clothes. Quickly, I grabbed the hood to cover my head, but suddenly, the rain stopped. The sound of raindrops pattering overhead made me look up. Cold wind blew, sweeping back the hood until it rested at the back of my neck.

Eyes that contained a galaxy pierced mine, and a jolt of electricity zapped my limbs.

"You," I whispered, unable to look away from his stare.

"You're surprised?" His voice was low and gruff.

My head bobbed.

"You called me."

Ripping my eyes off his, I gazed up, seeing the umbrella he was holding over my head. "You're the reason they let me go?"

"Who else?" He smirked.

I let my gaze drop to my feet. "No one."

The rain seemed to pick up, pounding more violently overhead and splashing the concrete around us, sprinkling my already ruined shoes with water.

I was so cold my knees ached, and every joint in my hands screamed because I'd clenched my fists for so long.

"You can go home now." The voice seemed far away, and it took a minute for me to hear him.

Pulling up my chin, I gazed back into his smooth face. "Home," I murmured wistfully.

A great crack of thunder boomed through the night, attacking the city and knocking me off my feet. Cringing, I ducked into the closest thing I could for protection as I was immediately assaulted by images and flashes of things I didn't understand.

Lightning streaked overhead, lighting up the sky bright white before sparking out almost as quickly as it appeared.

My sore hand curled around the front of Neo's black

jacket, the buttons on the many pockets poking my palm. The hand not holding the umbrella splayed over my shoulder and pulled me back, but I still clutched the front of his coat.

Tipping up my chin, I tried to focus, wondering why I wasn't able. "Home," I murmured once again. "I can't go home."

And with that, my mind and body succumbed to darkness.

Seven

Neo

Bang! Bang! Bang!

I tried to kick on the door as lightly as possible but still loud enough to be heard. With the adrenaline pumping through my limbs, keeping the kicks under control was actually a challenge.

Normally, I wouldn't knock. Normally, if I did, I wouldn't care how loud it was. The whole point of knocking was to get the attention of the people inside. The louder, the better, right?

Not when you had an unconscious princess cradled in your arms.

Granted, I would do well to wake her up, but I found myself trying not to disturb her. Trying to protect her from any undue stress.

I kicked on the door again, staring at the thick wood impatiently. *Suspicious bastards.*

"I know you're standing there, Fletch. Open the damn door," I announced, watching the girl. Her face remained turned into my jacket, long lashes sweeping against her near-translucent cheeks.

Light scuffling sounded, and I heard the small hatch open

over the peephole on the other side. I leaned toward it, scowling.

Several locks disengaged, and the light dragging sound of a thick metal chain slid back. The door creaked loudly when it was pulled back a few inches, and Fletch's golden eye peered through the crack. Surprise widened his stare, and he scrambled back, pulling the door all the way open.

I brushed past, tightening my hold on the bundle in my arms as I went.

"Is that a girl?" Fletcher gasped, shutting the door and scurrying so close he nearly collided into my back.

"Lock the door." I reminded him.

An impatient, almost petulant sound came from him as he glanced between the girl and the door. Arching an eyebrow, I silently asked if he really thought there was a choice.

His hair flopped as he went to lock up, making about as much noise as the construction crews around here working on the buildings.

"Did you say, girl—" Beau called, pushing back from his usual position to stand and turn. "What the hell happened?" The words rushed out, his legs carrying him to where I was carefully laying her on the couch.

Ignoring both Fletch and Beau, I slipped a pillow under her head and tucked her hands into her lap. Straightening, I saw the blanket tossed over the back of the couch and snatched it to drape over her body.

She was a small woman, her frame narrow and delicate, her stature petite. Even lying across our sofa, she barely took up half. She was still. Silent and so very pale.

Flashes of the past assaulted me. The echo of shattering glass, screaming. Then an overwhelming veil of sadness draped over my mind, blocking out the woman I'd just carried three blocks in the rain and replacing her with another time and place.

"Whoa, whoa." An arm slipped around my waist, and a solid body offered support I hadn't realized I needed until his cautious voice was beside my ear.

Blinking, I glanced beside me.

Beau's blue-green eyes were concerned. "Are you hurt somewhere?"

I shook my head. "No."

"Then—"

Shaking off his concern, I glanced back at the couch.

Why wasn't she waking up? Should I have gone to the hospital instead?

"Is that the girl from the bar?" Fletcher asked, pushing into my other side.

I nodded, and the three of us stared at her for long, silent beats.

"You know the rules." Earth's voice cut through the room.

I felt Beau and Fletch exchange glances, but I looked directly at my brother. "She literally passed out on the street. Was I supposed to just leave her there in the rain?"

Earth shrugged. "Not my problem."

"I thought she got arrested," Fletcher prompted.

"Of all the nights to not go down to the bar..." Beau muttered.

"She did." I confirmed with Fletch. "She called me to bail her out."

Everyone's stare swung to me. I felt their astonishment.

"You know her," Earth stated.

I shook my head.

"But you bailed her out anyway."

"She went to jail because of Fletch."

"That guy knew it was me! I had to do something! I didn't

think she'd actually get hauled in. Stupid Fig." He complained. "You shouldn't let cops in your bar, E!"

"Yeah, 'cause that wouldn't be suspicious," Earth retorted, then turned back to me. "No outsiders. No exceptions."

A faint echo of the memories I'd just relived bounced around inside me, sort of like how the scent of paint lingers as it dries. "I'll get rid of her as soon as she wakes up."

"Now."

"C'mon, Earth. It's just a girl. And a small one at that. She doesn't look too good," Beau concluded, glancing back at her.

"Why is she like that?" Fletch pointed at her. "Did she hit her head or something?"

"I'm not sure," I murmured. "She just fainted."

"She's probably faking." Earth guessed.

"She's very pale." Fletch leaned in, staring at her closely. "What's up with her hand?" He pointed to what looked like a sock that was matted with dried blood.

"Whatever is wrong with her isn't our concern. Wake her up and get her the hell out of here." Earth's footfalls were heavy as he walked across the room, his shadow following closely behind.

Both hands slapped onto the back of the leather couch, his torso leaning over. A disgusted sound fell from his curled lip, and his hand shot out.

I caught it.

Surprised, he glanced up.

Both of us leaned over, the sleeping girl drawing a line between us.

"Don't," I intoned.

His eyes narrowed. "Why do you care?"

"I don't."

Pointedly, he stared down at where my hand circled his wrist, keeping him from shaking her awake. Pulling free,

Earth crossed both arms over his chest. "As soon as she wakes up, she's out."

I nodded.

"This is the first girl that's ever been in our apartment," Fletcher said as if he were seeing some kind of magical creature.

I really should socialize him more. Actually, no. Fletch got lots of socialization on the streets every day. This was different. Part of me understood his awe. She was nothing like any of the people we usually saw. It felt like she was from a whole other world.

"Hey, Sleeping Beauty!" Earth barked, using his knee to kick the back of the couch. "Wake up!"

The muscles in the back of my neck tensed. Her eyelids did not flutter.

"Sleeping Beauty," Beau mused. "Maybe she needs true love's kiss to wake up."

Warmth coated the back of my neck. At my side, my hand balled into a fist. Unable to tell myself no, my gaze strayed to those perfectly shaped lips.

"Don't be stupid," Earth snapped, then hit the back of the couch again. "Princess!"

"What the hell is your probl—" I started to challenge, but I was cut off.

"Mmm." A soft sound purred from the small girl's throat. The hand not trapped by a sock rose to lightly touch her forehead.

She moaned again.

Dark, velvety lashes began to flutter.

Four men waited with bated breath.

Eight

Ivory

The veil of darkness cloaking my world lifted slowly, the shadows diminishing bit by bit. My lashes fluttered, and light and sound pricked my consciousness. A low moan tickled the back of my throat as I blinked, focusing.

Four sets of eyes peered down at me as if I were some kind of experiment.

"Agh!" I screeched, bolting upright and making everyone jump back. Another scream ripped out of me. "Agh!" I scrambled backward, pulling my knees into my chest.

Four strange men gathered around the large leather sofa I was squished against. The pounding of my heart was actually painful, and the back of my neck ached. I shifted, and so did they.

My mouth opened to scream again, but something slapped over my lips, keeping in the sound.

"Think of our eardrums, princess."

That voice… I knew it. Eyes following the sound, I felt my nose flare when they settled on Neo. I gasped against his palm, and my stare clung to his as I was pummeled by everything that happened since the sun rose this morning.

Everything was so vivid, as though I were reliving it all over again. To my embarrassment, tears flooded my eyes and slipped over my cheeks, trailing down until they met with Neo's hand.

The glittering onyx in his eyes melted some, sort of like a night sky giving way to day. The soft expression made more tears fall.

I shook my head, not wanting to cry. Not wanting to show any kind of weakness at all. I was far from weak.

"She's crying," a voice whispered rather loudly. "What do we do?"

The voice was a reminder I was surrounded. Pushing away Neo's hand, I swiped at the falling tears while the men stared.

"You." I gulped, pointing a finger to the smallest one of the group. "You're the one who got me sent to jail!"

"I didn't mean to!" he squeaked.

Levering myself up, I stood, my feet sinking into the couch cushions so I had to use the sofa back for balance. Standing on the furniture like this was entirely unladylike, but it made me taller than everyone else in the room.

"Do you have any idea what that place is like?" I yelled. "I'm going to have nightmares for the rest of my life!"

"You were sleeping just fine a minute ago," someone on the opposite side of the couch grumped.

My gaze swung to him. I knew him… "Gross bar guy."

His entire face scrunched up like he had a mouthful of sour milk. One of his eyebrows rose. "Gross bar guy?"

I shuddered. "You gave me water from the tap. You work at a place named after rotting fruit."

His arms crossed over his chest, and he glared. "I own that place."

I wrinkled my nose. "That's even worse."

He pitched forward like he would lunge at me, and I squealed again, falling onto the cushions.

"Back off, Earth," cajoled another guy I did not recognize, pushing the mean one back and stepping in front.

"I'm Beau." He introduced himself, offering his hand.

I stared between his deep-red hair, freckled nose, and outstretched hand for long moments before slowly reaching out my own hand.

His fingers were warm where mine were cold. The shake was brief, but his smile lingered on his lips. His bone structure was something people would pay millions of dollars for. Such sharp cheekbones and a strong nose.

"Wh-who are you?"

"I live here."

Shifting my eyes around, I noted the large room with brick walls, exposed pipes overhead, and the glow of computer monitors reaching toward us from the other side.

Heinous, frankly unnerving sound filled the room, and my body tensed. It was a cross between someone breathing like they'd just run an entire marathon and the sound of someone snoring.

Thump!

A heavy body fell onto the cushions, making the entire thing sag toward the new weight. Both my hands clung to the back of the couch as if I might be sucked into some weird portal.

The heinous sound grew louder, and a solid body jumped at me.

"Ahh!" I shielded my face with my arms. Expecting to be pounced on.

"Down, boy." Neo's voice was calm, and no attack ever came. "Are you afraid of dogs?"

Dogs?

As I cautiously lowered my arms, a big brown and white head filled my vision.

"Aww, hi," I crooned, forgetting about everything else to

reach both palms out toward the bulldog staring at me expectantly.

Neo released the hold he had on the dog's collar, and the big boy lumbered over until he was practically in my lap. The horrible sounds I'd just heard were from him, and they became more erratic as his tail and body wagged.

A big, sticky tongue came out and licked up the side of my cheek, making me squeal. "Ew!" I laughed but then went back to petting him.

His head was practically bigger than his wide, short frame. The underbite caused crooked teeth to stick out of his mouth and rest against his lips. His nose was smooshed in and had a scar…

I guess that explained the breathing.

"What's his name?"

"Snort," grumpy bar guy announced. "He's mine."

"You poor thing," I crooned to the dog who made more snorting sounds.

"Down," grumpy bar guy commanded, and Snort instantly left the couch.

The weight of four sets of eyes became heavy once more.

Swallowing, I tucked my hands in my lap. "Where am I?"

"You passed out in front of the police station, and I couldn't get you to wake up so I brought you here."

"Where's here?" I pressed.

"Our apartment," the little one announced.

"You all live here… *together*?"

His nod was eager, and it made his hair flop into his eyes.

"But *why*?"

"All right. She's awake. She's gotta go," grumpy bar man bellowed. Shoving forward, he grabbed my upper arm, hurling me off the couch.

My legs sagged the second my feet hit the floor, and I bowed into him.

He didn't try to help me. In fact, he let go.

I would have fallen right over if Neo hadn't been there to catch me.

"Earth." He grunted, supporting my weight.

"That was the agreement." His tone was unforgiving. "She's awake now, so she can find her way home."

I burst into tears.

Every sound in the room ceased to exist, even the heavy breathing of the dog. All that filled the apartment was the angst and trauma I'd experienced in the past day.

"He told me I couldn't exist anymore," I wailed, pulling away from Neo and covering my face with my hands. "At first, I believed him. Then I thought he was just a liar. But now I'm not so sure." I continued, my words a jumbled, watery mess.

More tears fell, and my voice cracked. "I don't even know where I am. I have no money, no ID, and…" I held up my injured hand. "He ripped off my entire nail!"

For dramatic effect, I pulled off the sock still covering my hand, but part of it was stuck to me with dried blood.

"Waaaah," I wailed anew. "And he butchered my hair!"

Four men shifted uncomfortably, the little one who'd gotten me thrown in jail slinking behind one of his friends and stealing glances at me every few seconds.

"Who would do that?" Beau said, his eyes wide.

"Your hair looks better than mine," I yowled and reached up to finger the chopped-up, once glorious strands. I sniffled, glancing back at Beau. "Is your color natural?"

"Out!" Earth yelled over the chaos. Storming closer, he pulled a twenty-dollar bill out of his jeans and thrust it at me.

I made a face. "People still carry cash?"

He muttered some *very* impolite words and dragged me toward the door. Flashes of color all over the walls blurred by me as he dragged.

"Stop stalling." He snarled and jerked me onward.

"Ow," I whimpered, reaching up to cup the back of my neck.

He stopped pulling and swung to assess me with unreadable eyes. "Don't play games with me."

"I'm not. My neck hurts."

Something brushed the back of my shoulder, making me cringe and lean toward Earth who was suddenly very surprised by my movement.

Feeling his astonishment, my stare lifted, my face turning sheepish. "Sorry."

"Let me see." Neo's voice was soft and smooth, a lot less menacing than Earth's.

"Oh. Neo." My voice was relieved when I realized it was just him.

"Hold still," he instructed, stepping up to grasp the hood on my jacket and pull the neckline down.

Small goose bumps rose along my arms when his bare fingers brushed the back of my neck, sweeping my hair out of the way.

"You're bleeding," he announced, grim.

"What?" I spun around, trying to see.

Beau and the thief laughed, but I didn't think it was funny. I was bleeding and didn't even know it!

Catching me by the shoulders on my third spin, Neo said, "You won't be able to see."

"But what's wrong with it?" I fussed, slightly dizzy.

"Looks like you were cut." Dark eyes searched mine. "With something sharp. Like a knife."

I gasped. "I told you he chopped off my hair!"

"With a knife?" Earth doubted.

My head bobbed. "I thought he was going to slit my throat."

"Someone really tried to kill you today?" Beau jumped in.

My lower lip wobbled. "First thing this morning. And now I can't go home. I can't—"

"Why can't you go home?" Earth scrutinized.

I stared at him without blinking. Wasn't it obvious? "He said I couldn't."

"Are you dimwitted?"

My mouth fell open and then snapped shut. "How dare you?" I raged. "If anyone is dimwitted in this room, it's you!" I started forward but swayed.

"Whoa," three of the men all said simultaneously while Earth stood there and glared.

Outside, loud thunder cracked, and the windows across the room rattled. "I don't like the rain," I whined.

Neo led me to the couch, easing me down. "You can stay here tonight."

"Hell no, she can't!"

"C'mon, Earth." Neo swung around toward his friend.

How could anyone be friends with that grumpy, uncombed villain?

"It's the middle of the night. It's storming, and she's bleeding in more than one place."

I remembered the stuck-on sock and looked at it dangling off my ripped-up, stumpy-looking finger. What a waste of the perfect nail color. And it still really hurt. In fact, my whole body hurt. It seemed the little nap I'd had only made the pain much easier to feel.

Gently fingering the crusty, slightly slick, but entirely sore cut at the back of my neck, I winced. A vivid memory of the shining blade whistling through the air as it swung down on me made me squeeze my eyes closed.

A gentle touch on my shoulder had them reopening.

I expected Neo.

It was the one who got me sent to jail.

"You." My eyes narrowed.

"Here." He held out a bottle of water.

Unexpected emotion swelled up inside me like a tidal wave. "This is the nicest thing anyone has done for me all day," I wailed, tears falling anew.

"I bailed you out of jail..." someone muttered sourly from across the room.

Beaming like a good boy, he uncapped the water and offered it to me. Sniffling, I took it, not caring in the least it was a totally unheard of generic brand, and took a long sip. Then I cried some more.

"What's your name?" I asked after I swallowed.

"Fletcher," he announced. "But everyone calls me Fletch." His eyes were the color of dark organic honey and appeared so innocent I immediately wanted to hug him.

"Thank you for your kindness," I said over his shoulder while we hugged. "I so needed it."

Fletch pulled back, smiling, his cheeks pink, eyes shy. "I'm sorry about getting you arrested."

Pursing my lips, I smacked him lightly on the side of the head. "Stealing is so bad! Don't do that ever again."

His face fell like a scolded, sad puppy.

I hugged him again.

"What's your name?" Fletch asked, gesturing for me to drink more water.

"Oh, it—"

"It doesn't matter because she's not staying!" Earth declared.

"Aw, c'mon, Earth. It's the middle of the night," Fletch whined.

"Kicking a girl out in the middle of the night in this neighborhood is going a little too far, don't you think, E?" Beau added.

"She smells good too!" Fletch put in.

I felt bad he thought I smelled nice in my current state. This boy was deprived.

Curious, my eyes found Neo. He was standing sort of in the center of everyone, his eyes watching everything, settling on nothing. Until he saw my stare.

They moved past, then came back and held. Our eyes locked just as they had under the umbrella before.

Authority shimmered in the air around him despite his battered jeans and T-shirt as he closed the distance between us. "C'mon, I'll help you clean up."

My body was so exhausted he didn't have to work at all to pull me off the couch, and once I was at his side, I had to concentrate hard so I didn't lean on him for support.

"This is my—" Earth started, his voice saltier than the ocean, but it was cut off abruptly.

"She's staying," Neo intoned. His voice was quiet. Calm. Final.

No one said a word when he took my hand and tugged me toward the bathroom.

Nine

Neo

"You can clean up in here," I offered, holding the door open so she could step into the bathroom.

Briefly, her eyes touched my face. Then she moved past into the small bathroom.

"Is this the only bathroom?"

"It's a one-bedroom."

"But four of you live here…"

I didn't say anything because we'd already told her that. Turning around, I grabbed a towel out of a cabinet on the wall and held it out. "Do you want to shower or just wash up?"

Her eyes strayed to the shower and then down at herself.

She called out lightly as I left the bathroom but didn't follow. When I stepped back into the main room, everyone was still standing where we'd left them just moments ago. Saying nothing, I grabbed a T-shirt and pair of basketball shorts from my stack of clothes.

"Are those for her?" Fletcher whispered loudly.

"I'm going down to the bar." Earth's words were punctuated by the locks being released on the door.

My footsteps stalled a little on the threshold of the bathroom. She was standing at the pedestal sink, staring in the mirror… or rather, at the top of her head.

Hearing me, she turned with a grimace. "I can't even see myself in this mirror."

"Shorty." I snickered.

"This bathroom is poorly designed."

"It's better than being dirty."

A loud boom of thunder shook the small window against the wall, and the girl cowered close.

"It's just a thunderstorm," I explained, my palm tingling with the urge to run it over her hair.

"Then why do the windows shake like that?"

"They're old."

"Oh." Straightening as though she hadn't been worried at all, she cleared her throat.

"I brought shorts because you'd fall down and kill yourself in my pants."

"Wouldn't be the first time I almost died today."

I paused. "Someone really tried to kill you?"

Her narrow yet perky nose wrinkled. "Do I look like I'm lying?"

"Is this not how you normally look?"

She gasped. The offense in her eyes was almost comical. "I can assure you that I do not ever look this awful." Turning back to the mirror, she pushed up onto tiptoes to see but still couldn't. Pouting, she turned back, leaning into the white porcelain. "This has been the worst day of my life."

The second those words were out, I saw the doubt cross her face. As if in her mind, she was thinking, *No, this is not the worst day of my life. There was something worse.*

"Worse than someone trying to kill you, getting arrested, and passing out on the street?" I responded to her expression.

"He cut my hair too."

I blinked. Her hair was clearly a big deal. More than almost dying? I didn't comprehend, but I wasn't about to argue. "Worse than that even?"

Her nod was sage. The beauty she clearly possessed turned precious. Her small frame, big eyes, and sulking attitude made her cute.

Without realizing the way she appeared, she reached up. Midway through the movement, she patted her shoulder and halted. Tears swimming in her eyes, her hand lifted higher to finger the definitely uneven black strands of hair.

"I can fix this," she told herself. "You can fix anything."

She was giving herself a pep talk. It made my heart beat unevenly. "Here," I said, thrusting the clothes at her.

"Thank you," she said, politely pulling the fabric against her chest into a hug.

"When you're finished, I can clean up that cut on the back of your neck."

"Do you have any bandages? Antibiotic cream?"

I faltered. We didn't have that stuff here. I didn't want to tell her that, so I just nodded.

"There's soap in the shower."

Still hugging my clothes, she nodded.

How could someone seem sturdy yet fragile at the very same time?

"Um, wait," she called out as I was closing the door.

I poked my head back in. "Neo." I reminded her.

"I remember." She nodded, lowering her eyes like she was suddenly shy. "Neo..."

My heart trembled. "Hmm?"

"Will you wait outside the door?"

"Sure." I agreed gruffly before quickly shutting the wood between us. All the oxygen I had left in my lungs exhaled.

What in fresh hell was wrong with me? Irregular heartbeat, wasting perfectly breathable air, going against house rules I helped create… and all for a girl whose name I didn't even know.

Ten

Huntsman

"The package was delivered," the shrewd voice informed me.

"Satisfied?"

The muffled sound of cardboard in the background gave me pause. It sounded like a gift unwrapping and not confirmation of a crime.

"Interesting proof you send."

I could almost imagine the person staring down at the blue ribbon tied around the bundle, the black strands of hair lying limp against the box.

"Would you rather I cut out her heart and send that?"

"I guess it would be no more identifying than this black hair."

"There's more."

Paper ruffled, and I knew the moment the smaller item was discovered.

Riiipp. The covering was torn away. A breath was indrawn.

"The color on her nails is exclusive, is it not?" My voice was bored. I didn't bother to point out there was also blood and DNA on the nail. I wasn't paid to point out the obvious.

"It's a brand-new color. Unreleased."

I knew that.

The voice continued, slick and satisfied. "Ripping off her nail *and* her hair. Probably didn't have to do much else to kill her."

I reminded myself I couldn't be disgusted because I was worse.

I grunted. "Satisfied?"

"And the body?"

"You'll never see her again."

"Payment has been wired."

I hung up, disabled the phone, then crushed it.

I didn't bother double-checking if the payment was there. It would be.

The people who hired me were no-conscience scumbags, but even they knew better than to cross a killer.

Eleven

Ivory

Go on strongly despite the fear. I repeated the phrase to myself like a mantra until the words were tattooed in my brain and I didn't have to whisper them anymore.

Today was hard. Harder than almost any day before it.

But I survived before, and I could again. All I needed was a good night's sleep and the sun. *Yes,* the second the rain stopped and the sun shone down over the city, everything would feel brand new and I would know what to do.

A shower would help too. Wash away the horrible grime the hunter left behind, the stickiness from the jail. I could even wash away the blood and tears.

I was afraid. Alone.

I could still be brave.

My eyes slipped to the door, my mind wandering to the man who promised to stand there and wait. He was nothing but a stranger. A necessity to get me through the night.

Glancing around to put the clothes on something while I showered, I found nothing at all. No vanity. No dresser or even a soft bench. I'd never been in such a small, primitive bathroom before.

The tiles on the floor were tiny and discolored, a few of them cracked. The sink was small, needing a cleaning, and the faucet dripped. The walls were white and actually probably had been painted recently. But not even fresh paint could give new life to a space where everything else was dying.

The clawfoot tub might be charming, but it was grimy. So grimy I thought about showering in my sneakers. Then I considered not showering at all.

Balancing my clothes on the edge of the sink beside the towel, I turned to grab the shower curtain…

There wasn't one.

These men showered in a clawfoot tub with no curtain? Making a face, I looked at the showerhead sticking out from the wall.

I'll spare you the details of its unfortunate state.

Wouldn't water get everywhere with no curtain or door? I gazed around, shifting from foot to foot for a while longer, my eyes oddly drawn to the chipped white mug near the sink. It had five toothbrushes sticking out of it. They were all just tangled up and shoved in the same mug. All of them were different colors… and one of them looked chewed.

Ew.

There was a plant on the back of the toilet. I didn't know why, but I took pity on it and gave it some water.

And I can tell you on good authority that the toilet paper in here… it was *not* two-ply.

They probably all had rashes.

A gentle knock came from the other side of the door. "Are you okay?"

"Yes, thank you," I called back.

I couldn't see my reflection in the mirror, which had its positive and negative sides.

Positive: I couldn't see what a mess I was.

Negative: I couldn't see what a mess I was.

If I couldn't see, how would I fix it?

I decided just to go for it and stripped off the ruined designer workout attire that I sincerely hoped I wouldn't see again. And you better believe I was having a meeting with the executives at Dior. This fabric was severely lacking. It didn't hold up at all to my near-death and jailtime experiences!

I decided not to shower in my shoes. I needed them to stay dry. And since I only had one sock on my foot, I couldn't shower in those either.

Making a whining sound, I tugged the sock off my injured finger, whimpering again when fresh blood started to well. Why did he have to go and rip off my entire fingernail? Wasn't that just too vicious?

How long until it grows back? How long until there will be enough nail to attach a false one? Should I have gotten stitches? What if it gets infected? What a waste of nail polish.

All these worries consumed me as I climbed into the tub, trying to touch as little as humanly possible. My limbs were freezing and weak, and I promised myself the warm water of the shower would make all of this suffering seem far away.

Finding the knob for the spray, I turned it on.

Nothing happened.

Frowning, I turned it the other way.

Again, nothing.

Irritated by this thing's lack of responsibility to do what it was supposed to do, I gave it a spin all the way around, using a little extra force. A stream of water shot out not from the showerhead above, but from the faucet coming out of the wall near the tub.

"Ahhh!" I screamed, scurrying back as water burst from around the spigot like someone hit it with a hammer and cracked the entire pipe. Sprays of water attacked my skin, and it was frigid.

I screamed again, trying to shut it off, but I swear the water started attacking with more force!

Half wet, half dry, and completely naked, I scurried back, my bare foot slipping on the bottom of the porcelain tub, my entire body flying.

"Oomph." I didn't know if it was the sound I made when I fell or the sound the person who caught me made, but it was the sound I heard.

A few low curse words rained down upon me like that friggin' spigot water, but just as fast, the sporadic spray cut off.

The loud sound of water being gulped up by the drain and dripping in the sink settled like a blanket over the previous chaos.

"What the fuck are you doing?" Neo growled, water dripping from his nose and pulling the long strands of hair down into his eyes.

"Me?" I gasped. "That thing exploded, and I didn't do anything!"

"It didn't explode."

"It did so!" I argued. "What kind of shower is—" I screamed again.

Neo fell back with the loud yell, but I went with him.

"What in the hell are you screaming for now?"

I hadn't hit the floor when I fell over the side of the bathtub. I'd fallen into Neo's arms.

And I was naked.

Naked. *Naked!*

Not even my massage therapist saw this much of my skin.

"I'm naked!" I wailed, tucking my arms over my chest and trying to conceal all of me.

"Should I have let the bathroom flood and you drown?"

"Don't look at me!"

He closed his eyes. "You don't have anything I want to see."

"How rude!"

"Rude that I don't want to look at you? Or rude that I should be trying to steal a peek and I'm not?"

"Put me down!"

Despite the fact that I was yelling at him, everything was wet, and his eyes were closed, Neo put me down with a gentleness that, for a moment, overshadowed everything else.

"Thank you," I said soft, still cowering to cover myself.

Eyes still shut, he grabbed the towel like he knew exactly where it was and held it out to me. Snatching it, I wrapped it around my body.

"Covered?" he asked, squinting open his eyes.

"Don't!" I shied away.

To his credit, he turned his back, reached into the tub, and turned on the shower in one go. This time, the water came from above, and it wasn't erratic. In fact, the water pressure was terrible.

"It's temperamental," he explained.

"I think it's possessed."

A laugh burst out of him. My stomach flipped a little at the appearance of his dimples.

"Hurry up. There's not much hot water." His voice turned gruff when the laugh disappeared.

I was climbing back into the tub as he was leaving. "Where's the shampoo and conditioner?"

"Soap's in the corner," he called, then snapped the door shut behind him.

Still clutching the towel, standing just out of the sad spray, I turned to see a bar of white soap. There was a hair in it.

It was official. This was hell.

12

Neo

How could someone so small make so much noise?

I'd known her only a couple hours, and I'd already witnessed this girl screaming (many, *many* times), crying, whining, yelling, *and* being polite.

She was giving me whiplash.

Maybe she had some sort of mental imbalance. Maybe Earth was right. Maybe I shouldn't have brought her home.

From the other side of the bathroom door, there was some noise. Straightening off the wall where I was waiting, I brushed my palms down the front of my jeans, expecting her to appear.

Rattle. Rattle. Scuffle.

I suppressed a sigh. "It sticks. Pull harder."

Her annoyed determination echoed behind the door, and I couldn't help but smile slightly. How did this girl function in her daily life? I'd never met anyone more prone to life-threatening idiocy.

And why did her fatal flaw make me smile this way?

Finally, the door gave way, the frame nearly shuddering as it jerked inward.

"Eek," she squeaked, falling backward as it swung in. Seconds later, her dark head peered around the edge, eyes settling on mine. Clearing her throat, she slipped around, hands wringing together in front of her.

All the annoyance, the whiplash, and thoughts of her being mentally imbalanced blew away as if I'd never even thought them at all.

I wasn't a huge man, but my shirt on her petite frame gave a different impression. The neck was so wide it exposed her collarbones and graceful neck. The shoulders hung low on her arms while the hem stretched down to nearly her knees.

It was a dark-red color, which somehow complimented her inky hair, paper-white skin, and rosy mouth.

Long, charged, but utterly silent moments passed between us. My heart was thumping, tongue dry. And my eyes… they wouldn't turn away.

"Where are the bandages?" she asked, her hands twisting together anew.

"Oh." I blinked, taking a step forward, and then blanked on the question.

"My finger is bleeding," she said, reminding me I was supposed to be doing something.

"Here." I held up the small plastic bag I forgot I'd even been holding. I'd sent Fletch down to the corner market to get the stuff we didn't have.

Her eyes drifted to the bag. "You went out and bought some?"

"Not me," I quickly informed. "I stayed here the whole time." It seemed important I tell her that, though I wasn't sure why. "Fletch went."

"How sweet."

She thought he was sweet? He was the one who got her sent to jail.

Annoyed, I thrust the bag out. "Here," I intoned as it swung back and forth on my finger.

"Thank you." She took the sack and went back into the bathroom, leaving the door partially ajar.

Placing the sack in the sink, she began rifling through, pulling out whatever Fletch purchased, and frowning as though she didn't know what any of it was for.

Where is this girl from? Mars?

I watched her struggle with the seal on one of the small bottles, then released a hefty sigh. "Give it to me," I said, stepping into the bathroom.

She relented immediately, watching as I used my teeth to rip the seal and peel it away.

Tossing the trash into the bag, then hanging the entire thing on the door handle, I held out my hand. "Let me see."

Cautiously, she surrendered her tiny hand, all of her long nails perfectly manicured and painted… all of them except the one that was missing.

Glancing at her, I noted the way she grimaced and stared sullenly at her messed-up finger. It was hard to imagine someone literally ripping it right off her hand.

"I fell," she explained almost like she'd read my thoughts.

"What?"

"I fell when he was, ah, attacking me. The nail broke, and I cried. He used the fact it was already weak and ripped it all the way off."

It took a second to find my voice. "I'm sure it hurt."

She said nothing but nodded emphatically. Was she commiserating with herself?

Kinda cute.

"Are you smiling?" She accused.

Removing any kind of look I might have been showing, I cupped her hand, pulling it over the sink. "Hold still."

"Ow!" she wailed.

"I haven't even sprayed it on you yet."

"It's going to hurt."

"It says it's sting-free on the bottle."

Her round blue eyes relaxed, her gaze completely trusting. "Really?"

Taking advantage of her distraction, I sprayed a generous amount over the raw and bleeding finger.

"Agh!" she yowled and tried to pull her hand away. My grip was stronger, so I held it in place and sprayed again. "Owww!"

I let go.

"You said it was sting-free!"

"I lied."

Her lower lip stuck out in a pout. "Blow on it." Her fingers waved at me.

"No."

A small whimper vibrated her throat, and she turned away from me, cradling the injured hand to blow on it herself.

Her shoulders shook between puffs of air.

Sighing, I pulled her around, cupped her hand like I was some kind of prince greeting a royal, and bent to gently blow air across the injury.

Her body sagged slightly against the sink, making me glance up. Those long dark lashes fanned against her cheeks, and the grimace of pain left her face.

I continued what I was doing until the antiseptic spray was nearly dry, then reached into the bag for some medicated cream and bandages.

"Hold still."

Squinting one eye and barely peering through the other,

she watched me uncap the cream. Straight white teeth bit into her lower lip.

"Why do you look like that?" I demanded. She shouldn't be biting herself like that.

"It's going to hurt again."

"No, it's not."

"You said that last time too."

"I'm not lying this time."

She still winced and tensed like I was about to pull her tooth instead of apply soothing cream and a bandage. Halfway through, the tension drained from her body.

"One more," I said, reaching for another bandage to cover the top of the finger that was still exposed. Finished, I glanced up. "Feel any better?"

"A little." She agreed. "I'm glad I don't have to look at it anymore."

"Turn around. I'll do your neck."

"I'm not wearing any pants," she blurted out.

Both of us looked down.

Even her feet were small and bare, her toes polished.

"I gave you shorts." I reminded her.

"I have a cut." Her hand hovered over her upper leg. "I was going to bandage it before I put them on."

"Let me see."

"I can do it!" she burst out, words breathless.

"Even with your finger like that?" I gestured to the one we'd just covered.

She seemed a little doubtful.

"Come on, then." I gestured.

My shirt bunched up in her hand as she tugged up the hem. There was indeed a cut and a few scrapes on the front of her thigh.

"What happened?" I asked, crouching down without thinking.

She jumped back like a bunny pouncing on a carrot and nearly fell over the toilet. "What are you doing?" she demanded, righting herself.

"Bandaging your leg. Do you want to sit on the throne while I do it instead?"

Sheer horror passed over her face, and her thigh appeared in front of me quickly. "Hurry."

Tension crowded the tiny bathroom that was also filled with the familiar scent of soap. Finished with her leg, I stood, motioning for her to turn around. I didn't have to tug at the shirt too much to reveal her neck. Instead, I tried to brush away her hair to clear room to work.

"Wait!" she exclaimed suddenly, reaching into the pocket of her discarded jacket and beaming like she'd won something fabulous as she came back with a hair tie.

Her fingers shoved through the silky, glossy strands as though it were an action she'd done a million times before. When she had compiled a short, oddly shaped ponytail near the base of her head, she made a sound.

"What?"

"It's stuck," she grumped.

"Huh?"

"Your stupid Band-Aid is stuck on my hair!"

Indeed, some strands were caught on the bandages I'd put on her finger.

"Hang on." I shifted closer. The fabric of my shirt she wore brushed against my jean-clad legs.

My entire frame dwarfed hers. Anyone behind me wouldn't even be able to see she stood there at all. "Why're you so small?" I asked, reaching for her hair.

There was a noticeable pause.

"Be careful. If you rip out any more of my hair, I will scream."

"Wouldn't be the first time," I commented.

Our skin collided, my fingers brushing lightly against hers to untangle the mess. Everything froze for an undesignated amount of time, and I swear we created our own energy—something that had never existed or been felt before.

Startling. Unexpected. Unmatched.

"Did you get it?" Her voice was hoarse, and it was affirmation she felt it too.

I made a sound. Timidly, she pulled her hand back.

"Wait," I called, circling my fingers around her wrist.

Her quickly indrawn breath made my stomach flip.

"I'll do it," I said, pushing past the currents competing with the task and slipping the hair tie off her wrist.

In seconds, I had her hair pulled up despite its uneven length.

"How do you know how to do that?" Blue eyes glanced over her shoulder.

"Is it supposed to be hard?" I picked up the spray. "It's going to sting again."

Both her hands wrapped around the edge of the sink and squeezed. Her intake of breath made me slightly angry.

The cut wasn't overly deep, but it wasn't a small prick either. Whoever did this had been using force.

"What's your name?" I asked quietly as I worked to clean up the cut and apply the cream.

"Why do you want to know?"

"Thought it would be good to know the name of the girl I just saw naked."

She moved with her gasp. She was incredibly dramatic, not just in mind, but with her whole body. "Ach!" she exclaimed, and I avoided being hit by one of her flailing hands just in time. "You said you didn't see anything!"

"Pretty sure I didn't say that."

"Yes-huh!"

"I said you didn't have anything I wanted to see. How would I know I didn't want to see it unless I already had?"

She gasped again and stomped on my foot. For a small, bare thing, it actually had some power. "Ow!"

"Take that back!"

Holding my foot, I laughed.

She raised herself to her non-impressive height, lifting her chin, and an austere aura seemed to bloom around her like a shield. "I'm leaving."

She brushed past as if I were beneath her.

I caught the back of the T-shirt, stopping her. "I still haven't put a bandage on your neck."

"Forget it. I'll just go to the hospital."

"Guess the reasons you were willing to go to jail earlier don't matter anymore."

Her head tilted and with it, the small ponytail. "You think I wanted to go to jail?"

"Seemed to me like you thought it was the safer option."

Her shoulders slumped. I actually didn't get any satisfaction from outsmarting her. That was a first.

"Am I still bleeding?"

"Yes."

"Are you lying?"

"Yes." Then I added, "But it's an open cut and really needs covered. You'll get a scar."

She gasped and hightailed it back to the sink. "Hurry!" She pointed to the area while holding her ponytail out of the way.

Another loud boom of thunder rattled the thin window as I was smoothing the bandage into place. Her body swayed back into mine. Without thinking, I cupped the side of her hip, holding her against the comfort of my body, offering a solid place to hide.

The second the sky turned dark after another lightning strike, she put space between us once more.

But the space she created was filled in by the sound of her soft, timid voice. “My name is Ivory. Ivory White.”

I wanted to crack a joke. What kind of pretentious name was that? I didn’t say anything. I couldn’t. The feel of her backing into me for protection clung to the center of my chest, making anything else impossible.

Swallowing thickly, I gathered up the trash lying in the sink. “It’s late and storming. Put on the shorts I gave you and come get some sleep.”

I left her standing in the bathroom, her body still turned away. She knew just as well as I did that she wouldn’t be going anywhere tonight.

Thirteen

Ivory

Five men in a one-bedroom apartment. Yes, I counted Snort. In my opinion, he was more human than his owner.

Math wasn't my best subject, but you didn't even need to know math to know this was an unbalanced equation. This entire apartment would fit in my living room, and I lived there alone.

"Where does everyone sleep?" I asked, standing in the center of the room, gazing around as a new kind of fear swept over me.

I was exhausted. Physically and emotionally. Not only had I been almost murdered, warned of potential danger, told to no longer exist, gotten arrested, and then passed out in the street, but I was now… here.

Standing in some drafty old building in clothes that were not mine, with cuts and scrapes stinging my body, and realizing for the first time that I was essentially surrounded by a bunch of strange men.

What in the hell was I thinking coming here?

Oh, right. I wasn't. I'd been unconscious. It didn't matter. I had nowhere else to go. So I had to make a choice to take my chances out there on the streets or stay inside… My thoughts led my eyes to float around the room.

Beau was across the way, partially hidden in some giant chair that faced several lit-up computer monitors, a headset pulled over his dark-red hair.

Fletch was sitting on the couch with a giant bag of chips in his lap. Whatever was on the flatscreen seemed to enthrall him to the point of not even realizing Snort was breathing heavily right beside him, hoping for a snack.

Earth was nowhere to be seen, thankfully, and Neo… *I don't see him anywhere either.*

An unsettled feeling stirred in my stomach, making my toes curl against the scratched-up wood floor. My breaths turned labored, and the strangeness of all of this began pecking at whatever shred of sanity I had left.

Blurred movement out of the corner of my eye made me whirl, my vision struggling to keep up with the quick change.

A strong grip curled around my elbow, steadying me even as I felt alarmed.

"What are you doing?" Neo practically demanded.

Blinking rapidly, my eyes focused, his dark features filling my line of sight. "Neo," I whispered, relief washing over me. "I thought you'd left."

"This is my apartment," he said as though I were stupid.

I felt kinda stupid in that moment. "Where were you?"

Two lines formed between his eyes and I expected him to be harsh again, but his voice was patient. "In the kitchen. Here." He offered a fresh bottle of water and was also holding a paper plate with a sandwich on it.

"What's that?" I asked, taking the water to unscrew the cap.

"A ham sandwich." He was back to talking to me like I was stupid. "I figured you might be hungry."

My stomach growled loudly, but I shook my head. "No, I'm fine. Thank you."

"Eat it anyway."

My eyes widened. “I said I’m not hungry.”

“And I said eat it anyway.” He challenged.

Despite my exhaustion, my hackles rose. “Don’t you try and tell me what to do!”

Neo picked up half of the sandwich made with white bread and held it to my lips. “Take a bite.”

How dare he! “I don’t know—*hmmph*.” My words were cut off when he stuffed a corner of the food into my mouth.

Utterly shocked he would do such a thing, I straightened, eyes wild with blue fire, and stared at him incredulously.

His dark eyes watched me, waiting. “Bite,” he whispered, reminding me he was still holding the food stuffed into my mouth.

My jaw obeyed even as my mind rebelled. Neo pulled back, glittering onyx eyes still on mine.

The sandwich sat in my mouth forgotten because I couldn’t focus on anything at all when I felt like I was being swallowed whole by an entire galaxy.

“Chew.” He reminded.

Snapping out of it, I made a face when the tang of mayo exploded over my tongue. The bread was too soft, and it stuck to the roof of my mouth. The ham, well, I wondered if it contained more chemicals than actual meat.

“Don’t like it?” he asked, unperturbed.

“I hardly ever eat sandwiches, and when I do, it’s from a gourmet bakery down the block that makes their bread fresh daily and imports their ham from a butcher in the Hamptons. It’s organic.” I chewed some more. “And I don’t like mayonnaise. I prefer aioli.”

“Here.” Fletch appeared, holding out a greasy bag. “Add some chips to it. Then the bread won’t stick to the roof of your mouth.”

“No, thank you.”

Snort leaped off the couch, his toenails click-clacking

over the wood as he came to my side. The snorting sounds he made intensified when he sat at my feet.

Plucking a piece of "ham" off the plate, I held it out to the dog. He snatched it up like he was starved.

"Better not let Earth see you do that." Fletch warned.

"Where is he?" I wondered.

"Downstairs at the bar."

"We're above the Rotten Apple?"

Both men nodded.

"Eat more." Neo shoved the plate at me.

"I couldn't."

"I'm not picking you up off the floor if you pass out again," he snapped, shoving the food more insistently.

I picked up the half I'd already taken a bite out of. "You can have the other half."

"Thanks!" Fletch said, grabbing it and shoving half into his mouth at once.

"Fletch," Neo growled.

Frankly, I was grateful he took it. I snuck another bite to the dog while they were arguing.

"I saw that," Neo informed like I'd been caught robbing a bank.

"Where does everyone sleep?" I asked, subconsciously taking a bite of the mushy sandwich.

"Earth has the bedroom," Fletch said, pointing past the bathroom. "I sleep on the couch, Beau's bed is on the other side of his desk, and Neo sleeps on the floor."

"On the floor!" I said, looking at Neo for confirmation.

He nodded.

"But aren't you uncomfortable?" I demanded.

"I have a blow-up mattress."

Was that supposed to make it better?

Going across the room, Neo grabbed a pillow and blanket from the corner, bringing it back toward the couch.

"You can sleep here tonight," he told me, putting the pillow on one end of the sofa.

"But what about Fletcher?"

"You don't even take up half the cushion. Plenty of room for both of us," he said, plopping back down on the other end to prop his feet up on the coffee table.

Teeth sinking into my lower lip, I wondered if it was too late just to leave.

Making a sound, Neo grabbed Fletch by his ear, hauling him off the couch.

"Ow, ow, ow!" Fletch wailed.

Beau glanced around from whatever he was doing and laughed.

"You can sleep on the floor with me tonight," Neo instructed.

"Aww, man."

Knocking at the door made my body tense, my eyes swinging around for Neo.

"It's just Earth." He promised, passing by to undo all the locks.

Earth stepped in a few seconds later, his dark, level stare landing on me. His entire upper lip curled, and he looked anything but friendly.

I barely batted an eye. I was used to people like him. All bark. No bite. The fact that Snort was dancing around his feet only proved it.

He made only a disgusted sound before going to his bedroom and shoving the door shut behind him.

"Get out the mattress," Neo told Fletch, his hand curling around my upper arm. "C'mon." He led me to the couch and pushed me down.

"I've never slept on a couch before."

"Think of it like you're camping."

"I've never been camping either."

Neo made a rude sound. "Go to sleep." He draped the blanket over me and turned away.

"Neo?"

The way his hand fisted at his side when I called his name made a funny feeling squirm around in my chest.

"Huh?" he asked without turning back.

"Thank you."

"No more talking," he rebuked gruffly and continued away, shutting off the TV as he went.

The room was plunged into darkness with the exception of the glowing computer monitors that kinda made me feel like I was onboard some weird spaceship.

Hey, the way this day was going, I wouldn't be surprised.

"I don't even know where I am?" I muttered, pulling the blanket closer around me.

"You're in the Grimms," Fletcher answered.

My nose wrinkled. "What's the Grimms?"

"Aren't you familiar with NYC?" Fletch questioned.

I peered through the dark at him as he helped Neo set up their bed. I wasn't sure how both of them would fit on the blow-up mattress, but I didn't want to ask. They all shared the same bar of soap, for crying out loud.

"Of course," I proclaimed. "I was born and raised here."

Forgetting the bed, he glanced at me. "Where?"

"The Upper East Side."

Fletcher made a strangled sound. I didn't know why. It was a perfectly respectable place.

"She's probably never been below 5th Avenue," Neo muttered.

"Of course I have!" I insisted. Then in a much softer tone, I said, "I think."

They both finished making their bed, and when they were settled, I stared across to where they lay. "So how far are we from there?"

"In terms of miles? Not far," Neo replied. "In terms of lifestyle? Light-years."

"The Grimms is the grittiest part of the city. The poorest. The ugliest."

Without thinking about it, I reached up and gripped the pillow.

There was an ominous but sad quality to his next whispered words. "Some people say once you stay here, you can't ever get out."

Does Fletcher want out? Does Neo?

Pushing back my uneasy feelings, I scoffed. "If you want to leave, call a cab and go."

"If it was that easy, you wouldn't still be here."

Fletcher's words made me uneasy, but Neo's?

They frightened me.

Fourteen

Neo

THE SKIES RUMBLED AND ROARED LIKE THE GODS ABOVE US were at war. Maybe they were. I had no idea what or who watched us from above, but thinking they were tumultuous and nonconciliatory sure seemed like a correct assumption.

Every time the wind rattled the windows, a boom of thunder shook the sky, or an overly zealous blast of rain splattered the building, Ivory moved.

She was a conundrum, Miss Ivory White.

On one hand, she was snotty, haughty, and carried herself with a monied air.

On the other, she was jumpy, nervous, and afraid of her own shadow.

A fish out of water. That's what this storybook beauty reminded me of. Flopping around, gasping for air, and looking for any drop of water that could make her feel like she wasn't lost. The second someone placed this fish back in its ocean, she would swim off with utter confidence and never look back.

That was the thing about a fish out of water. It could only survive in its own environment. If there wasn't someone there to put it back… it would die.

Craack! The sharp, sudden sound of thunder seemed to

rip open the earth with its unexpected violence. A high-pitched keening sound followed. Then everything in the entire apartment shut down.

The computer monitors that always lit up the room went black, plunging everything into darkness so opaque I couldn't even see my own hand when I held it out.

"Fuck!" Beau spat, the sound of his chair rolling across the floor and crashing into something disturbing the utter stillness of the dark. Another noise, which I assumed was his headset being flung onto his desk, followed.

Beside me, Fletcher was undisturbed. I'd never met anyone with the absolute ability to block out everything when he slept.

"Everything okay?" I called to my friend who was moving around across the room.

"Peachy."

"Backup?"

He made a rude noise. "Of course I'm backed up. My backups have backups. I just hope none of these motherboards got fried."

Hacker speak. I was used to it.

"Need some help?"

"Nah. I'll look at it in the morning when the power comes back on."

The light from his phone dimmed when he went behind his desk to the mattress on the floor.

The rain pelting the windows was the only sound in the room when I slipped from beneath the blanket and crawled across the floor. It didn't matter how dark it was in here. I knew this place like the back of my hand and maneuvered skillfully.

Ivory was sitting on the sofa, knees pulled into her chest, arms wrapped around them. I don't know how she managed to appear even smaller than she was, but she did.

A lump formed in my throat as my eyes made out her form in the night.

Her body trembled.

Her breathing was uneven.

Speaking seemed out of place here. Even just whispering her name seemed intrusive. Kneeling in front of the sofa, I reached out my hand.

She flinched when my fingers brushed the back of her hand. Her head lifted out of the shelter of her body. *Skin as white as snow...* Even in the darkness, I could make out her features because she was so utterly beautiful not even the shadows could disguise it.

I brushed away the wetness on her cheeks and tucked the hair in her face behind her ear. Pausing at the trembling of her lower lip, I debated on my instinct.

Her blue eyes watched and waited, curious as to what I would decide.

Screw it.

The pad of my thumb gently tugged the fullness of her mouth away from the sharp edges of her teeth. Performing light swiping motions, I soothed until the quivering stopped. Once her mouth was calm and still, the pad of my thumb rested at the center for long moments until I reached up to palm the side of her head.

Ivory surrendered to the light pressure I applied, her body lowering into the pillow. Lying on her side, knees still pulled in, she focused her eyes on me, never once looking away.

The weight of her attention was heavy. It muffled everything else as if this fish had been tossed back into the sea. But instead of rushing away, she'd brought me along. The water swallowed both of us, muting anything and everything, making it feel as if we were the only fish in existence.

Unable to deny the urge, I stroked the side of her head then tugged the blanket up around her shoulders.

Preparing to crawl back to bed, I rotated. Small, cold fingers closed around my bicep, making me turn back.

Her eyes pleaded.

I was in no position to deny.

Scooting close, I leaned my weight into the side of the couch. The hand around my bicep extended for something her small arm wasn't long enough to reach. I offered my hand, and she clasped on, tugging most of my arm into the cocoon of the blanket around her.

When our fingers linked intimately, her eyes drifted closed.

Fifteen

Ivory

The scent of coffee wafted into my dreams, promising something wonderful the minute I opened my eyes.

Imagine my surprise when I got a face full of nostrils.

"Agh!" I exclaimed, trying to move away. The weight lying across my body prevented the escape.

Snort, snort, snort. The dog's heavy breathing puffed in my face, and along with his nostrils, I got a good view of his crooked teeth.

"Oh, ew," I said, pushing away his snout.

His tail wagged, and it made me smile. The dog nudged my hand, and I scratched behind his ears, enjoying the softness of his fur.

Over his heavy breathing, the sounds of people moving around filtered in from what I assumed was the kitchen. I took a deep breath, wanting to appreciate the coffee scent that first enticed me to awake.

My nose wrinkled. It smelled burned.

"That's not the coffee, right?" I asked Snort.

He sneezed.

"Good boy," Earth said, appearing over the couch and praising his dog for blowing snot on me.

I snarled at Earth and patted the dog.

"Sun's up." He hitched a thumb over his shoulder toward the door.

"Guess that means your personality doesn't improve with daylight."

"Breakfast!" Beau yelled from the kitchen.

Snort leaped off me at the promise of food and tugged half the blanket with him. Air brushed over my legs, and I gasped, at first not remembering I had on shorts. Nearly rolling off the sofa, clutching the blanket, I tried to spread it over my bare legs.

Looking to where Fletch and Neo slept last night, I saw the mattress had already been put away.

How did I sleep through that?

Aware of the glare still being cast down at me, I sighed and sat up. Holding back a wince, I took stock of my body. I was sore in places I didn't even know existed. I couldn't tell if it was from what I went through yesterday or sleeping on this couch.

Probably both.

My neck was especially stiff, and when I reached around to rub it, breath hissed between my teeth as my hand closed over the bandaged cut.

Earth made a sound. Quickly, I glanced up to see if he'd noticed.

Oh, he had. Probably nothing got by this guy.

"I'll change and go," I said, my voice hoarse. My throat was sore.

He patted the top of the cushion, so I glanced over my shoulder.

"Breakfast," he grumbled and then went toward the kitchen.

I blinked. Blinked again. Did he just invite me to eat breakfast?

Rubbing my eyes, I looked around as if I were seeing this

place for the first time. The room was brighter now. The rain had finally stopped, so sun streamed in through the windows. The floors were scuffed, worn wood. The furniture was at a minimum, but the electronics around the room were all top-notch.

But what drew my eyes most, what I couldn't believe I'd actually not even noticed last night, was the walls. The brick walls were filled with color.

Actually, graffiti.

It looked as though some deviant snuck in and splashed paint all over the loft walls. Some of it was completely abstract, large pieces of color and shapes that all fit together to create movement and shape. The colors were electric, loud, and at times chaotic. Then my eye moved farther down and stopped at a giant dinosaur wearing headphones and a backward hat commanding a turntable.

Random words floated around the room. The corner was painted to look like the room cracked open and different-colored skeletons peered out.

I'd never seen anything like it.

Untangling from the blanket, I wandered around the space, staring at it all again, knowing that even if I stared for an hour, there would be something new to find. As I looked, my heart rate actually elevated as though the passion the painter put on these walls had the palpable ability to inspire.

Pulling my eyes from the dinosaur, I turned.

My heart slowed. Everything in me focused on the new piece of art that covered the entire wall the door was located on.

The vibrant color was gone as if a moment of sorrow leached away everything, leaving only black and white. Melancholy swelled inside me so thick my chest turned tight and a lump formed in my throat.

Moving closer to the canvas, my steps were hushed just like my breathing.

I felt as though I stood in front of a vast ocean; that's how greatly the sentiment in this piece moved me. That's how thoroughly swallowed up I was.

The edge of the wall was a bright garden, blooming and promising. The vibrant color that was everywhere else in the room was here, but very quickly, it faded away, the garden turning dark and overgrown. Prickles of wickedness crawled over my arms, and I tried to rub away the chill. Closer to me, something burned, something I should recognize, but it was being eaten up by flames that felt hot despite their cool color.

The fire was violent and greedy, destroying the sad and depleted garden. As if this evil were so greedy it wanted even the things that had nothing to give.

Tears swam at the edge of my vision as I forced my eyes to turn away from the fire, away from the destruction, and toward the white feathers that were painted so realistically I felt as though I could reach out and take one. They floated down from the ceiling against a sky so dark there weren't even any stars. The feathers trailed all the way past the frame of the apartment door, raining down to a portion of what they used to be.

A broken wing.

An angel wing lay torn in half, the feathers ruffled, the white turning gray. Or maybe, I thought, looking again, the wings were covered in ash from the fire blazing so close by.

The tears swimming in my eyes spilled over, trailing untouched paths down my cheeks. The center of my body tugged toward those feathers, toward the wings and that midnight sky. My stomach felt pained, and my fingers quivered.

It felt as though I'd floated close enough to finally touch, but when I did, something stopped me.

"What are you doing?"

I didn't bother to hide my tears when I turned to Neo. Like magnets, our stares attracted, the pull so strong I wouldn't have been able to move away.

For a moment, the emotions inside me, the emotions reaching out from this wall enclosed us like we weren't viewing this art. We were living it.

His fingers tightened on my wrist, an anchor in this strange reality.

"What are you doing?" he repeated.

"This painting," I said, finally able to break the spell cast over us. Pulling free, I backed up so I could look again. "I didn't notice it last night." Gesturing to all of them, I added, "Any of these."

"You were distracted."

"They're incredible."

His surprise was so pungent it was jarring. It was enough to pull my sight away from the art and focus on him. Dark hair was tousled, the shadow on his jaw shaved away. Paint splattered his jeans and speckled the shoulder of the black T-shirt he wore.

I'd just thought he was dirty last night; I hadn't realized the dirt was paint.

My mouth opened. Closed. Opened again. "Did you…?" I gestured around the room. "Is this your art?"

"You're surprised?"

"Well, yes." Realizing how rude that came out, I quickly said, "No, I…" My voice trailed away, and I gazed at him for help, hoping he would fill in the sentence.

He didn't. He stared arrogantly, watching me fumble.

I didn't know what to say. I was caught off guard, turned emotional by paint on brick walls. But it was more than that. Placing my palm against my chest, I rubbed. "I can feel it," I whispered, gazing back at the feathers. "This isn't just a painting. It's emotion."

The arrogance was gone from his face when I glanced back. Prickles of awareness and excitement skittered along my spine. Intensity radiated from the endless depths of his obscure stare. How eyes so dark could blaze with light was a mystery to me.

Without thinking, I rubbed at my chest again. The pressure there was stronger than before.

I didn't know how much time passed or how long I was lost and found in Neo's infinite stare, but coming back from that place he'd taken me was startling.

His hand was so warm it almost felt scalding when it wrapped around my forearm. "Breakfast," he insisted, tugging me along.

"But I was still looking—" I protested, trying to turn back to the painting.

"That's enough." His words rang with finality.

Maybe I was still spellbound by the art and its creator. Maybe his touch muted my desire to talk back. Maybe my body wanted coffee more than an argument.

Regardless, I surrendered to his demand.

Sixteen

Neo

She felt my artwork.

I felt her.

It had been easy enough to ignore until the lights went out. Until I crawled across the apartment floor to make sure she wasn't afraid. Her hand was so small when it beckoned me to stay.

Her trembling stopped.

She fell asleep.

And I sat there with nothing left to distract me from the way she made me feel. When the sun came up and life restarted, I thought perhaps I could go back to ignoring it.

I couldn't. Not when I saw her reaching out toward the painting as if she'd finally found a missing piece of her soul. A piece I created. A piece she seemed to need.

My mind reminded me I didn't need this. There was no room in my life. My heart whispered something else entirely.

"Sit." My voice was gruff, but I didn't bother to correct it. She made me feel entirely off balance, so she deserved to feel that way too.

Ivory hopped from foot to foot, staring at the chair I pushed her toward, and I wondered what made her hesitate. I wondered what this place looked like through her eyes. I couldn't imagine because honestly, wherever she came from was probably somewhere I'd never been.

"Do you drink coffee?" I asked.

Her little sniff was followed by, "Are there people who don't?"

I made a sound.

"Where's the espresso machine? I can make it myself."

The fork Fletch was holding clattered against his plate. Earth turned from the stove, and Beau poked his head up from rummaging in the fridge.

She blinked. "Why are you all staring?" She fidgeted with the hem of the shirt she wore. My shirt.

Earth tossed the spatula down, abandoning the eggs he was scrambling. Coffee sloshed around in a half-empty pot when he grabbed it out of the machine. The sound of the liquid pouring into a mug filled the space, as did the sound of the ceramic plunking down on the wooden tabletop in front of her. "Drink it or don't."

Ivory leaned over the cup, sniffing.

Beau left the fridge door hanging open and carried a bottle of creamer over to set it next to Ivory's cup. "You don't seem like the type to drink it black."

"I'm not a psychopath," she told him.

All of us suppressed a snicker, and Earth made a rude sound.

Ivory pointed to his back, which was turned away, and we nodded. Understanding lit up her face. "That explains a lot."

"Real men don't need creamer," Earth announced like he knew exactly the conversation we all had behind his back.

Sitting at the table, Fletch paused in reaching for the creamer. His lower lip stuck out in a pout.

"Except for you, kid," Earth announced, again not even having to turn around.

Fletcher was pacified, smiling while adding more creamer

to his cup than he had coffee. He held the bottle out to Ivory. "Here you go."

Wrinkling her nose, she took it and glanced down. "Do you have organic heavy cream?"

"That tastes like vanilla!" Fletch declared.

"Carbs and sugar." She corrected him.

"I like it," Fletch told her.

Beau grabbed the bottle from her and added some to her cup. "Try it."

Ivory was skeptical, but when Beau stirred it, then lifted the cup for her, she relented. She was definitely a snob, but she was polite.

"Thank you." Her prim voice was quite the contrast to this shabby mismatched kitchen and the clothes swallowing her body.

We all watched curiously as she sipped the coffee, waiting for even the smallest of reactions. After her second sip, she noticed the three of us staring.

"Well?" Fletch asked excitedly.

"Not bad."

"Sit, sit!" Fletcher insisted, pointing to a chair beside him, not the one I'd pushed her toward. Ivory sat, and Beau pulled up his chair to the opposite side so she was sandwiched between the two.

A plate hit the center of the table, making what was already sitting there rattle.

Fletch and Beau attacked the platter of scrambled eggs and bacon with their usual gusto, reaching across each other, arguing over who got the best piece of bacon, and threatening bodily harm.

Just a typical morning.

Blue eyes wide, Ivory sat back while they clambered around her, clutching the mug like a shield and watched them.

"Are you hungry?" I asked, grabbing a cup.

Beau and Fletch stopped what they were doing and turned to her.

Her smile was weak. "Don't mind me," she told them, lifting the mug to her lips. Lips that were still rosy red. I'd never seen anyone with that natural shade before. "I'm good with this."

They went back to being savages, and I poured some coffee for myself.

Turning from the stove, Earth dropped a plate in front of her. "Eat."

Her eyes rounded anew. "That's for me?"

Everyone stared in shock, Fletcher with bacon hanging from his lips.

"If you don't eat, you'll just pass out again and use it as another excuse to park it on my couch," Earth announced.

Life resumed around the table. I grabbed some food and sat down.

Despite the plate in front of her, Ivory remained pressed into the back of her seat, grasping the mug. A shiver shook her slight frame, and I squinted. Her arms and legs were covered with goose bumps.

Abandoning my food, I went into the living room and grabbed a few items, carrying them back to the kitchen. Without a word, I took her mug, giving it to Beau to hold. "Here," I said, thrusting out one of my flannels.

She practically grimaced at the red fabric. "I don't usually wear plaid."

"It's better than being cold," I barked.

She pushed her arms in, and I tugged it around her body. Next, I draped a blanket over her lap.

Her soft thank-you made me embarrassed, so I hurried back to my seat and avoided looking at her.

We all ate in silence. Well, except for the sound of Snort

breathing under the table. Out of the corner of my eye, I watched Ivory slip a piece of bacon off her plate and under the table to the bulldog.

When she reached for another, Earth's voice was like a whip. "Do not feed the dog bacon."

"But he's hungry," Ivory protested.

"He has food."

"He told me he wanted bacon."

Earth dropped his fork. "You talk to dogs now?"

"No. I just listen."

"Well, stop *listening* to Snort."

"Whose mug is this?" she asked a minute later.

I couldn't help but grin at the chipped mug featuring a giant green Care Bear on the front.

Beau laughed. Fletcher groaned. Even Earth, who was sitting there shoveling eggs into his mouth, cracked a smile.

"Not one of these mugs matches." Ivory went on when we all just laughed and said nothing. "So they must be specific for each of you, right?"

"All right, princess. Enlighten us." I encouraged.

"Earth has a black mug because it clearly matches his soul."

Earth glowered, which just made her point more valid.

"Beau's mug has an emoji smiley face on it because he's the friendliest."

"Hey!" Fletch took offense.

Ivory glanced at him, pointing out, "You got me arrested."

"On accident!"

"Actions are still actions!" she retorted, turning away.

Fletcher rubbed his head, frowning.

"Your mug has smudges all over it because you never wash your hands after you paint," she told me.

My mug was definitely splattered with paint.

"Your mug, though," she said, looking at Fletch, "all white..."

"I like it. It's mysterious. Just like me."

"More like he doesn't want to drink out of the mug Earth bought him." Beau snickered.

Under the table, Fletch kicked him.

"This is your mug?" Ivory asked, glancing between the Care Bear and Fletch.

"It's Lucky Bear," Beau answered.

"Are you very lucky?" Ivory asked him.

"Stupid bear," Fletch grumbled, turning back to play in his eggs.

"He's lucky he's stayed out of jail this long." I teased.

Fletcher took offense. "I don't need luck. I'm just good at what I do."

"And what is it you do exactly?" Ivory asked.

"He gets fired a lot," Beau said around a mouthful of eggs.

"I thought you said you were good at what you do," Ivory deadpanned.

We all laughed.

"Your food is going to get cold," Fletch mumbled, pointing to her plate.

She glanced at me, and I pointedly glanced at her plate. She sighed and began eating. "Mmm," she said after a moment. "These eggs are delicious!"

Earth froze, caught off guard by the compliment. "They're just eggs," he mumbled.

"Not so. I've had eggs by some of the best chefs in this country! I don't even normally eat scrambled eggs because I don't like them. What's your secret?"

Crossing his arms over his chest, he stared at her. "I cook them in fat."

I think he thought she would be horrified. "Fat makes everything taste better," she announced and ate more. "Did you know that fat will also help keep you looking younger and makes your hair shiny? Fat is essential to the body. It's why I like cream in my coffee." She picked up some bacon and took a bite. "Organic. And in moderation, of course."

We all sat there staring until Earth lowered his arms and cleared his throat. "It's cheap at the corner store."

"Here, have some fruit," Fletcher told her, sliding a bowl of strawberries toward her.

"Oh!" she exclaimed. "Those look very nice for this time of winter. But no, thank you."

"C'mon, just one," Fletcher said, picking one plump red berry out of the bowl by its stem to dangle it in front of her face.

Ivory shrieked and shoved away from it.

Fletch and his berry followed.

"No." She gasped, tangling up in the blanket and plummeting right off the side of the chair.

"Fletcher!" I growled, pushing back from the table.

Beau was already helping her to her feet, at the same time pulling her free from the blanket. I couldn't help but notice the way Beau's hand wrapped around her upper arm, how he used his strength to help steady her.

My back teeth gnashed together, and a feeling I didn't like wormed around inside me.

"What the hell?" I pinned Fletch with a look.

Grimacing, he lowered the berry to his side. "Who is scared of a strawberry?"

"I didn't mean to react so..."

"Dramatically?" Earth put in.

She gave him a look, then turned back to us. "I must still be shaken up from yesterday. And then when that berry came so close..."

"Did the killer threaten you with a strawberry *and* a knife?" Fletcher asked, eyes wide.

Kid was a moron.

"No," she said quite seriously, not even amused by his stupidity. "That might have killed me for sure!"

No one said anything. Beau finally released her, and something in my chest loosened.

"I'm highly allergic. Just touching them causes me to have a harsh reaction."

"Huy…" Fletch worried and tossed the berry onto the table. "I didn't know!"

"This is ridiculous," Earth grumped and left the kitchen.

Snort stared between his owner and the table, debating if he might get more snacks if he stayed.

"Snort!" Earth bellowed.

The dog scurried after him, his heavy breathing leaving a trail of sound behind him.

"Let me help clean this up," Ivory said, reaching for a few plates.

"No!" we all exclaimed at once, and I pulled her around so I could step in front of her.

"Why not?"

"We can't be sure what the strawberry touched," I explained. Pulling a chair back, I directed her into it and handed over her mug. "Just sit there."

Fletcher hurriedly scooped the remaining food from his plate into his mouth while Beau carried the dishes over to the sink.

Ivory wasn't even quiet for a full minute. "So Neo is a painter, Fletcher is good at getting fired, Earth owns the bar, and Beau… What do you do?"

A few looks passed between us.

Beau cleared his throat. "I work with computers."

"That would explain all the high-quality tech in this apartment."

Beau's red eyebrows lifted. "You know about tech?"

One of her shoulders shrugged. "Not really. But I know high-quality when I see it."

"So, ah…" Beau shifted, all our attention still focused on this strange girl in the middle of the kitchen. "What do you do?"

"Hey, princess!" Earth's voice carried in from the other room.

Ivory straightened. "Yes?" she called ambiguously.

"You're on TV."

Seventeen

Ivory

The headline across the bottom of the large flatscreen was assaulting, and even though I knew I was fully alive, I felt I was actually dead and was staring down at the world's reaction.

Elite NYC Heiress Missing – Presumed Dead!

"The Upper East Side, home to the city's most elite, is in shock this morning as it has been reported that the daughter of the late Arthur White, founder of the Fortune 500 company, W, is missing. A discovery of blood at her last known whereabouts has people assuming the worst.

"Ivory White, who is the sole heir of her father's dynasty, is also the CEO of her own fashion and beauty company, Reflection.

"It is being reported that Miss White was out for her routine early-morning run in Central Park yesterday morning and did not return home. She has not been seen since. Her bodyguard and driver, who were both with her at the park, say that despite the blood splatters that point to foul play, they saw no sign of any trouble and that the young elitist seemed to vanish into thin air.

"A missing persons report has been officially filed, and the police are asking that anyone with any leads or information at all

about the potential whereabouts of Miss White should call immediately."

I felt the stare of many eyes as the news anchor droned on about me as if everything I was could be summed up on a single sheet of paper. The photo filling the right side of the flatscreen wasn't my best, but looking at it further, I understood why it was chosen. The black Balmain suit, which featured a fitted skirt and textured jacket, and black Louboutin heels made it seem as if I were attending my own funeral. The oversized black sunglasses and long black hair made my white skin appear even more like snow.

Like I'm a ghost already.

I stood in between the kitchen and the couch, my feet having stalled out since I first saw the screen.

Something light brushed against my arm, and I glanced at Fletch, whose honey-colored eyes were awed. "That's you?"

It seemed to take all my effort just to swallow, so all I did was nod.

"Audra White, Ivory's stepmother, has yet to release a statement, and it is being reported she is being treated at home for shock. She has been in contact with the authorities and is doing everything in her power to make sure her beloved daughter is found safe."

I snorted. Earth stole a glance over his shoulder to where I stood. I shrugged.

"It is also being reported that the executives over at W and Reflection are all scrambling as stocks begin to plummet. An executive emergency meeting is being called for later this afternoon."

The screen flashed to a crowd of people (mainly reporters) gathered outside a very familiar high-rise building. The crowd parted, and a man in a three-piece gray suit stepped through, stealing the screen and all eyes the second he was visible.

It wasn't only his height that made him stand out in the

crowd, but the way he carried himself, the confidence that radiated around him. The dove-gray suit was tailored to fit his broad shoulders and lean waist. The pale-pink tie would have looked girly on anyone else, but not on this man. Everything else about him radiated masculinity, and even the color pink bowed down to it.

His blond hair was styled perfectly, but not so perfectly that he looked like an ass. He carried a leather briefcase, wore custom leather loafers, and accentuated everything with a somber but brave face as he pushed his way into the building.

My building.

"What are you doing, Ethan?" I whispered, moving closer to the TV.

"You know him?" Beau questioned.

My hands gripped the back of the couch as the picture changed and the reporter asked once again that if anyone had any leads to call.

"Of course, we will keep the city up to date as any new information or leads come to light about this breaking story."

Just like that, they transitioned into the weather as if everything that had happened to me since yesterday could be neatly summed up in a few sentences.

The silence in the room was jarring because quiet in a room with these four men and a snorting dog was something that hadn't occurred since I'd walked through the door.

Automatically, my stare went to the one whose silence seemed the loudest. He stood not very far away, but still, the distance seemed tremendous.

"You know him?" Neo's voice was calm and quiet, but it sent chills up my spine.

Words failed me, so I nodded.

"How do you know him?"

All four men stared, waiting for explanations and details.

Despite the weight of four pairs of eyes, I stared at only one. "I-I've known him a long time," I said, still ensnared by his stare. I couldn't really pinpoint the way he looked at me, but I guess it didn't matter because I was trapped there just the same.

"How do you know him?" Neo repeated, even more of an edge to his voice. It was different. He seemed different suddenly. The air around him shimmered with something new… something intense.

He's an acquaintance.

A friend.

I went to school with him.

Our families know each other.

All of these were absolutely true and accurate. But these were not what tumbled from my lips as I stood in the middle of four men, a loud-breathing dog, and paintings that seemed to wake up my soul.

"He's my betrothed."

The heat from the painted fire consuming the color off the wall just steps away suddenly seemed scorching. As if it were actually burning, I felt it's melting intensity reaching out, trying to consume me too.

Tension sucked all the oxygen out of the room. Our stares remained locked as my lungs nearly shriveled and my skin felt tight.

"Be-what?" Fletcher wondered close by, reminding me there were three other men in this room.

"Betrothed," Earth repeated, and my lungs constricted more.

I swore I heard something in his voice, almost as though he were disgusted but also not surprised.

I wanted to look at him, but I was still trapped by Neo's eyes.

"That's a big word," Fletcher whined. "I don't get it."

"They're engaged," Neo answered in that same calm yet monotone way.

All his animation is lacking. I wasn't used to seeing Neo so… flat. Usually, everything he did was with some sort of vigor.

"You're engaged!" Fletcher exclaimed.

A muscle in the side of Neo's jaw ticked once. Vaguely, I wondered where his dimple had gone. His eyes flicked away, dismissing me and making me nearly sag.

"That's your fiancé?" Beau asked, curious.

"Yet you needed to sleep on my couch." Earth's voice was sharp as a blade, filled with a thousand I-told-you-sos.

"No, I—" Before the words could even trip off my tongue, I was silenced.

"I have to go," Neo announced, walking across the room to jerk on yet another plaid flannel over his paint-splattered T-shirt and then snatch up a black leather jacket. His flannel was a dark shade of blue, and the unbuttoned ends hung below the hem of the leather. The color seemed to compliment his skin better than the red.

"Go where?" Fletcher wanted to know.

"I have to work."

Fletcher might have said something else, but a quick glance from Neo made whatever it was wither and die before it was even born.

He went to the door, dark hair falling over his forehead, and for a brief moment, it was like he was walking into his painting.

"Wait," I called out, panic suddenly gripping my heart.

Hand wrapped around the doorknob, Neo paused but didn't glance back.

I didn't say anything else because I didn't know what to say. I didn't understand the sudden turbulence inside me.

He left, the door slightly ajar, leaving me staring into that slim opening with a mighty urge to chase after and beg him to stay.

I didn't chase people. I didn't beg. So I stood there instead, wishing he would turn back.

"Don't be here when I get home." Earth practically snarled, pulling the door wide so he could leave as well.

He didn't leave it slightly ajar. He slammed it shut with finality, punctuating that it was time for me to go.

Eighteen

Neo

I WAS IN TROUBLE.

The kind of trouble I didn't know how to maneuver my way out of. And maneuvering out of trouble was my specialty.

Sometime between yesterday and this morning, I'd lost control of things I firmly had on lock.

Beneath my skin, I was hot and stinging like I was somehow burning from the inside out. The feeling was unpleasant, and the more I stood in this room, the worse it felt.

So I bolted. It's what I was good at, right? Making a mess then leaving. Not committing to anything other than what required no commitment.

My name on her lips stopped me, the burning under my skin intensified, and the urge to turn back scared me enough to push forward.

Out in the hall, I stomped to the stairs, chest tight, the back of my neck flushed.

He's my betrothed. Betrothed. Betrothed.

My hands fisted at my side. I knew exactly why I was boiling, and I hated it.

The long hallway at the bottom of the stairs ran alongside the Rotten Apple and at the end was a door offering escape.

Footsteps on the stairs tightened my stomach, and for a split second, I *hoped.*

Hope was a cruel emotion because the disappointment that usually followed forced a bereft feeling onto someone who didn't want to hurt.

"You should stay away until she's gone."

That bereft feeling I mentioned howled through me like a winter wind in an empty building. Closing my eyes briefly, I took a deep breath. Glancing over my shoulder, I stared at Earth.

"And why is that?" I challenged.

"We both know why," Earth deadpanned, stepping off the stairs and heading toward the door leading inside his bar.

"I don't know what you think you know."

"You're from two different worlds, and you have way more to lose than her."

I made a rude sound, swinging around defensively. How dare this asshole act like he knew how I felt? How dare he imply I somehow had more to lose than her?

"Oh, here I thought it was her someone was trying to kill."

"Some things in life are far worse than death." Earth's quiet words echoed down the hallway, filling the air ominously.

I rocked back on my heels and watched him end the conversation by disappearing into the bar.

He was right.

I knew better than most people that life could sometimes be far worse than death.

An entire party of emotions kicked off inside me. It was a party I did not want to attend, but it appeared that I was the host. Pissed off, I stalked to the small storage cubby underneath the stairs. Inside, I grabbed a small black bag, added a few items, and walked out of the building without looking back.

Nineteen

Ivory

"Where's your ring?"

The obscure question snapped me back to reality.

"My ring?" My face wrinkled as I stared down at my hands. My bandaged finger hurt almost as much as last night. I should probably change the bandage…

"You're getting married, right? That guy looked pretty fancy. Shouldn't you have a giant rock on your finger?" Fletcher jumped over the back of the couch, sinking into the cushions with a bag of chips clutched in his hand.

Didn't we just eat breakfast?

"I'm not getting married."

"But you said you are bequeathed."

"Betrothed." I corrected.

Crunch, crunch, crunch. "Yeah, that."

"There's a difference between being betrothed and being engaged."

Fletcher paused, a chip poised in front of his lips. Snort put his paws up on the sofa cushions to beg.

"Is this like a rich people thing? Because to me, getting married is getting married."

I was getting a headache. That coffee from earlier was not

cutting it. I longed for my espresso machine or the café on Fifth Avenue that had handcrafted lattes made from freshly ground beans from the best place in Costa Rica.

I could almost taste the deep, smooth aroma over my tongue…

"Maybe we should call Neo!"

I blinked, glancing up.

Beau's head popped up from behind his fancy computer monitors.

Fletcher pointed. "She looks like she's about to pass out again!"

"I'm fine." I assured Beau, lifting my chin.

He went back to whatever he was doing.

"My family is well acquainted with Ethan's. It was proposed when we were just babies that we would get married when the time came."

Fletcher's eyes widened. "Rich people don't get to pick their own husbands?"

I'd never heard it worded that way before, and the assumption stung… probably because I wondered if it was true.

"Of course we do."

"So you like that guy?" Fletcher's eyes went back to the television as though Ethan were still filling up the screen.

My stomach tightened. *As a husband?* "Of course. He has many fine qualities."

Fletcher nodded, digging into the chips once more. "I've never seen anyone look like that before."

"Like what?"

"Handsome. Like a prince." The second the words left his mouth, a fine blush spread over his cheeks, turning them a light shade of pink. Avoiding my gaze, he shoved five chips into his mouth and chewed loudly.

"You're going to choke." I scolded.

A crumb fell from his lips, and Snort ate it.

Across the room, I stopped at the side of Beau's workstation, straightening my shoulders and reaching up to fix my hair before remembering it was half gone.

"Excuse me," I said after a moment of him not noticing I was there.

Startled, Beau looked up, his green eyes going wide. Pushing one side of the headphones he was wearing off his ear, he met my gaze. "Yes?"

"Can I borrow some money?"

He started to choke on the air as if he couldn't believe I was asking for money. I felt my cheeks heat, embarrassed. I'd never had to ask for money before.

"Did I do it wrong?" I wondered aloud.

He stopped coughing. "What?"

"Asking for money, did I do it wrong? Is that not what you're supposed to say?"

Beau blinked. "Uhh…"

"I wouldn't ask if it weren't of utmost importance. And as you witnessed on the TV earlier, I am good for the money. I will be sure to pay you back. With interest."

Clearing his throat, Beau pulled off the headset completely. "How much do you need?"

I frowned. "How much to do cleaning supplies cost?"

"Cleaning supplies?" he echoed.

"Oh! Do you have some here? I didn't see any in the bathroom." I couldn't stop the small, indelicate shudder that went through me when I thought of my shower experience last night.

"Uh, there is soap in the bathroom."

You mean to tell me they all shower with that one bar of soap and *they clean with it too?*

Oh my. I would have to consult my physician when this was over. I might need an update on my tetanus shot.

I held out my hand, palm up. "Twenty dollars? No, thirty. Make it thirty."

Beau reached into his pocket and pulled out some cash. It really amazed me that people carried cash around here. I couldn't remember the last time I saw a five-dollar bill.

"Thank you!" I beamed, leaning down to peck a short kiss to his cheek.

His face turned nearly as red as his hair. "N-no problem."

"There's a small market down on the corner?" I verified, remembering Neo mentioning it when Fletcher went to get bandages.

Beau nodded.

I went into the tiny, grimy bathroom and reluctantly put on my leggings and shirt from yesterday. It was too cold outside to wear the oversized shorts Neo had given me. It was also a fashion tragedy.

When it came time to put on my jacket, I hesitated long enough to notice what I was doing. I didn't want that jacket.

It held bad memories. The fabric was ruined. It wasn't warm enough.

Someone might recognize me if I wandered around in designer clothing.

Dropping the jacket, I pulled the red plaid flannel around me, buttoning it up over my outfit. It could also be considered a fashion tragedy… but strangely, I didn't care.

Beau looked up when I approached him again. His headphones were still not back over his ears.

Smiling sweetly, I said, "Could I borrow a hat?"

Saying nothing, Beau reached under the desk to pull out a black baseball cap.

I put it on my head, adjusting the thingy at the back so it was tighter. "You really are the nice one."

He blushed again.

"I'll be right back," I called out, going to the door.

"You're leaving?" Fletcher exclaimed.

"Just going to the corner store. Will you leave the door unlocked for me?"

Both boys nodded mutely, shocked as if they'd never seen anyone go to the store before. I waved and let myself out of the apartment.

Outside in the quiet solitude of the hallway, I sagged against the door. My limbs felt weak, my hands trembled, and every thought I had seemed sluggish. I wasn't used to feeling this way… so out of sorts.

The news this morning had shaken me, leaving me even more confused than I already was. Everyone thought I was dead. They didn't even have a body, and they all just wanted to assume the worst.

Almost like they hope it is true.

And Neo… he just walked out. And when he'd gone, I'd felt…

No.

I cut off the feelings and thoughts completely. I didn't have time for this. I had to think. Plan. Decide what to do.

I could simply get a cab and go straight home. Let everyone know I was very much alive and breathing. That would be the easiest thing to do.

But would it be the smartest?

Trust no one.

I could not unhear the ominous truth in those words.

Pushing off the door, I left, going down the stairs, bypassing the entrance to Earth's bar, and stepping out onto the sidewalk.

The sky was gray and moody, still recovering from the storms that shook the earth all last night. Just thinking of them and seeing the way the clouds still lightly churned made an uncomfortable feeling worm around inside me.

Picking up my pace a little didn't help. I couldn't outrun what was inside me, but I was going to try anyway.

The street was narrow, dirty, and grim.

Most people don't ever get out of the Grimms. The whispered words last night haunted me, following me down the street like an invisible ghost. Something unforgiving and hard jammed into my shoulder, knocking me sideways.

"Ah!" I gasped, righting myself and looking up. A man probably twice my size, dressed in black with a matching cap pulled low on his head, glared even as he kept plowing down the street.

"Watch where you're going!" he growled, stomping away.

"But you ran into me!" I spoke indignantly.

His stomping paused briefly, and I scurried away because he wasn't someone I really wanted to speak with.

The corner store looked menacing as it loomed ahead. It was small and seedy-looking, the green paint around the windows and doorframe faded and chipping. The sign on the door was handwritten: *Corner Store.*

Not very original, but I supposed it was accurate.

The lighting inside seemed dim and kinda yellow, and my stomach twisted a little. Wind blew, brushing against my neck and making me shiver. When I flipped up the collar of the flannel, the edges brushed against my cheek, and a faintly familiar scent washed over me.

Some of the anxiousness making my fingers tremble relaxed, and just that little bit of release gave me so much relief tears sprang to the backs of my eyes.

Sniffling, I ducked farther into the shirt and tugged the hat down over my forehead.

The door to the place swung out, making me fall backward.

"If you aren't coming in, don't stand in the doorway," some woman snapped on her way out.

"Excuse me." I apologized, scrambling back up to grab the dirty handle before the door could close completely.

Inside the tiny box wasn't much warmer than the street, but the wind didn't blow in there. The aisles were narrow and crowded, but it seemed they had the things I was looking for. Letting the oversized flannel fall over my hands, I grabbed up a shopping basket and used Neo's shirt as a barrier between my skin and the handle.

Neo's shirt.

The scent that calmed me just moments before... *it was his.*

Squeaaak. My sneakers made a loud sound when I stopped abruptly in the center of the aisle, my arm dropping on its way to a bottle of cleaner.

He'd just left before. He didn't even say good-bye. I might not ever see him again.

He held my hand last night.

Somehow his scent had become a relief to me. Even in this strange and scary place, he'd become somewhat of a comfort.

More tears threatened the backs of my eyes, and I blinked them away.

Of course he was a comfort. He helped you when you had nowhere to go. It was perfectly natural to be grateful. Not just to Neo, to all of them.

Well, except maybe Earth.

That was why I was here. The reminder served to get me moving again, selecting some cleaning supplies, actual soap, and shampoo, and since I could, I splurged on new toothbrushes and this pack of plastic cups in several colors.

I knew I couldn't stay there any longer, that I was going

to have to figure out my next move fast. But I could think and clean at the same time, right?

Cleaning couldn't be that hard, could it?

And then I would leave those five grumpy misfits with a clean apartment. An appropriate thank-you for what they had done.

Twenty

Neo

Sounds of the city were so common to me that I almost didn't notice it anymore. Unless, of course, when I used it to my advantage.

Bumper-to-bumper traffic echoed between the tall, crowded buildings. Honking horns, revving engines, and crowds of people on the sidewalks all created a cacophony of noise unique to New York City. Scents of frying meat, roasting chestnuts, and coffee mingled in the constantly moving air. Steam rose from grates along the sidewalks, creating random puffs of clouds, and loud clattering floated from the side streets where workers unloaded supplies from trucks.

As if the scents and sounds weren't enough to bombard the senses, the visual distractions were also everywhere. Huge billboards blinked with animations and rotating pictures. Flashing banners and advertisements vied for attention nearly every few feet. People crossed the busy streets, moving in and out of stores and shops, barely watching where they were going.

It was all too easy for someone like me to pick out the tourists. They walked almost starstruck as if trying to decide where to focus their attention and failing to put it any one place, which resulted in them being half present at every given moment.

They walked less brusquely, with less purpose, as they tried to figure out where to go and what to see.

These people were ripe for the plucking. Perfect targets, perfect opportunities to remind myself exactly who I was and who I would never be.

Slam.

"*Oh!*" someone gasped.

I pulled back from my *accidental* run-in with a woman who was staring up at a giant M&M advertisement and not paying attention at all to who was around her. My hands went automatically to her waist, steadying her as any gentleman should.

"I'm sorry. Are you all right?" I asked, offering a worried smile.

She blinked. "Oh, I'm the one who's sorry. I ran right into you!"

"It's all right. Happens a lot." I smiled, the beanie on my head sinking a little lower above my brows.

"Oh." She paused, then remembered she was speaking. "Yes, well, there is so much to see."

"Well, as long as you're okay?"

She nodded, and I slipped into the crowd, crossing the street.

I wondered how long it would take her to notice the cash in her pocket was gone. It didn't really matter because I was already long gone too.

"Want me to take that photo for you?" I asked on the opposite side of the street. A man was taking a photo of who I assumed was his girlfriend as she posed in front of Radio City Music Hall.

"Thanks, man," the dude said, handing over his camera and rushing to get into the frame.

I took a couple photos, then returned the camera, walking away with my pocket a little heavier than before.

I went on like this for a while, choosing my marks, lightening their cash supply without them even realizing. When I felt it was time to move on, I headed in a direction I never went but didn't stop to question my motives.

I rarely came this far uptown, but I made it worth my while.

After making another pile of cash in Manhattan, my stomach reminded me I was running on empty. Grabbing a coffee and a hot dog from a nearby stand, I turned the corner, and all of a sudden, my location slammed me hard.

Tall trees rose up in the middle of the cityscape, grass and sidewalks where buildings might have stood.

I had come all the way to Central Park.

I stood there dumbly like one of the clueless tourists I'd just spent hours robbing blind until the clop-clopping of a horse-drawn carriage got too close and snapped me out of the trance I'd slipped into.

Hurrying across the street, I entered the park, eyes fixating on a woman jogging along a path.

All the work I'd done the past few hours to forget her vanished. Hell, I might even believe none of it ever happened if I didn't have a fat pile of cash in my pockets to prove it.

Cash that suddenly felt heavy and… *dirty.*

This is who you are. I reminded myself. An urban thief standing in the center of a majestic scene.

Earth's words taunted as I stood and stared. *You're from two different worlds.*

He was right.

I hated him for it.

I thought to run and flee but instead walked farther beneath the trees, letting them fold me closer, their welcome offering some sort of relief.

I realized all the running I'd been doing all day, all the stealing, all the reminding myself of where I belonged had only been a distraction.

Under my skin still burned, a tight knot fisted in my stomach, and now there was an unmistakable ache in the center of my chest. How ironic that I'd run out of the apartment, hell, out of the Grimms, trying to put distance between her and me, and where did I run?

To her world.

Anger, swift and pungent, consumed me, offering relief from the host of other ailments I'd been living with since that storybook princess walked into my life.

How could I let this happen? How could one woman—a devastatingly beautiful one—twist me up so tight in barely two days?

I knew better than this. There was no place for her in my world, and there was no place in her world for me. We were completely different, incompatible. She was snobby, naïve, spoiled, and couldn't function without people hovering around her, offering help.

I was a conman, a liar, and loyal to a select few. My world was gritty, and the only color I knew was the color that came from the spray-paint I illegally blasted all over public and private property. Everything else was black and white.

How dare she show up with those red lips and sapphire eyes?

How dare she make me feel like black and white was suddenly not enough? That *I* was not enough.

Self-doubt was something that plagued me. It had ever since *that* day. I understood who I was and who I would never be. I knew my place.

I accepted it.

Being here now, gazing around at her world, it all

unleashed. Feelings I thought I accepted bubbled up, spilled out, and made me feel like shit.

I knew I was a liar. But I never knew I'd been lying to myself, too.

Tossing my leftover food and drink into a nearby wastebasket, I headed for the exit. The very same trees that had welcomed me moments ago suddenly felt menacing, and oddly, it was as if I could hear the echo of their laughter.

You don't belong here.

Out on the street, another horse-drawn carriage rode by. The couple perched in the red velvet seat had a blanket over their lap and smiles on their faces.

I spun away, colliding with a man who was walking by.

"Hey!" he grumped, his body bouncing off mine. His angry eyes flashed to mine, and whatever he saw in my face melted the expression off his.

Ducking his head, he muttered an apology and went on with his life.

A cold wind blew, reaching to the edges of the park, trying to grab me with its icy, stiff fingers. My anger was still burning too hot, my emotions so raw. I let it try to grab me, the pricks of its clutches failing to pull me back.

On the corner, a man stood on his cell phone, not paying attention to anything around him. I ran into him harder than I needed to, the collision somehow giving me satisfaction. He stumbled forward, dropping his phone on the pavement.

"Hey!" he roared, spinning around.

I'd already emptied his pockets and slid the contents into mine.

He charged me, and I shoved him back. The sudden onslaught of his fist did not catch me off guard. My body dipped, skating beneath the intended punch before straightening with a smug smirk.

"Son of a bitch!" I could still hear him yelling when I made it across the street.

The next corner over was filled with vendors and people standing around buying hats and bags that were knockoffs of the real thing Ivory White probably had stuffed in her closet.

More anger licked my guts, making my feet and fingers tingle.

Practically looking for a fight, I shoved through the people and deliberately plucked a wad of cash out of a man's hand as he extended it to a vendor.

"Hey!" he said, indignant.

I smirked and grabbed the rest of the cash sticking out of his pocket. The man's nostrils flared, and his eyes became narrow slits.

Slap, slap, slap. My sneakers pounded the pavement when I took off. His shoes were equally loud as he gave chase.

"Stop!" he roared. "I'm gonna kick your ass!"

"Gotta catch me first," I yelled over my shoulder, feeling the rush of adrenaline flood my veins.

A group of women stumbled out of a shop ahead, filling the walkway with obstacles. I plowed right into the center, grabbing one by the shoulders, doing a full one-eighty.

"May I have this dance?" I inquired, offering a quick smile.

It was over before she could react, but her giggles floated behind as I continued to run.

"Thief!" my pursuer roared. "Stop him!"

Just my luck, a uniformed officer heard the man's pleas, and soon I was being trailed by more than one.

Another crush of people tried to slow me down, but I used the side of the building as a personal sidewalk before dropping onto the other side of the people and slipping into an alleyway.

"That way!" someone yelled, and I briefly glanced over my shoulder.

Big mistake. Looking back always slows you down.

The meaty hand of the man I'd robbed slammed down onto my shoulder, his fingers much nimbler than the ones of the cold wind trying to claim me back at the park.

Twisting away, I pushed ahead, but I could practically feel him breathing down my neck. A black Mercedes pulled out of a parking garage but stopped partway on the street. The footsteps chasing me slowed a bit.

I sped up, leaping into the air and sliding across the hood of the car like it was a Slip 'N Slide in the middle of summer. My leg buckled when I hit the ground, so I rolled with it, bounced up, and kept on running. The Mercedes honked, then drove off, another, much larger SUV pulling out after it.

The moment of distraction was all I needed. Dipping unnoticed into the parking garage, I dove behind a large cement pillar, my ass hitting the pavement and my lungs heaving for breath.

My beanie seemed to stick against the concrete when I leaned my head back, stretching my neck to allow in more air.

"He went that way!" the man yelled nearby, and I stiffened but didn't move.

"He's gone, sir." Another voice spoke, this one out of breath.

"He just robbed me blind in broad daylight!" the angry guy roared. "Do something!"

"Unfortunately, there isn't much we can do. This stuff happens a lot in the city. Next time, I would suggest not carrying cash, but if you do, put it in a pouch or something against your body so they can't access it so easily."

"You implying this is my fault?"

I grinned.

"Of course not, sir."

"Hey, fuck off!"

The slight scuffle of feet made me perk up and itch to glance around the pillar.

"That's enough, sir!" The officer's voice became much more official. Fig never sounded like this.

Fig was a moron.

"If you don't calm down, we will have to bring you in."

"I'm the victim!"

I grinned again.

A few minutes later, the party of pursuers broke up, and I was left with nothing but the sound of my own heavy breathing and the occasional car exiting the garage.

When I shifted, a scrape of metal clashing lightly against metal made me look down. I'd forgotten about the black bag strapped against my back.

Pulling it around and unzipping the top, I wrapped my hands around the cold cylinder of a spray can. The nozzle had a splattering of paint all over it already, and the weight of the can in my palm felt right.

Glancing around, I made sure no one was there. Once certain I was in fact alone, I raised the can.

Whoosh, whoosh. The light, familiar sound of spraying paint was somehow cathartic and exactly what I needed.

I lost myself for an unknown amount of time, switching between the few cans I'd packed, and just letting my hands and emotions work together. It was almost as if I were painting blind, guided by my innermost thoughts and sometimes my innermost demons.

I didn't always paint this way. It used to scare me how I would essentially check out and then come back to a piece of art I couldn't even recall creating. The time it first happened, I didn't even believe I'd been the one to paint, but the splatters on my fingers and jeans were undeniable proof.

Now I let my mind dump whatever it needed to, knowing that all the emotion locked inside me had to come out and this was the least painful way.

Sometime later, my arm dropped, the dull exhaustion in my shoulder a familiar ache. The world came back in a haze at first, as though I were leaving one place and arriving at another. My brain was fuzzy and my mind sluggish, but soon I was firmly back in the parking garage, fully present and staring at the empty cans littering the ground at my feet.

Shit. Being careless was a rookie move. I knew better than this. Especially here in an unfamiliar place.

What the hell is wrong with me today?

Kneeling, I packed up the empty cans, the metal balls inside clinking around as I stuffed them away. My finger ached from pressing on the nozzle, and dots of red, white, blue, and black were splattered all over my stiff hand.

Why these colors? What had I suddenly become possessed to paint—and practically in the middle of me being chased by police?

Zipping the bag, I flung it across my back and straightened, lifting my gaze. Every single emotion I'd been running from earlier rushed back tenfold. My vision blurred a little, then refocused on the art my hands and mind had created.

Skin so fair. Hair as black as night. Lips the color of a blood-red rose. The blue of her eyes identical to the blue ribbon tied in her hair.

"Snow White," I whispered, my voice startling. Shaking my head, I corrected myself. "Ivory White."

Indeed.

A storybook princess but in real flesh and blood.

I could steal and steal again. I could nearly get arrested, start fights, and walk through a world I didn't belong.

I knew we didn't fit.

I painted her anyway.

No.

I didn't paint her.

My hands had been mere tools for my heart. For my soul.

I stared at the artwork done in poor lighting on a crude cement wall. Even like this, she was beautiful. Even like this, you could tell she was practically royalty among men.

Exhaustion wrapped around me like a dark cloak, enclosing me in black and white. But no matter how tight that cloak squeezed, I still saw her in color.

Twenty-One

Ivory

I have discovered that cleaning is not for me. In fact, cleaning is hard. And gross. And time-consuming.

I would ask how so much grime could accumulate, but one only had to remember the men sitting around the breakfast table this morning and glance at the dog's chewed toothbrush sitting with the humans, and well… the question was no longer a question.

I decided I would give my cleaning staff a raise.

While I was always grateful for them, I'd never been this grateful.

In the midst of spraying and scrubbing and sneezing—my word, cleaning supplies were horribly pungent, and they filled the air with an unhealthy chemical mist—I'd made a decision.

The only decision I really could at this point.

I was going home. Back to the Upper East Side where I'd always lived and the place where I belonged. What other choice did I have really?

If I ceased to exist, then how would I live?

The hunter said to leave and never come back. Where would I go? What would I do? No money. No clothes. No home or friends. No food.

And let's be honest here. Should I really trust the word of a man who cut off my hair, ripped off my nail, and almost killed me?

Not exactly trust-inspiring.

But he didn't kill you, and he could have.

I scrubbed a little harder with that thought. Pain shot through my hand, making me wince, so I sat back onto my heels and gazed down at my throbbing finger. It was still bandaged, though the covering was half falling off and damp from my work. My wrist was still tender from my fall even if there was no visible bruising or swelling.

All my exposed fingers were red and felt raw from the scrubbing, my knees ached because I'd kneeled on them half the day, and my lower back burned from the strain.

A heavy sigh moved through me. With palms resting on my knees, I gazed around the tiny bathroom. There was a definite improvement. This place was almost usable.

Tossing the sponge down into the small bowl, I climbed to my feet. Everything was still old. The tiles were still tiny and cracked with some missing. There was no storage at all, and the window seemed awfully fragile.

But everything was clean and sparkling now. Well, as much as it could sparkle.

The pedestal sink was spotless, the window smudge-free. The floor and bathtub glistened. Not bad for a girl with very little domestic experience.

"Just one thing left to do…" I remembered, reaching into the bag hanging on the door handle. "Beau," I called from the doorway. "Beau, could you please help me?"

A few seconds ticked by, and I worried that maybe he had his headset on and wouldn't be able to hear, but then he appeared, red hair ruffled and green eyes wide. "What happened? Did you hurt yourself?"

"Me? You act like I'm clumsy," I mused, laughing a little.

He didn't laugh with me. It was kind of rude.

Thrusting the shower curtain I'd picked up at him, I pointed. "Could you help me hang this. I'm not tall enough."

A dumbfounded look crossed his face. Dividing his eyes between the curtain and me, he echoed, "A shower curtain?"

"I mean, don't you think it's silly you guys have the bar thingy to hang it on but no curtain? Water gets everywhere when you shower! Do you know how hard it was to scrub all the water splatters and soap off everything?"

Beau blinked. Once. Twice. The third time, he glanced around as if noticing the bathroom for the first time. "Woah," he whispered, staring. "You cleaned."

Resting my still-tired hands on my hips, I asked, "Well, what did you think I was doing most of the day?"

He shrugged.

"Well!" I demanded. "What do you think? Looks nice, right?"

He nodded, gaze fixing on the small window ledge, which was now lined with five different-colored cups. Each cup had a color-coordinated toothbrush sticking out of the top.

"Which one is mine?" he asked.

"Red." I confirmed, pointing down the line. "Green for Fletcher, yellow for Neo, and blue for Earth and Snort."

Beau's brows furrowed. "Earth and Snort are sharing a cup?"

"Well, he keeps saying Snort is his," I refuted. Served him right to share with a slobbery dog.

Beau pointed to a pink cup and toothbrush. "Whose is that one, then?"

"Mine," I said.

That surprised him, and I suddenly felt embarrassed. "It's not like I'm staying. But dental hygiene is important. I'll take it with me when I leave later."

When he said nothing, I pointed to the shower curtain still in his hands. "Can you hang it?"

"Uh, Earth might not like—"

"Hang the curtain, Beau," I ordered, my voice calm and austere. It was the same voice I used to conduct major meetings for Reflections.

I always got what I wanted.

Today was no different.

Minutes later, the yellow and white striped curtain hung straight, all the way down to the inside of the clawfoot tub.

Clapping, I beamed. "Thank you, Beau. It looks wonderful!"

"Can I go now?"

I nodded.

When he was gone, I picked up all my cleaning supplies, including the ones I used to dust and sweep the floor out in the main room and put them into a bag to sit neatly in the corner.

Neo still wasn't back, and now that I didn't have cleaning or thinking to distract myself, my mind drifted to him continuously.

It was time for me to go.

I really wouldn't get to see him again.

Glancing down, I took in Neo's shorts and my own T-shirt. I'd taken off his flannel before I'd started scrubbing. I couldn't possibly go home like this. It would be shocking enough when I walked into my building looking like I'd slept on the street!

I had time for a quick shower. It would be better to rinse off the grime and cleaning supplies anyway. They could give me a rash.

This time, I turned on the spray before I stepped into the tub. The water pressure was dismal, the heat of the water barely passable, but still, it felt wonderful to wash off. Since

I'd stocked the shower with body wash, shampoo, and conditioner, I made good use of it all, deciding to wash my hair.

Frankly, at this point, it couldn't look any worse.

When my skin was pink from a good scrub and my hair was dripping, I turned off the water and used a too-small, scratchy towel to dry off.

There was no hair dryer (these men were savages), so I toweled it off as much as possible, then wrapped up the chopped strands, piling the towel on my head.

Without any choice, I pulled my running leggings back on, my sneakers without socks, and picked up my T-shirt, wrinkling my nose. How could I put it back on? It was smelly and sweaty and… ew.

Making a split-second decision, I tossed it into the trash and pulled on the flannel, buttoning it up over my body. Since I was going home, it didn't matter if I tossed that shirt.

And if Neo didn't want me to borrow this permanently, then he should have come home and told me himself!

Indignant, I reapplied a bandage on my finger but couldn't reach my neck, so I left it bare. Taking the towel off my head, I finger-combed the damp strands as best I could, which really wasn't good at all, and moved to gather up my things.

I didn't have any things.

Guess this was it, then. Time to go.

Odd how since all of this happened, I'd done nothing but long for home, for comfort and safety. Now that I'd made the decision to go back there, I was suddenly stalling.

What is wrong with you, Ivory White?

Shaking myself, I left the bathroom, carrying the wet towel.

"Beau, where is the laundry basket?" I asked, popping into the living room.

He didn't even look up from the computer monitor, but

he pointed. Wandering off in the direction he pointed, I found the basket in the far corner of the room.

Their laundry looked like a mountain of unwashed fabric.

My nose wrinkled. *Why are they like this?*

After everything they'd done for me, I couldn't leave them with all this soiled laundry. Nearby was a large empty bag, so I shoved all of the clothes and towels into it, grimacing and trying to touch as little of it as possible the entire time.

The bag was half the size of me when I was done, but I tied it closed and appreciated my handiwork.

"Where's the washing machine?" I asked Beau.

His head still didn't tilt up. "Down the block."

"You mean you don't have a washing machine?" I was horrified.

"Down the block," he repeated.

I thought back to the laundromat I passed on the way from the corner store. Is that what he meant? Did they take their laundry down the street to wash it in a... *communal* washing machine?

The giant jar of quarters sitting near the now-empty basket was basically a giant unspoken yes.

I'd never been to a laundromat before. I'd never actually used a washing machine before. Or a dryer. I sent my clothes out for dry-cleaning, and my housekeepers did the other wash.

The only reason I knew the quarters were for the laundromat was because I saw it in a movie once. I'd thought it was just for the film. I didn't realize it was like for real.

Glancing at the bag beside me, I thought, *Maybe I could just send them some cash as a thank-you and they could send all this out for cleaning.*

Almost immediately, I dismissed the idea. Neo would be insulted. Handing someone money seemed awfully ingenuine. *Funny how I never thought that until now.*

"I'm going to the laundromat," I called, dragging the giant bag of stuff along with me. I didn't realize dirty clothes weighed so much!

Beau merely grunted, and I grabbed the cap I'd borrowed from him earlier and pulled it over my still-damp hair.

Halfway down the block, my muscles gave out, and I ended up dragging the bag the rest of the way. No one even offered assistance. What a strange world this was. There were people everywhere, but it seemed everyone was alone. No one smiled or offered a hand. The only interaction I'd had with anyone here had been when they were snapping or snarling at me.

Earth fit right in.

But not Neo... Neo isn't like this.

Stop. Thinking. About. Him.

The laundromat smelled of soap and was filled with the sound of running machines. There were so many of them. They were lined against the walls and much bigger than I expected. I stared for long minutes, suddenly overwhelmed and unsure of what to do.

A woman in a huge puffy coat, hat, and fingerless gloves shoved inside, brushed right past, and took up position at a nearby machine. I watched curiously as she dumped her laundry in, tossed in a pod-looking thing, and shut the door. Then she inserted some coins and pushed a couple buttons. The machine started going almost instantly.

Oh, well, that didn't look too hard.

"Got a staring problem?" she snapped, glaring at me.

I jolted and turned away, choosing a machine at the opposite end of the place. I didn't have any detergent, but there was a little vending machine that had some. I put in some money and then a little more to make sure I had enough.

The laundry was gross, so I dumped the bag into the large

machine, pleased when it all fit. It was a bigger load than the woman I'd watched put in earlier, so I put in a few extra pods of the soap to make sure it all got super clean.

Once it was all in and closed up, I put in the money it asked for and followed the instructions on the machine for which button to hit.

When the machine started up, I clapped for myself. A job well done always deserved some praise.

"What do you think this is, *The Price is Right*?" the grumpy woman yelled.

Maybe if she wore something less black and a little more flattering, she would be in a better mood.

There was a big sign on the door that said **Not Responsible for Stolen Laundry** that made me pause. Did people really steal other people's clothes? There was also a sign that read **Do Not Leave Clothes Unattended.**

There were forty minutes left on the machine, so I gazed around, eyes landing on a fashion magazine on a table nearby. The issue was a couple months old but it was better than nothing, so I snatched it up and sat down on a nearby bench.

Laundry was much easier than cleaning.

Swinging my feet happily over the floor, I opened the magazine and settled in to wait.

Twenty-Two

Neo

I hope she's gone.

Those were the words valiantly filling my head as I trudged up the steps to the apartment. I was tired and hungry, and the last thing I wanted was to watch her one-woman show of emotions. She was a freaking noise box: screaming, yelling, cowering from loud sounds, and screeching about dirt. Just the sound of her voice was enough to give a man a headache.

I let myself in, vaguely wondering why all the locks weren't engaged but not summoning up enough energy to care.

As I dropped my leather jacket and beanie on the floor near the door, my nose was assaulted with unfamiliar scents.

Snapping my head up, I scanned the room for whatever it was that was off.

Beau seemed unbothered, sitting over at his computers, so involved in whatever cyberworld he lived in that I was convinced this place could burn down around him and he wouldn't notice. The flicker of a small flame caught my notice, drawing me around the couch to the edge of the coffee table where I stared down.

A small white candle sat in the center of the completely

clear surface, a vanilla fragrance wafting up from beneath the flame.

The tabletop glistened under the sun streaming in from the window.

Wait.

It glistened?

Holy shit, the table was actually shining and nothing like chip crumbs, dog slobber, or cans and glasses filled the surface.

Gazing back at Beau, I practically gaped. *Did he clean?*

Emitting a strangled noise, I turned to the TV, and everything around it was also clean, the screen free of streaks, the floor around it spotless.

What the fuck…?

The entire room was clean. Dusted, the floor without shoe prints, dust, and dog hair.

"Snort?" I called, and the familiar sound of the dog's heavy breathing made me turn. I hadn't seen him before, but he was lying near the couch on a folded blanket that appeared to be laid out for him.

"Good boy," I told him because he was staring at me. He snorted and went back to his nap. Couldn't blame him. He looked hella comfortable.

Another wave of vanilla hit me, and I realized it was mixed slightly with lemon and this other scent I couldn't identify. It was kind of… harsh. Like bleach.

Intrigued, I went back down the small hallway and into the bathroom.

Well, I barely made it to the bathroom because I froze in shock at the threshold of the tiny space. I'd never in my life seen this bathroom look so *livable.*

The tiles were actually white—well, some of them. The sink shined with no smudges or toothpaste smears. The window was wiped clean, and the colorful line of cups and toothbrushes made a lump form in my throat.

Desperately trying to swallow it down, I turned away from the somehow charming sight. Turning away only made it worse.

There was a shower curtain, cheerfully hanging with wide white and yellow stripes. It curved around the inside of the now-clean clawfoot tub. Unable to resist, I peeked inside, seeing several bottles of body wash, shampoo, and a bottle of conditioner. Nearby was a basket of small washcloths.

My mother used to stock our bathroom with those.

I spun away, blinking down at the floor.

She couldn't have. She wouldn't.

Lifting my eyes, I saw the mirror. The bottom half was cleaned and clear, no streaks at all. The top half was exactly as it had been, smudged, splattered, and dusty.

She couldn't even see herself in that mirror. She isn't tall enough to reach it to clean the top.

My heart clutched so hard I bent, holding my palm against it until the worst of the constriction subsided.

Snort glanced up when I barreled back into the room. Beau looked up as I rushed him, green eyes widening as though he hadn't even realized I was home.

"Neo," he said, pushing one headphone away from his ear.

"She did this?" I motioned to the place.

Beau grimaced. "She made me help hang the curtain."

My heart squeezed again. "Where is she?" I asked, glancing toward the kitchen.

"She left."

My hand slapped onto the corner of the desk, my arm taking some of my sagging weight. "What?"

"Yeah, like an hour ago."

I didn't get to say good-bye.

How could she just leave like that? How could she walk out of my life as easily as she walked in?

You left first.

Numbly, I recalled the way she called my name as I'd fled the house in a jealous haze.

Yes. I'd been jealous. So fucking jealous. I couldn't admit until now just how insane it made me to hear she was promised to someone else.

She was gone. Back to her world.

Pushing away from the desk, I wandered back toward the couch, staring at the flickering candle, seeing how she left her thumbprint on literally everything in this apartment.

On me.

"She should be back in a few. Actually, she probably should have been back already."

I spun back. "What?"

"She took our laundry to the laundromat down the block." He pointed to where we had collected a mountain of dirty clothes.

Following his direction, I saw the spot was indeed empty.

"She went to do our laundry?" I repeated.

Beau made a sound.

"How could you let her leave like that?" I roared.

He glanced up, finally realizing I was having some sort of internal meltdown. Watching me warily, he said, "Didn't think it was a big deal. She went to the corner market this morning and was fine."

"Where'd she get the money?"

His cheeks flushed. "I gave it to her."

He gave her money. *Oooh,* unpleasant feelings wormed around inside me, making my tongue slide across the sharp edges of my front teeth.

"How could you just let her of all people roam around the Grimms alone?" I snarled.

Beau sat back, eyes growing wide. "I—"

"Someone just tried to kill her!"

"Uhh…"

My heart was beating triple its normal speed as I stalked over to the door, grabbing my jacket and hat and flinging it open. "You'd better hope nothing happened to her!" I declared, slamming it hard behind me and then breaking into a run.

Twenty-Three

Ivory

Turns out laundry isn't as easy as I thought it was.

Unless, of course, massive amounts of soap bubbles were supposed to basically explode from around the closed door and flood the tile floor at an alarming rate.

Oh my.

"What in fresh hell is going on out here?" a loud, frantic voice erupted from somewhere in the back. "Why are you just sitting there like that? Is your brain broken?"

I glanced up from the article on predicted trends for spring (I can tell you they were all wrong) and nearly fell off the bench at the way the old man was hotfooting it across the cramped laundromat.

Pressing the open magazine against my chest like a shield, I gazed at him warily from beneath the brim of the black baseball hat.

Does he know who I am?

"You GD millennials can't do anything right, can ye?"

Ye? Is that a word?

"Pardon?"

A loud cackle from across the room startled me again. Peeking around the magazine, I saw the grumpy woman dressed in black staring.

"I knew she was trouble from the minute she dragged that bag in here."

"I was here first," I said primly.

"Missy, you've gone and done it this time!" the man yelled, rushing by. "You're gonna pay for this!"

Following his rushed footsteps, I turned, and the loud gasp I let loose did knock me off the bench. The magazine lay forgotten on the floor as I sprang forward, eyes wide and mouth open.

"Oh my gosh! Your machine broke! My clothes!"

Ankle deep in fluffy white suds, the man glared. "Don't you dare try and blame this on my machines! This is all on you, operator error!"

"Me!" I gasped, completely offended.

"Have you never used a washing machine before?"

"Well, I—"

"Christ! How much soap did you use?" he hollered as white clumps clung to his brown pants.

"Is there a limit?"

A string of very impolite profanities burst out of him, and frankly, I found it shocking. Shouldn't someone his age have better manners?

Shuffling through the suds, which were basically covering the entire floor on this side of the room, he reached out and hit a button on the machine to make it stop.

I tried to see if the clothes were okay, but the entire window was blocked by suds. Even after the machine stopped, white soap continued to ooze from around the edges, sliding down the machine and adding to the mess on the floor.

"You!" The man fumed, his nose flaring like a bull's as he charged me. I skittered back but wasn't fast enough because his fingers latched onto my ear and tugged.

"Ow!" I cried out as he began towing me forward.

For such an elderly gentleman, he sure did have some muscle.

"Wait, no," I begged, trying to drag my feet when I saw where he was making me go. The suds on the floor were not very good for gripping, and I just slid along behind him like I was on some kind of surfboard.

"Eeek!" I squealed the second my feet and legs were consumed with bubbles and water.

When he roughly released my ear, the momentum kept me going, and I slid right into the wall of washing machines, bouncing off.

"Agh!" I fell back onto my butt, suds splashing everywhere and clouds of white filling my vision. Sputtering and soaked, I scrambled up, slipping and falling once more. Like a lightning rod, pain shot up my finger, but I pushed it away as I managed to stand. "Why would you do that?" I panted, putting my hands on my hips to glare.

"If I have to wear your mess, it's only fair that you should too," he intoned and then flung open the washing machine door.

Like a tidal wave, water whooshed out, splattering against the floor with a loud splash as droplets reached for everything they could find.

My damp shoes became soaked through, and the only pair of pants I had were saturated.

The tail ends of Neo's flannel suddenly felt heavy, and even though it seemed dramatic, the extra weight seemed to pull my shoulders down until they wanted to break.

The past two days had left me frightened. Confused. I felt like a woman lost in a strange world where nothing and no one was recognizable. I was abandoned by everything I knew and at the mercy of a place I didn't know how to thrive in.

I'd had enough.

Stiffening my spine and lifting my chin, I let the air

around me shift until it felt familiar. Keeping my gaze cool beneath the brim of the hat, I swept it over the older man and even spared a glance at the very rude woman. "This is all very uncalled for. Maybe you should let your patrons know how much detergent is too much."

The man blinked at the change in me, but then he snarled and pointed to a sign near the vending machine. It did indeed say how much soap to use.

Well. Maybe he should have made it bigger.

"Just call someone to clean it up and send me the bill."

The rude woman cackled. "You hear that, Fred? She's offering to pay for someone else to clean up her mess!"

"What do you think this is, miss, the freaking Hilton?"

I made a face. I wouldn't stay at the Hilton.

"The only person cleaning this up is you because you made the mess," he ordered.

Oh, I'd had enough of cleaning to last me a lifetime. "What kind of establishment makes their customers clean?" I admonished.

"You think you can pull out your fancy words and somehow act like you're better than us?" The woman advanced, eyes boring into me. "Just look at yourself. Can't even afford clothes that fit, can't use a washing machine, and carrying around a jar of quarters." She pointed to the jar I'd brought along. "Probably can't even hold a job."

I felt like a flower wilting in the heat. Except it wasn't hot. In fact, my fingers and toes ached with cold. I'd never felt so judged in my entire life.

Insulted and pissed off, I bent, scooping up handfuls of the bubbles, and charged, swiping them down the woman's neck and coat. They clung to her chin like a beard, and I smirked.

"You little bitch," she snarled, and my eyes widened.

Maybe I shouldn't have done that.

Skittering back, my soaked sneakers lost traction, and the next thing I knew, my feet were in the air above my head and I was once again part of the mess on the floor.

Momentarily stunned, I blinked up, white suds floating everywhere but suddenly blocked out by a giant looming black cloud.

"You're gonna pay for that," she intoned.

The woman came at me. I screamed as both my arms came up to protectively shield my face. Flashbacks of being attacked in the park assaulted me, the past and present all mushed together burning me with anxiety.

Hands latched onto my forearms and tugged. I cried out, curling closer into myself. "Please, no," I whimpered. "Please…"

"It's me, princess." The familiar voice broke through my panic, bringing with it a cascade of warmth.

Peeking around my arm, I saw Neo resettling his grip on me, gently tugging my arms away from my face.

"Neo?" I whimpered.

"C'mon now, up," he instructed, basically pulling me off the floor, depositing me on my feet.

A saturated strand of hair clung to my cheek, punctuated by a glob of bubbles. Neo clucked his tongue, eyes soft and warm as he brushed away the soap, then tucked the strand of hair behind my ear.

"Are you okay?" he murmured, voice meant only for me and eyes like the softest caress I'd ever felt.

Lips quivering, I held up my bandaged finger. "Pretty sure it's bleeding again."

The soft sound he made wrapped around me, comforting without a single touch.

Neo rotated, planting himself in front of me like a shield, everything about his body language shifting and growing hard. I wasn't afraid, though. In fact, I shuffled a little closer to his back.

"What the hell is going on here?" he asked, his voice cool and hard.

Both the woman and man stared at Neo in shock.

"You, ah, know her?" the woman stuttered, mouth agape.

"She's mine," Neo all but growled, making heat explode in my lower belly and a sense of relief chase it. His dark eyes settled on the laundromat man. "Fred?"

"Look at this mess! I come out from the back and she's sitting there reading a book while my machine practically explodes behind her, making a huge mess of this place!" When he yelled at Neo, it didn't sound the same. There was no real heat in the words, no aggression. It almost sounded like plaintive whining instead.

Neo glanced over his shoulder. "You make this mess?"

"I didn't mean to."

The woman snorted. "No one is that stupid."

I gasped. Neo shifted a little closer to me but kept his back turned.

I wished I could see the look on his face because the woman's eyes went wide, and then she pointed to her damp jacket. "Look at what she did to me!"

"You insulted me!" I shot out. "So rude."

"She said she would pay someone to clean up this mess." The woman criticized. "With what? That jar of quarters?"

Neo glanced at me again.

I sighed. "I'm tired of cleaning."

A ghost of a smile and some warmth passed behind his night-sky stare.

The door to the laundromat was open, being tugged at by the wind, and I shivered slightly as tendrils of cold air brushed against my soaked clothes.

Neo's expression shifted again. This time, concern deepened his stare. When he turned fully around, all his attention was back on me, and it felt like coming home.

Get a grip, Ivory. You've only known him two days.

"Why are you so wet?" he demanded, shaking me from my silly thoughts.

"Because he"—I jabbed a finger at the older man—"forced me into the water, then opened the machine so I'd get splashed. And she"—I pointed to the woman—"knocked me down again."

Shrugging out of his black leather jacket, he positioned it around my shoulders, and I couldn't help but snuggle in because his remaining body heat was delicious.

"Don't you think this was a little uncalled for?" Neo spoke to Fred.

"Well, I—"

"I know this isn't the first time this has happened. The machine is fine." He pointed at the open door. "Get me a mop and bucket, and I'll clean this up."

"You?" the woman exclaimed, incredulous.

Why was she even still here?

Neo turned. "What part of *mine* did you not understand?" he shot out. "You know in the Grimms, we take care of our own, Rhonda."

Ah, so the she-devil had a name.

Her face turned red. "I didn't know you had someone." She fished, looking between us.

Neo said nothing, just staring in stony silence.

Rhonda cleared her throat. "Well then, I guess I'll be going."

If she had a tail, it would have been tucked between her legs as she walked away to get her laundry.

Anger rose in me because she would concede to Neo but not to me.

"Don't forget your unfashionable and uncolorful wardrobe." I snickered.

The woman gasped, and Neo turned, slapping me with a hard look.

I wrinkled my nose and turned away.

Once the Godzilla of the laundromat was gone, Fred returned with a mop and bucket, apprehension on his face. "You really don't need to do this, Neo. This is my place."

Isn't that what I said?

"No worries, Fred. I'll have this cleaned up in a few. Sorry for the trouble." Neo looked at me, expectation in his gaze.

Clearing my throat, I glanced at the man who had thrown me into the suds. "I'm sorry as well."

Fred muttered something beneath his breath and shuffled off behind the counter.

Neo sighed. "What were you thinking?"

"I thought you left without saying good-bye," I blurted out, tugging the lapels of his leather jacket closer around me. It smelled like him.

He paused but didn't look up. "So did I."

We said nothing else as he transferred the large load of laundry into another machine and turned it on to finish what I'd started. Then he picked up the mop.

"I can do that," I offered.

"Sit," he barked, pointing to a bench.

I sat.

He worked fast, mopping up the suds and water, and frankly, when he was finished, the place looked cleaner than before.

Setting everything aside, he glanced up, eyes latching onto something outside. Without saying a word, he took off, rushing out onto the sidewalk.

Panic assailed me. Was he leaving again without saying good-bye?

Just as I was about to run after him, the door reopened and his dark head appeared, followed closely by Fletcher who carried a small case, making me wonder what was inside.

"Hey, Ivory." He waved. "Heard you had some trouble with the machine." He snickered.

I rolled my eyes.

"Sit here and wait until it's finished and then bring it all home," Neo said, pointing to the dryer where their clothes were now tumbling dry.

Fletcher nodded and then waved to the man who was staring from the counter. "Hi, Fred!"

"Good to see you, Fletch."

Why was that man nice to everyone but me?

Reaching into my lap, Neo's hand wrapped around mine, tugging me into his side. "C'mon, let's go."

Outside, the sun was lower in the sky, making the gray, heavy clouds seem even darker. The hand Neo wasn't holding curled in on itself, tucking farther into the sleeve of his jacket.

"You know them?" I asked, glancing back at the laundromat.

It was a horrid place I really hoped I wouldn't have to go in again.

He stopped walking, turning to face me as his eyes roamed my face and body as if inspecting every inch. "Everyone knows everyone in the Grimms, which is why you shouldn't be wandering around out here. You stick out like a sore thumb."

"I'm wearing a hat," I argued. And I certainly didn't look like myself in these crazy clothes.

Wrapping his fingers around the dark bill shading my face, he asked, "Whose is this?"

"Beau's."

A rough sound vibrated the back of his throat, and he pulled it off my head.

Gasping, I ducked, using his body like a shield. "You just said I stick out like a sore thumb, and now just look. You're ripping off my disguise!"

"A hat won't hide your storybook looks, princess."

He thinks I have storybook looks?

Let's not mince words. I knew I was beautiful. I worked hard to maintain myself. But somehow, hearing it from him made me feel it. Even standing on this dirty street in soaked, ill-fitting clothes and chopped-up hair, *I felt it*.

Sudden movement brought me out of my feelings but slammed me into new ones when Neo's hand slipped inside the leather jacket. The backs of his fingers brushed against my side, and my breath caught, body freezing in place as tingles danced across my skin.

Feeling his eyes, I lifted mine, and we stood in the center of the sidewalk in the fading light of day, eyes fighting each other for something I couldn't understand. Tension tightened my throat, and shyness nipped at the back of mind. I desperately wanted to avert my gaze, but I couldn't tear mine away from his even as a fine blush crept up my neck to bloom across my cheeks.

His hand was still inside the coat, barely brushing against my side. A forgotten touch that was anything but.

Blinking, he drew away, bringing with him a knit beanie in a shade of gray. I couldn't help but watch his long fingers when he lifted the cap and pulled it down over my head. He took his time adjusting it, settling it over my ears and making sure it was pulled down to practically cover my brows.

"Your hair is damp," he murmured, feet shifting so close that his sneakers bumped mine.

I opened my lips to tell him I washed it, but nothing came out but a breathless sigh.

When he finished fiddling with the hat, he didn't step back. We stood there practically sharing air, neither of us moving as the world went on around us but we ourselves were frozen in time.

When I felt the pull between us loosen, I tipped my chin back, gazing up at the baseball hat now on his head.

"That one concealed my face better," I told him.

His eyes caressed the beanie. "That one is mine."

A knot swelled up inside my stomach, so big and so tight it pushed against the bottom of my ribs. It ached, but not the kind of ache I wanted to run from.

An ache I'd never felt before.

"I'm glad you came back," I whispered.

Dark orbs bounced between my light ones, making my throat bob with every swallow. "You are?" His voice was raspy too.

I nodded. "Because now I get to say good-bye."

Twenty-Four

Neo

"Let's go," I demanded, tugging her up the street behind me.

"Go?" Her voice was breathless, and her wet shoes slapped against the pavement. "We need to talk. I want to say—"

"Later," I snapped. If she said the G-word one more time, I was going to lose my mind.

Fuck. I'd already lost my mind. I spent the entire day running away from her, trying to remember who and what I was and hoping she wasn't at the apartment when I got back.

I'd gotten my wish, and then what?

I nearly lost my damn mind. The ache I'd felt. The fear. Thinking she was gone and I'd never see her again.

When I realized she was still here, I couldn't get there fast enough, and when I saw her lying in a pile of suds, flinching away from the people standing over her, I nearly lost control.

Yes, I knew she had to go.

I wasn't ready for good-bye.

I didn't know what it meant, and frankly, in this moment, I didn't care. My pulse hammered with thoughts of her, adrenaline chasing desire in my veins, and her hand was so incredibly small in mine.

When we passed by the Rotten Apple and my apartment, I felt her twist around to stare back. "Where are we going?"

"Your clothes are soaking wet." I reminded her, my words punctuated by the jingle of a bell on an opening door as I ushered her into a small shop.

The floors were concrete. The window behind us looked out onto the sidewalk, and the lighting in here consisted of florescent bulbs without any covers.

Racks of clothes crowded the space, and a few shelves against a crumbly looking brick wall held even more folded garments.

Ivory's nose wrinkled as she gazed around. "What is this place?"

"I figured this would be like your motherland or something."

She scoffed. "Hardly."

"You've never been to a secondhand shop before?" I asked, curious.

"Of course." She sniffed, as though I'd somehow offended her. "Vintage pieces are great compliments to any wardrobe."

"I'm not talking about ten-year-old Chanel," I said sardonically.

Her entire face brightened, blue eyes lighting up beneath the beanie she wore. "You like Chanel too?"

Either my tone went totally over her head or she was choosing to ignore the way I'd poked at her. She was cute, though. How someone so achingly beautiful could even look cute was a surprise to me, but then I realized it was the beanie. *My* beanie.

"Pick out something to wear." My voice was gruff. "You're going to get sick running around like that."

Her small hand clutched the front of the flannel buttoned up around her. I barely had time to feel cocky about the fact she was wearing my shirt because I noted the dark stain on the Band-Aid around her finger. When she'd said it started bleeding again, she wasn't being dramatic.

"Does it hurt?" I asked, feeling my eyes darken as I stared at the injury.

Pulling her hand up, she looked at the wet bandage, which was starting to come loose. "It stings."

Without even thinking about it, I snatched her hand, roughly jerking her toward me. Stumbling, she fell into my chest as my hand curled around her much smaller one.

"Neo." Her voice was breathless. My name tumbling off her lips made it even harder to think straight.

Her fingers were cold against my lips, but instead of recoiling, I pushed closer, offering the warmth of my mouth. The hand that had curled into my shirt when she fell against me gripped tighter, and her eyes widened.

Our stares connected. My lips caressed the bandage, and her pupils expanded. A floating sensation erupted inside me, and my free hand curled inside the jacket around her narrow waist as if she were the only anchor that could keep me on the ground.

I heard her swallow, watched her bow-shaped lips quiver.

Kiss her, my pulse whispered, making the hand against her waist grip tighter.

Her eyes started to flutter toward her pale cheeks, and slowly, I lowered her hand from between us. Our chests rose and fell heavily. Every single breath she took I felt.

My face began to lower…

"Neo!"

I jerked back so fast Ivory went spinning out of my grasp, tilting dangerously toward the concrete floor.

"*Ah!*" She gasped, then followed it up with an, "*Oomph.*"

"I got you," I whispered, holding her above the floor, lifting her to stand on her own two feet.

"This is a surprise to see you in my shop—oh!" The

woman who appeared from the back suddenly noticed the small woman standing close to my side.

The woman looked at me in shock, her wide hazel eyes asking silent questions.

"Izzie, this is, ah, a friend of mine. We had a mishap down at Fred's, so I brought her in for some new clothes."

"Haven't seen you around here before." Izzie never minced words.

"She's new in town," I put in quickly. Who the hell knew what Ivory would blurt out? And frankly, I'd cleaned up enough of her messes for one day.

"I love your hair. It's very chic," Ivory told the store owner. "Who is your stylist?"

Izzie was taken aback for a moment before reaching up to finger the ultra-short blond pixie she'd had since I'd known her. "Oh, well, I cut it myself."

"Yourself?" Ivory gasped, stepping toward Izzie. "That's amazing! I would probably die without my stylist. I mean, just look." She went on, plucking at the hair sticking out from under my hat. "It's been only a few days since I saw my stylist last, and just look at what's happened!"

Izzie glanced at me, and I shrugged. I didn't know how to deal with her either. Sometimes she was like an alien from another planet.

And other times, I wanted to pin her against the wall and kiss her silly.

"So, ah, you're here for some clothes?" Izzie asked Ivory.

"Well…" Ivory glanced around nervously.

"Yes," I put in, placing a palm to the small of her back and directing her toward a nearby rack of clothes. "Pick something."

Ivory began wandering around, sifting through racks, and making some faces that frankly amused me. To be honest, her snobby, spoiled behavior stopped offending me not long after we met. Probably because I realized she didn't mean it in a snotty way. It was just how she was.

The more I was around Ivory, the more I realized there wasn't a mean bone in her body. If anything, she was sheltered and naïve. She'd grown up with a platinum and diamond spoon in her mouth and didn't know anything else. I couldn't exactly punish her for being the product of her environment when I was also a product of mine.

Careful there, Neo... Sounds like you're trying to blend two worlds into one.

"Where'd you find her?" Izzie asked, sidling up to my side. She was taller than Ivory. I didn't have to look down to see into her eyes.

"I told you she's a friend from out of town."

Izzie snorted. "And I'm the queen's long-lost daughter."

"I always knew you were too good for the Grimms," I quipped, winking.

She laughed, lightly slapping my chest. "Charming as always."

"Oh my God!" Ivory gasped from the back of the store somewhere.

Pulse spiking instantly, I took off, rushing around the racks, trying to see where she'd disappeared to. She was so small that all the displays hid her from sight.

"Princess!" I demanded, feeling as though hours had passed instead of seconds.

"Neo!" she exclaimed, and I spun, my shoulders sagging in instant relief.

She was tucked between two racks, my hat and jacket making it even harder to see her slight frame. Wide blue eyes stared at me with glee as she clutched a hanger in her hands.

"Look at this!" She bounced forward, waving whatever she had in her hand. "Look at what I found!"

"You're yelling like that over a sweater?" I demanded, my heart rate still not back to normal.

She gasped. "This is not just *any* sweater! This is an authentic Aurora cardigan."

"An a-whatta?"

Ivory tsked, lowering the fabric. "I guess you wouldn't know. You wear flannel."

Raking my eyes over her body, I smirked. "So do you."

Completely unamused, she turned to Izzie who was standing just behind me. "You know Aurora, right?"

Izzie shook her head. "Should I?"

"As the owner of this fashion establishment, you should absolutely!" Ivory grabbed the sleeve to look at the price tag. Her gasp made both me and Izzie jump. "Twenty dollars!"

"Damn, Izzie, don't you think that's a little steep?" I muttered. Leave it to the princess to find the most expensive shirt in the place. Did she have an antenna on her head for money?

"Steep? She's practically giving it away!" Ivory exclaimed, holding up the hanger. "Look at the stitching, the detail on the hem. The fabric! And it's nearly in mint condition. It just needs a good dry-clean, and it will be an essential piece to any wardrobe."

All I saw was a white button-up sweater with some fat stripes on one arm.

Ivory held it up, marveling at it some more, then flipped it around to look at the back, which had a large A on it. "Original Italian buttons and the signature A on the back." She sighed dreamily. Hugging the garment to her chest, she said, "It's just perfect."

Oh my God, she's being cute again. I have to stop this.

"It's too expensive," I declared.

"You said to pick something," she countered.

"Not that."

"But—"

"No." My money, my call.

The plump red flesh of her lower lip jutted out, and she hugged the shirt closer to her body. The leather jacket seemed to envelop her and the damned shirt even more, and it made me think of how she might look if it were my arms around her instead.

I sighed heavily. "Fine."

Her face brightened once more, and she clapped for herself. Or maybe it was for me.

Good God.

"Get some pants and come on. You're going to freeze to death."

She went off behind another rack, and I called after her. "And stop exclaiming like you're being kidnapped at everything you do and see!" In a much lower voice, I muttered, "Fucking giving me a heart attack every time."

Izzie was staring at me like I was the alien and not Ivory.

"What?" I snapped.

"You got it bad."

Shit, not her too. "I do not," I deadpanned.

"I've never seen you like this with anyone," Izzie remarked, then tilted her head. "Actually, I've never seen you with a woman ever."

I stepped closer, allowing a glint to come into my eyes. "Now that's not true, Izzie. You're a woman."

A pink blush blossomed on her high cheekbones.

I should stop right now. Truth was I'd always known Izzie had a little crush on me. She was beautiful and from my world. But I never pursued her. I never pursued any woman because I was better on my own.

"I never thought you noticed," Izzie murmured, taking a step closer.

Alarm bells went off in my head. Was she actually turning

my charm around and using it to hit on me? Why now? Why after all this time?

"Almost done!" Ivory called out.

Izzie's eyes flicked away and then came right back to mine, a small smirk on her lips and a slight glint in her stare.

Was she jealous?

Her hand slid up my chest, but I kept my eyes locked on hers. "Well, if you aren't interested in her, maybe you might be interested in me," she practically purred.

"Iz." I grabbed her wrist, stopping the perusal of her hand. "You aren't interested in me."

"I think you know that's not true." She arched into me.

I did know.

What I hadn't known was just how much I was *not* into her until this very moment.

She might be beautiful, and she might be from my world… but I didn't want her. I never would.

I caught her just before her lips locked with mine. My palms wrapped around her shoulders, holding her back. Surprise lit her catlike eyes, and they narrowed vindictively.

"I'm sorry, Izzie. I'm not interested."

Cocking her head to the side, she studied me. "That girl is high-maintenance, noisy, and completely wrong for you."

"I know."

"She's also annoying."

My mouth turned up slightly. "I know that too."

The thump of things falling nearby had me pushing Izzie away and spinning. Ivory stood there staring, all the items she'd picked up in a heap at her feet. Hurt glistened in her blue eyes, and teeth bit into her rose-red lip.

She heard Izzie insult her.

She heard me agree.

For a split second, our eyes connected, and it was as if she silently asked why. Why I would agree, and what had she done so horribly to deserve this hurt?

Suddenly, I was assaulted by what felt like a hundred flashbacks of her cowering beneath the hood in the bar. Of her standing in the rain, frightened and automatically seeking my shelter. I remembered how light she'd been when I carried her home and how last night, I'd held her hand so she could sleep. All those moments were punctuated by the memory from just moments ago and how vulnerable she looked on the laundromat floor.

"Thank you, but I don't think I'll be needing any of these items today." Her voice was calm and austere, matching her posture but not her eyes.

Maybe that's why she closed them briefly before stepping over the mess and escaping onto the street.

Twenty-Five

Ivory

Hurt, derisive looks, and whispering behind my back. I wasn't a stranger to any of those things. In fact, I was a victim just like everyone else. Money and power didn't give you a free pass from insults.

Sometimes it made you more of a target.

So did beauty and success.

I never minded. I knew in life you had to take the good with the bad.

Go on strongly despite the fear. My mother used to tell me this, and I told myself this now as I walked numbly down the sidewalk as wild cabbies whizzed past.

Fear could mean many things. Basically, it meant anything that could hold you back. Hurt was one of those things.

My mother's words had gotten me through most of my life, and I managed to somehow dodge the barbs trying to rip me open.

But this hurt.

His casual agreement with judgment from a stranger stung deep. Sure, we hadn't known each other long at all, but truthfully, I felt like he knew enough to not think those things about me.

High-maintenance. Annoying. Noisy.

Fine. Maybe I was high-maintenance, but when did I ever ask him to maintain me? I didn't! I could maintain myself. I'd been doing it for a long time.

I tried not to be annoying or noisy. I even tried to say good-bye before, and he dragged me into that shop! For what? To insult me? To let other people insult me?

I've had way worse. *So why does this hurt so bad? Why do I care so much what he thinks of me? And why is that woman in his arms like that? Is that his girlfriend?*

Pressing a hand against my aching chest, I thought I heard a dim yell from behind. I didn't turn back. It was time I went home. Back to my world where I knew how to handle my life and the people in it. Whoever tried to kill me was probably long gone, and even if he wasn't, I would hire enough bodyguards he wouldn't be able to get close again.

The sun was gone now, disappeared behind buildings and put away for the night. The sky was starless, not because of the city lights, but because it was still heavy with clouds. Anxiety sank its sharp claws in as I walked, beleaguered with thoughts of rain and flashes of just twenty-four hours ago when I'd been walking alone down this same dark street.

Now that the first rush of hurt and anger was passing, fear and anxiety invited themselves in. What if that huntsman was still out there? What if he found me while I was on my way home?

Tugging the hat lower on my head, I shrank into the leather jacket. My clothes were still wet, the night wind cutting through the fabric like a sharp knife through butter. When I got to the next street over, I'd hail a cab. The doorman at my building would pay when I got there, and then I could pay him back.

Just one more block and you'll be safe.

Instead of reassurance, a new wave of anxiousness

crashed over me. The back of my neck prickled with warning, and chills rose along my arms like an army of spiders with thousands of curious legs.

The urge to itch and fidget in my clothes was nearly unbearable, and up ahead, a streetlight exploded with a loud pop. I crouched low, my knees hovering over the cold concrete as my hands protectively caged my head.

The sound of glass splattering ground made me think of bones breaking, and darkness descended with ominous resolve. Still crouching, I waited for more sounds to erupt, for pounding footsteps or even his menacing voice growling that he'd found me at last.

Nothing came.

Cautiously lowering my arms, I found nothing out of the ordinary except a broken light.

Stuff like this probably happened a lot. The buildings were super old, so the streetlamps probably were too. They really should get some funding to revitalize this neighborhood.

Straightening, I started ahead, still feeling the uneven pounding of my heart against my ribs.

"Princess!"

A voice that seemed ingrained in me echoed behind me, stalling my feet.

"Wait!"

I couldn't talk myself out of looking back.

Neo was down the sidewalk, barely visible in the fading light but visible enough for me to know it was him. He rushed forward, his form becoming bigger the closer he got.

I didn't want to talk to him. In fact, just seeing him made me ache all the more. Turning my back, I rushed away, hoping he would get the hint.

He yelled my name again.

And he said I was annoying.

I started to run, ignoring the uncomfortable squishing of my shoes and slapping of the wet tails of the flannel against my thighs. The ground underfoot turned uneven, making my feet wobble.

The broken glass from the light scraped and moved under my sneakers as I rushed, making me stumble, but not enough that I slowed in pace. The shards scattered as I ran, focusing on the corner up ahead, telling myself that I was almost there.

Unpredictably, I pitched to the side. *No.* I was grabbed.

Shock made it hard to think, as did the violent way I was snatched from the sidewalk, suddenly flying over the ground to be swallowed by the shadows.

When my brain finally caught up, I opened my lips to scream, but something hard and unrelenting slapped over my mouth forcing back any sound I would have made.

Eyes wide, arms flailing, I tried to escape, but there was no escaping the shadows. I was being captured by something much larger than myself.

I heard nothing over the pounding of my heart, saw nothing but the darkness and the narrow alley I'd been snatched into.

The hand around my mouth was so tight my jaw ached from the pressure, and when my foot connected with a part of the kidnapper's body, there was a grunt and the pressure on my jaw grew impossibly rougher.

"I told you if I saw you again, I wouldn't let you go."

My entire body stopped fighting, realization slamming into me, followed closely by fear.

The huntsman. He was still here. Watching. Waiting. Intent on killing.

Why even let me go at all if this would be the result? The prolonged suffering and confusion were cruel. Instead of dying in the park in the middle of the city, would I instead die here in a dirty, dark alley?

"Ivory!" The frantic way my name was called surged life into my limp form.

Stiffening, I lifted my head, yelling out to Neo even though the attempt was blocked.

"Ivory White!"

Neo! I'm here. Please find me. Please don't let me die...

Grunting, the huntsman slid through a door I hadn't even seen, my arm scraping on the rusty metal frame. I yelled, but the sound remained muffled like all the ones before.

His boots echoed against the concrete at first but then turned silent, almost eerily so. How a man so large could move like a ghost was a mystery. He held me with my back against his front, lifting me so I couldn't see his face. Attempting to twist around only earned my jaw more pain, and his fingers to bit into the side of my hip.

This place was like a dungeon with stale air, trash-littered surfaces, and crumbling brick walls.

"Ivory!" Neo roared, his voice surprisingly close.

Did he know about this place too? Had he found the secret door?

The huntsman stiffened, the first time he'd ever shown any kind of reaction at all. Desperately prying my jaw open, I bit down on his covered hand, sinking my teeth into any meaty part I could.

Breath hissed beside my ear, but his palm didn't move at all.

The fingers on my hip tightened, and I knew I'd have a bruise. Despite my watering eyes and desire to shrink away from the pain, I resisted.

And then I was being stuffed into a small space that no human should ever fit in. The huntsman went in first, dragging me along with him, our arms scraping and struggling to fit.

Not only was I caged inside some tiny cubby, but I was farther trapped by this man's body, situated between his legs and arms. He gripped me like a vise.

As he kept his one hand locked over my mouth, I felt my nostrils flare, struggling to breathe.

Thinking fast, I began stomping my foot, hoping Neo might hear.

The man squeezed me tighter into his form, his chilling voice brushing threateningly against my ear. "If he finds us, I'll kill him too."

All fight left me, and my shoulders slumped. Fat tears welled up and spilled over my cheeks, dripping onto the glove covering most of my face.

"I told you to run. I told you to never come back."

I didn't answer. I couldn't, and really, was I even supposed to?

Sounds of Neo moving around in the dreary space nearby made me tense.

"Princess, just answer me."

My body stiffened, and more tears fell. I wanted to answer, but I wouldn't. I couldn't. The man crowding around me would kill us both.

Neo might have hurt me, but I would never want him to die.

I could hear his shuffling feet and low swears as he searched a bit more. It seemed like forever when he muttered, "*Fuck*," and his footsteps faded away.

Overwhelming emotion caused pain in my chest, a rock in my throat, and quaking in my hands. We sat there long after he was gone until I grew lightheaded from lack of oxygen and too much fear.

Abruptly, the hand left my face, and I sucked in great

gasps of air, trying to replenish my lungs. I ended up coughing spastically as dust and stale air filled my throat.

The hand clapped back over my face, and his gravelly voice filled my ear. "No noise."

I nodded, hoping he would let go, and he did. The shove he gave me was not gentle, but the space was too tight for me to fall.

"Go. Don't try anything stupid."

I crawled out of the cubby, grit and grime clinging to me with my every move. There were no windows and no light. My eyes could only make out large square pillars stretching from floor to ceiling, trash-littered floors, and bare walls.

The second I was free from the cubby, I pushed off from the floor and started to run. My legs felt like Jell-O. He said not to run, but I ran anyway.

Why should I listen to him?

This was my last chance at escape, my last chance to save my own life.

With a final burst of adrenaline, I lunged forward, stumbling into a cement pillar and sagging against it. Shoving away, I rushed forward, desperately trying to locate the door that seemed to have disappeared.

The ends of my hair swirled as I spun, and heavy footfalls angrily approached. I tried to evade. I failed.

In a moment of déjà vu, I was slammed into the hard wall, my cheek scraping and making me cry out.

"Please," I begged. "Please let me go."

I'd only heard the blade of a knife cut through air once before. Once was more than enough to ensure I would never forget, so tonight when he lifted his blade, I recognized the sound without having to see it glimmer.

He palmed my head like it was something insignificant, forcing it back to bare my throat.

"Don't worry. You'll already be dead when I cut out your

heart." His words were so chilling, so matter-of-fact, I wondered if I'd imagined them or if he really had spoken.

I squeezed my eyes closed, feeling death was horrific enough. I wasn't about to watch it too.

The blade was swift, so sharp it whistled through the air. I flinched and cried out, then fell to the ground.

Curling in on myself, I gasped and heaved for air, anticipating the warm ooze of my life's blood to bloom out.

It never came, but the sounds of a scuffle did. The sounds of grunting and running feet.

Pushing up, I peered through the dark as something large and fast materialized, coming right at me.

A blood-curdling scream ripped out, scraping everything inside me on its way past my lips. Desperate to get away, I tried to run, but my knees were weak and I couldn't stand.

A large body dropped beside me, and I shrieked, curling into a ball, trying to become so small I couldn't be seen.

I really didn't want to die, but honestly, why was it taking so long to get this murder over with?

"I got you." He promised, and warm hands slid under me, lifting as if I weighed nothing at all.

I looked up as Neo pulled me into his lap, cradling me there like it was the safest place I'd been.

"N-Neo?" my voice was raspy, throat hurt, and I didn't even trust my own eyes to tell me he was real.

"It's me."

My entire body went limp, relief making me cry. Aching fingers curled into the edge of the unbuttoned flannel he wore, holding on for dear life.

Murmuring soothing sounds, he stroked his palm over my hair and brushed away my tears. I breathed in, drawing comfort from his scent.

"I know, sweetheart," he crooned. "I got you now."

I tried to remember a time when I'd felt so safe, but a

specific moment was impossible to recall. I could only think of a person. My father. He'd always made me feel safe.

But then he died and left me all alone.

"Please don't leave me too," I whispered, curling even closer into his lap.

His body wrapped around mine, and unlike before when I'd felt trapped with the huntsman this close, with Neo, it was entirely different.

"I won't." He vowed. "I'll never let you go again."

Twenty-Six

Neo

"I thought you'd left."

Her voice was hoarse. The sound of it welcome but the strain a stark reality check of how close she came to dying. Again.

Funny how knowing about the first attempted murder didn't affect me the same as the second. Perhaps because I hadn't witnessed it or I'd doubted it even happened at all.

Perhaps because now her death felt like it would be *my* loss.

I thought I'd ached when she walked out of the shop. I thought I'd ached when I called her name and she kept running.

Those things were nothing compared to how my heart literally stopped when I saw her snatched into the shadows.

One moment she'd been there, the next out of sight.

Tendrils of panic still clung to me like wild vines trying to tug me beneath the earth. Even now with her safely ensconced in my arms, dread tapped me like a jagged, too-long talon, ready to draw blood.

"Neo?"

Her voice against my chest broke through the clinging chaos.

"I pretended to leave," I explained. "I was waiting for him to come out."

"How did you know we were still here?"

"There was nowhere else for you to go."

"I tried to get away. I couldn't find the door." She drew in a sobbing breath.

I'd seen. I'd watched it all. With a thundering heart and a violent urge to pounce, I'd watched this gentle princess claw and fight to live. "You did so well, sweetheart."

"If you hadn't been here, I'd be dead." Her voice was flat, almost accepting of her fate.

Fate has better plans for you.

"C'mon, we need to get out of here," I said, standing up, bringing her with me.

Her hands clutched my arms, head tipped back to stare up with wide eyes. "Do you think he'll come back?"

"He'd be stupid to."

"Did you see his face?"

Shaking my head, I replied, "No. He had his back turned to me the entire time and a hat and a hoodie over his head. I rammed into him from the side. He kicked me in the ribs and then took off."

She gasped, pulling back to hover her hands over my midsection. "You're hurt!"

"I'm not."

"Let me see!" she demanded, pulling up the hem of my T-shirt.

I had half a mind to let her undress me, but now really wasn't the time. "It's dark. You won't be able to see anything."

She made a face, and I tucked my arm around her, leading her toward the door.

"I didn't see him either, but I know it was the same man as before," she said, allowing me to guide her.

Keeping her body tucked behind mine, I stepped out into

the alley first, scanning to make sure it was clear. Finding it empty, I wrapped my hand around hers and tugged.

Halfway toward the street, I stopped, bending to scoop up a white bag I'd dropped.

"What is that?" she asked, curious. Her voice was still raw and painful-sounding, and I didn't like it.

"Your clothes." The words came out harsher than I intended.

"My clothes?"

"The ones you threw on the floor in the shop before storming off in a fit."

She gasped so hard she winced and yanked her hand free of mine. "I did not storm off in a fit."

When she wobbled on her feet, I automatically reached for her.

She evaded. "Do not touch me."

"Two minutes ago, you were wrapped in my arms." I reminded her.

Her face soured. "I was upset."

I raised an eyebrow. "You're not upset now?"

"Yes, but this is a different kind of upset!"

"And how am I supposed to keep up with your mood swings?" I wondered aloud.

She gasped, putting a hand to her throat. "There you go insulting me again." Her legs were still wobbly, making her look like a newborn calf trying to walk as she "stormed" ahead toward the street.

I could have easily caught up to her, but I decided to let her think she was leaving me behind. That lasted about four seconds until anxiety whispered at the back of my neck as she grew closer to the street. I didn't think the guy was out there, but I didn't want her going first. If I had to see her snatched away one more time tonight, there was no telling what I might do.

"Princess."

"Don't call me that," she called over her shoulder, still forging ahead.

"Stop."

She didn't stop, about to step from the alley. Just then, a man in all black walked past, his steps quick, stride powerful. She nearly collided with him, a shriek echoing around us.

The man barely spared her a glance as he kept going, but Ivory wasn't so unaffected. Fleeing backward, she locked her eyes on me, terror leaching what little color was left in her cheeks.

Planting my feet, I opened my arms in invitation.

She was so slight and weak that I barely moved with the collision. Her trembling arms wound around my waist beneath the flannel, fingers interlocking and pressing against my spine. Her face buried into my chest, and I swear if her legs weren't quivering so bad, she'd have wrapped them around me too.

We said nothing, just stood there in the dark with her in my arms as I tried to reassure her with my presence alone.

The wind blew, and she shivered, a signal it was time to go.

A low whine vibrated her throat when I peeled her off me. Chuckling, I kept moving, crouching in front of her. "C'mon, princess, your carriage awaits."

I knew she was exhausted when she didn't bother to protest, instead climbing on my back and wrapping her body around me from behind. Straightening, I lifted her a little higher and set off down the street toward the Rotten Apple.

Izzie's shop came into sight, and Ivory made a small sound, the arms around my neck tightening. "I don't want those clothes."

With a slight smirk, I asked, "Not even the sweater?"

She leaned forward, peering over my shoulder toward the bag I carried. "You bought me that sweater?"

The smirk turned into a full-blown smile. "It's *like* an Aurora."

She slumped back. "You're making fun of me again."

Oh, beneath that aloof exterior, she was so sensitive and easily hurt. Possessiveness rose inside me, overcoming all thought.

Reaching up and cupping one of her hands clasped around me, I lifted it, pressing a soft kiss against the palm. "I'm not making fun, sweetheart. I think you're cute."

"No one thinks I'm cute."

"No? Then what do people think of you?"

"They think I'm beautiful."

"Well, you are that too."

"You're bad at apologizing."

"Why should I apologize? I didn't do anything wrong."

A rude noise floated beside my ear, and her chin hit my shoulder as though she were going to pout. "She insulted me. Said I was high-maintenance, annoying, and noisy. You agreed with her."

"I agreed with her, yes. But to me, those things aren't insults. They're things I like about you."

"You must think I'm stupid too."

Without thinking, I kissed her palm again. "Let's talk about this later, princess. You've had a long night."

The smallest of sighs brushed against my ear, and her body settled even farther against mine. Her chin was still on my shoulder, her lips still near my ear when we finally approached the Rotten Apple.

"Is she your girlfriend?"

I was still holding her hand, and I gave it a gentle squeeze. "No."

Neither of us said anything else.

Twenty-Seven

Ivory

When Neo stepped into the apartment with me on his back, Beau's eyes widened, Fletch waved, and Snort danced happily around our feet.

My shoes made a squishing noise as water pooled out when Neo placed me on my feet. Earth came out of the kitchen, and a precarious feeling floated through the air when he stopped midstride and turned to glare.

There were four pizza boxes and a carton of beers in his hands.

"I thought I told you not to be here when I got back."

"I wasn't," I retorted.

His stare was stony and unpleasant. "You cleaned my house."

"I had to. You never do."

His eyes flicked over me, no doubt noting how ridiculous I looked. "What happened to your face?"

Worried, I reached up, fingering my cheeks until my hand brushed over a tender, stinging spot and making me wince. A vivid memory of being slammed against a wall—*again*—flashed through my mind.

"Someone tried to kill me again."

He grunted. "Pizza's getting cold."

Beside me, Neo relaxed. I hadn't even known he was tense.

Beau and Fletch both smiled, diving for the pizza and beer.

"Come sit by me, Ivory," Fletch yelled, already shoving food into his mouth.

Did he ever stop eating? If I ate that way, I'd be a thousand pounds!

Something brushed the small of my back, and I flinched, a low sound building in my throat. Neo didn't pull back or react to my sudden scare. Instead, the pads of his fingers pressed more firmly against me, offering solace.

"You're safe here."

I believed him.

"What if the huntsman comes here looking for me? You all could be in danger." I worried.

Seconds later, a body shoved between mine and Neo's, arms winding around my waist and hugging tight. Fletcher's honey-colored floppy hair tickled my cheek when he rubbed his nose against my shoulder. "You're worried about us?"

"Of course."

"Even Earth?" Beau grinned. He had pepperoni in his teeth.

Earth didn't bother to turn around to look at us from the couch. Instead, all I saw was the back of his dark head and the movement of the beer bottle tipping up against his lips.

"Of course," I answered instantly.

Beau's eyes widened, and he glanced at Earth.

"Well, I don't know why you all are so surprised. You've allowed me to stay here. You've offered me some sense of safety and a place to try and figure out my next move. You've all been very kind—some more than others—and I would never want anything bad to happen to any of you."

Fletcher made a sound and hugged me again, nearly knocking me over in his haste.

Grabbing him by the back of the neck, Neo peeled him off, giving him a hard look. "That's enough."

Unbothered, Fletcher went back to his seat and resumed inhaling the food.

"Hey, turn that up," Beau called, motioning toward the flat-screen.

Earth obliged, raising the volume as the same news anchor from this morning filled the screen. It took a moment to register what she was saying because I marveled that it had only been one day. It truly felt as if I'd been here far longer.

Missing Heiress – New Information

The headline scrolled across the bottom of the screen as the woman stood in some sort of power suit she really shouldn't have been wearing, holding a microphone and standing inside what appeared to be some garage.

"There has been a new discovery in the case of missing heiress Ivory White who disappeared yesterday morning while out for her daily run in Central Park. The Upper East Side's princess is presumed dead after the discovery of her blood in the park, and no one has seen or heard from her in nearly forty-eight hours. Authorities have not ruled this a recovery mission as of yet, but things were looking grim until just a short while ago when some locals made a discovery in a parking garage not too far from Central Park."

I felt all the eyes of the men turn to me, and I shrugged. "Don't look at me. I've been cleaning this pigsty all day!"

Feeling something, I turned to Neo who was pointedly avoiding my eyes while dividing his stare between the TV and the wall with a prominent grimace tugging at his lips.

"It's probably just some made-up crap by kids who want five minutes of fame," he said, going over to snatch the remote from Earth like he would switch the channel.

"Wait!" I gasped, putting my hand on his arm. "I want to see what they're saying."

"It could be important." Fletch agreed, still chomping. He had sauce on his chin.

"About an hour ago, a mural was discovered in the middle of a parking garage, and it immediately added another layer of mystery to this already clandestine case."

The camera moved past the reporter to focus on a wide cement pole that was decorated in colorful paint.

"That's you!" Fletcher exclaimed.

I couldn't even argue. It was undeniably me.

Moving closer, my body bumped the back of the couch as I took in the details of the painting, the dark hair that curled to hide the fact it was crudely uneven, the pale skin, red lips, and bow perched on my head like it could be a crown.

The colors were simple. Even the art itself was simple… but nothing else about it was. The simplicity captured things that not even "professional" art could have portrayed. I felt admired as I stared at the work. I felt as though whoever painted it knew me in an almost intimate way.

My stomach fluttered, and my fingers moved restlessly over the cushions on the couch.

How could something so roughly painted in a dim, gritty garage with only three colors look so… *captivating*?

"This image, which is clearly freshly painted and was not reported to be here this morning, has sparked new hope that perhaps Ivory White is still alive and whoever painted this might have information about her whereabouts.

"More grim theories are also circling that perhaps this is some sort of tribute to a beautiful life cut far too short or the work of a madman silently bragging about his kill."

As the reporter spoke to the camera, the painting could still be seen behind her while police, photographers, and other people moved around treating that pole like a crime scene.

The screen changed suddenly, ripping away the sight of the painting, making me blink. Another familiar image filled the screen, but it was much less captivating.

Audra White – Grieving Stepmother Makes Plea

My austere stepmother sat perfectly poised but also slightly out of sorts with a Hermes handkerchief clutched in her hand. Her top was black silk, the high neckline ruffled and subdued. Her blond hair had been pulled back, but not too severely so she still looked soft. Her makeup was done to perfection, not too glamourous but enough to highlight the fact that she was an extremely beautiful woman.

My relationship with Audra could best be described as tolerable, even though I'd known this woman longer than my own mother. She never precisely liked me nor I her. But we got along for my father's sake, coexisting in the same world but trying not to cross each other's paths.

She was so different from the memories I held close of my mother that I often wondered how my father could have such different tastes from one wife to the next. I never asked, though, because I didn't care as long as he was happy, and he always, always had a smile for me.

When he died, Audra remained composed. I assumed her emotionless, cold exterior was a front for her grief, as she was a woman who didn't like to show weakness.

Maybe that was why I was surprised to see her now. To hear the words she told the world.

"Please." She spoke, her voice filled with emotion. "If anyone out there has seen or heard from my stepdaughter, please call. She's the only family I have left." Pausing, she twisted the designer handkerchief in her fingers. When she looked up again, pure anguish filled her imploring gaze and actually made my heart squeeze.

Had I misjudged her all these years? Did she perhaps like me more than I assumed?

"I'm offering a reward for her safe return. A handsome amount for any clue. I just want her back safe and sound." Her voice broke, the cloth lifted to her eyes to dab.

My fingers tightened around the back of the sofa, and suddenly, I felt very selfish for not going home. For not calling to tell her I was all right.

I'd let a madman dictate how I handled this. I'd let him scare me into hiding.

Audra began to softly weep, her blond head bowing as sounds of suffering bubbled through the speakers. Suddenly, someone else was there, a man in a dove-gray suit and a pale-blue silk tie. His blond hair was styled neatly away from his face, his chiseled jaw completely smooth.

His arm wrapped around her shoulders, making her look fragile as he looked into the camera with eyes that matched his tie. "Ivory, if you can hear this, be strong. We're searching for you, and we won't ever give up."

"Ethan," I whispered, seeing the worry lines on his usually unlined face.

And then they were gone, the screen flashing back to the parking garage, the reporter, and the painting of me.

"We'll keep you updated as more information is released."

An ad for toilet paper burst through the heavy silence, dancing bears shaking their bums.

My emotions were all over the place, the faces of my step-mother and Ethan still flashing behind my eyes and the odd intimacy I'd felt when seeing that painting still humming through my veins. It took a moment to realize the TV had been muted.

It took a moment for the thick silence to penetrate my deep emotions. When it finally did, I noted no one was staring at me, the missing heiress of NYC.

Everyone was looking at Neo with varying degrees of shock and curiosity.

He seemed rather sheepish, avoiding every single stare. Uncomfortable, his shoulders rolled under the open flannel.

"After the hell you gave me earlier for letting her go to the laundromat," Beau said, making Neo wince.

I glanced back at the TV, then the walls bursting with Neo's art. The back of my neck tingled, and I stared at him.

His cheeks flushed.

And then I knew. The intimacy. How a painting could be so crudely done but still utterly captivating.

"You painted that," I said, not really a question because there was truly no other answer.

"Of course I didn't," he refuted.

Closing the distance between us, I grasped his hand to look down. Paint splattered his fingers, red, white, black, and blue.

"You painted that," I repeated, holding the proof in my hands.

Pulling his fingers from mine, he tucked them into the pockets of his jeans.

"It was beautiful," I said after a moment of awkward silence.

His eyes lifted, the darkness in them suddenly shining like the moon had risen. I offered a small smile. He didn't offer one back, but the glimmer in his eyes was better.

"You gonna eat or what?" Earth spat, breaking the moment.

Neo didn't have to be told twice. If anything, he was

beyond grateful for the escape. Setting aside the bag of clothes, he dove into the food.

"You need to wash your hands!" I scolded.

He paused, holding a slice against his lips.

I lifted an eyebrow.

Sighing, he put it down and went to the bathroom.

"Whipped," Earth muttered darkly, picking up Neo's slice and stuffing it into his mouth.

Placing my wet shoes neatly by the door, I padded around the couch. "Would it be all right if I cleaned up?"

"I'll save you a piece." Fletcher volunteered.

"Thank you."

My eyes went to Earth, and he lifted his eyes. "Put something over your face. You're gonna bleed all over dinner."

Bleeding! Forgetting his sour attitude, I raced off to the bathroom, nearly colliding with Neo on his way back to eat.

"You!" I gasped, pushing a finger into his chest.

"Now what?" he muttered.

"Why didn't you tell me my face was bleeding?"

"It's just a scratch. You'll be okay."

Pushing past him, I dashed into the bathroom, which was still surprisingly clean, to look in the mirror. Oh. Right. The mirror I couldn't see in.

"Neo!" I yelled.

"What?" he yelled back.

"How am I supposed to see myself with this mirror hung so high?"

"Shorty!" Fletcher called out, laughter in his voice.

A few seconds went by, and no one did anything.

"Neo!" I hollered again.

His stomping footsteps announced him, and then his scowling face came around the corner. Pizza in one hand, he reached out with the other, taking the mirror down from where it hung and setting it on the back of the sink, leaning against the wall.

"Ta-da," he sang around chewing.

"Chew with your mouth closed."

Leaning in, he chomped even louder right beside my ear.

"That's just disrespectful." I sniffed but ruined it when I started to giggle.

Neo pressed a kiss to the tip of my nose and disappeared, leaving me standing there shaken to the core. I didn't know how to react to him. How to feel about him. When at last I could breathe again, I turned to the mirror and saw my reflection for the first time in almost two days.

"*Agh!*" I screamed so loud the mirror actually quivered.

Thunderous noise followed, and four large men somehow crammed themselves in the narrow bathroom door.

"What is it? What happened?" Fletcher asked, crouching down as the others stood higher.

Neo's eyes were panicked, Beau was staring at the shower curtain I'd made him hang, and Earth's eyes were also suspiciously worried. He probably had something in them.

"What's wrong?" Neo worried, pushing through the men to lightly grab my arm.

"This!" I exclaimed, pointing at the mirror.

"What's wrong with it now?"

"There's probably a spider on it." Beau snickered.

I rolled my eyes. "Why would I be frightened of a spider? What did he ever do to me?"

"Then what's wrong?" Neo sighed as if he were losing patience.

"Why did no one tell me I looked this awful?" I demanded.

All the men blinked and looked around at each other dubiously.

"Easy." Earth finally chimed in. "We thought you looked like this all the time."

My mouth fell open, and then I rushed him.

Neo caught me around the waist, my legs still swinging over the ground I was no longer touching. "That was the meanest thing you've ever said to me!"

"Fix your face. You're bleeding," he deadpanned, not even worried in the least about my threats.

All three men left the bathroom, and Neo put me on my feet. An unexpected rush of tears filled my eyes, and I fought to keep them from spilling over.

It was a fight I did not win.

"Shh, shh…" Neo soothed, tugging me into his arms and holding my head to his chest.

I sniffled, wiping my tears on his shirt. "No wonder you insulted me and flirted with her," I mumbled.

Neo laughed, his clear glee ringing over my head as I stood there and cried miserably. He really was so rude. "I was not flirting."

"Whatever."

My hands clung to his shirt when he pulled me back, dark eyes seeking mine. I didn't feel like looking at him, so I shut mine, denying my stare.

Instead of arguing with me, I felt warm, wide palms cup my face. Emotion moved through me, making me feel weak and wobbly. The way he held my face so tenderly seemed to open up the floodgates of raw emotion lurking just beneath my surface, fighting hard to get out no matter how hard I tried to keep it contained.

How could he cradle me like this? How could such a small gesture make me want to crumble?

The center of my chest felt tight as though there were no room left inside me for even air to fill my lungs. Wet lashes clung to my cheeks as I squeezed my eyes shut, trying with all my might to keep him from getting in even further.

"Look at me." He beckoned. Oh, his voice was like the sweetest of apples, offering the most delicious snack.

I let loose a sound of refusal, squeezing my eyes closed even harder.

His low chuckle scraped across my insides like the strike of a match setting fire to my soul.

"Okay then, just listen," he mused. "Why would I flirt with her when you were standing just feet away? Even hidden by the clothing racks, wearing wet, dirty clothes, and with your hair all uneven."

"This is not helping!"

He chuckled again, and my God, why was it my favorite sound?

"Even then, you were achingly beautiful. A beauty I thought only existed between the pages of a storybook. Even on your worst day, Ivory White, you will always be the fairest of them all."

I opened my eyes and fell into his.

Are you lying again?

I couldn't lie about this. His black depths vowed.

His hands still cradled my face, and I couldn't help but nuzzle into his palm.

Gentle pressure was applied against the underside of my jaw, bringing my face back up as he began to lower his. My heart leaped into my throat, and every thought worrying me evaporated with anticipation.

"Fletch is gonna eat all this if you don't get out here!" Earth yelled.

Neo's forehead dropped, momentarily touching my shoulder. Disappointment curled my toes, and my teeth sank into my lower lip.

"Bad timing," he muttered, straightening away. The pad of

his thumb brushed against my mouth, tugging the abused flesh away from my teeth. “Next time.”

The moment shattered when he stepped back. “Clean up and dry off. I’ll save you some food.”

It wasn’t until he was gone that I remembered to breathe.

Twenty-Eight

Neo

I wanted to kiss her so badly I ached.

Distractions kept interrupting, and I allowed them to stay.

Because I knew.

With one thousand percent accuracy.

I couldn't deny that the moment our lips finally connected, my life wouldn't be my own anymore.

It would be hers.

Twenty-Nine

Ivory

I couldn't relax.

Maybe it was the loud-breathing dog anchoring my feet to the couch like an anvil. Maybe it was the death glare I got from Earth when he called for Snort to come to bed and the dog refused to leave my side. Could have been the pizza I ate for dinner. More likely, it was watching four grown men inhale said pizza.

I mean, I'd seen more civilized feedings at the zoo.

And look, in my defense, I had to eat the greasy carbs for dinner. It was that or pass out. I was tired of passing out. Besides, I was almost murdered twice. Hello, stress eating for one.

All of these were valid reasons, but I didn't think these were the explanation as to why I was lying on this lumpy couch in the dark, staring up at the ceiling. Why restlessness allowed me no peace.

At least the place smelled nice. The cheap candle I got smelled better than some of the ones I'd been gifted from major designers.

The light but constant tapping of Beau's fingers on his keyboard lent a nice cadence to the very dim room, but even that wasn't enough to lull my exhausted body and mind into slumber.

What's a girl gotta do to get some sleep around here?

Maybe I should have taken one of the beers Earth brought up from the bar to go with the pizza. I mean, it was gross, but it did offer poison. Maybe that would have knocked me out.

I felt my nose scrunch up just thinking about it. I think I'd pass on that kind of sleep.

The slightest shuffle drowned out everything else, and I struggled under the weight of the dog to turn toward the sound. The covers shifted on the mattress Neo and Fletch were sharing, and then a body sat up.

I knew immediately it was Neo. Somehow in this short amount of time, I'd grown some sort of instinct to recognize him without any help at all.

His upper body was bare, his skin standing out in the shadows. As he pushed a hand through his hair, his shoulders rose and fell with a single deep breath. My belly flipped a little watching his movements, and I recalled what it had been like being carried on that back.

Leaning down, he scooped up a T-shirt and tugged it over his head, the dark material of the shirt concealing the broad shoulders I'd been captivated by. Pushing up, he grabbed a pair of jeans, and my attention sharpened.

Why is he getting dressed in the middle of the night?

Almost as if sensing my curiosity, he glanced behind him, staring at the space where I lay. I pretended to be asleep, of course. Couldn't spy on him if he knew I was awake.

Hearing the rustle of the jeans once more, I went back to observing. The little hop he did when he pulled up the jeans made me smile. Neo disappeared into the bathroom for a few moments and then returned, grabbing a jacket and spinning toward me again.

Quickly closing my eyes, I willed my breath to be even as I felt him creep close. Snort shifted, glancing up at him, and Neo shushed him quietly.

My heart was thundering so loud I expected him to ask me why I was faking sleep, but he said nothing. Just stood over me, staring down.

Oddly, I didn't feel violated or even offended. If anything, my skin grew warm and the air around me shimmered with comfort.

I only need him closer to fall asleep.

The thought jarred me, nearly giving away the fact that I was not actually asleep. But Neo didn't notice because he'd moved away, and all the locks on the door started to slide free.

Eyes flying open, I stared at the back of the sofa, listening to him unlock the door. *He's leaving? At this hour? Where is he going? Is he coming back?*

Unmistakable panic flooded my veins, wiping out the sleepy feeling I'd only just achieved. When the door clicked shut behind him, I gasped, throwing off the blanket and rushing out into the hall.

"Neo," I breathlessly called, my bare feet slapping against the floor.

He spun back, looking like a prince of the night. Black ripped jeans. Black boots splattered with paint. Black T-shirt, black hoodie with the hood resting over a black jacket with a thousand pockets covering the front.

His night eyes seemed like wide orbs, which were illuminated with surprise as he stared from beneath a black knit cap pulled down to his eyebrows. His jaw was even shadowed with dark stubble, accentuating the strong line.

For a moment, I forgot to breathe. I forgot to think, and all I did was feel, pummeled by a million emotions coming so hard and so fast I couldn't even single them out.

"Go back to sleep," he said, his voice deep and raspy, exactly the kind of voice a prince of the night would use.

"Why are you leaving?"

"I have to work."

"I thought you went to work earlier today."

"I lied."

Then where were you? I wanted to ask but knew he wouldn't tell.

"Please don't go."

His throat bobbed, and his eyes glanced away before coming back to rest on me. "Go back to bed."

"I'm scared." It was true. I was. Everything was foreign here, and it seemed there was danger and chaos around every corner.

But he was an anchor. An anchor that made me feel like maybe I'd be okay.

"The others will protect you."

"I want you." The second the words exited my mouth, I nearly died from how they could be construed. Folding my lips in, I forbade myself from speaking again. I hadn't meant it *that* way, but it seemed if I tried to explain, I'd only make it worse.

I felt swallowed whole by his intense stare and oddly shy under the weight of his silence. I was normally not a timid woman. I owned who and what I was. I commanded a room whenever I entered.

But here with him, it was different.

Oddly enough, I realized I felt more vulnerable with him right now than I had in the clutches of the huntsman.

And that realization wrapped fear around my heart.

It was this intense fear that allowed me to break the spell I always fell under when I stared into his gaze. I turned back to the apartment, but something warm and firm encircled my wrist.

Instead of looking at him, I stared at where he held me, at the contrast of his warm-toned skin against my nearly paper-white.

Still holding lightly to my arm, he moved past, stepping into the apartment and leaving me in the hall. Feet rooted to the floor, I watched him move silently around the room, then approach once more. Closing the apartment door behind him, he held out the basic pair of white sneakers he'd gotten me at the secondhand shop.

I put them on along with a pair of his socks, which were long enough that they covered the hem of the black leggings I'd also gotten.

Any other time, I never would have put this on, let alone considered going out in public, but here I was, silently doing both without even asking why.

Once that was done, he handed over a black hoodie that looked a lot like the one he was wearing. I went to grab it, but he made a sound and lifted it carefully over my head, tugging it down until it fell to my thighs.

Finally, he held out a baseball cap, one I recognized as his instantly because it was splattered with paint. Once I pulled it down over my limp and frankly tortured hair, his hand appeared palm up, silently asking for mine.

I answered the same way he asked, by offering my hand, sliding it along his. When our fingers intertwined, my stomach felt fluttery, and a shaky breath silently rushed past my lips.

Outside on the sidewalk, my hand was still in his, the city sleeping softly around us. He walked, and I followed, not caring at all where we were going because I was with him.

Thirty

Huntsman

She did not heed my warning. She did not disappear.

So I took an approach I never had before. Snatching her off the street, trying to make her understand.

I thought she might flee. Still, she stayed.

The proof I'd sent of her demise could only work if she was forgotten like pages ripped out of a book.

Now there was a painting. There was hope she might still live.

The proof I sent would begin to look feeble. The reputation I'd carefully cultivated could be shattered by one girl.

I couldn't allow it.

She should have listened. She should have disappeared.

There was only one solution to stop this from getting too far out of hand.

Produce a body. But not just any body.

Hers.

Thirty-One

Neo

Trepidation shifted the way she walked, turning her cautious and more deliberate. Her always small but graceful steps were clumsier, and it felt like I was tugging her along instead of walking beside her.

Timid wasn't really a word I would use to describe Ivory. Even in her most vulnerable times, there was always a sort of arrogant confidence about her. I didn't mean that as an insult either, though if I said those things out loud, she would take it as one. Just like before.

Before when she got jealous.

She didn't actually say she was jealous, but I felt it. I saw it deep in her jewel-toned eyes and felt it in the way she clung to my back a little tighter when I carried her past the thrift shop.

Pleasure, a warm and fuzzy feeling, curled through my middle, making my stomach feel oddly light. Her jealousy satisfied me.

And so did the way her hand tightened around mine, her short strides quickening so her body was that much closer.

It wasn't that I wanted her to be afraid or wary, but I couldn't deny the enjoyment I got from knowing it was me she reached for when she needed more than her own confidence. The instinct to protect curled through my veins, reaching for my senses, tingling the underside of my skin.

The urge to protect wasn't necessarily new, but this was.

This felt new because I felt wanted. I wasn't obligated to protect Ivory. I wasn't asked to, and honestly, I probably didn't need to. But she came to me anyway, keeping close, allowing me to lead…

Trusting me.

I wasn't a man worthy of trust. I hadn't been for a very long time, and I knew she would probably rescind that trust when she got to know me better. But right now? Right now her body bumped into mine because my presence reassured her, holding her hand helped her sleep, and the bandages I put on her scrapes made me feel worthwhile. Like maybe the man I'd lost so long ago wasn't as misplaced as I believed.

This was a dangerous game I was playing—a game I knew I would never win. It was why I tried not to kiss her. It was why I tried not to fall too deep.

But how could a street rat like me, a guy with nothing to offer but paint-stained hands, resist when a woman like her made me feel I was actually enough.

Don't do this to yourself, Neo.

"Neo?" Her voice was sort of musical as it floated to my ear, carrying over the loud noise of the subway.

Retreating from the battle within my head, I let my gaze drift to the storybook girl.

How I wanted to fall into that book with her. How I wanted to get lost in her pages.

"You've never been on the subway before, have you?"

The way her eyes darted toward the silver bullet screeching to a stop beside us and then back at me was all the answer I needed.

"How could you live in New York City all your life and never once ride the subway?" I mocked.

Her hackles rose, as I knew they would, giving back some of her usual confidence. "Why would I ride this"—she gestured—"when I have a driver?"

I rolled my eyes. "You can't call yourself a New Yorker until you ride the subway," I announced. "Let's go."

Wide silver doors slid open all along the cars, and the hair around her neck blew back. Inside, the lights were harsh, and the hanging handrails swung back and forth.

"I don't know," she murmured, trying to turn away. *"Eek,"* she squeaked when my arms circled her waist and lifted, walking into the car.

She was lucky it was so early in the morning and not many people were squished in here with us. I wanted to laugh thinking about how she would have reacted if this had been normal hours because the car would have been jam-packed with people.

Her feet touched the ground again as the doors slid closed. "It smells in here. And why is it so dirty? Why do people put up with this?"

Spinning her around to face me, I merely smiled, knowing that all her complaints were because she was so stressed.

"Hold on." I warned, and the subway pitched forward.

She fell of course, not ready for the jolt of movement. I caught her, tugging her closer than I needed to, my blood heating when she didn't pull away. Instead, her cheek lay pillowed just beneath my shoulder, her hands holding on to my biceps for dear life.

A second passed, and she pulled back, staring out the thick glass windows. "We're going so fast!" she exclaimed.

We shot into a tunnel, and all the lights flickered out. The unfamiliar darkness made her bury her face against my chest.

A lump formed in my throat. *I am falling. I don't know how to stop.*

Clearing the tunnel, the lights came back on, but we stood there clinging to each other far longer than necessary. The next stop approached, and the change in speed caused us to wobble unsteadily.

When I tipped her head back, I couldn't see her eyes because of the hat, but her rose-red lips were on full display.

"Are we getting off?" she asked.

"Not yet." My voice was raspy, but I pretended not to notice.

As the doors opened and no new passengers got on, I led her toward the back where there was a bench seat in front of a window.

I sat first. Ivory stared at the empty space beside me as if it might have some kind of contagious disease.

Still holding her hand, I tugged, bringing her into my lap.

"Neo!" She gasped.

Locking my arms around her waist, I answered, "You can move over if you want to."

She didn't. She stayed firmly in my lap. "How much longer will we be riding this thing?"

"You in a hurry to get off?"

That earned me a shy glance and a glimpse at her blushing cheek.

Resting my chin on her shoulder, I couldn't help but hold her a little tighter. "Long enough for you to tell me something about yourself."

"What do you want to know?"

How to keep you. "Whatever you want to tell me."

"I own my own fashion company. We specialize in high-end couture and accessories. It's called Reflection."

"Why'd you name it that?"

Her face turned a little toward mine, and I didn't think

she realized her finger was playing with the strings between the rips in my jeans over my knee.

Just that slightest touch, her skin against mine, drove me crazy and made me work double time to hear the words she was speaking.

"Because to me, fashion is a reflection of who you are or who you want to be. It's the first thing people see about you, the first impression you give. And because I think everyone should love the reflection they see when they look into a mirror."

"And what about you, princess? Do you love the reflection in your mirror?"

"Sometimes."

The scoffing sound I made ruffled her hair, and she twisted around in my lap to look into my face, a scowl firmly on hers. "Why is that funny?" she demanded.

"Because you're so gorgeous. There is no way you can't know that."

"Your reflection is more than just the way you look," she admonished softly.

Ahh. I felt that.

Swallowing thickly, I couldn't resist tugging the cap off her head so I could see every expression that flickered across her features.

She ducked her head, fear flashing in her eyes.

Tipping her chin up so our eyes could meet, I reassured her. "No one is looking. It's just you and me right now."

I could have sworn I felt her tremble.

"So tell me, sweetheart." I began, keeping my voice for only her to hear. Tucking a midnight strand of hair behind her ear, I asked, "What is it about your reflection you don't like?"

We went through another tunnel, lights flickering off and

darkness hiding everything, including whatever expression she'd likely just made.

"There's this…unknown inside me I can't explain. Fear that lives deep within me, but it wears a cloak so I can't ever see its face. It makes me question everything, even myself," she confided.

I marveled at her honesty, again at the trust she offered as if baring her deepest secrets were no big deal because she knew I'd keep them safe.

My God, I wanted to be that for her. I wanted to be the man I saw reflected in her clear blue eyes. I wanted to shelter and protect. I wanted to hold all her secrets close and bear the burden of her worries so she wouldn't have to.

"And sometimes…" She paused, eyes finally skirting away.

"Sometimes what?" I cajoled, wrapping a palm around her hip.

"Sometimes I feel lonely like there are pieces of me missing, pieces I might never find."

I'm a thief. She is a princess.

Two different hearts. Two different worlds.

But here in this grimly lit subway, she sat in my lap, and here in this moment, our hearts shared a single beat.

"Something in me recognizes something in you," I whispered, caressing the bandage I'd applied over her cheek just hours before.

She didn't say anything. She didn't have to. Long, silent moments passed as the subway sped along, but we were suspended in time, lost in a world of our own.

When she finally looked away, it was all I could do to haul in a shuddering breath. My lungs burned as though we'd been kissing for hours and I'd forgotten to breathe. I *felt* kissed. No, I felt devoured, and the fog in my mind tried to convince me our lips had met.

"What about you?"

I blinked, pushing through the fog still hovering over my thoughts like a forest in the early morning hours. "What?"

Bow-shaped lips tugged into a smile. "Now you tell me something about you."

The harsh sound of metal scraping against metal was like nails on a chalkboard on crack, as the subway screeched to a stop. The voice over the speaker announced the stop and I stood, sitting Ivory on her feet. "This is us."

"Oh!" she exclaimed, spinning around to watch the doors slide open. "We're here?" she asked, as I pulled the hat low on her head.

"Hmm." I agreed. "We're here."

And just in time too. Because I didn't want to answer her question. I didn't want to become the villain in her storybook.

Thirty-Two

Ivory

Tall wooden poles with metal arms curving out like hooks at the top illuminated the night with yellow light. Their brightness only cast so far, leaving patches of shadows in between, giving everything a seedy feel.

The blacktop underfoot was faded and uneven, puddles of water pooled in the dips, but the flatter areas just appeared damp. A huge building spread out in front of us, a place that looked like nothing more than a massive garage. All the wide doors were lifted, and everything inside was wide-open concrete with concrete pillars and more harsh, unflattering lighting.

Despite the ungodly hour and the fact the sun was long from coming up, the place bustled, coming alive while the rest of the city slept. Shouts from men and beeping from what I assumed was the small tractor-looking things driving around filled the air. Piles of wooden pallets, empty boxes, and other unidentifiable objects were all piled around.

The scent in the air was unpleasant. Well, really, it was foul. A cross between fish, sweat, and damp air. Over to the right, river water came right up to the pavement with barely any kind of separation from land. The water lapped noisily against the meek concrete wall holding it back, and a few precarious and frankly frightening-looking rickety docks stretched out into the water.

Wind blew off the water, making me shiver as I stared toward the city beyond and the huge bridge that stretched over it. Even though the city was in slumber and the sky was dark, it wasn't truly black. There were still too many lights to give the sky the rich onyx that could be found in Neo's eyes. Overhead was murkier, a deep gray instead of black.

"What is this place?" I asked, pulling my gaze from the murky, rough waves.

"A fish market."

Startled, I focused on Neo by tipping my head back to stare at him fully from under the brim of my hat. Sometimes his eyes intimidated me, the secrets they held, the mysteries that begged to be solved.

I kept seeking them out anyway, unable to deny the urge to find something, anything, in their depths.

"A fish market," I echoed, trying to decide what in the world that meant. "Like a place where people come to shop for fish?"

He nodded.

One of those machine-type things collided with a pile of pallets, sending them crashing over and creating a mighty ruckus.

Startled, I jolted toward Neo, my fingers closing around the hem of his jacket.

"But why would anyone shop for fish at two in the morning?" I wondered, wrinkling my nose. And here of all places? No, thank you.

The corner of Neo's mouth lifted, and all my focus went to his lips. His lower lip was plumper than the top. He always looked to be pouting, but he rarely ever was. I thought about the way we stared at each other in the subway. I remembered how it felt to sit snuggly in his lap.

My own lips tingled as though they remembered the taste of him, yet how could they? His taste was just as mysterious as the secrets his eyes held.

"This is the time when we get our deliveries. Some come by boat." He gestured to the water. "Some by truck. We unpack them, get the fish ready and on ice, and then the vendors come to make their choices."

"Like restaurants?"

He nodded, pride shimmering in his eyes, and I couldn't help the pleasure I felt at his approval.

I mean really, I wasn't dumb. I owned my own company. Actually, I owned my father's massive company, *W*, as well. I wanted to snap that at him, but how could I when he was so pleased?

"Yes, a lot of the really good local restaurants get their supply here, and a few people who just live around here come down and get some because it's fresh."

My lips pursed. "So the fish are all dead?"

"Most of them."

My stomach turned queasy. "What about the ones that aren't?" I whispered loudly.

He laughed. It was a genuine chuckle that calmed the sickness quelling my stomach. Leaning down beside my ear, he whispered, "Do you really want to know?"

My head shook so adamantly I fell backward over my own feet. A squeal of alarm caught in my throat but never released because he caught me before I fell.

"How can a person be clumsy and graceful at the same time?" he murmured, breath fanning over my face.

I wanted him to kiss me. Like *really* kiss me.

Smacking his shoulder, I moved out of his grasp. "I am far from clumsy." I sniffed. "It's these cheap shoes."

"Neo!" someone yelled from one of the doorways. "We ain't paying ya to stand around."

"This place can't be that profitable," I muttered as he started away.

Turning back, he lifted a brow. "Actually, it is, and the pay is good because not many people are willing to do this kind of work."

My face scrunched up. "Selling fish? Is it hard?"

He laughed again, his white teeth flashing in the dimly lit night. They weren't perfectly straight and set just right from years of braces or dental work. They weren't whitened professionally until the brightness sparkled. Instead, they were slightly crooked and a little uneven, the color more natural. I actually found it a little charming.

"Come find out." His smile appeared again, an ornery glint in his stare and the dimples in his cheeks making his roguishness all the more appealing.

His fingers stretched between us, wiggling a bit, asking for me to take them.

Slipping my hand into his, I noted a boat gliding across the water toward the building. Apprehension filled me. "Neo?"

"Yes, princess?"

"We don't have to go in the water, do we?"

He stopped and turned, rubbing a thumb over my knuckles. "You don't like the water?"

"I can't swim."

This seemed to surprise him and make him grin like the Cheshire cat. "Whaaat? Something the princess cannot do?"

"I'm just really not a big fan of water."

A knowing look came over him. "Like rainstorms."

I nodded, an uncomfortable, murky feeling squirming around inside me. That feeling was there a lot lately, and I thought it was because, you know, someone tried to kill me twice. But why was it slithering around now, turning my stomach nauseous when the huntsman was nowhere in sight?

"Hey." His booted feet bumped against mine, and his voice gentled. "It's okay. You don't need to go near the water, okay?"

Nodding, I did my best to shake off the ominous feeling and smile brightly.

High-pitched whistling filled the air when we stepped into the building, and what felt like a million eyes turned to us.

Suddenly, I became conscious of our hands that clung together. I felt completely small and out of place.

"Who is this?" someone cracked.

"Looks like Neo has himself a girlfriend." Someone else chuckled.

I opened my mouth to deny it, but Neo squeezed my hand, silently telling me not to deny.

"Yep, she's mine, so go easy, okay, guys? She's never been to a place like this before, so don't make fun of her too much."

A few whistles and catcalls made me stiffen. How uncivilized. Didn't their mothers teach them any manners?

"She's awful tiny," a large man said, coming over, practically sizing me up.

I stood a little straighter, lifting my chin. "Maybe you're just large," I retorted, matter-of-fact.

He threw back his head and laughed. All the other men around us joined in. His beard looked as if it hadn't been groomed for years, and his cheeks were ruddy from likely working outside.

"Spunky," he said, laughter still glittering in his eyes.

"Times a'wasting," snapped another large, equally ungroomed man. He was wearing overalls and some sort of puffy vest over top. "I ain't got time for this."

"I'm sorry to interrupt you at your place of business, sir," I said, contrite. "What can I do to help?"

Neo made a small sound, and I slid him a glance.

Just why did he appear so amused?

The grouchy man was taken aback with surprise. "Well now, honey, I didn't mean to snap at you."

"Not at all. Time is money."

He looked as though he'd swallowed one of the fish he sold and shuffled off.

Beside me, the other man chuckled. "First time I've seen old Harold speechless." Holding out his calloused, slightly dirty hand, he said, "Nice to meet ya. I'm Kraken."

"Like the sea creature?" I wondered, shaking his hand.

Everyone laughed, the loud booming of it ringing up to the rafters.

"Just like that," he said, winking.

I nodded. "Nice to meet you, Mr. Kraken, sir."

A large semi with bright lights pulled into the lot, slowly making its way over.

"All right, everyone, let's get to work!" Kraken roared, making me step back into Neo.

"His real name is Craig," he whispered in my ear.

I giggled.

Loud, pumping music blasted overhead through speakers I hadn't even noticed. It was jarring for this hour of the day, and honestly, I couldn't imagine working while it was blaring. How did they even think?

"Put this on," Neo said, draping some kind of bright-yellow slicker around me.

"This is hideous," I announced, recoiling. "And it smells like fish!"

"Did ya think it would smell like roses?" One of the nearby men cackled, laughing like he'd made some epic joke.

"Come on." Neo urged, already buttoning it up around me. "You'll be thankful for this in a few minutes."

I put it on, noting the way it literally hung to my feet.

More laughter rang out. "Look at that little duck!"

"Neo's dating a shrimp!"

Scowling, I turned to Neo.

"Don't listen to them, princess," he said, amusement written all over his face.

Kneeling, he grabbed the hem and lifted it, tying it into a knot so the jacket ended just above my knees. Then he rolled the sleeves so my hands were free.

"Remember," he said sagely, "you asked to come."

Before I could ask why that sounded so threatening, Mr. Kraken was yelling again. "Line it up!"

All the men, including Neo, lined up starting at the back of the now-open semi, leading all the way to a giant table filled with pans of ice. Everyone was wearing a slicker like me, but all of theirs fit.

Scurrying after Neo, I watched as they began passing something down the line, sort of like a game of hot potato. Fascinated, I watched until suddenly, it was being tossed at me.

Thump!

I tried to catch it, but it was big and slippery and surprisingly heavy. I rocked back with the weight of it, scrambling to keep it from falling as it slipped and slid around against the slicker.

When I finally had a manageable hold, I looked down.

Wide, dead eyes stared back.

"Ahhh!" I screamed. *"Ahhh!"* The large, scaly, and slimy fish fell out of my arms, plopping onto the ground with a wet smack.

Thunderous laughter erupted around me.

"Neo!" I squealed, stumbling back as I stared at the wet

fish juices covering the front of my slicker. "Oh my goodness! Oh, ew!" I shrieked.

Pointing plaintively at the fish lying there, I demanded, "It's staring at me!"

"It's dead. It can't see."

"Then why are its eyes open?" I retorted.

"Because we ain't cut its head off yet!" one of the nearby fishmen hollered.

Gasping, I looked at Neo for confirmation.

Chuckling, he leaned down, lifting the dead fish that definitely was staring at me in accusation and tossed it on down the line where it eventually landed in one of the ice bins.

Before I knew it, another equally large fish was flying down the line. This time when it came at me, Neo intercepted, giving me a wink.

Oh, this place was gross. Still, his wink thrilled me a little.

Roaring music continued to vibrate the air. The men all sang along, slinging fish like it was nothing at all, falling into a rhythm that showed they had indeed done this many times before.

After watching for a while, I stepped back into the line, readying my stance.

"Oh-ho!" Kraken called. "Princess is back in the game!"

"Toss me a fish, Mr. Kraken, sir."

My body still rocked with the weight of it hitting my chest, but Neo was there, putting a hand supportively against the small of my back, and this time, I was ready for its slippery scales.

I also avoided eye contact.

After catching it, I turned and flopped it into Neo's waiting arms.

Cheering as loud as the previous laughter erupted, and everyone started to clap. My cheeks felt hot, but I joined in, clapping for myself.

Turning toward Neo, I said, "I didn't drop it this time."

"You did good, princess," he allowed, pride shining in his eyes.

"Here comes another one!" someone yelled, and I turned back so I could catch it too.

We worked like that for a while, me becoming part of the group, slinging smelly wet fish into the bins where they could be sold.

A huge tank of bright-red lobsters was brought in, and I ran over to stare at them, noting the giant claws. More types of fish were brought in, and the tables began filling up with so much seafood I was amazed.

Noting everyone seemed out of breath and tired after their hard work, I wandered around until I found a huge cooler filled with what I thought was water.

It wasn't water.

It was beer.

Drinking on the job was really not professional.

But they worked hard and they only made fun of me a little, so I filled my arms with the cans and began passing them out.

After a few trips back and forth from the cooler, Neo appeared. "Why are you giving everyone beer?"

"These men looked thirsty."

Those within earshot all cheered and held up their beer. "Bring her along anytime, Neo!"

He rolled his eyes. "Water is over there." He pointed across the open bay.

"Oh."

"Let her alone, boy," Kraken said, bringing a hand down on his shoulder. "A little beer never hurt no one."

"Now what does everyone do?" I wondered.

All the trucks had been unloaded, and those thingies that

they used to move heavy loads (they told me it was called a forklift) had stopped running back and forth.

"Prep the fish," Neo said.

Behind him, Kraken made a slicing motion across his throat and then rolled his eyes back in his head.

"I'll leave that to the experts," I said, shuddering at the memory of the fish staring at me accusingly.

I so loved sushi, but now I wondered if I would ever be able to look at it the same way again.

Kraken laughed and moved off, leaving me with Neo, his eyes sweeping over me from head to toe.

Glancing down, I tried and failed not to be horrified by the front of the slicker and how, umm, nasty it was.

"Thank heavens I didn't wear the Aurora," I said to myself.

"You surprised me tonight."

I looked up. "I did?"

Keeping his eyes focused on me, he nodded.

"Why?"

"For a little while, it was like you were a part of my world." He spoke so low I had to strain to hear him, but hear him I did.

"Maybe it isn't my world versus your world. Maybe it's just one world and we both live in it."

"Innocent," he murmured.

I scowled. "I'm not innocent. Both my parents are dead, and now someone is trying to kill me. I know I was raised with every advantage, but I work hard for my company and now my father's."

He cocked his head to the side, studying me. "Fair enough. Then…"

"Then?" I pressed, leaning forward.

"Then somehow you've maintained your hopefulness where mine vanished long ago."

I thought back to the painting on the apartment wall, how color leached from his world, suddenly becoming black and white. I saw the fire and the feathers… I felt the death.

"Whoa." Neo gasped, reaching out to steady my swaying form.

I glanced up, searching for his face in a sudden veil of haze.

"Princess." He worried, concern creating lines at the sides of his mouth. "What's wrong? What's happening?"

"I-I'm fine." I assured him, trying to clear my mind. "Just got a little dizzy for a minute."

Wrapping an arm around my waist, he practically hauled me across the wide space, guiding me down to sit on an unsteady crate. Seconds later, he appeared with a bottle of water, twisting off the cap and pushing it against my lips. "Drink."

The water was cool and soothing to my parched throat, making me realize just how thirsty I'd been.

After a few strong sips, I sighed, pulling away, and Neo pushed the bottle into my palm. With him kneeling in front of me, for once, I was higher than him, making his chin tilt up so our eyes could meet.

He hadn't shaved before we came here, and there was a distinct shadow on the lower half of his face.

"Hey." His voice was as soft as his fingers as they caressed my cheek. "You okay?"

I nodded and smiled. "Fine. Guess all the fish throwing made me a little shaky."

His chuckle quieted some of whatever was still clinging to me, acting like a warm towel fresh out of the dryer. "Sit here and drink all that, okay? Get some rest."

"What about you?" I worried, suddenly feeling like he was planning to escape.

"I'm not going anywhere, princess." He soothed me, somehow reading my emotions.

"You painted me," I blurted out.

Both of us jolted in shock.

"Why are you surprised? You're the one who spoke," Neo teased.

"I'm usually very good at thinking before I speak," I replied coolly.

Both of us fell silent, and when I couldn't take it anymore, I said it again. This time more deliberate. "You painted me."

He nodded.

"Why?"

His eyes lifted to mine, somehow seeing directly into the shadow the hat I wore created. "Because you were on my mind."

"Neo!" Kraken yelled.

Hearing his name, he jolted up, spinning around as though he'd been caught doing something illegal. "Yeah?"

"Last shipment's here. Bring it in."

Nodding, Neo stared off toward the water where a boat was docked. A moment later, he was before me, his large palm fitting over my knee. "I'll be right back. Just sit here and wait for me."

"Okay." I agreed, unable to keep my eyes from straying toward the unfriendly river.

Thirty-Three

Neo

A BREATHER WAS GOOD. A CHANCE TO WALK IT OFF.

Because, you know, walking off your feelings was *totally* possible.

I'm starting to sound like Ivory. That abrupt thought propelled my feet a little faster.

The boat ahead was equipped with a rotating light at the top, and as I walked, it arched around, shining its beam right at me. I recoiled a bit because it was very bright considering all the darkness around me. Shielding my eyes with my forearm, I waited as it moved along, sweeping across the empty lot.

Onboard, men were moving around, preparing the fish for transfer. Seeing the large containers already waiting, I stopped walking once more and decided to go grab a forklift to make it easier. Usually, I wasn't in a hurry, but tonight was different. Desire to be alone with Ivory, desire to know her more, to see how else she would surprise me, made me anxious to finish up.

I knew there would be screams and gasps when I brought her here. What I didn't realize was that she would win over all the old codgers who usually hated everyone and then actually stand in a line, slinging fish with the rest of us.

She was a surprise in every way. Usually, I hated surprises, but not this one. Not her.

After I parked the forklift near the dock, resisting the urge to look back at where I'd left her, my boots moved across the dock toward the boat.

The waves seemed restless, the water level higher than usual as it splashed against the wooden planks. One particular upsurge swelled, splattering across the toe of my boot. Almost as fast as it reached me, it retreated, the dark wave threatening to pull me into the murky depths along with it.

I wasn't intimidated. It would take more than that to ruffle me. Instead, I found myself pondering Ivory and her fear of water. I wondered what caused the trepidation. It almost seemed as if she didn't know either.

Fear lives deep within me. It wears a cloak so I can't ever see its face.

Her words came back at that moment, halting me where I stood. Those words hadn't seemed ominous in the moment, but now they were nothing but.

Unable to deny the urge, my body swung around, eyes searching through the dark, retreating the way I'd come.

The spot I'd left her sitting in was empty, no sign of her tiny frame covered in the oversized slicker in sight.

Stark worry quickened my breath, and I forgot about the fish, the boat, and the fact I was supposed to be working. Instead, I started back, needing to have eyes on my princess, to make sure she was safe.

Kraken's unmistakable booming laugh carried all the way out here, and I followed it across the market to where he stood with several other men. And standing among them was a princess in a yellow slicker.

My little duck.

A strangled noise broke from my throat, carried out to sea with the wind. Warring emotion swelled inside me—

ridiculousness because I'd had such a thought and tenderness because that was exactly what she looked like—and it made my heart expand.

I allowed myself a moment to stand there and watch how she commanded the attention of men who normally scowled at everyone, awed a little at her natural charm.

Someone on deck called out to me, and I was forced to pull away, hitting pause on the storybook to get back to real life.

Thirty-Four

Ivory

He's so different from any man I've ever met before. The thought echoed around inside me, touching all my hollow places and even finding room where I was already full.

It hardly seemed possible that just two days ago, I'd fled from my world, stumbling into his. How shocking the difference was here, how unfamiliar.

At first, I'd been so afraid, shocked even. Embarrassment pecked at me because I'd never thought to look beyond the place I lived. I never realized how different people could be.

My whole life, I'd lived with blinders on. My whole life, it was as if I only saw what I wanted to see.

Until Neo came into my world, splashing paint and color everywhere, making me reevaluate everything I knew. He was honest, blunt, and sometimes crude.

He didn't always shave, his teeth weren't perfect, and I didn't think he owned a comb. The plaid shirts he wore were practically abominations to fashion everywhere, yet if given the chance, I'd wrap myself up in one.

He lived with a band of misfits, people who, before all of this, I would have thought didn't fit in. Practically criminals, messy and startlingly ill-mannered.

Misfits who took me in when I had nowhere else to go.

Offered me a hand before they knew my name and my connections like it didn't matter who I was because I was someone in need.

Maybe I didn't fit in with them, but astoundingly, I badly wanted to. I liked them. Even Earth, who seriously needed anger management.

Most of all, I liked Neo.

Maybe I liked him a little more than like.

I knew I would have to go home. I'd already made that decision. But it wouldn't hurt to wait just a little bit more, right? To be a little selfish and stay at Neo's side.

I came from a world of extraordinary comfort, so imagine my astonishment when I discovered the most comfortable place I'd ever known was where Neo's eyes consumed mine. When we held hands and he pulled me down to sit in his lap.

Yes, I would go back to my world, but truly, I didn't think I would ever look at it the same.

I wanted to bring him with me, all of them. To somehow meld both worlds together. I mean, after all, we did reside under the same blue sky.

Neo thought it was impossible, and it hurt because it seemed he was willing to just let me go.

"Princess!" one of the fishmen hollered, making me pop up from my seat.

"Yes?" I called back.

"Come look at this beaut!"

Nodding enthusiastically, I hoped this beauty they referred to would not make me queasy. With these men, one could never be too certain.

Joining the men, I looked at their catch, which just looked like another giant fish to me, and exclaimed over its "beauty."

Just because I didn't see it didn't mean it wasn't there.

Truthfully, I felt a little sorry for all these fish whose destiny was to become a meal.

My eyes kept straying out toward the boat and the dock where Neo was. The forklift he'd parked sat waiting for him to load it up and drive back.

It hadn't been that long since he'd left me here to wait, but I was already anxious for him to return.

All the men moved off to clean fish and do other gross things I didn't want to see, and I used it as a chance to escape the crowd, moving toward the large open doors to wait for Neo. Even in the dark, I was able to pick out his form.

There was an energy about him, charisma that spoke on its own. He worked with a few men, carrying large totes toward the end of the dock, then going back to the boat for more.

All the men I knew would never do this kind of job. They would look down on anyone who did. These men might all be rough around the edges, but they weren't any less than anyone else.

Without realizing it, I moved just beyond the doorway, closer to Neo, not even heeding the warning of the lapping river against the shore.

When I realized where I was, enveloped by total darkness, out of reach of the yellow lights, a prickle of warning shot up my spine, tingling across my scalp.

The bawdy voices of the men seemed muffled, taken over by the sloshing water. A shiver wracked my body as I looked toward the opaque brown current, which seemed to whisper in forewarning.

A familiar yet starkly unknown feeling rose inside me, making my feet feel heavy and my mind weak. I'd carried this feeling with me for as long as I could remember. It usually only reared its sinister head when it rained or I was near water, but lately, it lurked just below the surface, threatening to swallow me whole at any given chance.

My feet, though delicate, felt like anvils anchoring me to the uneven pavement. The urge to run from my feelings, from whatever was trying to push through, screamed at me so loudly my fingers and hands shook.

I tried to go, but I was trapped in the darkness of the night and the shadows of my deepest mind. Unable to run, I frantically sought sanity, going immediately toward the boat. Toward Neo.

I saw him up on deck, the wind ripping at his slicker and tugging his hair. I thought I would feel better seeing him.

I thought wrong.

Flashes of a car wreck, of color leaching from the world… of plucked feathers stolen from an angel raining down from a black, empty sky…

The imagery was vivid, as was the overwhelming emotion slamming into my small body, rocking me on my feet.

Finally, I was unglued from my position, and I began to tumble. Everything around me shifted, the sky overhead becoming my only view.

And then I hit something hard, the jolt giving me a bit of clarity. Clarity that arrived too late.

I'd fallen into the arms of the huntsman, his face still hidden but his aura and intentions abundantly clear.

The starless abyss I stared up at was not the sky after all, but the huntsman who wore a cloak the color of midnight and a dark mask of the exact same shade.

This was perhaps the clearest view I'd ever had of this man who'd tried to slay me twice, but even as my lashes fluttered up at him, I saw nothing that could offer a clue to his identity.

Run! Fight! Scream! the voices in my head implored. I wanted to listen. Oh, I so badly wanted to flee.

His grip was like a vise, my body still captive of whatever knocked me off my feet.

How ironic this monster would be here waiting in obscurity for an opportune moment to strike.

He started to move, half carrying, half dragging me away.

My lips fell open, and a weak scream burst out. A gloved hand slapped over my mouth, cutting off the scrawny sound.

Scrappppeeeee.

The distinct sound of my shoe scraping over the pavement as I was hauled away seemed to break me from whatever spell I'd been under.

Life surged into my limp limbs, stiffening my spine and shoulders. A burst of adrenaline offered me a chance to leap out of his arms.

I made it only a few inches, the man having caught the back of my giant slicker to tug me back.

"Neo!" I screamed wild. "Hel—"

The cry for help was silenced by a hand slapping violently over my nose and mouth. Eyes popping wide, I fought and struggled, panic rising because, with his hand this way, I couldn't get any air.

Lungs burning, eyes frantic, I was hauled farther into the darkness toward the murky river. Dread curled up from my toes, trying to strangle me just like the huntsman's hand.

He wouldn't just toss me in the water... would he?

As if he heard my unspoken question, he leaned in, voice low and gravelly, ominously evil. "Should have learned to swim."

Fighting anew, I kicked and screamed against his hand, trying to bite him, trying to break free. My attempts only served to tire me out, the lack of oxygen beginning to mess with my brain.

Sluggishness tugged at me. The pain in my chest made me want to curl into a ball.

I tried to look for Neo one last time.

Just let me say good-bye.

It seemed Neo and I would continually be robbed of farewell because moments after that silent plea, my entire world went black.

Thirty-Five

Neo

"Neo!" The scream found my ears even though it probably shouldn't have made it this far. "Hel—"

The last part was cut off, and every single hair on the back of my neck stood at attention.

The tote I carried fell to the ground, the lid popping off and dead fish pouring everywhere, some even sliding back into the river.

Someone shouted in displeasure, but there was only one voice I was listening for now.

Not even knowing where I was going, I sprinted off the deck, desperately searching for the location from where I'd heard her scream.

I started to yell her name but clamped my lips closed at the last second, the unreleased yell burning my throat and making it impossible to swallow.

If someone was with her, I didn't want them to know I'd heard. I wanted them to think they would get away with whatever they were planning.

Forcing my body still, though my heart pounded inside me like a racehorse, I searched everywhere and then searched again.

In the back of my mind, there was a ticking clock. *Tick-tock. Tick-tock.*

If I didn't find her soon, she would likely disappear forever.

I shouldn't have brought her here. I should have stayed glued to her side.

Enough! I silenced all the screaming thoughts in my head and demanded my eyes to see.

There. A shift of movement, a little bit of bright in the night.

That yellow slicker was ugly as sin, but it had probably just saved her life.

Blinking, my eyes adjusted as I started forward, nearly tripping over my own feet. Her body was limp and lifeless. The man all in black carried her like a rag doll that belonged in the trash.

White-hot anger unlike anything I'd ever felt before blew up behind my eyes. Tears rushed to the back, trying to put out the flames but managing only to blur my vision.

It didn't matter. I wouldn't lose sight of her. I would keep my eyes on her even if I were blind.

"Ivory!" I roared, sprinting forward.

The man hauling her stiffened, glancing in my direction.

I didn't waste my energy on threats because I was past threatening.

Sensing my deadly manner, he turned away, lifting the limp little duck nearly over his head.

"Nooo!" I screamed, fear almost buckling my knees.

Horror overcame me as her slight, defenseless body met air, flying high for only a moment before plummeting, hitting the water with a splash, and being tugged down into its dark depths.

A sound that could only be described as animalistic

ripped free as I rushed toward the water, hell-bent on pulling her out.

A man cloaked all in black materialized in front of me, readying his stance as if he could stop me from getting by.

No one would stop me. Not even this harbinger of death.

Taking note of his posture, I shifted, leaping into the air as he lunged, my feet propelling me out of reach as I spun into a flip, landing with a smack behind him.

A sudden loud gasp and some clumsy splashing practically made me weep with relief when I saw Ivory's dark head pop above the surface of the water.

Cough. Cough. "Help!" *Splash. Splash.* "Help!"

"Ivory!" I roared. "Hang on!"

Something hard and firm hit me dead center in my back, knocking me onto my knees. I rolled with the hit, spinning around and kicking out one leg, tripping the asshole trying to stop me from saving her.

He fell but rolled into it, leaping right back up onto his feet.

Cough, cough.

I could practically hear her drowning. The sound would haunt me the rest of my days.

I can't let her die. I can't be responsible for one more death.

Surging forward, I moved to leap into the water, but a hand grabbed my slicker, pulling me back onshore.

"*Fuuuck*!" I screamed, ripping at the buttons and shedding the layer.

Something hard and heavy slammed into the back of my head.

"*Ungh.*" I gurgled as white light and darkness exploded behind my eyes.

Dark water came fast, plowing into my face and body as I smacked into the wall of river, everything burning, but I couldn't quite care.

For long seconds, everything went quiet, the muffling effect of the water muting everything else. My eyes were open, but I couldn't see. Cold penetrated suddenly, stinging my fingers and nose. The back of my head exploded in pain as warmth seeped out of my skull.

Something grabbed me, yanking me up, heaving me out of the water to drop me like abandoned trash on the pavement.

Through half-open, blurry eyes, I saw a shadow pause before slipping away, leaving us there to die.

Us.

Ivory.

Immense, thunderous pain echoed through me, and it seemed to take forever to form a single thought. But it was okay because all my thoughts were a single word, and I knew what I had to do.

Rolling over with a heave, I blinked the water and maybe blood out of my eyes at where she was slipping beneath the surface.

"Here," I croaked. "Ivory, come toward me."

Her pale hand stretched out for mine, but the distance between us was still too great.

Crawling farther toward the water, I moved until I was mostly hanging off the divider, stretching as far as I could go.

She made a sound, and I made one back. And then her hand slapped against mine, my fingers automatically grabbing on to never let go.

My body didn't want to work. I felt my brain and limbs begging to shut down. I denied the urge because I was it for Ivory. If I succumbed, then she would too.

Muscles burning with effort, mind nearly numb with pain, I pulled and shifted until her hand slapped the divider I lay across and she hefted her drenched, shivering form out of the water, falling beside mine.

"Neo!" She gasped, her voice sounding so far away.

I felt my lips try to smile. I hoped my muscles listened. Even dripping wet with no color at all, she was achingly beautiful. More beautiful than anything I'd ever seen before.

"You're okay," I slurred, eyes growing heavy.

Her palm slid against my face, but I couldn't feel it, just as I couldn't hear whatever words she said.

"You're safe now," I repeated, relief draining the rest of determination from my limbs.

Her face was the last thing I saw before there was nothing at all.

Thirty-Six

Huntsman

The business of killing paid well, and that's how I looked at this. As a business.

Every business had standards. A set of rules to follow.

1. Never compromise your identity.
2. Never kill for the same person twice.
3. Always get paid half up front.
4. Do your research on your target.
5. Finished your research? Do more.
6. Only kill who you are paid to kill.
7. Always finish the job.

And above all: **Never make it personal.**

I'd never had a problem following this simple code of conduct.

Until now.

Until keeping one rule compromised the others. Until this no longer felt like a business, but a nightmare I couldn't escape.

Thirty-Seven

Ivory

Concussion.

Ten stitches.

I'd never been more afraid in my entire life. And not because I almost died, but because Neo did it all because he was trying to save me.

My life wasn't worth his, and if he wasn't lying here unconscious, I would tell him exactly that.

I was frightened. Exhausted. I'd had just about enough of all of this.

And this hospital was… primitive.

The chair was pulled so close to the bed the arm would leave a dent in the mattress. The air was cold and sterile and there were no extra blankets, so all of the ones we had, I made sure covered Neo. He was still and silent, something I had never seen.

Something I never wanted to see again.

Usually oozing with sarcasm, mischief, and even sometimes with sadness, he always sparkled with life. His normally luminous eyes were hidden from me, all his secrets locked up tight with no chance of me finding the key.

Vivid images assaulted me, and I curled into a ball. I'd been drowning, slowly losing the battle with the waves, but

I'd barely noticed because he'd been ashore, screaming my name and literally flipping over a killer just to come and save me.

The hit to the back of his head should have knocked him out instantly. The doctor said if it had been just a little to the left, he might have died right there.

Neo didn't die or pass out. He pushed through the obvious splitting pain, the life pouring from his wound, and pulled me from the water before allowing himself to slip away.

I'd never met anyone so selfless in all my life.

Body still tight in a ball, I leaned against the mattress, resting my head near his prone body. A relaxed hand lay at his side, and I stared at it, marveling at the length of each digit and the strength I knew they possessed. Slowly, my own hand slid over the blanket, one finger reaching for his, hooking around his pinky and holding on tight.

"Please wake up," I whispered. "Please be okay."

A soft groan answered, and my body shot up to stare at his face.

His eyes were still closed, but his face was no longer relaxed. His brows furrowed in what could be pain, and his lips tugged into a grimace.

He groaned again, and butterflies erupted beneath my ribs.

"Neo," I whispered, watching him intently. "Neo, wake up."

Slowly, his lashes fluttered, opening only to recoil from the light. "Wh-what happened?" He groaned, raising a hand to press it against his forehead.

"Oh, Neo." I tried not to sob, but the relief of seeing him moving and awake was almost more than my heart could bear.

Thank goodness he was all right. Thank goodness my world could remain splashed with color.

Suddenly, his eyes shot open, and his shoulders lifted off the mattress. The abrupt movement caused pain and made him wince, but he ignored it, grasping my face between his startling warm palms so slightly unfocused eyes could scour every inch.

"Are you okay, princess? Tell me you're okay." His voice was raspy, and it made my heartbeat wild.

"I'm okay." The words were watery like my eyes, my lower lip quivering.

"Ah, sweetheart," he whispered, caressing the side of my head.

I started to cry even though I tried very hard not to.

His body lowered back to the mattress, but he still held my face so I was pulled along with him. My cheek pillowed against his chest, and I sniffled then gasped, pulling back.

"You're hurt!"

"My head, not my chest," he said, reaching for me again.

Leaning over the bed, I let him press my face against his chest. The sound of his heart was a lullaby.

Grunting with dissatisfaction, he tugged on my shoulder. "Closer."

My lashes were heavy and wet when I lifted my head.

"Come here." He beckoned, patting the space beside him.

I gasped and glanced at the curtain pulled around the bed, shutting us off from all the other beds lined around the room.

"Please."

Giving in, I crawled onto the bed, fitting myself against his body and melting immediately when his arm slid around my waist, holding me tight.

"Are you okay?" he whispered softly, lips grazing my forehead.

"Now that you're awake, I am."

"How long have I been out?" he murmured, the sound of his voice giving me goose bumps.

"We've been here about an hour."

There was a pause and then, "Here...?" Lifting his head, he took in his surroundings for the first time.

"We're at the hospital."

"What?" he yelled, making us both flinch.

"Don't you yell at me," I admonished, pulling back to sit up and glare.

"Why did you bring me to a hospital?"

"Because you were unconscious and bleeding so much." I felt my lip wobble again and willed it to behave. "You almost died saving me, and I'm so angry with you!"

His lips tried to pull into a smile, so he pursed them instead. "You're angry at me?" He pointed to himself as though I wouldn't know who he meant.

"What were you thinking fighting that man like that?" I smacked him in the chest.

"I'm a patient!"

"More like a test subject. This place is foul." I sniffed. "If you weren't bleeding so bad, I would have insisted we take you somewhere else."

"We?" His brows shot up, making him cringe again.

"Kraken and the other gentlemen brought us here. After you pulled me out of the water, I screamed and they came running. Thank goodness for them because I wouldn't have known what to do."

"Did you tell them someone is trying to kill you?"

"Of course not," I rebuked, looking away.

"Ivory..." He growled a warning.

"Well, they might have figured it out because when we checked in, I gave them my name."

"What?"

"The nurses wouldn't admit you without some sort of paperwork and insurance. You were unconscious, and I only have one name..."

He groaned. "So they know who you are."

"I'd already decided to go back home." I reasoned. "I can't disappear if I don't have anywhere to disappear to."

"You should have told me."

"I just did."

"Before now."

"You were unconscious."

His stern look made my shoulders slump. We both knew what he meant.

"I wanted a little more time with you," I whispered. "I wasn't ready to go back home yet."

"And now you are." His tone brought up my eyes. There was softness there but also distance.

A sense of longing curled through my veins. "Now I don't really have a choice."

Pushing into a sitting position, Neo gingerly fingered the back of his head. "How many?"

"Ten."

"What the fuck did he hit me with?" He wondered.

"Please don't ever do that again."

Hand falling away from his head, the dark orbs I'd longed so desperately to see just minutes ago focused solely on me. I loved the weight of his stare, the depth.

"Do what?"

"Risk yourself for me."

"I won't ever stand by and watch you slip away."

I sighed. "Neo."

Abruptly, the curtain closing off the rest of the world was ripped aside, and Kraken stuck his head inside. His beard seemed even more unruly under the hospital light. "The press is here," he said, eyes so wide we could see white all around the brown. "You really are her." His voice was awed as he looked me over.

"Hold them off," Neo said, pushing back the blankets covering his legs.

"Neo! Your head!"

"Has stitches," he said, bare feet slapping onto the floor. "I'm fine."

"You need to lie back down." I fussed, hovering around him like I would catch him if he pitched over.

I probably wouldn't be able to catch him. I'd try, though.

Neo pinned Kraken with a look that made me draw back, and Kraken cleared his throat. "I'll hold 'em off as long as I can." And then he disappeared, curtain swaying with the force of his exit.

"Did you mean it?" he asked, voice taking on an almost desperate tone.

"Mean what?" I echoed, watching him find his wet boots and jam his feet inside.

The rest of him was wearing a hospital gown.

It was his most ridiculous look to date.

"You want more time with me."

Wide, sincere eyes searched mine, imploring for the truth.

The truth was all I had to give. I didn't like to lie. "Yes."

Emotion passed over his features, and then he was reaching for my hand, pulling me away from the bed in the opposite direction from which Kraken had gone.

People looked up from their beds, seeing a woman with a pair of scrubs and wet hair being led away by a man wearing only a giant bandage on his head, a hospital gown, and a pair of wet boots.

"Neo," I said, still clutching tight to his hand despite the ridiculousness of this situation. "Where are we going? Now that news of me being alive is out, they will find me."

The elevator doors slid closed, the car smoothly sliding down toward the ground floor.

He tugged, bringing my body flush against his. "Just a little more time," he murmured, brushing the pad of his thumb over my lip.

"Okay." I agreed. "But where will we go?"

He smiled. "I know a place."

Thirty-Eight

Neo

Riding a subway in nothing but a hospital gown?

One star. Do not recommend.

But a man's gotta do what a man's gotta do. And when big blue eyes look at you and rose-red lips wish they had more time… your naked bum runs out of a hospital and onto the subway.

To be fair, I'd done far worse in the subway.

Don't ask me what. Some secrets I'll take to the grave.

"We look ridiculous," Ivory muttered, tugging the green scrub top around her as if it would somehow make her less visible.

"At least you have pants."

A hand pressed against her lips, muffling the giggle shaking her slight frame.

I couldn't help it. I smiled. "You look good in scrubs."

Making a face, her hand fell from her lips. "This is definitely not something I care to wear again."

"Our clothes were drenched, huh?"

Her throat worked, and both hands twisted in her lap. "Yours were also covered in blood."

The bandage on her injured finger must have fallen off, and it caught my eye as she wrung her hands. The skin was still raw and red. The place where the nail should have been was angry and sore-looking.

Her anxious movements stilled when my one hand fit over both of hers. Without words, gently untangling her fingers, I brought one hand into my lap, cradling it tenderly.

"Why are you warmer than me when you have on less clothes?" She wondered, staring at our attached hands.

"Because when you're beside me, my heart beats extra fast."

"When I told the doctor you stayed awake long enough to pull me out of the water, he was shocked. He said you should have passed out right away."

"You needed me."

"Thank you."

It wasn't the words that meant so much to me. It was the sincerity behind them and the way she punctuated such a simple phrase by resting her head on my shoulder.

We rode the rest of the way in silence, my hand holding hers, my shoulder supporting her head.

The second the doors opened revealing our stop, music floated inside the car, and even though many other sounds were trying to drown it out, I recognized it instantly.

"Do you hear that?" she asked the second we stepped onto the platform.

I made a sound of agreement.

"It's so beautiful."

"Come on," I implored, tugging her hand and leading her toward the sound.

The music grew closer, and Ivory became enamored. "It's so powerful it mutes all the other sounds down here," she observed.

I would have to agree. The air hummed with lustrous sounds of a deep, heart-ripping tone.

"What a beautiful melody, almost sad but also optimistic

in some notes. Whoever is playing must have so much passion in them, so much talent."

Glancing down, I asked, "You like it that much?"

"Oh yes. I've been to the symphony many times, and I've never heard anything quite like this. It's unique and utterly beautiful."

"Want to meet the musician?"

Sparkling blue eyes widened on mine. "Can we?"

Smiling my most charming smile, I tilted my head. "I think I could make that happen."

A small crowd of people gathered around the violinist despite how early it was in the morning. The melody being played was so beautiful that many people spared a moment to stop and listen.

We stood near the back, Ivory stretching up on her tiptoes, trying to see, and still, she couldn't. Frustrated, she slumped at my side.

Chuckling, I pulled her forward, tapping someone on the shoulder. "Excuse me, mate."

"Were you a pirate in your past life?" she asked totally randomly.

I paused only for one second and then winked, making her blush. "Maybe."

The crowd parted, and I let go of her hand to place mine at the small of her back and push her forward.

She gasped, body flinging dramatically back, then colliding with my chest. I was becoming more accustomed to her dramatics, so this time, I decided to use it to my advantage and wrap my arms around her from behind.

"Neo!" she exclaimed, pointing. "That's Fletcher!"

My chin brushed against her damp black hair with my nod. "He's good, right?"

"I wondered what was in that case he carried." Her voice was hushed.

"He can't hold a job, is lousy at stealing, but that boy can play a fiddle," I mused, feeling pride well up inside me.

I never meant to get so attached to my friends. Moving in with them was basically a means to an end. A way to survive.

Somewhere along the way, though, they became my family.

"Why would anyone want to be good at stealing?" She glanced up at me.

The bottom fell out of my belly, but I couldn't look away. "Because for some, it's survival."

Emotion passed between us, an emotion I couldn't identify. And then Fletch hit a flute-like note, drawing Ivory's attention once more.

I thought fleetingly of releasing her from the circle of my arms, but then she wiggled farther against me, snuggling closer, and all thought of pulling away vanished as if it had never formed.

The top of her head made a perfect resting place for my chin, and we remained silent as Fletcher continued to play, creating a story with his song, weaving notes together to create harmony. You knew by watching that Fletch didn't just play his violin.

He felt it.

He allowed it to reach deep inside and play out his most secret emotions, spinning them into an eloquent tune that was so powerful his entire body swayed. Many times, I wondered if it was him playing the violin or the violin playing him.

His hands stopped, and the music ebbed until there was nothing left and everyone started to move along, dropping cash into his open instrument case.

"Fletcher!" Ivory exclaimed, pulling away to rush toward him.

His entire face lit up with surprise, light-brown eyes

going wide. "Princess?" he called, lowering the violin off his shoulder. His eyes flickered to me but then went immediately back to the small girl rushing to his side.

"Oh my goodness, that was incredible! You are so very talented!"

His cheeks turned red, his entire aura bashful. If he could have hidden his face, he probably would have. Why the dude needed to act like that was beyond me. We told him all the time that he was good.

"Aww, shucks," he murmured, looking down.

"No, really!" She tugged on the sleeve of his jacket enthusiastically. "I've never heard anyone play like this before. Why are you down here in the subway? You should be on a stage!"

"Who would put me on a stage?" he mumbled.

"I would!"

His eyes lifted, searching her face. "Really?"

"Most assuredly." She confirmed.

Sometimes I wondered if she read a dictionary for fun.

Fletcher's floppy hair flounced when he threw his arms around her, swallowing her whole. He was the smallest of the four of us, but even he was larger than Ivory.

"That means so much to me," he exclaimed, sniffling into her hair.

"That's enough," I said, reaching between them for some separation.

Noticing what I was wearing, Fletch made a face, pointing to me with his bow. "Is that a hospital gown?"

"You will never believe everything that has happened!" Ivory exclaimed, totally stealing Fletch's attention once more. "Neo took me to the fish market, and they threw a giant dead fish at me!"

Fletcher made a strangled sound. "He took you there? For real? Aren't those fishermen scary?"

"Oh, they look a little brash on the outside, but Kraken is a true gentleman. He even helped carry Neo to the hospital."

Fletch's eyes bugged out. Drawing her toward his open violin case, he said, "Tell me more."

It was like the two were on a whole other planet. I swear they needed some tea and cookies in front of them, and it would be like an episode of *Golden Girls*.

"I don't think the subway is a good place for this conversation." I reminded them, arching a brow.

Ivory made a face. "He's probably right."

"But you were just getting to the good part." He pouted.

"We can tell you later. We were on our way somewhere," Ivory offered.

Swinging toward me, Fletcher gave me a look of surprise. "You're bringing her to the tower?"

Of course he would know. This was the only reason I would get off at the subway stop. My only confirmation was a nod.

"Whoa," he mused.

"What's the tower?" Ivory questioned.

"You didn't tell her yet?" Fletcher whispered to me. His voice was so loud it was not actually a whisper.

"I haven't exactly had time," I retorted, gesturing to my attire.

"Right." He scratched behind his ear, his eyes turning worried. "But you're okay, right?"

Fletcher was a lot of things, and when he looked at me like that, not caring about whatever trouble I'd probably gotten into but rather that I was okay, it just proved he was one of my family.

"Yeah, I'm okay," I told him, making the apprehension in his eyes dissipate. "But do you think, ah, I could borrow your jacket?"

"Oh yeah." His head bobbed. Quickly, he packed away his

instrument, closing up the case, then shrugged out of his jacket and tossed it to me.

Grateful, I tugged it on over the gown, realizing it only made me look more ridiculous, but hey, it was better than nothing.

"But what's the tower?" Ivory asked again, waiting for someone to explain.

"I'll show you." I promised, turning back to Fletch. "Look, the press knows she's alive. They're out looking, so be careful, okay?"

"Will do."

"C'mon, princess," I said, taking her hand and tugging her away from Fletch toward the stairs.

"Bye!" he called out after us, and Ivory turned back to wave.

The tower was a large brownstone building deep in the city that was so old it was considered historic, but it was cared for better than most other places I'd looked into.

We stood on the sidewalk, staring up at the building that really had no indication out front of what kind of place it was, which was also something I liked about it.

The face had lots of windows, but many of the rooms inside did not. It turned out the windows overlooking the street fetched a higher premium, one I wasn't lucky enough to be able to afford. Sometimes the sight of those windows left a bitter tang on my tongue because they were reminders of things I couldn't provide.

Potted mums lined the concrete steps leading up to the black double doors, and there was a welcome mat, which frankly didn't make me feel welcome.

Pausing with my hand on the knob, I drew in a ragged breath, the weight of what I was about to do suddenly making it hard to breathe. I'd never done this before. Never brought anyone here. The only people who'd ever visited were my roommates, and it took me a long time to even allow them.

A light, tentative touch settled over my arm. "Neo?"

Glancing down only created more turmoil inside me. She'd asked for this, right? More time. More of me.

Well.

Maybe not more of me. But maybe I wanted to give it.

Or maybe because I thought it would make it easier when she went back home.

Honestly, it didn't matter right now because right now I was ripe with apprehension.

"This is the tower?" she asked, still leaving her hand to rest on my arm.

I nodded.

"There's something inside you want me to see?"

"Not something. Someone."

Her bow-shaped mouth formed a little O. "Really? Who?"

"My sister."

Thirty-Nine

Ivory

Neo had a sister? He'd never mentioned her before. I always thought he didn't have a family, so hearing about this now was momentarily stunning.

Suddenly, a flash of memory from the night I was locked up in jail and had used up my one call to Neo filled my mind.

He called me Virginia that night.

"Is your sister's name Virginia?"

Neo stopped walking down the hall, peeking around with a suspicious look floating behind his eyes. "How do you know that?"

I smiled, suddenly feeling relief I didn't realize I needed. *So that's who she was.* "That night I called you from jail, you called me Virginia when you answered."

Realization dawned, and he grunted. "That's because no other girls call me but her."

That made me so happy I swear I heard a symphony of chiming bells in the back of my mind.

"Why are you smiling like that?" he asked, wary.

"Because I get to meet your sister!" I beamed.

When we were in the elevator traveling up, he turned to me, a solemn look stealing all the usual charm from his face. "When we get up there," he began, "please don't stare."

"Stare," I echoed. "Why in the world would I stare? Staring is rude."

"Just don't," he bit out, voice harsh.

I hadn't heard that tone out of him since we'd met in the bar. I'd nearly forgotten that side of him. It made me realize with crystal clarity that his charm and easy smile covered up a lot.

I fell into step behind him when he exited the elevator, walking down a long, very white corridor. The feeling here was clinical and kinda sad. When we passed by what looked like a nurse's station, I tugged on the back of his borrowed jacket.

"Neo?"

His feet stopped, and I collided with his back, bouncing off. With more agility than I ever possessed, he spun, steadying me with a single hand on my elbow.

"What?" There it was again, the harshness in his tone. But it was softened by the gentle way he still held my arm.

"Is this a hospital?"

Glancing at the nurse's station and then back, he replied, "It's more like assisted living. But they do offer medical care."

"Oh, so like a live-in care facility?"

He nodded.

Across the hall, loud yelling erupted from one of the rooms. Neo didn't react, but I was startled, making his hand tug me closer to his body.

"It's okay. That, ah… resident gets a little loud sometimes."

I nodded, stepping back.

"Hey, Neo!" A woman in all-white scrubs appeared. Her skin was a gorgeous glowing shade of mahogany, her hair a mess of bouncy dark curls that framed a face with exotic features and full lips.

"Emogen, girl," Neo said, all the harshness he'd been giving me gone as he stepped around and held out a hand.

The pair did some complicated handshake thingy that they'd clearly done a thousand times before because neither of them made a single mistake. Once that was done, they both laughed and Emogen pulled back, parking a hand on her hip to look him up and down.

Clucking her tongue, she finally spoke. "Boy, what have you gone and done now?"

Neo chuckled, holding out his arms so she could get a better look at his incredibly awful attire. "You don't like my new look? I thought you knew style!"

"Oh, I know style, and that is not it," she announced, shaking her head.

"Exactly!" I sang, glad someone agreed.

Her deep eyes switched to me. "And who might you be?"

"Hello." I started forward, but Neo put out his arm, holding me back.

"How's V?"

Emogen seemed to forget I was there. "Oh, she's her usual sunshiny self. I almost need sunglasses when I go in her room."

"Any news?" His voice dropped a little with the question.

The nurse sighed. "I'm afraid not."

Neo's head bobbed as though he weren't surprised, but I could feel disappointment wrapping around him.

"Go on back. I'll see if I can rustle up some scrubs for you. Gowns are not a good look on you, my man."

He held out his fist, and the two knocked them together. "You're the best."

"I know!" she hummed, moving off down the hallway.

A large part of me wanted to be insanely jealous of whatever her relationship with Neo was. They were obviously familiar with each other. But I knew it was wrong to be jealous, and I told myself not to be.

Warm fingers circled mine, slipping between each of my digits, tangling together. Looking down, I noted his golden skin against my pallor and then glanced back up to see him watching me.

"I want you to meet my sister," he said, voice soft. "She's most important to me. The reason for everything I do."

"I would love to meet her."

He nodded, and we walked, a few of the other patients calling out greetings to him from their rooms. He stopped and spoke to all of them, making them laugh and smile.

He remembered details about them, asking about small things like their favorite book or show on TV. He even helped one woman water a plant beside her bed.

Watching him made me swell with emotion so thick my chest ached under the pressure. Someone had just tried to kill him. He'd been unconscious and had ten stitches in the back of his head. But here he was, laughing and being sunlight for other people.

Most people I knew would write a check and think they'd helped save the world. But watching him now, I realized that watering some tiny plant and offering a few moments of undivided attention was far more valuable than money.

"Princess?" I heard him speak my name, but it didn't register until his face came down on my level and his nearly black stare dove into mine. "What's wrong?"

"I admire you," I confessed, my tongue controlled by my feelings.

He straightened as a sudden "deer caught in headlights" look morphed across his face. "What?" His voice was hoarse.

"You try to conceal it, but the kindness in your heart is beautiful."

Rocking back on his heels, he said nothing.

I caught him off guard. Has no one ever told him this before?

A change came over him, twisting the surprise into something else, something darker and more difficult to read. "You wouldn't say that if you knew me."

He seemed so sure I faltered.

"Her room is here," he said, voice not cold, but not warm either.

Halfway across the hall, I called out to him. He stopped and waited for me to catch up to his side.

"Neo," I asked, hands wrapping around his wrist, "your sister, why is she here?"

I felt a probing sidelong stare, watching the muscle in the side of his jaw jump.

"She's paralyzed."

He left me standing there stunned, walking away without offering any kind of information or detail.

Paralyzed.

"V!" he called out, snapping me back.

Bell-like laughter chimed out into the hall as he disappeared inside the room.

"There's my girl!" I heard him practically sing, and I couldn't stop the smile forming on my lips.

There was not one ounce of harshness or even intensity in his tone just then. It was all charm, all warmth, and all love.

More laughter floated out, drawing me to the doorway where I watched Neo spinning around with a girl in his arms, carrying her bridal style as her arms looped around his neck.

The young woman had insanely long wheat-colored hair that floated out around them with every turn Neo made. Her feet were covered in pink socks, and she was dressed in a blue T-shirt dress.

"I'm dizzy!" she squealed, tightening her arms around his neck, dark lashes squeezing closed.

Laughing, Neo stopped spinning but made no move to put her down. Instead, he kissed the top of her head, smiling down. "You're not gonna puke on me, are you?"

"Would serve you right if I did!" she announced, her eyes finding me and widening. "Hello." Her voice was friendly despite her curiosity.

"Hello," I echoed, unsure what to say or do.

Clearing his throat, Neo introduced us. "Virginia, this is Ivory. Ivory, this is my little sister, Virginia."

Virginia's eyes widened farther as she divided her stare between me and her brother. "You came with Neo?"

Nodding, I said, "I hope that's okay."

"Of course!" she exclaimed. "I just—Neo never brings anyone here!"

"Hey, that's not true." He admonished her.

"Fletcher, Beau, and Earth do not count."

"It's so lovely to meet you," I said, moving into the room.

When she patted his shoulder, Neo moved to the wheelchair sitting in the center of the room to carefully place his sister on the seat. Once she was sitting, he reached down to tug the hem of her dress down to cover her thighs.

Her hair was so long it nearly reached the floor over the back of the chair. It was sun-kissed and shiny, not at all like the midnight strands on Neo's head. Her eyes were brown, but they weren't as dark and mysterious as his.

The chair moved soundlessly, closing the distance between us, and her arm stretched out. Placing my hand in hers, we greeted each other.

"You're so pretty," we both said at the exact same time.

Then we both laughed.

"I look a mess!" I said. "I mean, just look at me, wet, unwashed hair, borrowed clothes, soaked shoes…"

"Well then, I can't imagine how beautiful you must be when you're put together," Virginia said kindly.

Neo made a sound. "She's practically unreal."

I felt myself blush, and Virginia's mouth dropped open. Embarrassed, Neo scratched the back of his head and turned away.

"Your hair is absolutely stunning," I said, reaching out to touch the silky strands but remembering my manners and pausing. "May I?"

"Of course," she said.

"It's like liquid sunlight," I whispered, awed. "How long did it take to grow?"

"Forever," she mused. "But I can't bear to cut it. And it gives me lots of practice for braiding."

"Oh, you braid it!"

Virginia nodded enthusiastically. "Oh yes, I've learned all kinds of braids. And I love to add flowers."

"Oh, you have to show me."

"Really?"

"Absolutely!"

"Okay, but first, I have to know. How do you know my brother?"

He coughed, and I paused. "Well, that's a long story."

"I have lots of time," she said, gesturing to her room like she had nowhere else to be.

My gaze went to the far wall... which was filled with an incredibly vivid painting. Taking a breath, I faced it completely, feeling as if I were being sucked into a whole other world.

The sky was blue and filled with fluffy white clouds, the sun's rays shone down over a beautiful valley filled with blooming flowers in vibrant shades of purple, pink, and yellow. Tall trees stretched up, their branches enticing any observer to climb to the highest point. Bluebirds flew and butterflies romped.

In the center of it all was a tall tower reaching up toward the sky like a giant birdhouse. The roof was thatched, the windows arched and circling the entire round form.

"This is magical," I whispered, standing before it, trying to take in every detail.

"Since I don't really get to go outside much, Neo brought it inside to me."

It was Virginia who spoke but Neo that I turned to. Our eyes locked, and so many unspoken words passed between us. The pull to go to him was nearly undeniable, the heaviness in my heart and quickening of my breath all his fault.

"Makes you really feel like you are kept up in a secret tower and not locked away in a hospital." Her words broke the tether between us, and I turned back to the girl.

"Have you been here a very long time?"

She smiled a sad smile. "It's been awhile."

"But not forever," Neo said, going to her side, kneeling by her chair.

Virginia smiled, nodding at her brother with obvious affection in her eyes.

Emogen stepped into the room. "Knock, knock!" she called. "I found some scrubs for you, Neo."

"Ah, you always come through." Neo grinned, moving to take the offered garments.

"I didn't do it for you," she informed him cheekily. "I did it so the residents here weren't traumatized from having to look at you."

"You know you like me," Neo teased, leaning in to give her a cheeky smile.

Emogen laughed lightly, pushing him back. "Go change. You doing good, girl?" she asked, turning to Virginia.

"Of course!" She agreed, smiling bright.

"Well, it's about time for physical therapy. They'll be up to get you in five."

Virginia pouted. "But Neo just got here."

"I'll hang out 'til you get back."

Virginia turned to me. "You will too?"

"Of course," I said.

Emogen went back to work, and Neo excused himself into the bathroom to take off the hospital gown.

The second he was gone, Virginia pounced. "What happened to my brother? Why is he dressed like that? What's that bandage on his head, and are you his girlfriend?"

"Oh my," I declared, sitting on the end of the bed. "Well, your brother had an accident and hit his head." I began, thinking Neo might not like it if I told her someone tried to kill us. "He was at the hospital for stitches, and that's why he has the gown on. We left in a hurry, so he didn't get a chance to change."

"And?"

"And…" I echoed.

She leaned closer, anticipating what I would say next.

Are you his girlfriend?

"I'm not his girlfriend. We're just… friends."

Virginia made a noise and grabbed a basket of flower clips off a painted dresser. The entire room was filled with hand-painted furniture that made the room feel a lot homier and a lot less clinical.

There was even a braided rug in the center of the room with all the colors of the rainbow. The bed was covered in pillows and stuffed animals and a blanket that looked soft and warm.

Framed photos of Neo and Virginia sat everywhere, as well as photos of the siblings with two older people who I assumed were their parents.

Where are they? Why aren't they here too?

"I'll do pigtails today," she said, parting her hair perfectly on the first try. "It will keep it out of the way in PT."

I couldn't help but glance down at her legs, which were thin and unmoving. Remembering what Neo said about not staring, I glanced away quickly.

"It's okay," Virginia said, her voice soft. "Neo probably didn't tell you anything."

I shook my head. "Are you in pain?"

Virginia paused her braiding. "That's not usually the first question people ask."

"It's not?"

"Most people want to know how I got like this."

"I'd rather know if you're in pain."

Virginia went back to work. "I'm not. I can't feel anything at all from the waist down."

"I'm sorry," I whispered, knowing it was the wrong thing to say and my apology really meant nothing, but I was sorry just the same. She was such a beautiful, cheerful young woman, and it made me sad to think of her being limited to that chair.

"Neo thinks I'll get out of here someday. He works so hard to make it happen."

"But you don't think it will?"

She glanced at the bathroom door, then back at me. "It's not that I don't want it to happen, but I don't want to get my hopes up."

"So." I paused, then went on. "There is a chance you might walk again?"

"A slim one," she said. "Ta-da!" She smiled brightly, gesturing to the completed braid on the one side. It was a gorgeous fishtail style that she loosened a little so it was fluffy and perfect.

"You did that so fast!" I exclaimed.

Pawing around in the basket of flowers, she came out

with a few purple ones and clipped them into the braid. Finished, she went to the next side to begin.

"You're that girl, right?" she said after a minute of braiding.

"What girl?"

"The one on the news. Ivory White. The missing heiress."

"I—well, yes, I am."

"Something bad happened to you, right?"

"Nothing I can't overcome," I told her confidently.

She nodded. "You must be really special."

"How do you mean?"

"Because my brother brought you here. He's been helping you."

Ah, so Virginia also knew what a big heart her brother hid inside him.

"Yes. You're right." Then I felt myself blush. "I meant you're right about him helping me. Not that I'm special."

Virginia smiled brightly. She really was so beautiful. *And trapped inside this tower. Inside that wheelchair.*

"Well, you must be because I saw how my brother looked at you."

I was about to ask how he looked at me, but the bathroom door came open and Neo strolled out wearing a pair of black scrubs.

The color only made his midnight hair and eyes seem much darker.

"Who's ready for some PT?" A man also dressed in black scrubs entered the room.

He did not wear them the way Neo did.

"Hey, Jake," Neo greeted. "Take care of my little sister."

"Always do." Jake agreed, giving Virginia a wink.

"Can't I skip it today?" she grumbled, clipping the last of the purple flowers into the other completed braid.

Both braids fell over her shoulders and curled into her lap.

"'Fraid not, sprite," Jake announced, going to the back of her chair to smoothly push forward.

The nickname was cute, and it made me smile.

Leaning down, Neo kissed her forehead. "I'll be here when you get back."

She nodded. "Bye, Ivory," she called, waving.

When she was gone, the room was silent, and Neo and I stood staring across the distance between us. I wanted to ask so badly, but I could tell that whatever he said might change the dynamic between us.

Still, I wanted to know. I wanted to step forward no matter where the path led.

"Thank you for bringing me to meet your sister," I said, my bravado still not giving me enough courage to ask.

"Just ask, Ivory. Ask, and I will tell you."

Pressing my lips together, I nodded, feeling nerves bundle at the bottom of my stomach.

"What happened to her, Neo? And where are your parents?"

The pain that flashed through his eyes struck my heart, but I didn't call back the question. I just let it hurt while I waited for his reply.

Forty

Neo

Freedom. *The first taste of freedom was sweet when that small plastic card was handed across the counter and placed into my proud hand. Smiling as satisfaction filled my body, I carried it out to where everyone was waiting, holding it up the second I cleared the door.*

Mom and Dad both cheered, and Mom waved me to stand beneath the giant DMV sign so she could get a photo.

I was still smiling when a small finger pointed at the card, which was now my most prized possession, and the irritating laugh of my little sister rang out.

"Is that the best picture they could get of you?"

Spinning I pinned her with a glare. "Hey,"

Virginia shook her head and snickered. "Not good, Neo. Not good at all. Better not let any girls look at that."

Her shriek filled the air when I lunged, and of course she hid behind Dad because he'd block any attempts I made at payback.

"Leave your sister, alone," Dad mused as if he thought his daughter were precious.

Precious, my ass. She was a menace!

"Let me see," Mom said, reaching out for my newly printed driver's license.

I held it out, and she beamed down at it.

"Your sister is right," she deadpanned.

My jaw dropped.

Her light laugh floated along with the spring air. "You shouldn't show this to any girls because then you'll have a line of them to choose from."

It took a second, and then her words sank in. I felt my cheeks heat.

Mom laughed again and patted me on the cheek. "My Neo could never take a bad photo. He's as handsome as a prince."

"Gross." Virginia gagged, still hiding behind Dad.

"See if I ever drive you anywhere," I shot out.

"How about me?" Mom asked, bumping her shoulder against mine. "Will you drive me out for ice cream?"

I smiled.

"Everyone in! Neo is driving. I'm paying, and the ladies will just make us look good," Dad declared, motioning us all toward the car.

I'd driven a lot over the last year while I had my permit. But this would be the first time I drove as a full-fledged licensed operator. As a man who passed his driving test. Freedom was definitely in the air today. I could feel it at my fingertips and tickling at my toes.

"So can I borrow the car tonight?" I asked once we all had some ice cream and were seated at a white table outside the shop.

Dad laughed. "Already making plans?"

I held up my phone. "I want to catch a movie with David."

"Just David?" Mom asked, her eyes sparkling.

I licked at the ice cream cone in my hands and suppressed a smile.

"He wants to show off his license to Sarah," V teased, ice cream on her lower lip. "He thinks it will make her like him more."

Well, she said it. Not me. "I'm the first one in my class to get my license."

"So it's not just David?" Mom pressed.

"It's a group of people."

"Well..." My parents shared a look. "I guess it would be okay," Mom said slowly. "But no goofing off in the car, and be sure everyone wears their seatbelt. And home by eleven."

"Eleven!" I practically choked on the ice cream.

"Do you want the car or not?" Dad intoned.

"Fine," I muttered, then texted my friends.

After finishing up the ice cream, V dragged us all into some nearby shop with a bunch of frilly clothes and music that made my ears feel like they were bleeding.

"I can't believe my baby is old enough to drive," Mom said before I climbed into the driver's seat to take us home.

Pausing, I smiled down. Even though I was sixteen, I was taller than her.

"I'm bigger than you." I reminded her. I reminded her of that a lot.

Her eyes crinkled around the corners when she smiled, and her fist went lightly into my stomach. I doubled over, pretending to be hurt.

"Who's taller now?" she mocked.

"Ha-ha," I retorted, standing back up. Suddenly, she hugged me. Normally, I would have cringed because we were in the middle of a parking lot and she was my mom.

But today I didn't. Today, I hugged her back.

"I'm proud of you, Neo. I love you."

"Love you too, Mom."

"Dad! Mom's playing favorites again!" Virginia called from inside the car.

"You are my favorite son." Mom agreed.

"I'm your only son."

"That too."

The drive home was pretty quiet with the music my sister chose filling the car. "Ugh, V. Not this song again. For the love of God, play something else."

"It's my favorite!"

I reached for the volume, turning it way down. "You have crap taste."

"Turn that up!" she demanded.

I glanced in the rearview mirror to where she was in the back seat. Our eyes met, and she began to say something—

SLAM!

The impact was sudden and drowned out all other sounds. It was as if the gravity binding us to the ground was suddenly void, and the entire car floated upward, rotating around and around. A sudden queasy feeling ripped through my chest, but other than knowing it was there, I couldn't comprehend. It happened so fast, but each second felt agonizingly slow.

Pavement, trees, the sky... it all blurred together until all I saw was white, until all I heard was deafening silence and the hum of sirens somewhere far away.

My eyes were the first to flutter open. Everything hurt. Everything hurt so much I almost tried to go back to sleep.

But then I remembered. An instant replay of what just happened stole over everything else. Adrenaline shot through my veins like a dose of epinephrine, and I blinked furiously, trying to focus.

The world was upside down. Everything was twisted and bent.

There was blood. So much blood.

The eyes of my mother were open and staring in horror as if death were not nearly as peaceful as we had been led to believe.

Death.

"Mom," I tried to yell, but my voice was a weak whisper. "Mom!"

I prayed and clung to the hope that her pained expression would shift. That her open, horrified eyes would blink and reflect pain instead of a moment frozen in time.

She didn't move.

Crimson matted her hair. Her body seemed frail.

"No." I choked.

Turning my head, ignoring the pain, I looked for my father... who was nowhere to be found. In the place he should have been was nothing but shards of glass.

"V," I moaned, trying to glance past our mother who I realized was partially twisted around my little sister, a mother who wanted to protect her child even in death.

"V!" I roared, this time my voice a little stronger.

The seatbelt I was wearing kept me in place. Blood rushed to my head... or maybe out of it. I couldn't tell whose blood was whose anymore. I couldn't tell what was happening.

A small whimper from the back seat was like another shot of adrenaline into my heart.

"Virginia," I croaked, trying to reach back to where she was.

"Mommy," my sister called. Then again.

Our mother didn't answer.

"Wake up!" she yelled. "Wake up right now!"

"V," I said, struggling with the seatbelt, trying to get back to where she was.

"I can't move, Neo!" She panicked. "I can't move!"

"I'm coming." I assured her, tears flooding my eyes, blurring everything worse than it already was.

My sister started to cry, and then reality slammed into our entire family in a way it never had before.

Turned out the freedom I'd gotten that day was not at all the kind of freedom I wanted.

"I THOUGHT MY SISTER COULDN'T MOVE BECAUSE OUR MOTHER was pinning her in place." My voice rasped as I continued to tell my story. All I could do was shake my head and stare at my hands clenched together in my lap. It seemed just like yesterday instead of nearly seven years ago. I felt the pain like it was brand new.

A small, cool hand slid over my clenched ones, somehow fitting between the tension tightening my grip. For long moments, all I could do was stare, marvel at the whiteness of her skin compared to the warm tone of mine.

Seized by sudden panic, my breathing lurched, shuddering inside my lungs. A low wheezing sound was released from between my lips as I grabbed Ivory's face between my palms. "Why are you so white?" I freaked. "Why is your skin so pale against mine?"

"Neo?" Her eyes flickered with concern, the blue focusing on me as if I were the only thing in the world she saw.

"Why?" I gave her a small shake, demanding an answer.

Flashes of my mother lying dead in that crumpled car assaulted me, memories of her pale, lifeless skin taking over my brain. Then I recalled my father lying on the side of the road where he'd been flung from the car, his body so pale it was almost blue. They'd both been so colorless that day, no life left inside them at all.

"Neo!" Ivory's voice whipped through my panic like a hot knife through butter. Her image replaced the ones I was reliving, her eyes not nearly as lifeless as the ones I continued to see.

"Why are you so pale and cold?" I whispered. "I can't lose you too."

Her face turned into one of my palms. Tears I didn't even know she'd shed smeared against my skin.

"I'm here." She verified, her hands sliding across mine. I held her face, and she held me. "I'm alive. I'm not going anywhere."

I had to work extra hard to swallow, then swallow again. Tears swam in my eyes but remained unshed. "I killed them,"

I whispered. "I killed both my parents… And my sister… she might never walk again."

Ivory tugged at my hand, but at first, I refused to move it away.

"Neo," she whispered, captivating me with her rhythmical voice and storybook blue gaze. "Do you trust me?"

I nodded slowly, the only thing I was capable of doing.

She tried again, and this time I allowed my hand to be tugged down, completely enraptured by the way she commanded my every move. My heartbeat hitched when she pushed my palm against her chest.

"Feel that?" she asked, her voice like a sweet melody. A melody I tried to grip tight to, a melody I tried to only hear.

But…

My mind raced.

Heart thumped.

Ribcage ached.

Soul… *hurt.*

Rose-red lips lay upon mine. Everything quieted. Reprieve from the cage of anxiety I was locked in set me free. Eyes opened, I stared at her in wonder. Hers were closed, and though I knew she had to feel my stare, she didn't look.

She didn't break the kiss.

Her midnight lashes didn't even flutter when her mouth grabbed for mine a little more firmly. Those rose-red lips I loved so very much wrapped around my upper and tugged.

Awe kept me quiet as she kissed. I watched, completely stupefied that the ability to quiet my most savage inner demon lay within her. Within a girl who was so small and gentle she probably wouldn't hurt a fly. Still, she commanded me.

My lips began to move with hers, accepting what she was giving, swallowing it down as though she were the only thing that could fill me up. At some point, my eyes slipped closed.

At some point, I stopped thinking completely and allowed myself just to feel.

I didn't know how long we kissed. Time stopped the moment I realized her power. She pulled back but didn't go too far. My one hand, still clutching her face, made sure of that.

I took immense pleasure in the unfocused look filling her eyes, dropping my gaze to the lips I'd desperately wanted to taste and finally did.

Rubbing the pad of my thumb over her lower lip, I asked, "How'd you do that?"

"Do what?"

"Bring me back to life."

A hint of a smile tugged her bow-shaped mouth before she ducked her head. "Feel that?" she whispered, catching me off guard once more.

I didn't have to ask because her hand patted over mine. She was holding my palm against her chest.

Against her heart.

Indeed, I felt it beating, proof of life.

Emotion clogged my throat. "Didn't you hear everything I just confessed?"

She nodded, eyes shimmering with unshed tears. "I felt as if I were there."

It was hard, so incredibly hard to pull away from her. But denying myself was better than hurting her. I paced away, leaving her to sit alone. Leaving a space beside her I desperately wanted to fill.

"Then how could you kiss me like that? Knowing what I did."

"I'd kiss you again if you'd let me."

My body stilled. I kept my back turned, afraid if I looked at her, if I saw any trace of sincerity in her eyes, I would succumb.

"I killed my parents. I left my sister disabled and stuck in this place," I said, gesturing around the room.

"That's not what I see."

I scoffed. "No? Then tell me. What do you see?"

"I see a boy who became a man in the blink of an eye. I see a man who asks himself every day why he lived when the people he loved most died."

Pain. Her words were like a thousand sharp daggers penetrating my heart.

"I see a man who works endless jobs no one else wants so he can take care of a sister he loves."

Anger lit me up inside. Anger because she tried to paint me as some kind of angel. As a victim. I wasn't any of those things. In fact, I was the very opposite.

I didn't bother covering the anger in my voice. Instead, I let it make my words harsher. "I steal. I lie. I take from people when my shitty honest jobs aren't enough. And FYI, my honest jobs? They never make enough."

"You paint with sadness, despair, and hope. Your art breaks me, then puts me back together with just a single look."

I felt rather than heard her move. She was so small and graceful she was like a cloud drifting across the summer sky. Because I refused to turn, she stepped into my line of vision.

I stared at my feet.

"You painted her an entire valley so she doesn't feel locked up. You came and got me out of jail and carried me to your home when you didn't even know my name. Your friends are loud, irresponsible, and need a serious class in hygiene, but they're loyal to you, as you are to them."

She was breaking me. Weakening my resolve. It pissed me off. I tried so hard not to let her in, this princess who'd wandered out of a storybook and stepped into the Grimms.

Gripping that anger tight, I held it like a shield. She didn't flinch when I looked up. She stood there against the backdrop of the painting I'd done for my sister, looking exactly as I thought of her seconds before.

As if she belongs in a storybook.

"I'm a criminal."

"Yes. A very good one."

What an odd thing to say. My hackles rose even more. "How would you know?"

"Because you stole my heart… something no one else has ever been able to do."

I made a sound. I was pretty sure it was the shattering of all the control I had left.

"There you go again," I growled, stalking forward.

Her blue eyes widened, and she took one step back, bringing her body up against the painted wall. "What?"

"Offering me life when I'm trying to cling to death."

Dark hair framed her pale face as her narrow chin angled up to meet my eyes. "You're too good for death, Neo."

Her words caused me more pain.

Pain only she could take away.

My hands slapped the wall on either side of her head. Bending so I was closer to her level, I felt the soft breath from her lips brush across mine.

"I'm gonna kiss you now, princess," I whispered. "But I don't kiss like a prince."

She closed her eyes and pouted her scarlet lips in a dare.

Challenge accepted.

Forty-One

Ivory

There was a difference between kissing Neo and being kissed by Neo. There was a difference between reaching out in comfort and being devoured by flames.

It was even more incredible when both of those things, comfort *and* desire, could be discovered in a single pair of lips.

He didn't kiss like a prince. Instead, he kissed like the thief he claimed to be. Shoving me into the wall until I could literally feel every brushstroke his paintbrush had made, he robbed me completely.

Robbed of sight because all I could do was feel. Robbed of every breath inside my lungs, every single beat of my heart.

It felt as though he'd stepped off the edge of a tower and we were both free-falling, our limbs intertwined as we tumbled through the meadow he'd created. No longer did we exist in the physical world but instead in a world of our own making, and it didn't matter where or when we landed because I would be with him.

His tongue stroked over mine so earnestly I could do nothing but answer his call. Heat spread through my body, and I stretched against him like a cat in the sun. My hands that had been clutching his biceps slid up so my arms could loop around his neck.

Shifting, Neo changed the direction of the kiss, barely lifting his mouth before devouring me once again in a completely new assault.

A small moan built in my throat, but he took that too, swallowing it down greedily, deepening the kiss so I would make another. Against my hips, his fingers flexed, and then he lifted, picking me up as if I weighed nothing at all.

Locking my thighs around his waist, I delved my fingers deep into the black strands of his hair. When his tongue retreated, my fingers tightened, and I felt him smile against my lips.

"Oh, I'm not done yet, princess. Not nearly." His words were like rumbling thunder in a stormy sky. The only storm I'd never felt frightened by.

Sucking my lower lip between his, he tugged and licked until it began to swell. In retaliation, I nipped at his mouth, piercing his delicate skin with the blunt edge of my teeth. He jolted back, surprise glittering in his onyx eyes. The tip of his skilled tongue slid over the bite, and one of his thick brows arched.

"Feisty," he murmured, the word catching between us because his lips came back to mine.

The metallic taste of blood bloomed across my tongue, and honestly, the flavor enhanced his kiss all the more. In the distance, there was a sound, nothing my brain fully registered until my captor lifted his head.

"Oh, uh…" a voice stuttered. "I'll come back."

Suddenly, my lips were alone, and I stared at the way his hair stuck out all over the back of his head. *Proof my hands were just there.* Seeing that coupled with the sound of his raspy voice, I realized we were no longer alone.

The bravery of the girl willing to bite her lover suddenly

disappeared, leaving behind someone shy who ducked into the one who held her.

The sound of the door closing made him turn back. Peeking up from where I basically hid, I watched him smile.

"Your sister saw us?" I whispered.

He nodded.

Groaning, I dropped my forehead onto his shoulder. The husky note in his chuckle made my thighs clench around his waist.

"She's gone." He promised, dipping low.

Pressing my fingers against his forehead, I stopped him from getting any closer. "You should put me down now."

His eyes narrowed. "I don't want to."

"We're in public."

"There's no one else in this room but us."

"This is your *sister's* room." I spoke, emphasizing the word sister.

A distasteful glint came into his stare, his lips twisting into a disgruntled snarl. "You started it."

"And I'm the one who's ending it."

My legs untangled from around his frame, but Neo took his sweet time sliding me down his body, making me ache even more than I already was.

The second my feet hit the floor, my knees gave out. When I clutched him for support, he lifted, pushing me back into the wall as my legs wrapped around his waist again.

"One thing about me," he murmured, grazing my earlobe with his teeth. My entire body hummed with desire as I tried to hear the rest of what he spoke. "I don't like to be told what to do."

His lips devoured me once more, coaxing mine open, delving his tongue deep to explore all the places he'd yet to feel. Giving up all my weight to him and the wall, I surrendered to the onslaught of the passion curling between us.

One hand palmed my butt, kneading the flesh and making my quivering thighs tighten around his waist.

Pain shot through my injured finger when my hands clawed at his back, but I ignored it and tightened my grip even more.

When his hips rolled into my core, I whimpered, head falling to the side. Neo kept kissing, his lips moving across my jaw, face burying in the side of my neck where he sucked a sweet spot I didn't even know existed.

A persistent knock broke us apart, my chest heaving when Neo turned to glance at the closed door. "What?"

"People are here looking for Ivory," Virginia whisper-yelled.

His head whipped back around, and our eyes collided. The gentle way he cupped my cheek was far different from the way we'd just kissed.

"Guess our time's up, princess."

"And then what happened?" the officer questioned.

"I met Neo and his friends. They've been graciously allowing me to stay with them while I try and figure out what to do."

"Why didn't you come to me? You know I can protect you," Ethan admonished.

"Yeah, well, I have been," I snapped, out of patience. Leaving my sister's side, I went to Ivory, grasping her wrist and tugging her away from Ethan and next to me.

"I'm afraid we are wondering the same thing, Ms. White. Why didn't you come to the authorities?"

"Because the man who attacked me told me I couldn't. He said I had to disappear and that if he saw me again, he would kill me for sure."

"And you believed him?"

"He cut off all my hair, yanked off my fingernail." She held up her bandaged finger. "And threatened me with a knife."

"How horrible!" Ethan gasped.

Seriously, who wrote his lines?

"And I was planning to come back… but he tried again. Twice."

"He's tried to kill you three times in the past two days?"

Ivory nodded, leaning a little closer to me, so I shifted, offering to take some of her weight.

The other officer looked at me. "And you are?"

"Name's Neo," I answered.

"He saved my life twice. If it wasn't for him, I'd be dead." Gasping, she pointed to the bandage on the back of my head. "Look at what the huntsman did to him! He just got ten stitches."

"Why do you keep calling him the huntsman? Did the assailant tell you that's his name?"

"He's hunting me," Ivory replied as if it made perfect sense.

Everyone nodded, so maybe it did.

"Did you get a look at his face? Could you identify him, work with a sketch artist—"

"Whoa, whoa, officers. She's clearly been through a major ordeal. Can some of this wait until she's had some food and a shower?" Ethan asked, concern darkening his chiseled features.

"The press is here," Emogen announced from the doorway. "They're looking for a missing heiress?" Her wide dark eyes moved to Ivory, widening farther.

"This is definitely not the place for an interrogation." Ethan confirmed, a total air of confidence and leadership ruminating about him.

"I agree. I prefer not to be photographed like this," Ivory said.

"We will escort you home."

"Not necessary," Ethan put in. "I already have my team of bodyguards downstairs."

Of course he did.

"Perhaps you could come to my high-rise later this evening. I will be happy to cooperate then." Ivory obliged.

"That would probably be best. If you come to the station, it will be inundated by press."

"Thank you so much for your time, gentlemen. You are very heroic in your duties. This city is lucky to have officers like you watching over us," Ivory told them sincerely.

Both officers flushed and cleared their throat. No one was immune to Ivory White and her charm.

They left the room first, and then Ethan draped an arm across her shoulders, sheltering her into his side. "Let's go." His voice was gentle.

Virginia was giving me dire, desperate looks, silently asking me how I could just stand there and watch Ivory be taken away.

But maybe she wasn't being taken away so much as being brought back to where she belonged.

"If I could kick you, I already would have," V practically hissed in my direction.

My face turned sour and so did my stomach as I watched Ethan escort Ivory out.

"Wait!" she said, stopping them both and pulling from beneath his hold.

Sapphire eyes turned back to me, emotion deepening the normally bright blue to something deeper. "It's best if I go now." She spoke, staring only at me. "If I don't, the press will never leave you and your friends alone."

I said nothing at all.

Clearing her throat, she spoke again. "And I've already put you in so much danger. I'm very sorry about your head."

Virginia made a threatening sound, promising some sort of evil retribution if I didn't act right.

I smiled my best smile. "I have a hard head, so it's okay."

Disappointment flashed through Ivory's eyes, and I felt that singular emotion down to my core.

"Will you tell the misfits good-bye and thank you for me?"

I nodded. "Sure."

Why was my throat tightening up? Why did my palms itch and my feet want to not stay in place?

"Okay then," she said, turning toward my sister. "It was so lovely meeting you, Virginia. Perhaps I could come visit you again sometime?"

I made a sound, about to cut that off instantly, but Virginia spoke first.

"Will you? Oh, that would be so fun!"

"Of course. Maybe you could braid my hair." Why did her voice sound watery and thick? Why did it sound like she was about to cry?

"Definitely!" Virginia agreed brightly.

"Ivory," Ethan called from the doorway. "If we don't go now, the press will catch us."

I felt her stare back on me, but I avoided it.

"You don't have anything else to say?" she asked, and I knew it was directed toward me.

"Nope."

Her momentary pause felt like a year-long journey, and then she turned and walked away.

"Thank you for everything. Thank you for saving my life," she said from the doorway, likely from Ethan's embrace.

"Just a regular day in the Grimms," I called back, looking down at my feet.

And then she was gone, and it felt like she took all of the oxygen in the place with her.

"You are so stupid!" Virginia reproached. "How could you just let her walk away like that?"

"She's better off," I murmured, the words actually painful to speak.

"Well, considering the look of hurt on her face when you just treated her that way." V swore. "Maybe you're right."

Suddenly, the pain was too much. The piercing ache in my heart threatened to split me in two. Regret so bitter and thick rose up the back of my throat. I would likely taste it for weeks. Springing into action, I raced out into the hall, eyes scouring everywhere for a glimpse of her black-as-night hair, rose-red lips, and skin as fair as snow…

She was gone. Vanished as if she'd been only a dream.

The pain in my heart was too raw and too real for her to have been a mere dream.

When I raced down the hallway and into one of the "nicer" rooms in The Tower, Mrs. Regina looked up from her bed.

"Mind if I borrow the window?" I asked, rushing to it without waiting for a reply.

Some of Ivory's dramatic tendencies must have rubbed off on me because my palm flattened against the windowpane as I stared down at the street.

An immaculate white Mercedes was parked at the curb, not even in a parking space, but I guess a guy like Ethan could park wherever he chose.

I watched him pull open the passenger door, motioning for Ivory to get inside. She hesitated, and the wind blew, ruffling the strands of her hair. Ethan shrugged out of his sports jacket, carefully draping it around her slight frame. She was swallowed up immediately, buried beneath the expensive fabric.

He motioned for her to get in again, but she turned back instead, gazing up at the brownstone. My palm made a godawful squealing sound as it dragged down the glass and I dropped onto the floor away from the window.

"Boy, what in heaven's name are you doing?" Mrs. Regina asked, giving me an odd look.

"Shh!" I pressed a finger to my lips.

She tsked and went back to whatever she was watching on TV.

My heart still racing, I slowly straightened inch by inch. Ivory was no longer standing on the sidewalk but was now bundled into the car. I watched Ethan move around to the driver's side and climb in.

Seconds later, the sparkling white luxury car slid smoothly away from the curb.

The prince came to claim his princess, and I let her go without a fight.

Forty-Three

Ivory

The tile was cool underfoot, the walls echoing with silence, and the night view of Central Park and the city around it was attractive as always. The entire day was spent answering question after question, explaining and then explaining again.

People were downright worried and mourning what they thought was my loss, so when I reappeared, everyone wanted to call, text, and visit.

We'd managed to keep everyone away. I was in no condition to be seen right now. I wanted to be put together. I wanted to be the Ivory White everyone knew.

Even if something inside me was changed. Altered.

Not the same.

Besides, even if I did feel different, it was no excuse to go on looking this way. I was positively a mess.

Once I'd gotten rid of my personal physician, police, security, Ethan, *and* had a lengthy call with my stepmother (who would be visiting soon), I was finally blissfully alone.

Bone-deep exhaustion clung to me like a heavy cloak, trying to drag me into its endless depths as I ran a hot bath filled with soaking salts and expensive bubble bath that

Louis Vuitton had sent over the second word got out that I was actually discovered alive.

There was also an entire rack of couture clothing filled with new releases from my favorite luxury brands that had been delivered by security, literally wheeled right into the penthouse for me to peruse at leisure.

It was incredibly sweet, even if I knew they were just hoping I would be photographed in the clothing when I finally faced the press and went into my company.

As the tub filled the spacious bathroom with soothing scents, I wandered through the house again, dragging my fingertips over the luxurious fabrics of my furniture, the sleek Tiffany lamp in the living room, and the imported marble island in the kitchen.

Browsing briefly through the rack of clothing, I put my favorite pieces toward the front and then gazed wearily at the boxes of shoes that had also been sent to match each piece.

Tomorrow Marco, my stylist, and his team would be here to fix my hair, give me a much-needed manicure/pedicure, and help erase the mess my skin was in.

In the bathroom, I shut off the faucet and flipped on some soothing instrumental music. As I stepped into the deep soaking tub, a violin began to play.

Tears I didn't know I'd been holding back burst free, accompanied by a low sob.

Once I started, I couldn't stop. Deep wrenching cries echoed around me and made my chest heave. Shoulders ached from the tension, and my nose ran, mixing with the saltiness of my tears.

I let myself cry. Sometimes a girl just needed to.

I'd been through a lot, and now I was finally home. Finally safe.

But it wasn't relief making me cry. Or even the trauma of almost dying three times.

It wasn't even my heinous hacked-up hair.

It was him.

Neo.

I could still feel the distance between us when Ethan came to take me away. How jarring it was to be clinging to his lips, practically melting into his body in one moment and the next him barely batting an eye when I had to go.

He didn't even try to stop me.

He didn't ask to see me again.

It almost seemed he was relieved I was finally going.

I cried harder. Fat tears dripped into the massive amount of bubbles floating around my body.

It might have been easier to convince myself it was better this way if my lips didn't still tingle from his. If all day long, I hadn't pressed them together, trying to taste his tongue or relive how overwhelming it was to kiss him.

He had a horrible sense of style. He always had paint all over him, rips in his jeans. His hair needed cut, and sometimes he couldn't bother to shave.

He was also grumpy, prone to lying, and living with three other men.

I missed him already. I missed all of them. Even Earth, who was probably throwing a party because I was no longer there.

Crying out the worst of it all, I leaned back, completely spent, allowing the warm water to caress my skin and alleviate all the aches I felt.

Keeping my freshly bandaged and professionally doctored finger out of the water, I let my eyes slip closed, blocking out the flickering light from the candles.

A great sigh moved through me, but the second I truly relaxed, my mind attacked with memories of being tossed into that cold dark river. My nose began to burn, remembering the water I'd swallowed. The water I'd been soaking in suddenly felt like an attack.

"*Agh!*" Gasping, I sat up so forcefully that a little bit of water sloshed over the side, the bubbles making a distinct *plop* on the floor.

I pressed a hand to my chest, gulping down oxygen, more tears rushing to my eyes.

"Maybe a bath was a bad idea," I murmured to no one, then sighed with shame. "But this is such a luxurious bubble bath."

It was absolutely a far cry from the scary, possessed shower at Neo's place.

The bottom fell out of my belly with just the casual thought of Neo. Was he so ingrained in me already that he filled my head?

Afraid to lie back and let flashbacks pummel me again, I chose instead to wash, using all the luxurious products I loved so much.

I even shampooed and conditioned my hair twice. It wasn't easy with just one hand, but I managed. Soon, I was wrapping up in a giant, soft towel.

Imported body oil added the moisture back into my skin, and I also combed through a special conditioner into my strands, hoping it might make it look less horrifying to Marco in the morning.

The scratches on my cheek still stung a bit, so I took extra care, then pouted a bit when I rubbed over the knife cut on the back of my neck.

Inside my walk-in closet, everything was perfectly organized, and the scent of fresh jasmine floated softly in the air. I wandered through the racks and browsed the drawers, looking for something to sleep in and finding nothing at all.

Sitting on the lounge near the large island, I pondered what it was I was looking for.

The image of an ugly red flannel flashed behind my eyes.

Gasping, I stood. "An entire closet at your disposal, and that's what you look for? Ivory White, get your mind right," I scolded, marching to a nearby drawer to pull out a black silk nightie with spaghetti straps. The hem was short and lined with black lace, the smooth feel of the fabric whispering over my skin.

Slipping on the matching robe and a pair of Givenchy slippers, I went to the kitchen for some Perrier.

The penthouse was dark, the moon providing most of the light through the large windows. The quiet was something I relished, but tonight, for some reason, it seemed too quiet. I felt too alone.

After pouring water into a glass, I pondered, making some green tea to help me relax but ended up traveling to the window to stare down at the city forest.

The last time I'd been there, someone had tried to kill me. Shuddering, I recalled what happened in that ominous tunnel, feeling as though it had been so long ago, but really, it was just days.

Thump.

My ears perked up.

Bang!

Spinning around, I searched for the cause of the noise.

No one was there. Inside my apartment, all was still.

Thump. Thump. Thump.

Rattle. Rattle.

Was that the front door?

Panic assailed me, my heart beating so fast it made me nauseous. Had the huntsman found me? Was he trying to get past my bodyguards?

Was coming home a mistake?

More scuffling sounds and even a grunt echoed out.

Setting aside my glass, I crept into the entryway, staring at the door. The chain rattled, knocking against the thick wood.

My hands shook, legs trembling. Instead of running away, I took a breath and moved forward. If it really was the huntsman, I needed to know.

The door shuddered, and a startled cry ripped from my throat.

"No one is permitted entrance," I heard one of my guards nearly shout.

Furrowing my brows, I closed my hand around the handle.

"Stay inside, Ms. White," the guard called, obviously hearing me undo the locks.

I probably should have listened.

I didn't.

Instead, I turned the knob and swung open the door.

Forty-Four

Neo

"*Neo!*" That gasp could only come from one princess. "What in the world are you doing?"

Still keeping hold of the bodyguard, I glanced up. "These are your bodyguards?" I reproached, disgust in my tone. "Where did you find them? Mary's School of Dance?"

Ivory rushed out into the hall, smacking my arm. "Let go of him! How dare you?"

"Ma'am." The bodyguard pinned to the floor glanced over his shoulder. "Go inside. We have this handled."

Glancing across the hall, she saw her other bodyguard slumped on the ground, rubbing his head.

Her eyes widened, and my heart skipped a beat. How could I have missed blue eyes this much in only one day?

"Did you do that?" she demanded, pointing to the downed man.

"He's not unconscious," I refuted.

A rude sound was released, and she smacked me again, then grabbed my arm, forcing me to let go of the guard. "Get off him!"

I stepped back, releasing the man dressed in a penguin suit, watching as he stuffed the black earpiece back in his ear.

"Requesting backup." He spoke into his jacket.

Planting her hands on her narrow hips, Ivory glared. "What in the world are you doing?"

The tie on her robe came loose, and the sides fell open. All of her creamy white thigh was suddenly on display and so were her collarbones and pale chest.

"What in the hell are you wearing?" I demanded, scowling.

"My nightgown," she said as if it were obvious.

"Nightgown, my ass," I muttered, stomping forward to take her hand, pulling her toward the wide-open door of her apartment. "I've seen Victoria's Secret models wear more."

"I would never wear Victoria's Secret." She sniffed.

A hard hand slapped down on my shoulder, yanking me back, and because I was gripping Ivory, she fell back too.

Shaking off the inept guard, I caught her around the waist, using my body as a shield.

"You're fired." I snarled at the men.

"You can't fire them!" Ivory announced, straightening.

Reaching around, I pulled her robe closed. I mean, it might as well have been see-through, so I glared at the men. "Eyes up, mates."

"They are perfectly respectable gentlemen." Ivory defended them.

"They're really good at taking an ass-whipping too!"

Down the hall, the exclusive elevator dinged, and several more security guards looking exactly like the two already here burst forward.

"Good heavens," Ivory muttered wearily, pressing a hand to her forehead. I noticed her injured finger was newly bandaged in a discrete yet very effective style.

"Let's go." A gruff man grabbed my arm, yanking me back.

I didn't fight because for the first time, I realized how tired she looked. How her eyes were ringed with red.

"Wait!" Ivory gasped, reaching out a hand to stop them from hauling me from the building.

"Ma'am, this man was trying to gain access to your home. He assaulted two of your bodyguards."

Ivory pinned me with a serious look. "Apologize."

"What?" My mouth fell open. "No way."

"Fine. I'm going to bed." She turned, her tiny frame engulfed by the large casing of her front door.

"Fine," I bit out.

Ivory turned, as did all of the security guards.

When I said nothing, Ivory made a sound, and I sighed.

"I'm sorry I beat you up and almost knocked you out," I mumbled to the two men.

"And?" Ivory pressed.

"And what?" I whined.

"Next time, you will use your words and not your fists."

"I'm not five."

Ivory pursed her lips, straightening, and that austere air wrapped around her.

I repeated what she told me to say.

"Let go," Ivory told the guard holding me.

"Ma'am?"

"I know him. Let go."

"We advise against allowing anyone inside—"

"The last time I checked, this was my penthouse and I was employing you," she said coolly.

All the men straightened and agreed.

"I don't want to be disturbed the rest of the night. I'm tired."

"Of course, Ms. White."

Ivory went inside, disappearing, and I stood there wondering what to do. A moment later, her head peeked around the door. "Are you coming?"

I raced inside, not having to be told twice. After she

closed and locked the door, she turned, leaning against the wood. Her robe was falling open again, a total distraction.

"What are you doing here, Neo?" Her voice was whisper soft, eyes guarded.

"I didn't like the way we left things."

Pushing off the door, she started to walk away. "You seemed pretty glad to get rid of me."

She was utterly capable of being aloof and cold. I could see how this behavior worked in her favor probably all the time.

Not tonight.

Not with me.

I'd experienced the warmth beneath the surface. I knew the innate kindness at her core.

Her body spun when I grabbed her wrist and tugged, breath rushing out the second she collided into my chest. She smelled good. Expensive, unique. *Mine.*

"I lied."

Fusing our lips, I denied any chance we could keep speaking and ruin it all. I didn't trust my mind or words, but it seemed my heart knew exactly what to say.

All day, I drowned in regret. All day, I kept myself from running after her. However, when the sun bid the day good night, the darkness somehow concealed all the reasons I'd let her go.

The open-mouth kiss went on, Ivory's lithe body pulled tightly against mine. Our lips were slick with arousal. Hunger dripped off the tip of my tongue. She must have tasted it because she opened even more, inviting me to search for what I craved.

Stroking against her again and again, I nearly purred with deep pleasure whenever her tongue would slightly retreat, forcing mine to give chase and pull her back again.

I devoured her until I couldn't think straight, until

nothing else mattered but the connection we'd forged in such a short time. The interval at which my heart beat made me feel like I might explode.

Thump-thump-thump-thump. T-thump. Pause. *T-thump. Thump-thump-thump-thump.*

The smacking of our separating lips echoed overhead when we finally parted, but my hands stayed clamped around her hips, keeping her plastered to my front.

Gasping for air, her head falling back, she gazed up with a heavy stare. The usual bright blue was deeper and far less noticeable because of her blown-out pupils. The rose-red lips were still red as ever but swollen and quivering.

Pressing a kiss to the corner of her mouth, I continued, peppering more kisses along her jaw. Ivory tilted her head back, revealing the column of her graceful neck.

Burying my face into the smooth skin, I licked and sucked, enjoying every single little gasp and moan falling from her lips. Reaching her collarbone, I nudged the black silk with my nose, but it didn't grant as much access as I wanted.

With a rough sound, I wrenched back, leaving Ivory to sway unsteadily on her feet. It only took a moment to nearly rip the robe off her body, the unwanted silk pooling around her bare feet like she was standing in some sort of enchanted puddle.

"Up," I demanded, my voice foreign to my own ears, then lifted, her body wrapping around mine like it knew exactly where it belonged.

With her in my arms, legs wrapped around my waist, I yanked away the thin strap of the nightgown and attacked all of her velvety fair skin.

Like some sort of siren, she gasped and arched, her head falling back but every other part of her pushing close.

As I gripped her shoulder and ass, my mouth went right

to one of her offered globes. Ivory's breathy gasp tightened my cock the second my wet mouth surrounded her erect nipple, dampening the satin and sucking deep.

The room buzzed around us as I altered between flicking my tongue over the hard pebble and nipping softly with my teeth.

"Neo," she half moaned, half whined.

Lifting my head, I placed a gentle kiss at the center of her throat. "Where's the bedroom, princess?"

She pointed, and I swiveled around to follow the direction. She slumped forward, resting her cheek on my shoulder, her arms tucked between our bodies so her fingers could twist in my shirt.

Tenderness welled up inside me, mixing with the hammering need to claim her and producing some kind of intoxicating cocktail.

Her bedroom was huge and probably too fancy for my tastes, but it was also dark and I was too occupied to care what it looked like. The giant bed in the center of the room practically glowed with the pristine white bedding it was made with, beckoning me with its purity, challenging me to taint it.

As I moved her to the bed, her arms and legs tightened around me, clinging as though she were afraid I might disappear.

"I'm right here." I soothed, tenderness overcoming my burning need because I couldn't bear the thought of her being afraid.

Reassured, she let me sit her on the foot of the bed. My heart tumbled over when I saw just how small she looked practically swallowed up by the voluminous, fluffy bed. Her legs were so short they didn't even try to touch the floor, and her two bare feet curled in on each other, making her look like some kind of fairy.

"You make me ache," I confessed, the words actually stinging my throat.

Her head bobbed, silently saying she understood, and when our eyes connected in the dim light, I knew it was true. The very ache I felt bruising my heart was mirrored in her gaze.

The satin of her gown was cool and slippery when my fingertips grasped the hem, clinging to every curve and swell of her body.

"Don't show yourself to anyone else dressed like this ever again," I demanded, jealousy making me seethe.

The only reply I received was the lifting of her arms, a quiet invitation. The whispering of the fabric made the base of my skin tingle when I pulled it over her head, tossing it away.

She wore nothing at all underneath that dark silk. Ivory's skin was completely bare, glistening under the moonlight the way freshly fallen snow looked on an untouched field. I knew she was nervous by the way her fingers dug into the blanket at her sides, but she sat calmly and unashamed, allowing me to stare.

Kicking off my shoes, I nudged closer, dropping to my knees. Our breathing was heavy, the tension in the room so thick I could likely scoop it out of the air and hold it in my hands.

Her knees brushed my chest when I leaned even closer, the rapid rising and falling of her breasts hypnotic. I didn't think. I couldn't. Instead, relying on instinct, I did what seemed more natural to me than breathing.

Leaning in, I pressed a kiss over her heart.

Her skin was cool and smooth against my burning lips, but underneath, I discovered her heart beat as erratically as mine.

My eyes slipped closed. I left my mouth upon her skin, lingering there, trying to catch my breath.

Just moments ago, I'd been desperate to get inside her, desperate to fill this insatiable desire only she had ever made me feel.

And now I had her naked on a bed made of clouds. Instead of pounding into her until bliss was all I knew, I bowed at her feet. I kissed her chest, trying to reach deep into her heart.

It scared me. Scared me so deep that I began to pull away.

Small hands caught me, and though her grip was delicate, it was as if I were chained in place. Her eyes sought mine, but I refused to share my stare, choosing instead to gaze at the floor.

A gentle caress started at the top of my head and gently dragged down, brushing through my hair and making my scalp explode with thousands of tingles. My eyes slid closed when she grasped my ear, massaging it between two fingers and then giving the lobe a gentle tug.

Everything beneath my skin was buzzing, creating a fog I couldn't possibly think around.

Hands slipped under the flannel I wore, pushing it down my shoulders and back. I watched the fabric fall to bunch around my waist.

I glanced up.

I surrendered.

The flannel disappeared somewhere, as did my shirt, jeans, and boxers. My skin wasn't flawless like hers. It didn't inspire poetry or even a second look. But she stared as if it did. She studied me as if I were a painting and she wanted to take in every last brushstroke.

Discovering I wasn't as brave as her, I felt a flush rising up the back of my neck, creeping toward my ears, and leaving me to feel like I was on fire.

My hands landed on either side of her, and we both moved back, sliding up the bed as one even though we didn't touch. The bed enveloped her in a way that made me jealous, cradling her body in a way only I was meant to do.

My possessive growl filled the space. I grabbed her and rolled until I was the bed she lay on.

"*Agh…*" She gasped the second our bodies melted together. Skin to skin, chest to chest.

She was soft and smooth, whereas I was coarse and scarred.

With her enclosed in my hold, one of my thighs pushed between hers.

This time it was me who gasped when I felt the evidence of her obvious desire right against my thigh. I breathed in even as I caught her lips again, cradling the back of her head and kissing until her entire body went limp against mine.

Pulling back, I kissed over her shoulder, scraping my teeth along her skin, leaving a trail to prove I'd been there.

Pushing my thigh harder into her core, I hear her loud gasp cut off by her biting at my chest. Moaning, I pushed her head closer, encouraging her to continue as I rocked my thigh against her already wet center.

Need hammered through me, boiling my blood and overruling everything else. Soon, we were rocking together, bodies seeking more as our lips kissed everything they could reach.

When it became too much, she whined, sticking out her swollen lip in a pout.

Rolling, I pinned her into the mattress, looming over her so I was all she could see.

Her legs parted automatically, and I settled between them. Gentle fingers whisked down my sides, playing over my back and reaching down to flirt with my bare ass.

"Tell me you want this," I said, holding on to what very

little restraint I had.

She nodded.

Placing a finger beneath her chin, I forced her stare up. "Say it, princess."

"I want you."

The separation I held between our bodies withered, my throbbing, erect rod nestled against her crotch.

We gasped, stilling at the contact and then moving to rub together. I shuddered, feeling her wet warmth coat my shaft, and nearly came right there.

No. You won't come until you are enveloped in her slick heat.

Forcing myself up, I reached between us, dipping two fingers into her welcoming core. Her body arched up in pleasure before collapsing back down.

I wanted to play longer. I wanted to taste her flavor, but I was also impatient, my cock slick with pre-cum and my hands shaking with need.

Ivory reached for me when my fingers slipped free, and I came over her instantly, thrusting deep with no warning in one long push.

Our moans mingled, floating up to the ceiling, and I took a moment to nuzzle her neck before pulling back to move.

Pulling out until just the swollen tip was left inside her, I plunged deep again, watching her mouth fall open but no sound come out.

Her hands groped for me, clutching and then patting, asking me for more.

I obliged, setting a pace that maybe was too vigorous, but the way she moaned my name said otherwise.

We fell into a rhythm, our bodies moving in mutual pleasure, a mix of sweaty skin, sloppy kisses, and satisfied moans.

I wanted to stay in her forever, but her tight heat held me just right and the familiar tingle in my lower belly told me my climax was drawing near.

Grasping a pillow from nearby, I jammed it beneath her hips, tilting her up for more access. The second my tip hit against a bundle of rough nerves deep inside her, she nearly came undone.

Smiling, I did it again. And again.

"Neo..." Her voice quaked, unfocused eyes searching for mine.

Cupping her cheek with one hand, I let her find me. "Let go, sweetheart. It's okay."

Thrusting deep, I rocked against her sensitive spot, and beneath me, Ivory came unraveled.

What a beautiful mess she was with her head thrown back, neck exposed, and chest flushed. Her eyes closed, mouth open soundlessly. Just the vision she made, the feel of her body clenching around me, shoved me over the edge.

I came so hard that spots swam before my eyes, and a dry shout filled the quiet room. Even after I came back from wherever I'd spiraled off to, my cock still quivered inside her, twitching from shock, my entire body satiated and heavy.

Rolling away, I drew in a lungful of air and sighed.

Ivory shifted, and I turned my head, meeting her shuttered gaze. Rolling onto my side, we faced each other, long black strands of hair stuck to her damp cheek.

When I pushed them away, she refused to meet my stare.

"Are you shy?" I whispered, secretly reveling in how cute she was.

"Of course not," she insisted, looking everywhere but at me. Her cheeks were pink, her lips thoroughly kissed.

"Then look at me." I beckoned.

She kept her eyes averted. "Well, maybe a little."

A warm chuckle bubbled from deep within as I pulled her close. Ivory burrowed into my chest to hide, and I allowed it because I really wanted to keep her in my arms.

Doubt started to prickle at the absolute bliss coursing

through my veins, making me pause. "I didn't hurt you, did I?"

The concern in my tone made her look up. Her eyes were still slightly blissed out, but she seemed more coherent than before. "Oh no! You didn't. I—"

Despite her refusal, more worry assailed me. "You what?"

She ducked into my chest again, but this time, I pulled her back. "Tell me."

Staring at my chest, she whispered, "It's never been like that before."

"Like what?"

"So overwhelming."

As soon as the words were out, she scurried back into me, and I folded her close, stroking the back of her head. My own head was throbbing, but I was pretty positive I hadn't busted any of the stitches.

Even if I had? *Worth it.*

What? I'm a guy.

"Overwhelming in a good or bad way?" I asked, putting the stitches completely out of my mind.

"Good." The word was muffled, her breath warm against my bare skin, but I heard and grinned into the night.

I don't know how she knew, but suddenly, I was being smacked on the back.

"Ow!" I complained, still holding her tight.

"Don't be smug."

I laughed.

"Neo," she whined.

Still laughing, I kissed the top of her head. "It was like that for me too."

She pulled back, seeking the truth in my eyes.

I let her see, and when she did, she smiled.

Forty-Five

Ivory

Skilled fingers trail up my calf, moving past my knee to sensually explore the softness of my inner thigh. Humming in delight, I shift, opening up, granting more access because the way he touches is absolutely addictive.

Shivering with delight, his fingers continue to stroke, but he adds the soft touch of his lips. They feel plump and slightly wet as if I am so delicious the taste of me makes him salivate.

The tip of his tongue peeks out, cool against my burning flesh, leaving a trail of shivers in its wake. Arching up, I offer myself like some kind of meal, gasping with my own hunger when his lips close around one erect nipple, tugging and sending shots of electricity all the way down to where his one hand still plays between my thighs.

Strands of his hair brush over my chest, heightening every single touch he graces upon my skin. Panting, wanting more, I reach out for him, meaning to pull him over me, meaning to disappear beneath his body and get lost in his lips.

My hands meet air and panic assails, turning all my heightened desire into need, turning my hands greedy as they search for him once more...

My eyes shot open with a gasp. A sheen of sweat made me feel sticky, and the pounding of my heart was deafening in the quiet room.

Blinking up at the ceiling, I fought for breath, fought for composure.

How could I compose myself when my body was warring between desire and panic? Between wanting and loss?

"Neo," I whispered, rolling toward him for comfort.

He wasn't there.

The blankets fell to my waist when I pushed up, and uneven strands of hair clung to my sticky cheeks. Holding a palm against my chest, I measured how my heart raced and stared again at the space where Neo should have been.

The dream floated back, the warm desire it contained beckoning me, reaching out and offering me something far better than reality.

For a moment, I almost succumbed, but then I shook my head. *Was last night just a vivid dream?*

Emotion filled my chest and prickled behind my eyes. It couldn't have been. It felt too real. My body felt too… satisfied.

Confused, I glanced down, fisting my hands in the blankets.

A flash of color caught my eye, making me sit up a little straighter, focus on myself a little more. Red plaid flannel buttoned up around my body, the top few buttons left undone.

My stomach dipped, and my hands left the covers, grabbing the fabric to make sure it was real. There was absolutely nothing red plaid in my closet. In my entire penthouse.

Still clutching the shirt, I let my eyes roam the dim room, landing on the black nightie and robe I'd put on after my bath last night. They were on the floor in a heap, tossed aside and forgotten.

Don't show yourself to anyone else dressed like that ever again. His voice echoed through my mind.

A vague, hazy memory of him pulling this shirt around me, of me sighing when the scent folded me close, chased the back of my mind, tingling my belly with butterflies.

He'd buttoned it around me, kissing my temple before pulling away.

It wasn't a dream. Neo had been here, and we'd spent the night doing things in this bed that were so good it was no surprise I'd at first thought I'd awakened from a dream.

Stumbling out of bed, I padded across the floor. "Neo?" I called, voice still sleepy.

He wasn't in the bathroom, so I went out to the kitchen and eventually searched the entire apartment, only to find he wasn't there.

The more I moved, the more aware I was of places aching that had never ached before.

How could he just leave after that?

Finally admitting that he truly was gone, I went back into the bathroom to study my reflection and the red flannel hanging to my thighs.

"If he hadn't left this shirt, I might actually think it had all been a dream," I mused, noting a small dark mark just below my ear.

Clutching the edge of the counter, I gasped and leaned closer to the mirror. "A hickey!" I declared. "Never in my life," I said, offended... but then a smile curved my lips.

The doorbell rang, and hope blossomed in my chest, the flannel floating behind me as I rushed toward the door, not bothering to call out to whoever was there.

Neo. My heart sang.

"Oh," I said. The obvious letdown in my tone was not missed by the man who was not Neo standing on the other side.

"Agh!" Marco gasped, jumping back so the two women accompanying him had to do the same. Pressing a hand to his chest, he swept his dark eyes over me from head to toe. "It's even worse than I thought!" he announced, coming forward once again. "Thank God I brought reinforcements."

The women behind him made sympathetic sounds.

"Marco!" I exclaimed, still processing that it was not Neo but my stylist instead.

"Oh, you poor thing!" he crooned, rushing forward to sweep me into a hug. "There, there." He patted my back. "I'm here now."

"I missed you too," I said into his shoulder.

Pulling back, he held me by the shoulders to look at me in pity. "I mean, I expected you to be bad, but this…" His eyes widened when he took in the flannel. "Is that a synthetic fabric? Dear Lord."

Releasing me, he snapped his fingers, and a familiar paper cup was passed into his hands.

"Here, darling. I stopped by your favorite café down the block for this latte. I should have gotten a double shot."

"Ahh!" I exclaimed, making gimme hands at the cup. "You really got this for me?"

His head bobbed. "Mm-hm. Organic heavy cream, no sugar, just the way you like it."

The first sip was like heaven on my tongue. No, seriously, I heard angels sing. "Ohmigod," I rushed out, sipping again. "Now this is coffee."

"Girls!" Marco snapped around, all business. "Get set up. This is going to take awhile."

The two ladies went ahead of us into the apartment, going off to do their usual setup.

Clicking his tongue, Marco lifted a strand of my hair, his eyes sad. "Who took a machete to your hair?"

"The man trying to kill me," I said around another sip.

"*Agh!*" He nearly fell back, pressing a hand to his chest. "So it's true. Someone really is trying to kill you?"

I nodded, and because Marco could truly understand, I held up my bandaged finger. "And he ripped off my nail!" I wailed.

"No!" He gasped again. "Not the nail!"

My head bobbed, lower lip pouting.

"Well, he'd better never meet me in a dark alleyway because, honey, the things I would do!" Marco announced, snapping his fingers.

Tears filled my eyes. "I missed you," I said, suddenly turning emotional.

"Oh, baby," he said, pulling me in for a hug. "Don't you worry. Marco is here now. I'll take care of everything."

Sniffling when he pulled back, he stared at the flannel again. "Where in the world did you get that?" Holding up his hand, he stopped my answer. "I don't need to know. Just go take it off. Burn it. You can't feel like yourself if you're wearing that."

I took another sip of the heavenly coffee and went off to change.

"Who kidnapped you anyway, Paul Bunyan?" Marco muttered, moving into the apartment.

Inside my walk-in, I slowly stripped off the flannel and, without thinking, lifted it to my nose. Neo's unmistakable scent filled my senses, tingling the base of my spine. Echoes of pleasure whispered beneath my skin, making my eyes slide closed.

A noise out in the other room brought me back, and suddenly, I felt incredibly silly for standing in my closet, clutching the shirt of a man who'd slipped away so quietly that if it weren't for his shirt, I might still doubt he'd been here at all.

Forty-Six

Neo

The dark chased away my doubts.

The sun shone light on them once more.

I never claimed to be anyone I wasn't. I never said I would stay.

But slipping out of her penthouse left me feeling ashamed and somehow dirty, not at all like the man I was.

Still, I kept walking, slipping into the city as though it were my own personal shield. Awash with guilt, imagining her face when she opened her eyes and I wasn't there.

Truthfully, I wanted to stay, but I knew where I belonged.

Wasn't it easier to walk away from something before it was taken away? Before you were left alone?

I thought last night would feel like a good-bye, a way for us to get over the chemistry constantly trying to pull us together.

Last night didn't feel like good-bye.

It felt like a beginning.

And fear took over. Fear sent me fleeing.

There was no happy ending for a princess and a misfit. That wasn't how the story went.

Forty-Seven

Ivory

"*Mirror, mirror on the wall, who's the fairest of them all?*" Marco beckoned, self-satisfaction dripping from his voice as he stared at my reflection.

The little storybook quote left me with a small pang in my heart because it made me think of Neo.

Smiling, I gazed at him in the mirror instead of myself. "Well, I think it's you."

"Flattery will get you everywhere, my dear." Marco preened, giggling.

He really was a gorgeous man. Tall, broad without being bulky, and a flawless deep complexion. His dark hair was cropped super close because he often said he was too busy doing his clients' hair to bother with his own. And because, "I look damn good in any style."

Marco always wore makeup, dressed with flair, and exercised so the skinny jeans and trousers he favored always looked good. He was single even though he often said he was "ready to mingle."

Marco's high standards and ambitious work schedule didn't allow for a lot of mingling.

"You're done," he announced, waving his hand with panache, acting like he was some sort of fairy godmother.

Maybe he was. I did look *way* better.

My fair skin no longer appeared colorless but plump and healthy. Newly shaped brows framed my blue eyes, and the scrape on my cheek was hidden with expertly applied foundation.

My black hair was no longer limp and haggard but glossy and cut into an asymmetrical style so it was slightly longer in the front than the back. Originally, I'd planned to get extensions, to reclaim all the length I lost.

I didn't want that anymore. Somehow, it didn't feel like me.

What length I did have was layered to compensate for the hack job I'd been subjected to, and Marco used a styling wand to add loose curls that looked just the right amount of messy and polished.

Even my nails had been overhauled, getting a complete treatment, and painted with a gorgeous shade of red. Red was a power color, and I needed all the power I could muster right now. The missing nail was still covered and would remain so until it was healed.

"I don't know how you did it." Awe laced my voice.

"You look just like your old self," Marco agreed. "No!" He immediately shook his head. "Better!"

The two assistants made sounds of agreement.

Turning toward the ladies, I took their hands. "Thank you both for your hard work today. You've always done such a fine job, and I don't think I've ever shown my appreciation properly."

Both women's eyes widened.

"You've always been very kind." One disagreed.

"Of course, but I can do better than kind." I gave their hands a little squeeze. "If there is anything you ever need, please ask. You've done so much for me. I will be happy to return the favor. I will add a little bonus to your pay from

Marco as well. Please forgive me if I've ever seemed ungrateful."

Both women shook their heads adamantly. "No. No, you haven't!"

"Well, consider this a thank-you, then, not only from me, but from those you work with who are ungrateful."

Surprise made my eyes widen when both women swallowed thickly, clearly emotional.

"Thank you," one whispered.

They began packing up, and I turned back to the mirror, studying my reflection once more.

Marco came up behind me, his large hands completely covering my shoulders. "Are you ready for today? Are you sure it's not too soon?"

"I can do this," I said with more confidence than I felt. "Everyone knows I'm back. The media is camped out downstairs, and you know the stocks took a hard hit when I went missing."

"This is why I'm an artist," he said, tsking and making a sour face. "Business hurts my brain."

Sometimes business hurt my brain too, but it was also part of who I was. I owned two successful companies, and while I was also an artist like Marco, I wore more than one hat.

Ooh, I should get some new hats. They would look charming with this new haircut.

The press conference later today was happening fast, but it was absolutely necessary in many ways.

Once the two assistants were completely packed and out of earshot, I turned back to Marco. "Okay, spill the tea."

"The tea, you say?" He raised a brow.

"You know everyone, and you work with everyone. The second I went missing, rumors started to fly, and you've heard them all."

"A good stylist never repeats what is told to him in confidence," he informed.

We both laughed.

Marco plopped down on a plush chaise, crossing one leg over the other. "Well, girl, Jessica up on Park told everyone you had to go to rehab, so your publicist concocted this scheme so people didn't find out you're really an addict."

"She's still salty I got invited to the Chanel private show and she didn't."

Marco bobbed his head. "Malory from Gucci is telling everyone you ran off with someone you met online."

I laughed.

"Of course, there are the obvious rumors, that you got kidnapped and were being held for ransom."

I made a sound of agreement. That was to be expected.

"And of course…" He went on, waving a hand, dismissing the rest. But he did it without looking at me. "There's all the other ridiculous chattering among the rich, bored NYC housewives."

"Marco."

His gaze remained averted.

"Tell me."

"I'm sure it's just silly gossip like everything else."

"If it's stilly gossip, why aren't you talking, and why aren't we laughing?"

He pursed his lips. "Some of the elite have been whispering that perhaps Audra had something to do with it."

I felt my forehead crease. "My stepmother?"

"Mm-hmm." Marco pulled out a bottle of water and took a sip. "Apparently, Audra was insanely angry your father left W to you and not her."

"But my father left her more than enough money and their homes. What would she want with his company? She isn't even interested in business."

I thought back to when my father first passed away, trying to remember the reading of his will and how Audra behaved. I couldn't remember. How could I be expected to? My father had just passed away. I was overwhelmed with grief and fear.

His passing left me with no parents and a stepmother who always just tolerated me because she had to.

Not that she was ever outright mean. She was always just cool and aloof. It wasn't something I ever really focused on because my father had always been so warm.

But... *murder*? That was extreme.

"That's why I said it was all the baseless chatter of elite housewives."

I must have appeared shaken because a sound of distress ripped from his throat.

"Now look at you all upset. This is why I didn't want to say anything. Those stodgy old ladies wouldn't know truth if it hit them right in their liposuctioned asses."

I smiled. "Of course, you're right. I mean, it's absolutely preposterous to think Audra would have anything to do with what happened to me."

"Look at the time," Marco announced. "I would stay, but I have a full day. Beauty waits for no one."

I accompanied him to the door, thanking him again for his magic.

When he was gone, I leaned against the door, suddenly feeling overwhelmed and weighed down. Without even thinking about it, I went straight to my walk-in, hugging the flannel into my chest.

It was ridiculous that I found comfort in this item, considering the man who left it didn't even bother to say good-bye.

We never said good-bye.

It was also ridiculous that when I looked up into the full-length mirror, my reflection confirmed what Marco declared. I was just like before.

But I wasn't.

I was different somehow. Changed.

A single tear dripped from the corner of my eye, streaking over my cheek to cling precariously off my jaw. There was a horribly queasy feeling churning in my belly, splashing up into my throat.

The rumors and theories Marco dished were all comical and borderline absurd. Leave it to those whispering hyenas to come up with something so outlandish it still lingered in the back of my mind.

Probably because I knew. I knew bored, rich housewives who had nothing better to do but look for gossip and spot scandal were sometimes terrifyingly right.

But Audra… a killer?

The huntsman knew your name. Knew where to find you in the park. Told you to never go home again.

Could it be?

Forty-Eight

Neo

I AVOIDED EVERYTHING AND EVERYONE, CHOOSING INSTEAD TO take job after job and pickpocket in between.

The fish market wasn't the only odd/unwanted job in this city. Bike messengers made good money because the job was hazardous. Some construction crews took walk-on men when their projects were busy and they couldn't keep up. The pay was under the table and all in cash, just the kind I liked.

I worked all day until it was well past dinner and my stomach demanded fuel. Tucking deep into my jacket, I walked with a bowed head, not having to look at where I was going because I knew these streets like the back of my hand.

My stomach grumbled loudly the second the obscure noodle place was in reach. Lifting a hand to the woman behind the counter, I pulled out a nearby chair and sat down.

I was used to being tired, but this was a new kind of exhaustion. The kind that weighed me down, left me feeling out of sorts and somehow lost. Though I'd worked all day, the way I felt was not from labor.

A large white ceramic bowl with steam curling from the top slid in front of me. The spice of the sauce prickled my nose and woke me up just a little.

Straightening, I smiled widely at the woman. "You know just what I like, Nettie."

Beaming, she tapped me lightly on the cheek. "Added an egg for ya, on the house. You look worn out."

"When are we gonna get married and run off to the Caribbean?" I asked, taking her hand and holding it like I might propose.

She giggled like the schoolgirl she no longer was. "Hush now and eat it all."

"Yes, ma'am." Releasing her hand, I unwrapped a pair of wooden chopsticks and snapped them apart to dig in.

This place was tiny, old, and off the map, but it had the best ramen in the entire city.

When Nettie brought me a glass of water, I glanced up, slurping some of the long noodles hanging from my lips. "Yhank yhou," I said around the food.

She giggled again and went back to the counter.

I ate in peace for long moments, letting the spice burn my tongue and make my nose run. The over-easy egg on top added extra flavor to the already flavorful dish.

Nearby, there was a small TV mounted on the wall, and a flash on the screen caused me to look up.

The food in my throat stuck there like a rock. The noodles still between my lips dangled forgotten and no longer as tasteful as before.

She filled up the screen, making my heart jump a beat and something inside me yearn. She appeared almost unreal. My skin suddenly tingled, reminding me with stark clarity she was very, very real.

Even though she scared me like hell, even though staring at her on TV right now reminded me we were from different worlds, I couldn't deny how we'd been together just last night.

Ivory stood outside, the bright sky making it obvious this

was a playback from earlier in the day. Reporters and people crowded around, hanging on every word she said, cameras flashing left and right, but she didn't flinch at all.

Poised and composed, she stood, somehow large despite how small she really was. White high heels raised her off the ground, and the light-blue one-piece outfit she wore sparkled when the sunlight hit it just right, making her sparkle like a diamond.

The top had thin straps, exposing her collarbones, making me want to demand she put on a jacket but, at the very same time, graze them with my teeth.

A delicate necklace hugged her throat, and her hair ruffled in the breeze, brushing her neck.

She'd wasted no time at all putting herself back together again and stepping in front of the camera. I expected this to make me angry, for my cynical heart to sneer.

But I wasn't.

I already knew this was who she was. I couldn't hate her for it. How could I blame her for moving through her day just as I had done?

I watched her lips move, the volume too low for me to hear what she said. I didn't need to hear her words, though, to see what apparently no one else did.

She was exhausted just like me. The world she knew was altered just like mine. It didn't matter that she went back to normal because that normal no longer existed.

The chopsticks made a distinct echo when I placed them over the edges of the bowl, pushing the partially eaten ramen away.

Picking up the water, I downed the glass, eyes never once leaving the TV.

She smiled. She spoke. She posed.

Ethan stood off to the side, wearing a dress shirt and tie.

She was telling everyone she was back and safe. She

might have even been recounting some of her ordeal. She was assuring her stockholders that business was wonderful and their precious money would remain piled in their accounts.

Her dazzling beauty captivated everyone.

But underneath the beauty, Ivory was frightened and felt alone.

The camera zoomed in, Ivory looked up, and I felt her eyes like a punch in the gut. The empty glass hit the tabletop, one of the chopsticks falling onto the floor. Scraping back the chair, I dug into my pocket, tossing down some cash.

Nettie called out, but I didn't turn back.

The sun was gone again, the dark alive.

Forty-Nine

Ivory

THE TWEED BALMAIN JUMPSUIT WAS TUCKED AWAY IN MY collection. The white pumps lined up beside the rest. My skin was fragrant with the scent of fresh jasmine, and though I had a closet filled with glorious nighttime attire, I was wrapped up in red flannel.

The press conference was successful, stocks already starting to rebound. I knew it would be a few weeks of damage control, but it wasn't anything I couldn't handle.

Then why do I feel like this?

Lights sparkled across the city, creating a one-of-a-kind view that never looked quite the same.

A low knock echoed through my home, making me glance over my shoulder.

Rap, rap.

Rotating, I padded through the penthouse lit only by burning candles placed here and there. Leaving the chain on the door, I pulled it open, peeking out.

Luminous onyx eyes.

Shadowed jaw.

An unspoken question.

The door clicked closed when I pushed against it, and I paused to press against the thundering in my chest. My hand was unsteady when I reached to slide the chain free, fumbling twice before finally getting it to give.

I opened it only enough for him to slip inside, silently watching him replace all the locks.

The loud slap of his jacket hitting the floor made my eyes go wide, but they melted shut just as fast because the second he touched me, I turned soft.

The tip of his nose was cold when it pushed into my neck, and the sound of him breathing in deep made the rhythm of my heart heavy.

He was wearing another flannel, this one green and black.

When I slipped my fingers into his hair, they bumped against the bandage covering his stitches.

Distracted, I glanced down to frown. "You haven't changed this yet? I'll do it now."

"Later," he purred, grazing his lips across mine.

We stumbled into a deep kiss, our bodies tumbling into bed. His tongue was balm to my ache, the weight of his body grounding me in place.

The way he nibbled on my lower lip before capturing the top to do the same made my toes curl and body arch.

The flannel rode up on my hips, revealing my thighs. His body sank into mine, making me gasp against his mouth.

His erection was already pulsing, and we moved together despite the barrier of clothes. Delving under his shirt, my nails dragged lightly over his skin. The little shiver I was rewarded with made me do it again.

When he flicked his tongue against mine, a hint of spice burst across my mouth, making me tug at his clothes. His glittering stare never left mine when he pulled back to disrobe. Neo wasn't a huge man, but he was well defined and lithe. The sinew of muscle under skin sent my tongue sweeping across my lips, wanting to taste.

When the button on his jeans popped open, I pushed

forward, grabbing the waistband to help work them down. When he was free, his throbbing length stood out, promising pleasure, making my lower belly quiver. Too beautiful to be ignored.

I wrapped my hand around his girth, sliding slowing up his length and back down again.

Before I could go farther, he pushed me down, slowly unbuttoning the flannel before parting it to finally reveal my skin.

Trailing his lips down my body, he dipped his tongue into my belly button before continuing its venture.

Thick, warm fingers parted my folds, making me squirm, the room filling with my breathy gasps.

I was so exposed with him, not just in this bed, but in all ways. I wasn't sure I wanted anyone to see this much of me, but with him, it was like I didn't even have a choice.

A long, thick stroke up my center chased all thought from my mind.

I moaned, my thighs coming together, but Neo pushed them open, licking me again.

Settling into a rhythm, he treated me like some kind of meal, a meal so good it made me want a bite.

I was shaking with need when he lifted his head, sliding up my body and leaning down. His tongue stroked over mine the way it had in other intimate places. I could taste myself, a taste I never wanted until now, until he fed it to me.

With a single thrust, he sheathed himself inside me, our moans breaking our mouths apart.

Tears pressed against the backs of my eyes when he pushed his arms between my back and the mattress, holding me tightly against him.

His breathing echoed against my ear. Our bodies moved as one. Too soon, bliss came to claim me, making my nails dig into his back.

Not slowing the rhythm or changing pace, Neo turned his head and kissed my temple.

Fireworks exploded, unexplainable pleasure rocking my every cell. I clung to him as wave after wave of climax pummeled me and then as it washed over him.

His grunts and moans against my ear were almost as satisfying as the orgasm that just ripped through me as well as the warm throbbing I felt between my legs.

We lay together in quiet bliss for a long time, sticking together with sweat, sharing the same air.

"Shower me," I demanded but in a very undemanding tone.

Hair fell into his heavy-lidded eyes, and his lips were plump from kissing. "Shower you?"

I nodded.

His brow lifted. He was so roguishly handsome. "And why should I?"

"Because you're the one that made me a mess."

He smirked at that, not at all sorry, if anything, entirely proud. Sliding down my body and off the bed, he wrapped his hand around my ankle and tugged.

Blankets fell into a heap on the floor, but I never did. Neo lifted me against him, carrying me into the shower.

"This shower is bigger than our entire bathroom," he said, sitting me down in the center.

I hit a few buttons, and water sprayed from several angles. Grabbing a bottle of body wash and a loofah, I thrust it at him.

While we washed and rinsed, we got to know each other's bodies in ways we hadn't even in bed, touching everywhere, lips lingering. Steam from the shower filled the air around us, offering a buffer from the rest of the world, giving us a gift I hadn't realized we needed.

Wrapped up in oversized white towels, I directed him to

sit on the upholstered bench while setting out everything I needed to take care of the wound on his head.

I didn't ask if it hurt because he'd just lie, and the little hiss he gave when I started to clean it was answer enough.

Actually, there were a lot of questions I wanted to ask. There were a lot of words we needed to say.

I said nothing. He said nothing.

But the way I felt when we were finally back in bed and I was curled up tight against his chest?

It said so much.

Fifty

Neo

I left again before she woke, leaving behind another flannel, knowing it wasn't enough but unable to do anything else.

Fifty-One

Ivory

Thunder growled overhead, the ground vibrating under its threat. Impenetrable clouds crowded the night above, trapping every bit of heat and moisture in the air. Humidity so thick and stagnant tried to choke me as I ran, feet slapping against the pavement, joints aching with the furious pace I set.

I was sticky with sweat and fear but pushed on, cutting through the clingy atmosphere, wondering if it was an accomplice to the figure giving chase.

Clad in a long, concealing cloak, the figure blended in with the night and moved at an unhurried pace, causing excess panic because no matter how fast I ran, they still managed to be right behind, and no matter how well darkness concealed, I still saw.

A violent neon bolt of electricity cut down from the sky, the cracking sound so brash I tripped, slamming into the ground. Burning with new scrapes and cuts, my arms shielded my face as the sky shook with thunderous delight.

Even after the bolt faded, the sky still glowed portentously, electricity lingering in the air. Sheets of icy, stinging rain released from the clouds, drenching everything they touched. Shaking and nauseous, I pushed up to run again, but the fall removed any lead I'd managed to gain.

A strong but oddly bony-looking hand clamped down on my

shoulder, my yelp surely muffled by the monstrous storm. Flipping me onto my back, the huntsman hovered close, staring down from inside the opaque hood.

"Who are you?" I screamed, anger making me lunge.

Both my wrists were caught in just one of his hands shackled around me like mighty chains.

And then I was flying.

Falling.

My body suspended by nothing as it spiraled through the pounding rain and flashing lightning.

Slamming into something hard and unforgiving, back bowing, body arching, feeling like I might break in two.

Deafening silence enveloped me, the storm raging no more, the huntsman nowhere in sight.

Instead of falling, now I was floating, enveloped in some kind of void where everything was muffled and dark. In the murky light, a pale hand drifted close. I stared, transfixed by how white it was, almost as if it were nothing but bone.

Bubbles filled the space around me, bursting from my nose and mouth.

Realization smacked hard and panic seized my chest, forcing my mouth open. Water gushed its way down my throat.

Flailing, I struggled and searched for the surface but only sank deeper. A car appeared, half submerged in water, taillights looking like two menacing red eyes.

Pushing through the water toward the car, I beat a weak fist on the window.

"Help!" I screamed, the dense water seizing the sound.

Ignoring the heaviness in my limbs, the burn in my lungs, I hammered on the glass, begging whoever was inside for help.

Something came to the window, long dark strands of hair swaying with the current, swimming without care.

"Hey!" I screamed again, just wanting them to see me.

The body turned, hair still slithering around her like snakes and parting to reveal a child.

Skin as fair as snow, hair as black as night...

A bloodcurdling scream ripped free, a shriek so fierce it was no match for the water. Images burst behind my eyes, flickering so fast it was hard to even comprehend them all.

Rain. Night. Car. Woman...

Death.

THE FORCE OF MY GASP SHOT MY ENTIRE BODY UP OFF THE BED. Tears streaked my cheeks, dripping onto my chest. Sweat clung to my skin, and my throat burned as if I'd been screaming for real.

A dream. It had only been a dream. A nightmare.

The horrible images and indescribable fear still clung, lingering just below the surface of my mind, promising they weren't finished with me yet.

Shuddering, I turned toward Neo, craving his security, desperate to feel safe.

My arms met air.

My heart nearly broke.

A sob ripped out of me, echoing through the empty room. He'd done it again. Come to me in the night and left at the break of day.

How could he make me feel so incredibly secure but be so ridiculously fickle?

I need him.

Something I didn't want to admit. Something I didn't even like.

It didn't make the need go away. It didn't make me want him less.

The change I recognized in myself? It was him.

Did he not feel the same? Was I just someone to visit in the night? Someone to find pleasure with between the sheets?

He's scared. Just like you.

But why won't he reach for me like I just tried to reach for him?

More tears slipped free. Lingering fear mingled with fresh hurt as I sat in the center of my empty bed.

One teardrop fell from my damp lashes, splashing against my chest, against the green material buttoned up around my body.

He left another flannel.

Why bother leaving behind a piece of yourself if you didn't want to stay?

Fifty-Two

Neo

My hand froze just before connecting with the solid wood of the door.

I knew it was wrong to be here. I couldn't stay away.

The daylight hours drained me, my mind spinning around and around. Heart trembling constantly as war raged within. By the time darkness enveloped the city, I was weak and worn out, no longer wanting to resist the incredible urge to find her for peace.

Yes, it was ironic. The very woman causing this war was also the only one who could offer a reprieve.

Behind me, a throat cleared, reminding me I wasn't alone. Lowering my hand, I glanced back, the security guards offering bland, unapproving stares.

I didn't care what they thought of me.

But Ivory… I cared too much. *Which is why you shouldn't be here.*

Flexing my hand at my side, I debated another moment before rapping my knuckles against the wood.

There was no use in listening for the sound of her approach because she was so light and graceful that she never made a sound. My ears strained anyway, listening for even a hint of her, hungry for the faintest of echoes. The locks unlatched; the chain slid free.

Her body was illuminated from behind when she opened the door, hair so black it shone with a hint of blue. A long pale-pink robe was belted tightly at her waist, not offering a peek of what might be underneath.

She rested her eyes on mine for long moments, and a prickle of relief unclenched my heart. Stepping back, she granted access, and I slipped through the half-open door, pushing it closed behind us.

There was a ribbon in her hair, tied into a bow. The tails draped perfectly over her dark locks, and I desired to tug the ends and watch the fabric fall, whispering softly to the floor.

All that could be heard was the heaviness of our breath as we silently danced around each other without moving our feet. The days were so long, the nights incredibly short.

The dark-pink tip of her tongue peeked out, swiping over her lower lip.

I was on her in milliseconds, directing her backward until she was against the wall. The silk under my palms when I grasped her hips was smooth and slick, forcing me to hold her tighter.

The tongue she tempted me with moments ago disappeared, and I chased after, coaxing it out so ours could tangle and play. Stretching onto her tiptoes, Ivy opened a little wider, inviting me deeper.

Humming with greedy bliss, I moved to slide her up the wall, only to be halted by both of her palms. The smacking sound our lips made when she pushed me back was like a cold slap to my face.

"We need to talk first," she said, words breathless, lips glistening with shared passion.

"Later." I promised, lowering my face to hers.

Denying, her face turned so my nose brushed her cheek.

"Is this all I am to you?" she asked, taking my moment of distraction to slip from between my body and the wall.

"What?" I asked dumbly, desire-ravaged brain trying desperately to catch up.

"Am I just a plaything for your desires, a place to spend your nights?"

Yikes.

I deserved that. I did. I also deserved the pain it caused. But even so, I argued. "That's not fair," I rasped, rubbing the back of my neck.

"And you leaving every morning before the sun comes up is?"

The small catch in her voice made me look up, made my heart clench. Hurt shone in her beautiful blue-hued eyes. I was hurting her.

Why doesn't she understand how hard this is for me?

"What am I to you?" she asked, bold, her confidence shining through.

I felt the words more than I heard myself speak them. "You're someone I want desperately but cannot have."

"You never asked if you could have me."

"Because it's not you who denies me."

We both fell silent, my words like a heavy weight.

"It's all of me or none of me," she finally said, raising her chin. "I'm not some cheap clearance item nobody else wants."

"You mean Ethan?" I growled, jealousy fisting my hands at my sides.

"Ethan is my friend. Nothing more. Our parents might want us to get married, but Ethan is not who I want."

I wanted to give in. I wanted to succumb so badly I actually took a step forward.

The hope that blossomed in her eyes hit me like a ton of bricks.

"We're from two different worlds." I reminded her.

"I don't care."

A harsh sound ripped from my throat. "Yeah, because you have everything to give, and I have nothing to offer."

"All I want is your heart."

Anger and frustration welled up inside me, creating so much pressure in my chest I felt like I might burst. "And I said I have nothing to offer."

"Your heart is more available than you think," she whispered.

"What the hell would you know about my heart?" I growled, then immediately regretted the words.

She didn't even flinch, a princess staring down a dragon, her crown not even slipping. "I've seen it in your paintings, in the way you care for your sister. I saw it when you protected Fletcher at the bar and when you carried me home in the rain before you even knew my name."

"Stop." My voice was ragged, soul weary.

"And most of all," she said, floating closer, "I've seen it in your eyes when you're in my bed and inside my body."

"I have to go," I spat, boots stomping heavily toward the door.

"I know you're scared. I am too. But I want you despite the fear. All of you, just not in the dark."

My hand was shaking when it wrapped around the door handle.

"Don't come back until you can give me what I want." Her voice was so strong, and it made me feel even weaker.

"Then I guess I won't be back." I flung the words, not really wanting to hurt her, but hoping she might feel my pain.

"I'll be waiting," she whispered softly, promising she still wanted me despite my ire.

Refusing to look back, I bolted away from all her words

and my desires. Fleeing into the night with the taste of her lip-gloss lingering on my lips.

Fifty-Three

Ivory

Another nightmare robbed me of sleep. Another night I reached for a man who'd left me alone.

I didn't need him. I was capable and strong-willed. Able to make it on my own. So no, I didn't need Neo. But I wanted him.

I couldn't even be angry at the way he behaved because deep down, I understood. Perhaps if I hadn't seen the man he truly was, perhaps if we hadn't somehow lived a year in just a few days. If I hadn't met his sister and heard his story…

But I did, and those things couldn't be erased, not by a few harsh words or the way he ran so hot and cold.

So yes, I could understand his actions, but that didn't mean I had to suffer for them.

A girl had to have standards and set a clear line. I knew my worth, and there was nothing wrong with charging full price. I paid full price for a lot of items that weren't even as good as me.

Neo had to accept where I came from just like I had to accept where he was from. We were an unlikely match, but to me, it didn't matter. It didn't matter where you started out. It only mattered where you were going.

I wanted to go there with Neo.

I felt like he wanted that too, but fear held him back. I thought about the painting on his apartment wall, the car, the lack of color, and the angel wings. Death still had a hold on him, I wasn't sure it would ever let him free.

I would wait just as I vowed.

Go on strongly despite the fear. The words my mother imparted were never far from my heart. So even though I would wait, even though I was afraid, I would go on.

I had a company to run, a new collection to organize, and there was also the matter of the man trying to kill me.

Or woman. More specifically, my stepmother.

Now that I was home from the short-lived exile and the most pressing tasks had been dealt with, it was time to meet. Time for me to look into her eyes and really ask myself if Audra was the type of woman who would go as far as murder to get what she wanted.

But what did she want?

Didn't she already have everything? I just couldn't wrap my head around the gossip that she was behind this. Truthfully, though, bored, rich housewives were sometimes more perceptive than the FBI.

And not only that, but there was this… tingle somewhere inside me. A nagging intuition whispering that I actually knew the truth.

Sharp pain radiated from the base of my skull to throb behind my eyes. Inhaling sharply, I massaged my temples, shying away from the tendrils of darkness teasing my spine. The lurid dream that kept me awake half the night resurfaced with the headache, making me feel worse.

My palms turned clammy with the sense of foreboding rising within me like mist on a rainy night. Going into the kitchen, I reached for the small, rarely used bottle I actually never remembered until moments like these.

Yes, I'd had moments like this in the past, the beginnings

of a panic attack. But usually, I was very good at distracting myself and keeping them away.

I very rarely needed the anxiety medication my doctor prescribed, but today was not that day. Taking out a small white tablet, I put it on my tongue and swallowed it down with a glass of cool filtered water.

"The stress of everything that has happened is getting to you." I assured myself. "It's nothing to be ashamed of."

Insides still feeling heavy, I sat at the island, drawing in a deep breath. What I needed was a plan because if I had a plan, then I had a way to be in control.

How do you plan to control the fact that your wicked stepmother wants you dead?

Well, that was a very negative thought. It was also very alarming that my subconscious seemed convinced it was her behind the huntsman.

"Maybe start with something more manageable first."

As the medication started to work, my muscles unclenched, proving how tight I'd been. The pain behind my eyes turned to a faint throb, making it easier to think.

I'd deal with Audra later.

First, though… I would say a couple good-byes.

Fifty-Four

Neo

An unfamiliar black SUV slid to the curb right in front of the Rotten Apple, shiny and out of place.

It was the kind of SUV that would make everyone in the Grimms suspicious some kind of drug raid or sting operation was about to go down.

Earth didn't deal in drugs or allow them into his bar, so I knew it wasn't that. It wasn't happy hour, and he didn't have any well-off investors.

That left only one thing.

One thing that I didn't really need any of the above information to know because I felt it. I felt her even from all the way down the block.

Pressing up against a building, tugging my hood up to conceal my head, I stared, covertly waiting with intense anticipation to lay eyes on the girl I told myself I didn't want to see.

I really should work on my habit of lying.

A man dressed in black trousers, a black dress shirt, and some kind of smart driving cap stepped from behind the wheel to jog around to the passenger side, opening the back door.

I cursed the tinted windows for delaying the vision I

wanted. The first thing I saw was a pair of black heels stepping out onto the pavement, the soles of the shoes a vibrant shade of red. Fine-boned pale ankles stretched up, but the door blocked the rest of the package.

Moments later, she stepped from around the door, and everything else fell away.

Ivory White was dressed all in black, the above-the-knee dress showing off her pale legs and thin frame. One shoulder was exposed, the other covered with a wide black strap. Loose curls fell to her shoulders, swaying slightly in the breeze. Oversized round black sunglasses shielded her eyes, and her lips were her signature red.

The only color besides her lips came from a large satin cobalt-blue bow on her head.

She looks just like my painting.

The handles of an oversized black bag draped over her forearm, and she smiled warmly at the driver before pushing back some wayward hair.

I didn't want her to smile like that at anyone but me.

Another man I hadn't noticed until now got out of the passenger's seat, stepping close. One of her security.

Rolling my eyes beneath the hood, I scoffed. *Useless.*

Surprisingly, she waved him off, but he didn't move far, planting himself on the sidewalk right in front of the bar.

Surprise caused me to straighten off the wall when she didn't head toward the side entrance leading up to the apartment. The sharp clipping of her heels against cement rang down the street, reaching my ears as she walked straight to the Rotten Apple door, pulling it open and disappearing inside.

I blinked. Blinked again.

What the hell was she doing?

Fifty-Five

Ivory

"We aren't open yet," the familiar gruff voice called, Earth not even turning around.

"As if I'd come here to drink anything," I retorted, stopping in the middle of the empty bar.

Beneath the army-green T-shirt, he tensed, shoulder blades drawing together. Slowly, Earth abandoned his task, rotating with his usual grouchy look pasted firmly in place.

His ambiguous stare flicked over me from head to foot, taking in my appearance, then dismissing it to settle on my face. "I thought you went home."

"I came to repay the kindness you showed me," I said, scrunching up my nose. "Well, that *some* of you showed."

He made a rude sound and went back to whatever he was doing behind the bar. "Neo ain't here."

My stomach dipped at the mention of Neo. It had only been a few days, but I missed him. The ache and longing only seemed to grow deeper as more time passed.

I didn't come here to see him today. In fact, I came at a time I thought he might not be here. Regardless, disappointment still pinched my heart upon hearing he wasn't home.

It is better this way.

"I'm not here for Neo."

Pausing in his actions, Earth's head tilted and then looked up. "Maybe if you were, he'd be in a better mood."

"Is he okay?" I asked, knowing I shouldn't.

He grunted and didn't answer, which I thought was entirely rude. The sound of my heels was sharp against the floor as I closed the distance between myself and the bar, slapping a hand down on the top.

Instantly regretting it, I pulled back, making a face. "You should wash this."

Funny how his eyes were as dark as Neo's, but they didn't have the same effect when leveled on me.

Tipping up my chin just a little more, I clenched my fingers around the handle on my bag. "I asked you a question."

"And I didn't answer it."

"Just tell me if he's okay," I said, done with the passive-aggressive rapport we so easily fell into.

"If he wanted you to know, he'd tell you," he replied, the words harsh but his voice quiet.

I supposed that was true. It hurt to hear, but I didn't show it. My pain wasn't something I wanted to show to Earth, and it wasn't Neo's responsibility to bear.

Opening up the black denim Prada tote over my forearm, I pulled out a white paper bag, setting it on the bar. "Even though you didn't want me here, you didn't push me out. I want to thank you for that, for giving me a place to stay when I had nowhere else to go."

"I don't want your gifts." His voice was brusque.

"It's for Snort," I protested. "Surely, you wouldn't rob your dog of a gift."

His lips pursed, and I smiled. Turning, I caught the eye of my bodyguard still out on the sidewalk and motioned for him.

A few moments later, the man came inside, carrying a large box and setting it next to the bag.

"Thank you," I told him.

He nodded and went back to his position outside.

"That for Snort too?" Earth asked, curious.

"It's for the bar," I said, gesturing for him to look inside.

The second the flaps were open, he made a sound, glancing up. Reaching in, Earth pulled out a familiar green bottle with the Perrier label across the front. His eyebrow rose. "Seriously?"

"It really is bad business to not have quality water. Now you have some," I announced. Then, taking a chance, I said, "And maybe next time I visit, I'll actually want to have a drink."

"You aren't welcome here." The bottle made a light clinking sound when he pushed it back inside the case with the others.

Ignoring his foul attitude, I went around the bar, watching his eyes widen exponentially.

"Thank you, Earth. You have a terrible disposition and probably scare everyone you meet, but underneath it all, I think you are a good man."

He took a step back. "No. I'm not. I'm rotten to the core."

He really believed that. Maybe he was right.

I hugged him, slipping my arms around his waist and squeezing tight. He was so shocked he didn't even push me away. He was like a vibrating live wire, standing there motionless as though he couldn't believe I'd actually touch him.

Pulling back, I smiled up. "Rotten or not, I actually like you anyway."

Genuine surprise filled his usually indecipherable eyes. It kinda made me proud that I could ruffle the feathers of a man as rigid as him.

"I have work to do," he muttered, glancing away.

I could have sworn I saw a very faint blush fill the apples of his cheeks.

"Make sure you give that to Snort," I called, heading for the stairs.

Peeking over my shoulder, I stole one last glance at him before disappearing out of sight. He was still standing there, unmoving, staring at the gifts I'd left behind.

UPSTAIRS, I KNOCKED AND LISTENED TO ALL THE SHUFFLING OF someone approaching the door and then turning all the locks.

Fletcher's honey-colored head poked out, and a big grin broke over his face when he saw me waiting.

"Princess!" he exclaimed, flinging open the door and throwing his arms around me.

I laughed, his wild, floppy hair tickling my face as he hugged me tight. "We thought we would never see you again!"

"Oh, I thought we were friends," I admonished.

"Well, you're a rich, fancy, important woman. Why would you want to be friends with us?" Fletch asked, leading me into the familiar apartment.

I hadn't spent a ton of time there, but it was enough that I felt a wash of homesickness, momentarily leaving me unable to speak.

Fletch noticed my silence and perhaps the look on my face as I stood in the center of the room, taking in all of Neo's art splashed on the walls, the familiar glow of Beau's monitors, and the deep sound of Snort's breathing.

"Is everything okay?" He worried, putting a hand on my arm.

Somewhere close by, the sound of a chair rolling filled the room, and then Beau was standing before me too.

Blinking back unexpected tears, I took in the two men and smiled. "Oh, no. I just missed you."

Sharing a look between them, they suddenly rushed me, and the three of us were squished together in some kind of three-way hug.

"It's a princess sandwich!" Fletch declared.

I laughed, feeling lightness fill me. I really had missed them so much. My apartment was so quiet, quiet in a way I never noticed before.

Once they let me go, I lowered to pet Snort who was drooling heavily on my Louboutins

"Did you come to see Neo?" The question earned Fletch a smack from Beau. "Ow," he whined, rubbing the back of his head.

"Be nice," I admonished. "Actually, no. I came to see you. I wanted to thank you for everything."

"We didn't do anything," Beau said, scratching his head underneath the beanie perched on his red hair.

"Of course you did!" I exclaimed. "You were my friends when I needed them. You let me stay here and made me feel safe." Reaching into the black bag, I pulled out an envelope and handed it to Beau.

Curiously, he took it, peeking inside. A choked sound ripped from his throat, and he looked up, green eyes wide.

"Just paying back the money you let me borrow. Plus interest, of course."

"What about me? What about me?" Fletch asked, bouncing from foot to foot.

Beau raised his hand to smack him again, but I made a tsking sound and his hand lowered.

Pulling out a small card, I extended it to Fletch. He took

it, frowning. "Ivory White," he read, then looked up. "Is this your business card?"

I nodded. "Yes. I really meant it when I said you are the most talented violinist I've ever heard. I would love to work with you."

"But you aren't a musician or a producer," he said, wrinkling his nose.

"No, but I still have some ideas."

He slid the card into the back pocket of his jeans. "Thank you."

The disappointment in his voice could not be disguised, and it made me laugh. Reaching into my bag again, I pulled out something else.

Fletcher's eyes lit up when I passed the brightly colored item into his hands.

"This is for me!" he said, far more excited over a simple mug than an offer for a job.

Laughing, I nodded.

"Look, Beau!" he said, holding out the two-toned mug. It was covered in different Marvel comic strips, and across the front in large yellow font, it read: *I Have Issues*. The inside of the mug was bright red.

Beau laughed.

"Now you have your own mug that fits you," I said, feeling warmed by his delighted response.

I rocked on my heels when he rushed me but didn't fall because Beau steadied me with a hand to my back. Fletcher hugged me tight, and I could have sworn I heard a few light sniffles near my ear.

"Thank you, princess. I love it!"

"You're welcome." I beamed. It wasn't an expensive gift. It wasn't designer, but it made him so incredibly happy.

Another wave of homesickness washed over me and, with it, unmistakable sadness. I never knew my life had been lacking certain things until I left it behind and came here. Now I was supposed to let it go? I was supposed to go back to my wonderful but somehow lonely existence?

Tears rushed to the corners of my eyes, and I blinked, trying my hardest to keep them hidden. "Well," I said, trying to sound cheerful. "I just wanted to stop by and thank you for everything. If you ever need anything, anything at all, please call me."

Fletcher nodded, eyes round and wide as he clutched the mug into his chest. "Are you okay?"

Frowning, Beau took a small step closer.

Smiling, I stepped back toward the door. "You need to dust again. It's already starting to gather."

They were quiet when I went to the door, but then I remembered.

Inhaling a deep breath, I gathered my courage and turned back. Reaching into the bag one last time, my fingers clutched the fabric I'd stuffed inside. Just touching it, knowing what I was about to give up, made me want to weep, and a familiar tingle of panic swelled in my gut.

Both men's eyes went to the red and green flannel shirts as soon as I tugged them free. We all stood there a moment, thick silence filling the room while I clutched the clothing, willing myself to give them up.

Clearing my throat, I draped the shirts over the back of the couch. "Would you please make sure Neo gets these?"

"Uhh…" Fletch stuttered as if he, too, didn't know what to say.

Beau stepped in, saving the entire situation. "Sure thing. I'll make sure he gets them."

His voice was calm and clear, an anchor in the sea in which I was drowning. Gripping that anchor, I smiled, released the shirts, and stepped back.

Awkward silence descended again, so I went to the door, pulling it open. "Thank you again."

Just moments ago, I'd been homesick and wrought with anxiety about leaving, and now I was rushing down the stairs, past the bar, and out onto the sidewalk. The only thought in my head was to leave.

The moment I appeared, my bodyguard approached, guiding me to the waiting SUV and ushering me inside.

"Miss?" my driver said, glancing in the rearview to where I sat.

Summoning a smile I didn't feel, I answered, "Back to the Upper East Side, please."

The car drifted away from the curb, slowly going down the street, leaving behind a place I was going to miss and passing by a man standing at the end of the block, clad in all black and lurking in the shadows.

I was so busy trying to calm my tender heart that I didn't feel him watching as the SUV drove away.

Fifty-Six

Huntsman

The people who hired me were no-conscience scumbags, but even they knew better than to cross a killer.

Remember when I said that?

Apparently, there was an exception to this.

That exception stepped inside my place of business dressed in a black velvet cloak tied together by a black satin ribbon just below their chin. Even though the hood was lifted and the fabric draped in a concealing fashion nearly to the ground, I still knew who she was upon first sight.

Shock rippled through me first because this was something that never happened. My identity was a closely guarded secret, a well-kept mystery. No one knew who I really was despite the many attempts to find out.

No one had ever come looking for me. No one had ever dared.

So to see this person now, standing there staring from beneath the shadow of the velvet covering, arrogant superiority radiating off her like a thick, sickening perfume, was definitely surprising in a world where I was never surprised.

I wouldn't ask how they found me. I wouldn't give them the satisfaction or even the knowledge that I didn't know. If this person located me, I would act as if it were because I allowed it. I would never show weakness, not ever.

"Coming here is an ill-advised move," was all I said, my voice low and deep.

"Taking money for a job you were paid for and not doing it is imprudent."

"Do you think your classy words make you less trashy?"

"Do you think crossing the most powerful woman in this city makes you smart?"

Coming out from around the counter, I stepped toward the woman, burrowing my eyes into the shadows of the cape, not showing an ounce of the satisfaction I felt when she wavered on her heels.

"If you were the most powerful woman in this city, Ivory would already be dead," I taunted.

Her intake of breath was so sharp and deep the fabric fell back, revealing her face. White-blond hair could be seen at the top of her forehead, all of it swept back under the concealment.

Her skin was flawless but made up, the foundation she wore lighter than her actual skin tone as if she were trying to appear purer than she actually was.

Her eyes were blue but nothing like those of her step-daughter, and her cheekbones slanted harshly, giving her a sharp appearance.

"How dare you?" she hissed, voice cold.

"What are you doing here, Audra White? Why would you darken my door?"

Alarm flashed over her face when I spoke her name loud and clear. Only after quickly ducking back under the concealment of the cape did she speak.

"Your door is already black. I paid you for a job, a job you failed to do. I want it completed."

"No."

She cackled. "No?"

"No."

"You are in no position to refuse. I could have you locked up for the rest of your life in a cell like the animal that you are."

Unfazed, I raised a brow. "And how will you do that, tell the authorities that you hired me to kill your stepdaughter?" As I spoke, I stepped closer and closer until I could bend down and peer into the hood.

She was a mean woman… but I was far meaner.

She knew it. She saw it in my stare, felt it in the air.

"Go ahead and try me," I whispered sinisterly. "You'll find out just how good at my job I am when I want to be."

"Did she pay you? Did she offer you more than I did to spare her life?"

"No."

"Her charm. Her beauty," She muttered, pulling her gaze away from my intense one. "I shouldn't have underestimated it. It casts a spell over everyone, including her father. *Gah.*" She choked as my hand filled with the black velvet, yanking so hard she was no longer on her feet.

"Don't ever come here again. Don't ever contact me. Don't breathe a word of any of this… to anyone. If you do, I'll kill *you*."

Eyes practically popping from her skull, skin turning as white as her fake makeup, she gasped. "Did she… pay you to kill… me?"

"I would kill you for free." I snarled, releasing the hold on her garment and watching her fall to the floor.

Beneath the velvet, she panted and scrambled, standing up like she hadn't been knocked down at all. "How dare you threaten me this way? You know who I am."

"Yes. And as I already said, if you were as powerful as you think, she would already be dead."

The atmosphere in the room turned dim and sinister as if the extreme change in her demeanor could affect the very air.

Eyes flashing, lips pursing, her spine straightened and fingers that showed her age reached out to point at me. "You're right. Years ago, I was much smarter. If you want something done, it's always best to just do it yourself."

My eyes narrowed. A chill crept up my spine.

"Stay out of my way, and I'll stay out of yours," she intoned, the cloak spinning around her legs like slithering, loyal snakes before billowing out into a black cloud escorting her out the door.

I stood there a long time, thinking of how this happened and of how many rules I broke. Never once did this job ever bother me. Never once did the conscience I thought I didn't have rear its ugly head.

I was bothered now.

Closing myself in my small office in the back, I glared at the white paper bag sitting on my desk. Angry, I overturned the contents, staring down.

Picking up the white fabric, I unfolded and held it up. It was a small onesie made for a dog. On the back was a drawing of a mirror and the words, *The most beautiful reflection in the mirror is yours.*

I dropped the shirt as though I'd been burned, my stomach twisting with disgust.

It landed on a small black box I hadn't noticed at first. Taped on the lid was a folded piece of paper, and I snatched it up, nearly ripping it in half while unfolding it.

Earth,

Please don't be mad, but I wanted to give you something.

XO ~ Ivory

Ripping open the lid of the small box, I stared down at a glistening bright-red apple charm attached to a long silver chain.

Everything on the desk rattled and fell over when my fist slammed into the wood. Grabbing the necklace, I wrenched open the door and stalked back out into the bar.

Chest heaving, I stood in the center, not knowing what to do with the sudden overwhelming emotion pummeling me from every angle. Everything was so fucked up. How could I let things get this far?

My eyes fell onto the giant sign hanging behind the bar. My bar.

Rotten Apple: Poisoning Guaranteed.

My hand was shaking when I glanced down to the apple charm clenched tightly in my fist.

Yes. Poisoning guaranteed. But the poison wasn't the beer.

It was me.

Fifty-Seven

Ivory

I rescheduled my late-afternoon meeting because I was too drained to attend. I'd give myself the rest of the day to regroup, and then tomorrow I would return to normalcy. Whatever that was.

Ensconced in my penthouse, towering above the city, I poured a glass of red wine and sipped at it slowly while staring over the view.

Funny how everything was exactly the same, but it all looked so different.

Sighing, I set aside the glass and went to my walk-in to change out of the black dress hugging my body. It felt suffocating and uncomfortable, and I wanted it off. Once it was removed, I stood in fresh undergarments, pondering my choices.

Going for comfort, I selected a pair of yellow satin trousers with white piping on the outer seams and around the round pockets. The loose material floated over my body, whispering softly against my skin when I moved. Next, I pulled out an oversized pale-blue shirt. It was an updated, more casual version of a dress shirt. The material was all cotton, and I left the few top buttons undone so I had room to breathe. Since the shirt was oversized and long, I tied it at the waist, knotting it into a bow.

Removing the satin bow from my hair, I finger-combed through the loose curls and exited my room barefoot. The sudden chime of the doorbell changed the direction I was headed, a surge of adrenaline spiking through my veins without warning.

Neo.

Had he gone home to find I'd been there, that I returned his shirts? Was he upset he missed me…? Did he miss me?

I missed him.

No, it hadn't been that long. But still, I missed him.

Grabbing the door, I pulled it open, hope making it impossible to breathe.

Disappointment shattered that hope, my whole body sagging. The person standing there was not Neo. In fact, it was someone I really wasn't prepared to see.

"Ivory, dear? Is everything all right?" My stepmother fretted, the cape she wore moving around her feet as she stepped closer.

The security behind her also stepped forward, concern written on their features.

There was a brief but noticeable pause during the time it took me to swallow and pull myself free of the crushed hope. *Maybe he doesn't miss you at all.*

But then I spoke. "Oh! Audra! Of course, everything is just fine. I was just surprised to see you there. I wasn't expecting you."

"Do forgive me for not calling first. But I don't think a mother needs an appointment to see her daughter. Especially after everything she's been through!"

A mother?

"And I just felt so remorseful that I wasn't able to come sooner. The shock of your disappearance, your attempted murder, and then reappearance... Well, I just could barely process it all."

Imagine how I must feel. "Of course, it's been a difficult time." I empathized. "Please come in."

Holding the door wider, I stepped back, allowing her to glide in. Her pale hair was pinned away from her face in a style she often favored. Audra was a very beautiful woman. Classic beauty radiated around her, and usually, wherever we went, she was the most beautiful in the room.

Despite her age, she looked young, and beyond that, she always acted as if she were in her prime.

"I brought this basket of treats," she said, gesturing to a huge wicker basket piled high with fruit. "I'm sure you could use the nutrients."

"So kind of you." I thanked her, gesturing for us to move into the open kitchen.

Placing the basket on the counter, Audra untied the satin holding the cape around her.

"Would you like some tea?" I asked.

"That would be lovely." She agreed, draping the velvet over one of the stools.

She was dressed in a long pencil skirt in a classic houndstooth pattern. It hugged her slim hips impeccably and was paired with a long-sleeved deep-burgundy sweater with pleating at the shoulders to give it a very tailored feel. The sweater itself also hugged her body and was tucked into the waistband of the skirt to show off her trim waist.

"Please tell me how you're doing, dear. You look positively exhausted," she implored, perching onto a stool with perfectly straight posture.

Before, I probably wouldn't have thought twice about the remark. I mean, I *was* exhausted, and she did seem concerned. But now I was suspicious. The rumors Marco shared ran rampant through my thoughts.

"It's been a long several days," I said, pulling out teacups, saucers, and a wooden box filled with a selection of teas. "The police questioned me several times."

"Were you able to tell them anything helpful? I can't bear the thought of that *criminal* out there plotting another attack."

"I don't think I was any help," I replied sadly, pouring steaming water into each cup.

When we were settled beside each other and our tea prepared, I turned my full gaze onto my stepmother. "I just can't imagine who would do something like this."

Making a tsking sound, she reached out to touch the ends of my hair. "And your hair," she said sadly. "It was so beautiful."

"Ethan told me you contacted him right away when I went missing so he could cover my business."

"It was the least I could do. I hadn't given up hope, not even after they said you could be dead. I knew you'd come home, and I didn't want you to have to worry about the businesses."

"Well, I don't do the daily operation for *W*. You know that. I own the company, but it's run by the team of directors Daddy put in place before he died."

"Your father was very thorough in planning for anything that could have happened."

I made a sound of agreement and sipped my tea.

"I still miss him every day," she said, her voice filled with emotion. "He meant everything to me."

My cup made a delicate clang when I set it on the saucer. A pang of something hit me upon hearing the feelings in her words.

Placing aside her own tea, she reached out, covering my hand with hers. "This is why I am so grateful you are home and well. I wouldn't have been able to bear another loss. It comforts me so to have you here, to have a piece of your father still in my life." Tears swam in her eyes, making them glisten and shine. Her nude-painted lips turned in as she composed herself and then released them, letting out a shaky breath.

That little pang of something was guilt. Guilt that I could ever think so low of her. It was true she was usually indifferent, cool, and we weren't close, but to think she was trying to kill me?

There really wasn't a reason. As she just said, my father planned for everything—even his death. She was taken care of for the rest of her life. She wouldn't want for anything. Killing me would give her nothing.

"I know we've never been close." She went on, patting my hand. "And I apologize. I don't have any motherly instincts, but I've always been proud of you and I'm relieved you are all right."

"Thank you," I whispered, emotion piercing my heart. I hadn't realized how I'd longed to hear that. How much I'd wanted her acceptance.

Both my parents were dead. I was an only child... All I had was my stepmother. Perhaps the silver lining in all of this chaos would be a stronger relationship with her.

Sniffling a bit, she smiled. "How about some fruit?" she suggested, glancing at the giant gift basket.

"It does look delicious." I agreed, eyeing a particularly shiny red apple.

"Don't these apples look gorgeous?" she said, following my gaze. "I told them I wanted the best they had, and they certainly delivered."

"It all looks amazing." I looked over the various selection of fruit.

Reaching into the back of the basket, she grabbed a knife, then reached for the apple.

"You brought a knife?" I asked, surprised.

"The company I ordered this from said they put one in every basket."

"Of course."

"Frankly, I think it should include a diamond tiara, considering what I paid for it." She laughed.

The knife slid easily through a section of the apple as she cut out a small piece for herself and then handed me the rest of the plump-looking fruit.

"Don't you want more?" I asked, taking what she offered.

"There's plenty. Besides, it's a mother's joy to see her child fed."

A weird feeling tingled the base of my spine.

Setting aside the knife, Audra took a bite of the apple. "Mm," she said around the snack. "It's delicious."

"It certainly looks it." I agreed.

"Try it, try it," she insisted, pushing my hand and the apple toward my lips.

My teeth cut through the crisp fruit, juice exploding over my tongue. Sweet tanginess filled my senses as Audra smiled. Chewing, I returned her smile. "Very delicious."

Juice dripped down the back of my throat, creating a tickle.

My tongue started to swell, the rapidness with which it blew up creating immediate panic to seize me.

Clutching the apple, I started to wheeze, air becoming something so hard to find. Lifting a hand to my throat, I began to gag, my lips turning numb and a fuzzy feeling stinging my entire body.

Heaving, I was desperate for air.

Frightened, I reached for Audra, the woman I'd just given the benefit of the doubt. She slapped my hand away and cackled.

"Stupid girl!" She cackled again. "If I had known you

would be this gullible, I would have just handled you myself long ago!"

The sound of my throat rattling filled the room. My tongue felt so wide and hot I wanted to vomit. My hand flailed, searching for relief, and hit the basket. It tumbled over, fruit spilling everywhere.

Nearly collapsing on the island, I wheezed, reaching around for something. Anything. Numbly, I noticed my hand bump against something.

Through tear-soaked, blurry eyes, I saw it.

The strawberries.

Beneath all the fruit in the basket Audra had brought was a pile of bright-red strawberries.

Angry, I wrenched up, ignoring the way the room swam and the way my lungs screamed. Grabbing the basket, I threw it at her.

She cackled again, her laugh wild and chilling.

With that last burst of strength, I collapsed, sprawling onto the kitchen floor with the apple still clutched in my hand.

"Stupid, stupid girl." Audra preened, staring down at my struggling form. "All I had to do was rub that berry all over that apple, cut up some with that knife, and then pile all the *safe* fruit on top. You had no idea."

The apple! My sluggish, oxygen-deprived brain worried. I was still touching it. Still poisoning my body.

It seemed to take forever to pry my fingers away from the red flesh, but when I did, it fell out of my palm beside me.

My entire body felt as if it were on fire, burning from the inside out. My skin hurt, my face hurt, and I couldn't breathe or swallow.

Tears leaked out of my eyes, rushing over my cheeks and dripping onto the floor I lay on.

"W-w-why?" I gasped, wanting to know why I had to die.

"Yes, your father left me more than enough money," Audra answered right away, probably eager to spill the hate she'd carried around for so long. "But when he died, so did a lot of my power."

I couldn't understand. My brain just didn't comprehend.

Gasp. Rasp. Wheeze. If only I could get to my EpiPen. If only…

"That stupid man left you W and with it, all the power. But it's not you who's to be the most powerful in this city! It's me! I earned this! It's my time to enjoy everything I worked for. If you had died all those years ago like you were supposed to, then all would already be mine!"

Everything went quiet. Her screaming, incensed tone dropped away as if I'd been plunged into the depths of an ocean, the water so deep and thick it muted every sound.

Dry, cracked lips moved, but no sound came out. Tears stopped falling as though my body had nothing more to give.

My heart squeezed, lungs seared, and my vision began to fade.

Mirror, mirror on the wall... who's the most powerful of them all?

I stared up, straining to see the woman who hated me enough to kill. The last words I would ever hear echoed within my head. *If you had died all those years ago like you were supposed to...*

Darkness.

Fifty-Eight

Neo

Curiosity nearly starved me, but I endured. Even though I knew she was gone, butterflies still buzzed beneath my ribcage, and an unsteady feeling hummed through my limbs when I opened the apartment door, stepping inside.

It was almost like I could still feel her presence. Her scent and aura still lingered in the air. The second I stepped inside, a wave of homesickness slammed into me, staggering in intensity. Why would I be homesick while standing in the middle of my home?

Why did I inhale deeper, trying to claim what was left of her scent?

I missed her so much I'd turned into some kind of desperate rodent searching for crumbs.

Beau and Fletch looked up, disappointment filling their gazes when finding only me. Like they, too, missed her presence and wanted it back.

Beau grunted. "I was starting to think you were never coming home."

"I've been working a lot," I mumbled, but everyone knew what I was really doing was hiding.

"Ivory was here," Fletcher announced, holding up a

colorful mug as though he'd won some award. "Look what she gave me!"

The tightening of my heart made it hard to swallow as I took in the gift. "She came by to give you a gift?" I asked, trying to keep my tone even.

Fletch nodded, but then his face fell. "Seemed like she wanted to say good-bye."

A cold wind howled through my suddenly hollow heart.

"Don't be dramatic," Beau scolded. "It was more of a thank-you."

Swallowing, I nodded, my eyes zeroing in on the familiar red and green shirts draped over the back of the couch.

A pregnant pause filled the room. Then Beau cleared his throat. "Ivory asked me to give those to you."

"How'd she get them anyway?" Fletch wondered out loud.

Fingertips brushing over the green shirt, I remembered the way she looked tucked into her cloud-like bed, wrapped in my shirt.

She brought it back... "I have to piss," I declared, taking myself into the bathroom and slamming the door.

My fingers throbbed from gripping the edge of the pedestal sink so tight, my head hanging between my shoulder blades as emotion pummeled my heart.

I had no right to feel angry or hurt because I was the one who left.

Sniffing, I looked up, catching my wrung-out reflection in the mirror. *Mirror, mirror on the wall, who's the stupidest of them all?*

"You," I whispered, spinning away in disgust.

My eyes landed on the row of cups and toothbrushes... specifically the pink one. Longing so potent filled me up so there was no room for any fear.

Why was I doing this? Why was I pushing her away?

I stalked into the other room, pacing, feeling like a lion

trapped in some kind of too-small cage. Fletcher started to speak, but I growled, which sent him scurrying off into the bathroom for safety.

"I don't know what's going on between you two," Beau said quietly, "but if it helps at all, she clearly misses you."

"It doesn't," I snapped.

"Maybe it should."

The door banged open without warning, slamming so hard against the wall that everything nearby rattled dangerously.

I spun, whatever I would say to Beau forgotten. Fletch ran out of the bathroom as though there could be some freak earthquake, his footsteps halting when he saw Earth darkening the room.

The bartender's near-black eyes glittered dangerously, his chest rising and falling with heavy breaths. The fingers at his sides were pure white from the force with which he clenched his fists. Even my churned-up mood seemed to pale in comparison to the gale-force storm raging inside him.

It was something... something I'd never seen before. *Wickedness.* It was the only way I could describe it. And while no one in this room was pure of heart or clear of crime, this felt different.

Yet somehow *familiar.*

Tingles of warning exploded at the back of my neck, racing up and down my spine, muddying my thoughts.

"Earth?" I questioned, leveling my complete attention on the keyed-up man. "What's wrong?"

A sharp inhale of breath.

A shadow of dread behind his intense stare.

The tingles morphed to full-blown screams. Just as I was about to shout, his chest puffed out with a great inhale.

"It's her stepmother. She's going to kill her. We might already be too late."

One second of suspended time that felt like one thousand years paused everything, shock silencing all but then dropping as if I hadn't just aged exponentially in the flash of a moment.

"What?"

"It's Ivory's stepmother. We have to go."

Beau's chair banged against the wall when he stood, abandoning his workstation without a second glance. Fletcher leaped over the back of the couch, not questioning anything Earth said. Both of them rushed to the door, making enough noise for an entire herd of elephants.

But I just stood there rooted to the ground like someone had turned my legs to stone. As if my body were still frozen in that deferred moment.

"How do you know?" The question scraped out of me, its edges sharp, leaving the taste of blood on my tongue.

"That's not important right now!" Earth barked, turning to usher everyone out.

But it was. I knew its importance down to my core.

Fletcher and Beau stared between us, suddenly sensing my mood.

Fletch glanced at Earth. "Earth?"

Earth stiffened but didn't retreat. "Because I didn't do it for her."

I—*What?* It made no sense. I struggled to understand, but even so, I moved, feet light, flying over the ground, knocking into Earth and pinning him against the wall. Despite my trouble comprehending, adrenaline and anger were fully present.

Earth knocked me away, halting the impending attack with his words. "She might already be dead."

My vision flickered, turning everything in the room to black and white.

No more color. No more life.

I rushed out of the apartment, hearing everyone else close behind. Snort's heavy breathing followed us down the stairs as we raced out onto the sidewalk.

"How are we going to get to the Upper East Side so fast? Traffic this time of day is always jammed." Fletch worried.

Pulling out his phone, Beau said, "We can run for a while. I'll order a car to meet us halfway."

I started to run, but something slammed into the middle of my back. An unexpected flashback from the night at the fish market flooded my racing mind. Pain radiated through my skull as I recalled the hit, remembered falling...

"Follow me," Earth ordered, hand gripping the center of my back, half dragging me until my feet got with the program and I began to run.

"We don't have time for this!" I roared, wondering why we were going deep into some random alley and not toward the main street.

"Help me." Earth grunted, throwing his weight into a large dumpster against the building.

All of us did as he asked, the giant metal bin sliding out of the way to reveal a garage door. A door I didn't even know existed.

"What is this?" Beau asked.

Earth hit a code, and the door lifted, revealing a small space.

Beau whistled low the second the vintage black muscle car came into sight. It was equipped with some obvious upgrades, filling the hood with chrome.

"Let's go," Earth declared, rushing to the driver's side, Snort hot on his heels.

Breaking glass, weightlessness, blood, vacant eyes... death.

More flashbacks barraged my mind, twisting my stomach and making it hard to breathe.

A loud slapping against metal sound snapped me out of it,

and my head shot up. Earth was pounding on the roof, signaling for me to get in.

A vision of Ivory swam behind my eyes and, with it, fear I never wanted to feel again. Feet pounding over pavement, I jumped into the car as the engine roared to life, the rumble so intense the entire car vibrated.

"You gonna be okay?" Earth asked, flicking me a look of concern.

"Just go."

He didn't ask twice. Hell, I was surprised he asked at all. The car squealed out of the hidden parking space, fishtailing slightly with the excessive speed he started with. The alley filled with smoke from the exhaust and spinning tires as he fired ahead, not even pausing before drifting out onto the road.

Sounds of that night from seven years ago filled the back of my mind, and bile burned my esophagus. Gripping the handle above my head, I gave Earth a look. "Faster."

Steering expertly through the streets of New York City, Earth maneuvered the car none of us knew he had through alleyways and over curbs and disobeyed every law and sign as he went. The loud purr of the modified engine drowned out everything except the thrashing of my heart.

Vicious memories from that long-ago night and the more recent one when we were attacked at the fish market clashed in my head, blurring together to create one giant nightmare.

Every moment that passed by made me sweat harder, made me wonder if we were too late.

I was selfish. Cowardly. I wanted her so badly, but I walked out. I let fear and pride rule my actions… but they had never been able to rule my heart.

And now here I was, racing to the woman I loved despite trying desperately not to. It didn't matter that I was too afraid to fall. I fell anyway.

And now she might be dead.

Taken away like almost everyone else.

At least they knew how much you loved them. But Ivory could die thinking I didn't care. Thinking she didn't mean anything at all.

"Hurry up!" I roared, pounding on the dash.

Moments later, Earth muscled the car up over the side-walk, forcing people to dive out of the way. The car had barely stopped, and I was already out, leaping over the hood and racing inside the building.

The doorman tried to stop me, but I evaded, slamming my hand over the elevator button repeatedly.

"You can't just barge in here!" he yelled.

"Call up to Ivory White's penthouse. She's in danger!"

"Danger?" The man wondered. "Nonsense, she's with her stepmother."

How did Earth know? Impatience roared through my body, panic pummeling me, and I nearly fell into the elevator doors when they sprang open.

"Wait!" Beau yelled, stopping the doors from closing as the rest of my friends pushed past the shocked doorman.

"Call the police!" I screamed again as the doors closed.

Inside the elevator, we were quiet, but it was far from silent. If anything, it felt like I was standing in a room filled with screams. When the car finally stopped, I nearly forced the doors open, racing into the hall.

Bodyguards stood on post. All of them knew me. All of them stiffened when I rushed close.

"Open the door!" I roared.

"We can't—"

My fist stopped the rest of the words, and the man slumped to the ground.

Swinging around to the other guard, I was about to

demand the same, but the door opened from the inside and every single man crowding the hall turned.

A woman wearing a midnight-colored cloak came out, the fabric billowing around her like there was some kind of force moving around.

The lights in the hall flickered, making an eerie buzzing sound.

Though her footsteps paused, the cloak still wafted around her. Gazing into the shadows of the fabric, I prayed I'd see familiar red lips and pale skin.

I didn't.

I saw a woman who might have been beautiful if it weren't for the pure evil in her stare.

Shock rounded her eyes before they glinted. "Intruders!" she declared, a bony finger appearing from beneath the length of the cloak to point with a coffin-shaped nail. "Get them!"

Chaos erupted, but I left it all behind, pushing into the familiar home.

"Ivory!" I screamed. "Ivory White, answer me!"

Silence echoed back, making my knees weak.

Racing around the corner, my foot collided with something small and firm. It skittered across the floor from the force of my kick.

An apple.

It wasn't the only piece of fruit on the floor, though. There was more. A few oranges lay haphazardly around, a few stray grapes. Just as I stepped farther, my feet halted.

Strawberries.

Big, fat, brilliantly red strawberries were scattered everywhere.

In the center of it all was Ivory, sprawled lifelessly on the hard floor, lips no longer rose red but blue like death.

Falling to my knees, I bumped into another piece of fruit,

a piece that was close to Ivory's limp, open hand.

A polished apple missing a single bite.

She bit into that apple, not suspecting it had been poisoned. Poisoned by berries she likely hadn't seen until it was too late.

Knocking away the offending fruit, I took her face in my palms. Images of my parents dead on the street tried to pull me under, tried to steal what little sanity I had left.

Fuck those taunts and fuck that panic. If I let them pull me under, then Ivory would be lost too.

"Ivory!" I shook her, watching her head loll to the side.

Not only were her lips blue and puffy, but hives marred her limbs.

Leaning down, I tried to listen or feel for breath. Brushing her hair away, I searched for a pulse.

It was so faint, so barely there that I would have missed it if I hadn't felt a tiny beat of hope before the others rushed in.

"What happened?" Beau worried, dropping on her other side.

"Call 9-1-1! Now!" I roared, tilting her head back and using my finger to sweep her airway. "Find me an EpiPen. There has to be one somewhere!"

Security rushed in, but I paid them no mind, already administering CPR.

Please don't die. Please don't go.

Noise and people moved around us, but I remained focused on Ivory, on bringing her back.

"Here."

An EpiPen was thrust under my nose just as I was going back in to give her more breaths. I glanced up, meeting Earth's serious, stony eyes.

Knowledge passed between us.

There was so much I had to say to him... So much anger...

You don't have time right now. Snatching the pen, I pulled it open, yanked up her shirt, and jammed it into her stomach.

I told myself to be gentle, but the fear was all too real. She'd likely have a bruise from how hard I pushed it in, but honestly, a bruise was better than a funeral.

Nothing happened, and a sound of immense frustration echoed around us. The pen slapped against a nearby wall, clattering to the floor, and I went back to CPR.

I was still working, sweat dripping off my forehead and slipping between my shoulder blades when someone pulled me away from her.

Glancing over my shoulder, I saw Earth, and I started to fight.

I fought like hell, trying to get free, trying to get back to her side. The sounds of my wheezing filled the room as I struggled. My lungs lacked air because I'd given most of it to her.

"Neo, the EMTs will help her now!" Fletcher said. His frightened honey-colored stare swam in front of me, brown hair falling over his forehead.

I blinked.

"Look," Earth, said, swinging around to show me that the emergency responders were indeed surrounding Ivory.

I slumped, the fight leaving me instantly. I might have fallen if Earth hadn't still been holding me up. But then the brevity of the situation slammed into me hard, and I yanked free, standing on my own two feet.

Beau was still on the other side, staring down at Ivory as the men worked.

"Is she…?" My voice shook.

"She has a pulse but is unresponsive. The sooner we get her to the hospital, the better," someone answered.

Ivory was lifted off the ground via a stretcher, oxygen already strapped over her nose and lips. She was so small and fragile-looking but still so beautiful it broke my heart.

What have you done, Neo?

I should have been here. I shouldn't have been such a coward.

"I'm coming with you," I called, following behind them as we left the penthouse. One of the bodyguards opened his mouth, and I shot him a look that shut him up.

Out in the hall, a few of her guards were on the floor, nursing obvious hits they'd taken. Fletcher shifted from foot to foot at the elevator, holding it open for us.

I didn't notice the woman until I had to step over her body sprawled in the middle of the hall, the cloak spread out around her like black blood seeping out of her. The hood fell back to reveal white-blond hair wildly framing a face that suddenly seemed older than before. The lines creasing her mouth and eyes aged her. Her lips were crinkled as if they'd spent much of their life being pursed in judgment. One hand had fallen palm up near her face, the fingers bony and wrinkled.

This woman thought she was a queen, but in reality, she was nothing but a wicked witch.

Over my shoulder, I sought Earth, knowing why seeing that woman made me also think of him but still unable to fully admit it to myself. "You did that?"

"She deserved it."

I wouldn't disagree.

"I'll stay until the police haul her away."

A fleeting thought of whether he should be here when the cops arrived filtered through my mind, but I pushed it down and followed Ivory into the elevator.

That wasn't my problem right now.

Before the doors were even closed, I turned my back, reaching between the EMTs for Ivory's cool hand.

All that mattered right now was her.

Fifty-Nine

Ivory

Gray clouds filled the sky like thick smoke, an ominous warning something was brewing. Something sinister and inescapable.

Even as an innocent child, I felt the eeriness awash in the air. I felt it reach for my bones. But as any innocent child, I felt safe with my hand in my mother's. With the smiles donning both our faces.

"That was the best show yet!" I declared. The fancy dress we'd bought just for this night out flounced around my knees.

"I have to agree," Mommy said, blue eyes shining like jewels no jeweler would ever be able to find. At least that's what Daddy always said, that Mommy had the most beautiful sapphires in her eyes.

Her black hair was pulled loosely at the nape of her neck, a curtain of shining bangs making her eyes shine even brighter. Her dress was royal blue, the shawl around her shoulders custom created.

"I wish Daddy could have come with us," I said as everyone made their way toward the front of the theater.

"Me too, sweetheart, but he had an important meeting. Next time."

My daddy was always busy with work, but it was okay because it gave me and Mommy extra time together.

Stopping in the middle of the aisle, she leaned down so we were at eye level. "How about we get some ice cream?"

"Frozen hot chocolate!" I declared.

"Hmm, you drive a hard bargain." Mommy laughed and then agreed.

On the way home, pride swelled in my tummy because I hadn't spilled any of the frozen treat on my new dress, and we got to sit at the best table in the house.

"What show will we see next?" I called up from the back seat.

But mom didn't answer. Instead, she was whispering with our driver.

"Mom!" I called out. "Mommy!"

Sudden bright lights shone into the back of the car, making me squint and turn. A car was so close to us it made me scream.

Bang!

My small body flung forward. If not for the seatbelt, I would have hit my head. Groaning, screeching metal and squealing tires filled the night, drowning out all the happy feelings and thoughts I'd been filled with.

"Mommy!" I cried, tears streaking my face.

"Get down!" Mom said urgently, her reassuring hand trembling as it pushed me down toward the floor. "Get down there and don't get up."

"But Mom—"

"Go on strongly despite the fear," she whispered, lowering her face to mine. "It's okay, peanut. You can do it. Everything will be okay."

Nodding, I did as Mommy said, making myself small on the floorboard of the car as another crash made me cry.

"They're trying to run us off the road!" The driver grunted, and the sudden jerking of the car made all the frozen hot chocolate I'd just drunk threaten to come right back up.

"Whatever happens, please save Ivory!" Mommy begged.

Thunder exploded overhead, drowning out everything else and making me shake. Lightning so violent and bright cracked down and lit the interior of the car.

It didn't matter how loud I sobbed. The terrible raging storm drowned it out, and then the car was fishtailing, swerving all over the road, and a weightless feeling lifted me as though I were being sucked into a tornado and tossed around by the angry gale.

Pain radiated in my side when I hit the seat, and then I was tossed up, my head smacking against the glass...

Darkness.

Sheets of rain pelted the car, loud metallic booms waking me from my unconscious state. With the sky rumbling overhead, my body quaked as I pushed up, feeling sick to my tummy.

"Mommy?" I called out.

She was reaching out for me, her long, slender fingers extended between the seats. I grabbed onto them, not liking how unusually cold and stiff they felt.

Why didn't they wrap around mine?

"Mommy," I said, giving them a tug.

She didn't respond. I sat up, and the tinkling of something falling drew my eyes. Diamonds littered the floor and my dress... everywhere I looked.

"Pretty," I whispered, reaching for one of the jewels. "Ouch!" I cried the moment it pierced me, blood welling across my finger.

Not diamonds. Glass. Broken glass.

Calling for my mother again, I crawled between the seats, trying to see why she wasn't answering.

She was hunched over the middle of the car, arm still reaching for me, dark hair covering her face. All her pretty skin was stained red. Drops of the deep color were splattered everywhere.

Screaming, I grabbed her arm and shook, ignoring that now my hand was smeared with red too.

"Mommy! Wake up! Wake up, Mommy!" I pushed her, and she rolled slightly, her body slumping into a new position.

My scream raged war with the pounding storm as her empty

eyes stared straight ahead. Red streaks marbled her face, making her look like she was wearing some sort of scary Halloween mask.

"Mr. Tom!" I cried, looking to our driver, hoping he could wake Mommy.

A huge gash ran across his head, his face completely unrecognizable and more blood on his outsides than in.

Heaving, I fell into the back seat, vomiting everything in my tummy everywhere.

Crying, sniffling, and gagging, I pushed up, terrified by the storm, even more so by the death inside the car.

Across the road, light shone, streaking through the unrelenting rain like beacons of hope in the night.

"Help!" I screamed, beating on the window, feeling like I might throw up again.

The window slid down, and the storm seemed to clear just enough for me to see a woman staring back. A woman I kind of recognized but didn't know from where. I yelled for help again, crying harder than before.

The window rolled back up, and they started to drive away.

A sick feeling I didn't understand clawed at my already sore throat, but then the car turned back and I thought everything would be okay.

Instead of slowing, the car seemed to speed up, the headlights shining so bright I had to lower my face and hide my eyes.

Crash!

The car groaned and moved again, slamming into something hard and unforgiving. Suddenly, water started seeping in through every crack and crevice. Icy-cold drops forced their way in like an army, swallowing up everything inch by inch.

I screamed and panicked, all the private swimming lessons I'd had forgotten in a second. As I flailed about, water gobbled up the car, my limbs stiffening as cold wrapped around tendon and bone.

Breathing was nearly impossible, and my throbbing head made it hard to see.

"Mommy!" I gasped, the water weighing down the dress I'd loved so dearly. "Mommy, please wake up."

Cough. Cough. Choke.

Water tugged at my mommy's hair, swallowing it and pulling it under.

Her lips were blue, her eyes vacant.

But then her voice, a voice I would know anywhere, filled my head.

Go on strongly despite the fear, Ivory. Go out the broken window. Go!

I sobbed and cried, clinging to her prone fingers, not wanting to let her go, but wanting to do as told.

The car groaned, sinking a little deeper into the murky water that promised to have me for dinner if I didn't escape.

With one last look at my mother's face, I swam toward the window, holding on to her fingers until I couldn't anymore.

Water swallowing me, I held my breath and pushed through the broken window, somehow forcing my way through the water. Pushing, swimming... leaving my mother behind in the grim abyss.

The rush of air and violent coughing ripped apart my throat. Mud clung to my exhausted arms and legs, anchoring me to shore.

Vaguely, I stared back, teeth chattering, mind foggy, seeing the car I'd just abandoned gobbled up and swept out of sight.

There was no strength left for me to scream or cry. But inside, I shrieked and wailed until everything was gone. My anguish, my trauma, the blood... all of it drained away, perhaps swallowed like my mother, sinking to the bottom of the gloomy river where it would lay forgotten...

Until now.

Sixty

Neo

Ivory White lay still and motionless, inky hair fanning out across a snowy pillow, slender fingers linked, palms resting against her belly. Midnight lashes fanned across her cheeks. Red hives blotched what skin we could see, and a blanket hid the rest.

Even in sleep and trauma, she was more beautiful than anyone else, her pure and generous heart unmatched.

Four men stood soberly around a hospital bed, heads bowed as the sound of beeping monitors filled the silence. A normally snorting dog was also quiet, his head resting on the leg of the princess he'd grown to love.

Four misfits who trusted no one but each other, living in the middle of the Grimms behind a bunch of locks and defined by their crimes.

A goofy pickpocket who couldn't keep a job, a grouchy bartender who didn't like anyone, a recluse techy who barely looked up from his monitor, and a closed-off creative who wanted to love but was afraid.

She changed us all with just her presence. With her ridiculous words, screeching voice, and surprisingly kind acceptance.

We all loved her… But me?

I loved her most of all.

"What if she dies?" Fletcher suddenly wailed, sniffling, head hanging low.

"Don't say that!" I snapped, the very thought causing too much pain.

The door to the private room pulled open, and a nurse dressed completely in white strolled in. "My goodness! What are you all doing in here?" She gasped. "Dogs aren't allowed in the hospital!"

"It's fine, Ellen." A familiar voice made my face contort. "Just put an extra cleaning charge on the bill, and I'll be sure to pay," Ethan said smoothly, coming into the VIP suite right behind the nurse.

"But, I—" she argued, staring. No doubt, she noticed that we weren't the normal type to be visiting someone in a VIP suite.

"These are her friends. They found her and brought her in time. If not for them, Ivory might be dead."

The nurse's eyes went wide, and she nodded. "Well, I guess if Ethan says you're all welcome…"

Yes, because Ethan is her betrothed. Oh, the sour, unpleasant taste those thoughts released. Curling my lips, I couldn't even hide my displeasure.

"It's what Ivory would want." Ethan's voice was suave. In a surprising move, he gestured to me. "And this man is the one that Ivory loves."

The woman gasped. "But I thought—"

Ethan chuckled. "Yes, everyone thought that because we allowed them to." He agreed, winking at the nurse.

She turned to me. I felt my cheeks flush, but I didn't deny it. I would never deny the way I felt ever again.

"Would it be all right if I checked her vitals?" the nurse asked me instead of Ethan.

Stomach somersaulting, I agreed, gesturing for everyone

to move out of her way.

"She should be waking up soon," the nurse announced a few moments later before taking her leave.

Ethan approached, dressed in yet another suit with a bright-green tie and making me wonder if the man ever wore anything else. He extended a hand between us.

Locking eyes, I took his hand, shaking it firmly. "I love her too." I confirmed, staking my claim, not backing down.

He smiled, two dimples flashing, and yep, his tooth sparkled under the light. "I know."

Not exactly the reaction I expected. Not at all the reaction I would have given if I were in his shoes.

"Do you have a problem with that?" I challenged, testing his resolve, wondering just how big of a fight this was going to be. Not that it mattered. Victory would be mine. I was in Ivory's life now, and I wasn't leaving.

Ethan pursed his lips, almost amused. "Should I?"

My tongue slid over my front teeth. That smug look made me itch to deck his pretty-boy face. "Well, if I were you, I definitely would have a problem."

"Good thing you aren't me."

This asshole... Taking a menacing step toward him, I was intercepted by Fletch, who collided against my chest and bounced back.

Tripping over his own feet, he tipped over backward.

Oomph. His breath rushed out, and his eyes were squeezed closed as though he were anticipating a hard fall.

When none came, one eye squinted open, and then the other followed suit. "I expected that to hurt," he murmured.

"I'm not as hard as the floor."

Fletch's golden eyes nearly fell out of his head as he realized he hadn't hit the floor because someone caught him. Partially reclined into a broad chest, his wild hair clinging to that stupid green tie, Fletch tipped his head back, gazing up at the man who was still supporting nearly all his weight.

"You caught me," Fletcher said rather unnecessarily.

"Well, it was either that or watch you fall," Ethan replied, his hands looking so big wrapped around my friend.

Fletch's Adam's apple bobbed, and then he made a sound I'd never heard him make before.

He giggled.

Fletcher full-on giggled like… like some schoolgirl.

Shocked, I swung to look at Beau, who was also mind-blown and staring as though he'd entered the twilight zone.

"Up you go," Ethan said, his smug arrogance nowhere in attendance when he basically picked Fletch up and put him firmly back on his feet. "All good?"

Fletcher's head bobbed, his messy mass of hair bobbing with him.

"You should probably learn how to use those feet." Ethan pointed, and Fletcher blushed furiously.

On instinct, I turned, seeking out Earth to see if he was also watching Fletcher act even more absurd than normal. But the second my eyes landed on him, on the way he'd slipped into the back of the room, I remembered.

I remembered why we were here and that right now, Earth… was not my friend.

Turning away, I pinned Ethan with a glare. "How'd you know Ivory was here?"

Unbothered, he replied, "The doorman called me when the EMTs left the building with her."

Of course he did. Ethan probably got a call from everyone around Ivory when she so much as sneezed. That just pissed me off more.

Pulling out a cell from the inside of his jacket, he continued. "That reminds me. I need to try Audra again. I did before, but she's not picking up."

"She's not going to," Beau informed, his voice taking on a hard edge he normally did not have.

Ethan puzzled, forehead creasing. "Why?"

"Maybe because she's the one who put Ivory in here," I said.

Genuine shock contorted his face. "What? I thought Ivory had an allergic reaction."

A rude sound burst from my throat. "Yeah, to something Audra gave her that was tainted with strawberries."

He gasped. It was very dramatic. I was beginning to think it was a requirement to be overly dramatic on the Upper East Side.

"She wouldn't."

"You really believe that?" I questioned, tilting my head to the side. Did he really not know Ivory's stepmother was a witch?

"I mean, everyone knows Audra is a cold woman… but murder?"

He seemed sincerely surprised.

I didn't know him well enough to know if he was just a really good actor or if this was the truth. My instincts told me I could believe him, but the sight of Ivory lying in a bed made me doubt even myself. With her safety on the line, I needed more than just my instincts.

When I rotated, my eyes found Earth once more. He stood in the corner, almost lurking, just watching everything unfold.

Watching as if the bastard hadn't caused this.

His face flickered when he felt my gaze but didn't return the stare. An ache I didn't want to feel or acknowledge squeezed my chest and, with it, the bold rush of anger.

Still, I stared at him. Still, his word carried weight.

"He involved?" I asked, my voice rough and low.

Everyone's attention sharpened, Beau and Fletch dividing their gazes between me and Earth.

Bristling, Ethan spoke, "Involved in what?"

Earth's eyes flicked to Ethan, then to me. Unspoken truth passed between us. He knew I knew, and now there was tension between us that never existed before.

"No." He confirmed.

I believed him. Maybe after everything, I shouldn't have. But I did. Besides, why lie now that I knew? My fingers ached from the ferocity with which I squeezed my fists. They ached even when I unclenched them and turned away.

"What is going on here?" Ethan demanded, voice rising. "I want an explanation."

A barely audible sigh ended all conversation, every eye in the room turning to the sleeping beauty. Gently scooping her hand off her middle, I cradled it between mine.

"Ivory?" I whispered. "Ivory, wake up."

Another soft sound had us all leaning in, soundlessly watching as her long dark lashes began to flutter.

Endless moments stretched on until her eyes opened completely, her blue stare hazy when it landed on me.

"Princess," I whispered, relief making my voice weak. "You scared the hell out of me."

She blinked again, but then a sleepy smile curved her bow-shaped mouth. It was as if someone opened a cage filled with butterflies, releasing them all into my stomach where they went wild.

"You're here," she whispered.

"Of course I am."

"I've been waiting," she confessed, making the same butterflies erupt again.

How could I have ever made her wait?

Stroking her cheek, I swallowed. "I know."

"How are you feeling?" Ethan asked, moving up near her side.

Her eyes widened, confusion replacing the haze. "Ethan? What are you doing here?"

As if becoming fully aware, she glanced around, noting the IV taped to the back of her hand.

"Where am I?" She worried, starting to sit up too fast.

"Easy," I urged, gripping her shoulders and guiding her back down. "Take it easy."

"What happened?" Her eyes latched onto me, fear blazing in their depths.

"You ate something that touched a strawberry." I began, fury contaminating my emotions once more.

She gasped, a hand covering her mouth in shock. After a moment, her hand slid away. "The apple," she whispered, attention turning inward as memories clearly came flooding back. Shimmering eyes found mine. "Audra…"

"Shh." I soothed her, pushing her the rest of the way into the pillows. "We know. It's okay now. You're safe."

Her fingers wrapped around my wrist, their length not even able to reach fully around, clinging desperately. Her eyes implored I listen to her words.

"I remember." Her voice quaked, tears pooling in the corners of her eyes and immediately spilling over.

The pain radiating off her was palpable, so strong it dulled the fury eating me alive. Despite the tumultuous emotions attacking me, my voice remained gentle. "Remember what, sweetheart?"

More tears slid across her cheeks. More pain pierced my heart. "I remember when—" A choked sound left her throat. "After I took a bite of that apple."

The grip on my wrist slackened, and her teeth made sharp clacking noises as they began to chatter. Eyes glazing over as though whatever tormenting her was just too much, she began slipping away… limbs going limp, lashes falling against her cheeks.

Not again.

In a desperate attempt to pull her back, I did the only thing I could think of.

I kissed her.

Sixty-One

Ivory

My mother smiling. My mother screaming.
Drowning. Dying. Slipping away.
Breathing. Warmth. Anchored in place.

The faint brush of a tongue was unmistakable. The tip gliding along my lips, not asking for access but offering something far more valuable. The reassuring caress folding me in warmth and security, embracing everything I was feeling and telling me it was okay.

I didn't have to run anymore. I didn't have to protect myself so fiercely.

Reaching out, I answered the soft kiss, deepening it just a fraction. He didn't stop or pause when I took what he gave. Instead, his arms tightened all the more.

The watery grave trying to swallow me turned into friendly sunbeams on a spring day. A meadow filled with pink daisies, their petals brushing against my sun-kissed skin.

Withdrawing slowly, our lips parted, and I stared up at him with quiet awe. The worst of the storm quelled, my heart no longer consumed by chaos.

"It worked," someone whispered nearby.

"What worked?" someone else whispered.

"True love's kiss."

The infinite, glittering universe existing in his stare never wavered from mine. "Did I bring you back?" The husky quality of his words raised goose bumps along my arms.

I nodded. *You brought me back.*

"Where do you keep trying to go?" Neo asked, slightly chiding even though he spoke gently.

"Me?" I scoffed. "You're the one who walked out."

The smile on his lips was faint just like the stubble on his chin. "Touché."

"I'm not trying to go anywhere," I confessed. "It's my subconscious way of protecting myself."

"Protecting yourself from what?"

"From the past," I echoed, the chilling memory that flooded me like a nightmare when I lay dying on the floor rising within me again.

Suddenly, it all made sense. The unfamiliar panic that rose up out of nowhere, the way sometimes flashes of memory would attack and confuse. My phobia of rain, hatred of water.

I'd thought those things were just who I was.

No.

They were a product of something terrible a child should never endure. And because of that, my young mind repressed it all, locked it down deep, and threw away the key.

Until a single bite of a poisoned apple exposed the truth.

I groped for Neo's hand. Our fingers entwined together, and his strength rallied my own. Touching a brief gaze on everyone in the room, I didn't speak until my eyes came back to his.

"Your painting. The one where color seeped from your world…" I began, knowing it seemed like an odd place to start but feeling it was actually perfect.

Neo nodded, allowing me to lead.

"The car accident. The angel wings," I whispered, the claws of trauma scraping over my already abused heart.

He was there, enclosing his free hand around our linked ones. My skin was chilled, but his was warm and he rubbed gently, offering me every ounce of heat he contained.

"That morning I saw it, I felt it so deep. So deep I couldn't understand why it felt like it was part of me. But now I do."

Neo nodded, encouraging me to go on.

"It's a representation of what happened to you, right? To your family. How your world went from color to black and white."

He nodded again, visibly swallowing at the painful reminder. I understood how he felt. I understood in ways I hadn't before.

"It happened to me too," I confessed, crying again.

Crooning nonsensical sounds, he leaned in, brushing at the wetness, trying to soothe my pain even when he was filled with his own.

"Audra killed my mother when I was a little girl. She tried to kill me too."

The reaction from the men around us erupted, but Neo stayed still. Leaning close, placing his arms on either side of me, he used his body as a shield. "She tried to kill you before today?"

Chin wobbling, breath hitching, I went on. "They said it was a car accident. That it was just some sort of unfortunate thing. Daddy always told me he was thankful I hadn't been with her…" My eyes sought his, holding on. "But he lied."

Shock rippled over his features, but like a tree rooted in the wind, he stayed. "What do you mean?"

"I was with her. We were driving home from the theater. It was storming terribly. Great groaning thunder, pelting rain. The sound of it was so loud on the roof of the car that I started to cry. I was in the backseat, my mother and driver up front. Suddenly, someone screamed, and there was a violent jolt at the back of the car. The second time it happened, Mother shoved me onto the floorboards and told me to cover my head."

The sounds of crunching metal and then a horrible *bang* filled my ears.

"I waited for my mother to call out, to tell me it was okay to get up. But the silence stretched on, and I was so frightened."

Flashbacks of the repressed night assaulted me still. The blood. Her outstretched hand. The broken glass.

I was suddenly enveloped in a familiar scent. Comfort wrapped around me and, with it, a feeling of safety. "Stop," Neo begged, holding me tight but also cradling me with care. Cupping the back of my head, his fingers massaged my scalp as if he could banish the horrible memories. "You don't have to relive this again"

But I did. I'd been keeping it buried my whole life. It was time to face the truth, to face what that wicked woman had done to my mother and to me.

"I do," I insisted, pulling back so he could fully hear my words. "People need to know what she did. *I* need to face what she did."

"Audra?" Fletcher asked, his voice reminding me we weren't alone. For a little while, I'd fallen into a place where it was only me and Neo.

Briefly, I glanced around to where four men stood, faces drawn, eyes wide as they, too, heard everything I described.

"That wicked woman," I fiercely told them all. "I remember looking out the window in the back seat, through the pounding rain, onto the dark street."

"What did you see?" Beau asked.

"The car that ran us off the road sat nearby, headlights

streaked with the heavy rain. Pounding on the glass, I screamed for help. One of the windows slid down, allowing me a glimpse inside. It was her. Audra. She had a scarf around her head and I didn't know who she was at the time, but I recall her impassive face quite clearly."

"Your stepmother ran you off the road," Neo reiterated, his face a mask of anger.

"She killed my mother because she wanted my father." I confirmed, still having trouble believing it myself. "And she didn't want a stepdaughter, so she tried to kill me too."

"But you didn't die," Fletcher pointed out.

"I beat on the window and screamed her name. I was so confused when she just rolled the window back up like she didn't even see." The memory made me tremble, so I held on to Neo a little tighter. "The car started to drive off, and I started to cry. But then it made a wide turn, and I thought it was coming back..."

Neo's breath caught, and pain flashed in his eyes. He knew what I was going to say. He understood.

"It slammed into ours again, flipping it into the river. And then it drove off and never came back." As I stared off into nothing, my voice sounded like an echo in the vacant hollows of my broken heart. "I managed to swim free of the car, somehow ending up on the edge of the river. But that's all I remember." Glancing at Neo, I said, "I can't remember."

Wrapping me close, our bodies swayed on the bed as he whispered comforting, near-silent words against my ear. The brush of his breath over my skin made my eyes droop closed, exhaustion whispering in my limbs.

"You're not going to leave again, are you?" I asked, wanting his comfort so badly but afraid it wouldn't last.

"Never again," he vowed.

Pulling back, pursing my lips, I looked over his face. "Are you lying?"

My entire face was cradled in his palms. The intensity of his stare made my stomach flip and my heart beat rapidly.

"I would never lie about forever."

As I snuggling back into his chest, another tear dripped down my cheek. This one wasn't from pain, though. This one came from relief.

Sixty-Two

Neo

EXHAUSTION PULLED HER DOWN SO QUICKLY THAT WHEN I LAID her sleeping form back against the pillows, the tears streaking her cheeks weren't even dry.

Heart constricting, I dabbed at the dampness, taking care not to irritate her already red and aggravated skin.

It seemed entirely unfair that one trauma would make her recall another. Unfair she had more than one trauma to live with at all.

Everyone remained quiet as I pulled away, staring down at her vulnerable form marred with hives, swollen lips, and puffy eyes.

I was almost too late.

The still atmosphere rippled when I spun, eyes landing heavily on Earth. A large part of me was still in denial, unable to even comprehend the truth the other parts whispered.

It couldn't be true. *Can it?*

"Outside. Now." I growled the words, anger reverberating in every syllable.

"Where are you going?" Fletcher asked immediately, trailing after me as I went to the door. He flinched when I turned back, the wildness in my eyes stopping him cold.

"Stay here. Watch Ivory." Then I looked at Beau and Ethan, indicating the order was for them too.

Yes, we all deserved to know what Earth had done, but this felt so personal. I felt so raw. I wanted to look into his eyes and hear the truth.

I want none of what I'm thinking to be true. Just tell me I'm wrong.

Not waiting to see if Earth would follow, I stalked out into the hallway, the silent, sterile environment almost shocking in contrast to the loud chaos inside me. The VIP wing of a hospital was somewhere I'd never been before, but besides being larger, fancier, and less crowded, it wasn't much different than any other hospital. Feeling Earth's presence following me, I moved into an empty room across the hall, rotating as he stepped in behind me.

The collar of his black coat was turned up around his neck, its sharp edges framing his defined jawline and somehow accentuating his high cheekbones. His inky strands seemed wilder than usual as if he'd been tugging at them in anguish. His crescent-shaped onyx eyes were too dark to appear shadowed, instead appearing shuttered, not revealing a single answer.

Earth had always had a hard edge about him. He was intense and harsh from the day we met, but everything about him commanded respect. The truth was no one really liked him, and I always thought he liked it that way.

Except, of course, for me, Beau, and Fletch.

Actually, most days, we probably didn't like him much either, but he was our family. He had a soft spot for animals and a soft spot for Fletcher. He worked endlessly at the Rotten Apple, and though he might deny it, he was surprisingly a good friend.

At least I'd thought he was.

I never asked much about his past or his private

thoughts. None of us asked much about our lives before we all moved in together. All four of us had skeletons hanging in the closet, but it didn't matter. There was an unspoken understanding that bonded us all together. A code we all lived by.

Brothers before others.

Because in the Grimms, if you didn't have loyalty, you didn't have anything.

The rips in his black jeans flashed the skin beneath when he shifted, his black shoes light on the floor.

"It was you," I said, laying it all bare.

"Yes."

"Why?"

"Because her stepmother hired me to."

"You kill people for hire?"

"Yes."

Earth was a lot of things, but never had I thought he could be a killer.

And learning that was exactly who he was didn't scare me. It enraged me.

When I shot across the room, my fist connected with tissue and bone, snapping his head to the side. With an angry yell, I shoved, his back colliding with the wall. I hit him again, this time drawing blood from his lip.

"You son of a bitch," I growled, plowing my fist into him again.

Chest heaving, my breath wheezing, my arm wound back again, only to drop midway to his jaw.

He isn't fighting.

He isn't pushing me away.

He is letting me beat him.

The realization took all the steam out of my fist, and it fell to my side.

The hand gripping the front of his shirt shoved off,

leaving behind a wrinkled mess of the black T-shirt covering his chest.

"Why aren't you fighting back?" I yelled. My entire being itched for a fight. There was so much rage and worry pent up inside me. So much betrayal. I wanted to feel it explode from my knuckles against his skin.

Despite the strong desire and the rapid thumping of my heart, I couldn't.

"I deserve it."

Nostrils still flaring with every breath, I let out a harsh laugh. "No. No, you don't get to act contrite. Like you're somehow the victim."

"I told you not to bring her into our house. I told you not to get involved."

My eyes went wide, and I took a menacing step forward. "You're blaming me now?" I spewed. "Like it's my fault Ivory is lying in that bed!"

I swung again, but he caught my fist, squeezing my already sore knuckles. The sole of my boot connected with his middle, the force of the kick making him reel backward and let go of my hand.

Eyes burning like hot coals, he launched forward, and we locked together in a scuffle.

Blows were exchanged, but the only ones I felt were the ones I let loose on him. Grunts filled the air. High-pitched whines from shoes squeaking over the slick floor punctuated the fight.

Slipping from his hold, I slammed him into the floor, throwing my weight into his body, looming over him with a curled lip.

"Is this what you wanted?" he taunted, voice raspy and teeth stained with red. "You wanna fight?"

Straddling his waist, I let my shoulders slump, anger draining away. This wasn't what I wanted. Not at all.

"You pulled me out of the water at the fish market," I said.

"You were going to drown."

"Yeah, because *you* knocked me in the back of the head."

"I would never kill you."

A rude sound erupted from my throat, and I hoped it masked the feelings of hurt swirling inside me. "Unless someone paid you to."

"No," he said, his voice taking on his familiar harsh tone. "Because you're my family."

I slid off him, sagging beside where he lay, resting my elbows on my knees. "Ivory is my family now too."

"That's why I didn't do it. Why I warned you."

"You're a son of a bitch." I wanted it to sound hot-headed and mean. Instead, it came out low and wounded.

"Yeah."

"Neo?" Her timid, raspy voice reached across the room, evaporating everything else.

"Princess," I called, jumping up the second I saw Ivory standing in the doorway. She was always pale, but the pallor of her skin wasn't as it should be. "What are you doing out of bed?" I worried, rushing to close the distance between us.

"I thought you left."

I couldn't even blame her for worrying about me disappearing. I'd made her like this, and it was my responsibility to teach her I wouldn't do it ever again.

"I didn't leave. I'm right here." I spoke gently, lifting her off her feet, cradling her against my chest.

Small arms loosely looped around my neck, and a small sigh left her lips when she cuddled closer. Possessiveness roared through my veins, and the need to protect nearly blinded me, which was why I probably didn't notice when she lifted her head to look at me.

"You're bleeding!" She gasped, the pad of her thumb swiping over my lower lip, concern darkening her tired eyes.

"What happened?" Gazing across the room, she saw Earth still sitting on the floor. "Are you fighting?"

"You should be in bed." I tried to distract her.

"Why are you in here? What's going on?" she demanded as if I hadn't spoken at all. Leaning around me, she gazed at the man who literally tried to kill her. "Earth?" she questioned, completely in the dark.

Look, we all know I'm a bit of a liar. Fine. I'm a raging lie-aholic.

But there are lines even I will not cross.

So here I stood, stuck in the middle of my brother and the woman I loved, willing to overlook skeletons from the past but unable to overlook the fact he'd tried to turn Ivory into one.

"You gonna tell her, or am I?" I asked.

"Tell me what?" Ivory probed, dividing her stare between us.

There was a long, charged silence where I waited. I waited for him to do the right thing… to be even just a fraction of the man I thought he was.

Disappointment washed through me the longer he didn't speak, and I began to ask myself yet again how I could be so wrong about someone.

But then Earth unfolded from the floor, lifting his chin to settle his unwavering gaze on Ivory.

"I'm the huntsman. I'm the one who tried to kill you."

Sixty-Three

Ivory

I felt drowsy, muddled, and hopped up on antihistamine.

But I was not delirious.

Or maybe I was.

"Did you just say you're the huntsman?" I whispered, nearly choking on the words.

Earth nodded, not an ounce of sarcasm in his stare.

"No," I said, struggling to believe. "It was Audra. She's the one. She hired someone..." My voice trailed away, eyes settling on Earth.

"It was me she hired. I was there in the park that day. In the tunnel. I slammed you into the wall and cut your hair. I told you to run and never come back."

"No," I whispered, shaking my head in disbelief. "No. You wouldn't."

"I attacked you in the alley, and I threw you in the river."

Under me, Neo's body stiffened, rippling with emotion I couldn't process. Trying to process my own was overwhelming enough. Arms shaking, I tightened my grip on him, burying my face in his neck.

A thought struck me. So horrible it made my stomach heave.

I pulled back so violently Neo had to react quickly so I

didn't fall from his arms. "Did you… did you know about this?" I asked, feeling like my entire heart depended on his reply.

"No," he said surely, lifting me a little higher in his arms. "I didn't know until today."

His eyes mirrored the shock I felt. The betrayal.

Eyes filling, I hugged against his neck, burying my face under his ear. "Oh, I'm sorry. I'm so sorry."

"Why are you sorry, princess? You're the one who almost died," he whispered against my ear.

"Because he's your friend."

"You need to be in bed," Neo said, not responding to what I said, carrying me and my IV pole from the room.

"Wait!"

His feet halted at my cry.

Peeking over his shoulder, I spoke to Earth. "I want to speak with you."

He followed along. I kept my eyes on him the entire time, making sure he wasn't planning to run off while I was trying to think of the questions I wanted to ask. But I could only come up with one.

"Why?" I asked when I was back in bed with a white blanket pulled up to my waist.

Neo sat on the side of the mattress, one arm draped around me so I could use his body as my pillow. The IV in the back of my hand pinched, and my skin felt tight and burned.

"I told you your stepmother hired me."

Beau, Fletcher, and Ethan all reacted, mouths dropping open in shock.

"No way," Beau swore, staring at Earth as if he were a stranger.

"What's going on?" Ethan looked at me for some type of explanation.

So I told everyone. "Earth is the huntsman Audra hired to kill me."

"Earth would never do that!" Fletch demanded, chin lifting, stubborn determination in his eyes. Turning to Earth, his gaze softened just a bit. "Right?"

The huntsman's jaw clenched, and then his eyes dropped toward the floor. "Sorry, kid."

Fletcher's lower lip wobbled, and he spun away from the room, going to a nearby window to try and disappear behind the sheer white curtain. It didn't do a good job of concealing him or the soft sniffling sounds he made.

Earth gazed after him but didn't say a word.

Beau stood there in stony silence, and Ethan shook his head. "I can't believe she would go this far."

"I had trouble believing it at first too. Until she handed me a poisoned apple and outright tried to kill me."

"That's my fault too," Earth said quietly.

"What do you mean?" Neo asked.

"Audra came to see me earlier today. It's the first time a, ah… client has ever been able to figure out my identity. She walked right into the bar and told me to finish the job."

"But she's the one that came to my penthouse," I said.

He shook his head. "I told her I was done, that I wouldn't do it."

"And so she decided to," I whispered, remembering how she cackled about getting it done herself.

Silence descended, laying like a thick blanket over the room.

Glancing back up at Earth, I repeated my single question. "Why?"

"I told you," he growled, prickly as ever. "Audra—"

"No." I cut him off. "Not why you tried to kill me. Why *didn't* you?"

The curtain Fletcher was unsuccessfully hiding behind

rippled with his movement. He didn't turn around, but his head tilted and I knew he was listening to everything being said.

"I broke the rules." Earth finally spoke.

"What rules?"

"I let it get personal."

"So you've done this before?" I asked, my voice quaking.

He didn't answer, but really, he didn't need to. We all knew he had.

"Are you saying you, ah, like her, and that's why you didn't…?" Ethan implied, dividing his stare between me and Earth.

Neo reacted instantly, a rough sound ripping from somewhere inside him. Like a sleeping tiger, he jolted up, lunging toward Earth.

Shrieking, I grabbed the back of his shirt, my tired arms unable to do much in the way of keeping him back. "Neo, no. *Please.*"

He stopped, but his shoulders were tense and his body vibrated with anger.

Or was it jealousy?

"Neo," I beckoned softly, calling him back.

His eyes were soft when they turned, and I patted the empty space beside me. Once he was seated, I reclined, giving all my weight to him, hoping it might hold him in place.

Earth stood silently waiting, and when I looked up again, he dropped another bomb. "I knew your father."

This one was more explosive to me than even his murderous side job.

"Y-you knew my father?" I whispered, forgetting I was holding Neo down to lean forward toward Earth.

At the back of my hand, the IV tugged, and I let out a small involuntary whine of discomfort. Reaching around,

Neo pulled the stand, tugging it closer to the bed so it wouldn't create so much pull.

"I—" Earth started but stopped almost immediately. Under his clothes, his shoulders moved restlessly, and his eyes trailed toward the floor. Whatever he wanted to say was clearly difficult for him, or maybe it was just private.

I wasn't sure how to offer comfort or even if I should. All I knew for certain was that I wanted to hear how he knew my father.

Fletcher appeared, sliding up to Earth's side, snaking his arm through his. Surprised, Earth looked at Fletch holding on to him, receiving a timid smile in return.

"You can tell us." He encouraged, looking like a giant puppy.

In a surprising action, Earth ruffled Fletch's floppy hair, fondness echoing silently around the room.

With a great exhale, Earth spoke. "I ran away from my life in Asia when I was very young. With a little bit of help, I was able to make it here. I thought things would be easier here. Better. But it turns out life is hard no matter where you go, and when you're a kid with no support, no money, and no green card… life sucks."

I thought about a smaller version of Earth, maybe a softer version, running through the Grimms, hungry and with no one to care for him. It made my heart ache.

Neo turned restless, shifting where he sat more than once, and I knew beneath his anger, he ached too.

"I couldn't get a job, so I stole everything. Pickpocketing became a way to live." Earth looked up, avoiding the stare of his brothers but looking at me instead.

Nodding, I silently asked him to go on.

"One day, I got cocky, and I thought I could prove how good I was. So I went to the Upper East Side… and I snatched a wallet."

My breath caught, and tears already began pushing at the backs of my eyes.

Nodding, Earth continued. "Your father caught me red-handed. His bodyguards snatched me off the street and put me in the back of his car with him."

"Then what happened?" I asked, imagining my father dressed in a tailored suit and sitting in the back of his car. I missed him. I missed him so much.

Earth cracked a small smile, and it made me wonder what he would look like if he smiled with all his face. "He told me if I was going to steal, I needed to do a better job."

I giggled.

"I thought he was going to take me to the police station, but he didn't. He asked me how old I was, where I lived, and he listened to my answers. He didn't turn me in. Instead, he drove me to some old building he said he'd just bought and hadn't had time to do anything with. He told me I could stay there, and he helped me get a green card. I got a crappy job and didn't steal… as much. A year later, your father showed up at the building. I thought I was going to get kicked out."

"What happened?" I asked, totally invested in every detail.

"He signed the building over to me, told me that he wouldn't have gotten where he was if no one had helped him. He said to make something of myself and told me not to steal."

"The building…" Neo began.

"Is the Rotten Apple." Earth confirmed. "And our apartment. I own the entire building because Ivory's father gave it to me."

"But if you own that place, then why do you make us pay rent?" Fletch wondered.

Beau rolled his eyes.

"My father helped you," I repeated, love swelling in my heart. "He was a kind man. It's why my mother fell in love with him." The story that Earth told was completely believable because it was exactly the kind of man my father was.

"Yes. He did. He was the only person in my entire life who ever gave me a chance."

"And you repaid him by trying to kill his daughter," Neo growled.

"No." Earth's eyes flashed, cold enveloping the room. When they came back to me, I shivered. Suddenly, I recognized the aura permeating the room. The familiar chill to the air, the way my skin hummed with danger.

His roughness, his strong build.

Earth. He really is the huntsman.

"When I was first hired, I didn't realize who you were. I took the job, did my due diligence, as I always do. When I realized, I hesitated... but a job is a job, and I'm a professional."

"You, sir, are not a professional," Ethan declared.

"I thought I could do it." Earth talked over him. "When I was... in that tunnel with you."

Neo's body stiffened, and I placed my palm on his thigh to hopefully quiet some of his turmoil.

"Go on." I urged.

Earth's voice strained. "You called out for your father."

I remembered. He was the person I thought of before I was about to die. The man who occupied what I thought was my very last thought.

"I couldn't do it. You hadn't done anything... and I felt I owed him a debt."

I gasped, remembering that day. "You said the debt you owed my father was repaid!"

Earth nodded.

"It was you!" I gasped again, finally allowing myself to believe completely.

"I cut your hair and took your nail to send to Audra as

proof of death. That's why I told you to disappear and never come back. I thought you would listen. Turns out you're way stupider than I thought."

"I am hardly stupid!" I argued, indignant.

"You came to my bar," he deadpanned.

"It's not like I knew you were the killer!" I shot back.

"Stupid," he muttered.

"Why didn't you say something then?" Neo asked, teeth clearly grinding.

"Because I didn't know you'd bring her home."

"But he did," Beau said. "And you tried to, ah, off her again."

"Twice," Fletch pointed out.

"That second time, I was just trying to scare you off. I thought if you knew the huntsman was still around, you'd run."

"And the fish market?" Neo asked, voice tight.

Earth said nothing, and a sick feeling sat like a rock in the pit of my stomach. He really would have done it that day if Neo hadn't been able to pull me out.

Gasping, I realized something. "You hurt Neo!"

"I was trying to keep him out of the way," Earth mumbled. "I didn't want to hurt him."

"But you did." My voice was fierce. "And he has stitches! Did you even apologize?"

Earth jolted, taken aback. "What?"

"Did you apologize for what you did to him?"

His silence was a clear no. "You really have no manners," I admonished.

Ethan made a sound of agreement.

"An apology won't change what I did," Earth deadpanned.

Neo's body was strung tight like a string on Fletcher's violin that was about to snap.

"No, but it's a beginning to try and make up for what you did."

"He can't make up for trying to kill you," Neo refuted, voice cold and flat. Not at all the voice I was used to.

"But you didn't want her to die," Fletch insisted, clearly still struggling with the fact someone he looked at as a hero could be so corrupt. "You're the one that warned us about today. You're the reason we got to her in time!"

Some of the heaviness lifted, and a little bit of hope bloomed within me. "Is that true?"

"It doesn't matter," Earth replied.

I looked up. "Neo? Is that true?"

He nodded.

"And Audra?" Trepidation curled within me, a rising darkness trying to claim the light. "Where is she? I need to tell the police."

"Shh…" Neo mollified a portion of my anxiety, stroking down the back of my head. "She's already been arrested."

Vague memories from earlier today replayed in my mind, her cloaked figure cackling but then walking away… leaving me to die. "I thought she left."

"Earth knocked her out in the hallway," Fletch announced, proud.

"You did?"

"She pissed me off."

"But you're here." I wondered. "Aren't you worried she will tell them everything you've done?"

Earth shrugged. "She has no proof it was me. And even if she was going to try and prove it, ratting me out would also be an admission of guilt on her part. Hiring a hitman isn't exactly the reputation that power-hungry crow wants."

"She definitely wants power," I whispered, shivering at the things she'd said when I'd literally been suffocating to death.

What a terrible woman. To stand over the body of someone who was her family and cruelly watch her struggle to live.

"But she already is powerful. She's one of the richest women in this city," Ethan murmured.

"She never said anything to you, Ethan? Never made you question her when I was missing?"

Ethan was quiet a moment, then shook his head. "No. When you went missing, she called, and I came to help at the companies, knowing everything would be in chaos. She stayed in her penthouse, claiming she was too distraught to leave. I know she spoke to the authorities, and then we did that television appearance when there was some hope you could be alive."

"She's cunning and jealous of you," Earth said. "She knew with you around, she would always be second best."

First my mother, and now me. I wondered if she ever loved my father at all or if she just saw him as a means to an end.

He deserved so much better. So had my mother.

"I will see her in jail." My voice shook with conviction and confidence. I wasn't ever one to abuse my power or even flaunt it. But for this, I would.

I would do everything within my capabilities to see that malevolent woman locked away. Forever.

Sixty-Four

Huntsman

The rules I had were *not* made to be broken. I broke them anyway.

Never compromise your identity.

Not only did my hire find out my identity, but I confessed to a room full of people who I really was. Willingly.

Only kill who you are paid to kill.

Okay, maybe I didn't kill anyone I wasn't paid to kill… but I would kill Audra for free. She really pissed me off.

Always finish the job.

I failed at this three times.

Never make it personal.

Oh, it was personal.

Now all that was left was to take my punishment.

"You. Stay there," Ivory ordered, probably thinking I was about to run off since the cops were on their way.

I wasn't.

It felt as though I'd been running my entire life, and I was tired. I made my choices. I broke the rules. Now I would pay the price.

"Everyone else, gather around." She gestured, fanning out her thin, pale arms as if she would pull them close.

"Be careful." Neo warned, holding on to the IV line as

though it might somehow yank free of her arm and thrash wildly about.

I really didn't think I'd see the day that closed-off painter would let anyone in.

But I understood. Probably better than anyone. Because here I stood, my shattered life around me, but I couldn't regret not killing Ivory White.

She was too good and pure to be ended so violently. Would I have been able to kill her if not for the debt I owed her father?

I didn't think so. But I would never say that out loud. Some secrets were meant to stay buried.

Everyone gathered around, forming a small circle of bowed heads as they all whispered and talked, leaving me to stand on the outside looking in.

Fletch's head popped up, gaze swinging around to stare at me. His eyes were wide, his lip in a pout. As he stared, Beau reached up to palm his head and pull it back down with everyone else.

I'd done a lot of bad things in my life. I wasn't really sorry for any of them. But I was sorry for something.

Hurting my brothers. The three men who'd accepted me without any pause.

I'd betrayed them too. And it would be a lie if I said knowing they probably wouldn't have accepted me if they knew who I really was hurt.

No. I had no right to be hurt because I did this to myself.

I hurt anyway. All my life, I didn't have anyone until the three of us formed the bond that I'd just severed.

No wonder I was a huntsman. I was really good at killing things.

The low sounds of whispers floated through the room until finally they all broke apart. Neo didn't look at me, his body language still rigid and pissed off. Everyone thought Fletch was the softest… but he wasn't.

It was Neo. Neo had a heart he'd strung barbed wire around to protect it from pain. He would never forgive me.

Awkwardness descended, stifling the room.

"I'll wait in the hall," I said, starting forward.

"You should leave before the detectives arrive." Ivory spoke, halting my progress to the door.

"What?" I asked, staring at the small girl in the center of the bed. Snort was snoring heavily near her feet.

Traitorous beast.

"You shouldn't be here. We can answer all the questions."

Blinking, I glanced around at Beau, Fletch, and even Ethan nodding in agreement. Neo wasn't agreeing, but he wasn't disagreeing either.

"You need me to tell cops she hired me." I reminded her.

Ivory shook her head. "No. I don't. She tried to kill me earlier today. My word will be enough. I'll just say she confessed to hiring someone and then trying to do it herself when they failed. And I can tell them about my mother."

It took a minute for me to fully understand, and even when I did, I had to ask, "Are you saying you aren't turning me in?"

"Well, that depends," Ivory said, her voice prim.

Fletch made a sound like this was not how things were supposed to go.

"Are you going to keep trying to kill me?" she asked.

My shoulders relaxed. "I've already tried three times, and I still haven't been able to get rid of you."

Neo made a low growling sound, but Ivory smiled.

"So no?"

"No." I was sincere. "I'm done."

"Thank goodness. I'm so weary of people trying to murder me."

Neo made another grumbling sound. Ivory reached for his hand. His enveloped hers completely, and a lump formed in my throat.

"Why would you even believe anything I say anyway?"

"My father saw good in you. I see it too."

"We all do." Fletcher jumped in.

"Well, I don't even know you," Ethan muttered.

"What you did was really shitty, E." Beau spoke up. "We're all pissed as hell."

I didn't say anything.

"But you're our family." He went on.

"And family sticks together." Fletcher finished.

Emotion welled up inside me, tightening my chest, creating a buzzing sound between my ears. Turning, I looked directly at Neo, who'd remained silent and motionless up until now.

"What about you?"

"What about me?" He challenged.

"You okay with this?"

He still didn't meet my eyes, looking at a spot just over my shoulder, jaw tight and brows drawn. "It was a group decision."

I never said I was a good man, and yes, I said I would take my punishment, but that was before I knew I had another option.

Never in a million years would I have thought they could possibly… "You can forgive me?" I whispered, scarcely able to say the words.

It was too much to conceive, maybe even more than I would be able to do.

Fletcher rushed across the room, his body knocking into mine when he wrapped his arms around me in a tight hug. His cheek was buried against my chest as he hunched around.

He was the most affectionate man I'd ever met... and I should have hated it.

But I didn't.

"I forgive you," he said into my shirt.

I patted his back, kinda grateful for the kid.

Everyone else just looked at us.

Beau cleared his throat. "Might take the rest of us a little longer."

I nodded. This was more than I expected.

"But we don't want you to go to jail. So get out of here." Beau finished, gruff.

Glancing at Snort, then back to Ivory, I said, "He'll hang out with you a little longer."

Smiling, she nodded.

Partway to the door, I stopped again, retreating to the side of her bed. Across the mattress, Neo watched with a narrow gaze, practically daring me to touch her.

Kneeling, hands resting on the side of the bed, I gazed into her blue eyes. "I don't deserve this, but thank you."

"You can repay me by living a better life."

I nodded. "I will."

"Go on," she said, shooing me toward the door.

I went, my limbs unexpectedly heavy, my heart an odd mix of achy and full. I was a selfish, bad man... but some people liked me anyway. I didn't know how to feel, so I was left as a horribly mixed concoction of emotions.

"Earth."

Partway down the hall, Neo's voice brought me around. His face was shuttered, eyes mysterious. There was a bit of dried blood smeared on his lower lip, and his knuckles were red.

"I'll turn myself in," I heard myself say, but once the words registered, I knew I meant them. "If that's what you want, I'll do it."

Surprised flickered in the depths of his onyx eyes, but then it was gone, all his emotions hidden away. “I don’t want you in jail.”

Slowly, I nodded.

“But I’m not like Fletch. I can’t forgive you. I can’t forget what you’ve done.”

“I know.”

“You were my brother, and you betrayed me.”

“I know.”

We stood staring at each other for long, silent moments.

Clearing my throat, I said, “I’m sorry.”

“Sorry doesn’t mean anything.”

“No. It doesn’t. But someone told me it’s a beginning to make up for what I did.”

“Ivory’s a lot kinder than me.”

“I don’t expect you to forgive me. I’m not even asking you to,” I told him. Hitching my chin down the hall, I said, “She’s waiting for you.”

I was walking away when his voice rang out again. “I’ll try.”

I stopped but didn’t turn. My vision blurred a bit as I stared down at the floor.

“I can’t promise anything, but I’ll try to forgive you. Just… If you ever do anything like this again, it’s you who will end up in the river, and I won’t pull you out.”

“I wouldn’t expect you to,” I whispered, my heart squeezing with the painful sensation of hope.

I heard him turn and walk away, so I continued on. The distance between us grew, but a strange sensation of brotherhood remained.

Sixty-Five

Neo

She called out in her sleep, voice filled with panic and sorrow. Soft blankets fell to my waist when I sat up, gently tugging her fitfully sleeping form into my lap.

"Ivory," I whispered, rocking us in the center of the bed. "Wake up, princess."

"Neo," she whimpered, damp eyelashes fluttering.

"I'm here." I promised, tucking her a little closer.

A soft sigh left her rose-red lips, and her troubled, sleepy gaze found mine.

"It was just a dream." I assured her, dragging my fingers through her hair.

"Another one." Rolling into my chest, she flung one arm around my neck.

Warmth and love spread from my middle, filling my limbs all the way down to my toes. "It's only been a week." I reminded her, hand gliding over her back. "It's going to take a while to get over everything that happened."

"I know." She sighed, tugging back so we could look at each other.

"You want to talk about it?"

She shook her head.

Pulling her in, I tucked her head beneath my chin, rocking us gently once more.

Her fingertips whispered over the bare skin on my arm, arousing and relaxing me at the very same time. The soft scent of jasmine always clinging to her skin surrounded my senses, enclosing us in a bubble where only we existed.

"Neo?"

"Hmm?"

"Would you have come back if Audra hadn't tried to kill me again?"

Ripples of shock went through me, no clue until now she'd even wondered this. Slipping my hands around her, I tugged, but she whined and clung even closer. Almost as if she were scared of my answer, as if she wanted to hide her face away.

Sighing overhead, I lightly palmed the back of her neck. "I was always on my way back to you. I couldn't stay away."

"Really?" Her voice was muffled against my bare chest.

"I think that's why I left so many flannels. Leaving pieces of myself until I was ready to stay."

"I was afraid you wouldn't come back."

"I know, baby. I was stupid and selfish."

"You were afraid."

I made a sound of agreement.

When she pulled back, her stare touched mine. "Are you still afraid?"

"Love is scary. Part of me will probably always be scared."

Her bow-shaped mouth turned down, and the small pout was so cute I smiled. "But you know what someone told me once?"

"What?"

"We should go on strongly despite the fear." She smiled, her porcelain skin nearly lighting up the dark bedroom.

Pressing our foreheads together, I inhaled, drinking in

her scent, her presence… her love. "I love you more than I'm afraid."

"I love you too."

Ivory's lips brushed mine, pulling back with a silent plea. Answering, I pulled her back in, locking our mouths together and rubbing my tongue over her lower lip, asking for entrance. As soon as she parted them, I swept inside, both of us making soft sounds of satisfaction.

Tongues twirling together, I explored her mouth lazily, relearning every inch as if I didn't already know my way around. Lips gliding together, we kissed, saliva mingling, shared breath filling our chests. Trailing my hands down over her back, I dipped one beneath the hem of my flannel to glide over the softness of her skin.

She was warm and pliant in my lap, her lips giving and engaged.

She gasped when I rolled, pinning her into the mattress, rising to slowly undo every button along her chest. When at last the buttons were undone, I parted the material around her, revealing all of her smooth skin.

Night air brushed over her nipples, making them pucker. Dipping low, my tongue stroked up her abdomen, swirling around her small, perky globe before latching onto the hardened pebble and sucking lightly.

Her groan tightened my cock, body arching up to push her flesh deeper into my mouth.

"More." She panted, and I was only too happy to oblige.

Fingers dancing over her ribs and waist, I kissed and sucked until she squirmed beneath me.

Parting her legs, I settled between them, coming back for another soft kiss, trailing down her neck to suck deeply just under her ear.

Fingernails dug into my shoulder, and I rocked into her core, my hard length finding her softness.

Reaching down, Ivory tugged at my waistband, whimpering with need.

I loved watching her usually together exterior come undone. I loved playing with her until she was a begging mess beneath me.

"What do you want, sweetheart?" I beckoned, teeth grazing over her collarbone.

"You."

"You already have me."

She made a sound of irritation, hips reaching up for mine.

Pulling away, I sat up between her thighs, making her startle with the sudden loss of body heat. Through half-closed eyes, she watched me, a beautiful pink blush spreading out all over her pale chest.

"Tell me," I commanded, reaching down to lightly pinch her nipple.

"You." She panted. "Inside me."

My boxers disappeared somewhere in the room, and I peeled the shirt off her arms, tossing it away too. Dipping my fingers between us, I found her slick heat nearly dripping with readiness and groaned out loud.

When I swiped across her center, she quivered, and I used her natural lubrication to stroke my already throbbing cock.

Leaning in, I latched onto the inside of her thigh, peppering kisses there, enjoying the way her throat vibrated with every little suck I performed.

Pain prickled through my head when she pulled my hair, impatience getting the best of her.

Chuckling hoarsely, I came over her, my swollen head nudging her entrance. Eyes rolling back in her head, she looked like a beautiful mess.

One long stroke joined us, our groans mingling like the rest of us.

When she reached for me, I went to her, not a single inch

between our chests. Wrapping her up in my arms, I began to move, her tight, wet heat making me throb.

Our bodies moved in tandem, rocking and sliding together, heavy breaths and deep moans filling the bedroom.

"Neo," she whimpered, body tightening under mine.

Instead of plunging deeper, I pulled back, balancing my weight on my palms, staring down. "Look at me."

Her eyes fluttered, the blue barely visible because her pupils were blown wide. My arms shook with the effort to stay above her, to not move within her walls.

"I won't go anywhere without you ever again. I swear."

She pulled me back down, and my hips snapped forward, driving me so deep.

Both of us let go at once, spiraling into pleasure together.

Body spent, I rolled, carrying her with me so she was draped over my chest. I felt the tremble in her thighs and the thundering of her heart, making me smile smugly at the ceiling.

"Bet Ethan never did that."

"What?" she murmured, her voice husky and deep.

"Nothing," I said, pushing her cheek back onto my chest.

"Are you jealous of Ethan still?" She giggled.

"No." I scowled.

"I never slept with Ethan."

My head left the pillow. "Seriously?"

"Ethan isn't interested in me."

"Every man is interested in you," I rebuked, unable to get too salty because my body was so satisfied.

"Not every prince wants a princess." She giggled again.

"Huh?" I grunted, staring up. When it clicked, shock made my head rise again. "Are you saying Ethan is gay?"

"I'm saying you shouldn't worry about other men because the only one I want is you."

Cupping the back of her head, I kissed her, possession

rippling through my middle. "Good. Because you're mine, and I'm never letting you go."

"Two people from two different worlds, but love doesn't care," she whispered, tracing small circles over my chest, her breath tickling my skin. "Love will bind us together forever."

Gathering her close, I peppered her face with gentle kisses until she curled into my neck and sighed with happiness. Happiness I thought I would never know again.

This raven-haired beauty might have stepped from between the pages of a storybook, but I realized I didn't have to be a prince to love her because we're all stories in the end.

And it's up to us to give our stories a chance.

Epilogue

A few months later…

Ivory

Nerves buzzed around inside me like a bunch of bees, occasionally bumping into me, stinging and making me catch my breath.

Today was a departure for me. I was stepping way outside of the box.

Well… Okay, I'd been living outside the box for a while now. Maybe this was more of me dragging the box back into my world?

No.

Our world.

This was me mixing our worlds to create something shared. Something better.

"Are you ready?" Charles, my trusty right-hand man, asked, bustling up beside me with about three clipboards balanced in his arms. There was a headset over his head and a small mic reaching toward his lips.

"Of course," I said, putting on that air of confidence I always wore.

In truth, I wanted to vomit, but *never let them see you sweat.*

He ran off, shouting something to one of the models, and I pulled in a calming breath.

Warm arms and a familiar scent enveloped me from behind. Leaning back, I soaked in some comfort before pulling free and turning to face him.

Neo looked amazing in my new collection, which really wasn't a surprise considering most of it was inspired by him.

And today was the day I would reveal it to the world. I wasn't sure if the Upper East Side was ready for street couture, but I was about to find out.

The entire line was inspired by my adventures in the Grimms, by the people I'd met and things I'd seen. My goal was to bring some of that to the Upper East Side… with an upscale feel of course.

The tailored jacket Neo wore was made of plaid, but the fabric was superior quality and the cut accentuated his broad shoulders and lean waist. His jeans were belted, accented with paint splatters, and the white button-down he wore beneath the jacket had my logo embroidered on the breast—a mirror.

Across his chest (but under the jacket), he wore a black leather bum bag, the strap angling over his chest. The pocket of his jacket was filled with paintbrushes.

Not even the harness strapped over his outfit could detract from the way he pulled the outfit off. He was exactly what I wanted to convey, street attitude with high style.

"Be careful, okay?" I said, tipping back my chin to gaze up at him.

Smiling, Neo tugged on my loose curls and pecked a kiss to the tip of my nose. "You too, princess. Those heels look dangerous."

I was wearing one of my original designs as well, a pair of pleated, high-waisted jade pants cuffed at the ankles. Tucked in was a silk print top with a modern, colorful paisley pattern. The sleeves belled around my elbows, the silk flowing whenever I moved. The boatneck accentuated my collarbones, and the hot-pink heels strapped to my feet were the perfect finishing touch. Nearby on a rack, I had a long hot-pink trench coat to pair with the outfit.

The models began to line up, all of them wearing gorgeous street couture presented by Reflection. I was proud of this collection. It gave me a feeling of coming full circle.

"Gotta go!" Neo said, rushing off before I could even yell good-bye.

I'd come to realize I would never have the chance to say good-bye with Neo… because there would never be another good-bye.

Behind the scenes, I watched everyone take their places, and then suddenly, the show was beginning.

Music, heavy on the beat, started up, and lights flicked on, illuminating the white runway and stage. The only decoration was an oversized mirror with an ornate gold frame against the back wall.

The music continued to vibrate through the space, creating energy and a bit of anticipation. The crowd that sat in the dark started to buzz and then hushed when a man in a harness dropped from overhead, scaling the back wall.

I watched proudly as Neo pulled out a few cans of spray paint and started turning the white walls into incredible pieces of art right before everyone's eyes.

Another spotlight flicked on, and the strong hum of a violin cut through the music, mixing and mingling with passion to create a brand-new beat. Into the spotlight stepped Fletcher, also wearing one of my designs.

He swayed and moved with the rhythm he played, the music coming from him and not the instrument in his hands.

And then the models were walking. Moving down the runway like they were in fact on the street. Even though the rows of guests were in the shadows, I still watched their faces and reactions, the entire place humming with life and vibrancy.

At first, I thought there was more shock than anything. The edgy, colorful designs were unexpected, but then everything began to shift. The painting Neo was creating before their eyes began to take shape, and the music Fletcher played began flowing through their veins.

By the time I walked to the end of the catwalk, the applause was so deafening that tears blurred my vision.

"May I introduce Fletcher." I spoke into the mic, turning to point at Fletch. He beamed, cheeks all pink, and took a small bow. "And our resident artist who actually hand painted a few of our limited-edition pieces," I said, turning to the other side of the stage. "Neo."

But he wasn't there.

The clapping began to fade, and people started to whisper.

Peering backstage, I looked for my lover, but he was nowhere to be seen. Suddenly, wild applause erupted, and I spun back toward the crowd.

My ankle chose that moment to roll, and the hot-pink heel tilted underfoot.

My life practically flashed before my eyes as horror filled me at the thought of busting my well-dressed behind on the stage in front of everyone who was everyone in fashion.

But I didn't fall.

Neo dropped from the ceiling, harness still snug around him, scooping me up and placing me back on my own two feet.

More applause erupted, and I laughed as he smiled alongside me.

"Neo, everyone," I said, a little breathless.

Plucking the mic out of my hand, he put it against his lips, dark hair falling over his forehead and a charming smile, filled with dimples, on full display. "And your designer, Ivory White."

The dull roar of whistling and cheers rose around us as I gazed through the crowd to find Beau sitting in the audience right beside Virginia, who was beaming so brightly. It meant so much to me that they were here, that all the misfits came to my world.

No… that they embraced our new world.

Gazing toward the back into a dark corner near the door, I smiled, unable to see Earth but knowing absolutely he was there.

He said he wouldn't come, but family always showed up for family. Maybe you might ask how I could forgive someone who did something so bad?

But you know what? He did good things too. Maybe he's the villain in your eyes, but in mine, he was just a man who deserved a second chance.

Neo pushed the mic back into my hands, and I smiled at the audience, making sure I ended the show as I always did.

"Remember, the most beautiful reflection in the mirror is yours."

Neo's lips brushed over my ear, his whisper creating small tingles all along my scalp. "No, princess, the most beautiful reflection in every mirror is most definitely yours."

"You're biased," I whispered back.

"You're damn right." He confirmed, sweeping me off my feet, kissing me for all the world to see.

You know what I'm going to say next, right?

We lived happily ever after.

AUTHORS NOTE

Once upon a time, there was an author...

It's me. I'm the author.

And though I've written roughly fifty titles, the act of writing never gets any easier (for me). *Mirror, mirror on the wall, can this girl even write at all?* The past fifty projects don't really feel like proof of anything because I often taunt myself with the "you're only as good as your next book" thought.

So I struggled. A lot. I can't really describe it fully, and I won't bother to bore you with a note trying to. But the fact remains that I have struggled this year with writing. Not really writer's block, but confidence? Motivation? Inspiration? Validation? Maybe I struggled with those things.

So here we are in late August, and this is my first complete novel of the year. Truth is I started this book back in January. I made it about 30k in and then stopped. I didn't write for many months, but finally, I put my butt back in the chair and picked this book back up again.

I won't lie. This was a struggle. I doubted myself the entire way through, and I doubt myself even now that it's finished. I will say that I tried my very best, and I tried to put emotion into this book in whatever the characters were experiencing in the moment. I really try to make the reader feel and not read. You know? I want you to experience the world, just not have me tell you about it.

I don't know if I was successful here, but I did try. I also worry that many of you waited so long for a new book and this will be a disappointment. If you are disappointed by this book, I am sincerely sorry.

Also, this was a bit of a departure for me because I've never done a "modern fairy tale." It wasn't something I ever thought I would do, but then one day, I thought to myself, *I want to write about a girl in a house full of boys.* And here we are.

Another odd thing... Snow White is actually my least favorite fairy tale. But that's the one I chose to tell in my own way.

What can I say? I do weird things.

A few other fun facts about *Ivory White*: Originally, I titled it *Ivory White in the Slammer.* Ha-ha. This title still really amuses me. I love that she got thrown in jail and that she called a stranger she didn't even like or know. Alas, I dropped the *in the Slammer* part because that was a lot of words to put on a cover. And if you haven't noticed, I usually always only use one-word titles.

Also, the cover for this book is not the original draft. I had a cover done back when I first started this. It was finalized and everything, but I doubted it too. When I picked this book up again and wrote more, I felt it didn't fit the way I wanted it to. I felt it was a little too dark for the story, and I was worried readers would expect one thing and get something else. So I had a completely new cover designed. I hope you like it! I know I do!

As for the characters... Well, I like Ivory's duality. How she is sort of a spoiled princess on one hand but, deep down, kind and soft. I love how she can command a room but also have vulnerability within her.

Neo is also an interesting character to me, and he actually surprised me a bit as I wrote. To be honest, I think of him as a cross between Flynn Ryder and Aladdin. Charming, roguish, and well... a criminal. LOL. But what surprised me about Neo was the fear buried deep in him. Sure, I knew he would be "damaged" because of his past, but he isn't really. He is just very afraid. Afraid to love and lose. Afraid to let people in. When he loved and left Ivory, I was kinda shook. I even thought about not writing it that way. I worried people would think he was just using her for sex. Or he was acting out of character. Maybe some of you do think that, LOL. It's okay if you do. But I couldn't change it because I feel like this is true to who he is. It was what he whispered in my ear. He wanted her so badly he couldn't stay away, but at the same time, he was so afraid to reach out and grab her. It was kind of a surprise because really, he comes off as aloof and carefree in the beginning. But deep down, he really isn't.

Earth was also a surprise... I did not know in the beginning that he would be the huntsman. But then it came to me, and I was excited and also surprised. I do hope to write a book entirely for him. I hope you look forward to that. I actually plan to write a book for all of the misfits, but I'm not announcing anything officially because it's too much pressure for my writer heart, ha.

Anyway, this turned into a long author's note, but I haven't written one to you all for so long! I want to sincerely thank you for all the encouragement you have sent my way in the last few months, the patience and support you have shown me. Thank you so much for reading this book. If you enjoyed it, please consider leaving a review online.

I know 2020 has been an epic year of chaos for everyone,

and I hope you are well. I hope you have found some escape and entertainment between the pages of this book.

See you on the next one!

XOXO,
Cambria

ABOUT CAMBRIA HEBERT

Cambria Hebert is a bestselling novelist of more than fifty titles. She went to college for a bachelor's degree, couldn't pick a major, and ended up with a degree in cosmetology. So rest assured her characters will always have good hair.

Besides writing, Cambria loves a pumpkin spice latte, staying up late, sleeping in, and watching K drama until her eyes won't stay open. She considers math human torture and has an irrational fear of chickens (yes, chickens). You can often find her running on the treadmill (she'd rather be eating a donut), painting her toenails (because she bites her fingernails), or walking her chihuahuas (the real bosses of the house).

Cambria has written in many genres, including new adult, sports romance, male/male romance, sci-fi, thriller, suspense, contemporary romance, and young adult. Many of her titles have been translated into foreign languages and have been the recipients of multiple awards.

Awards Cambria has received include:

Author of the Year 2016 (UtopiaCon2016)
The Hashtag Series: Best Contemporary Series of 2015 (UtopiaCon 2015)
#Nerd: Best Contemporary Book Cover of 2015 (UtopiaCon 2015)
Romeo from the Hashtag Series: Best Contemporary Lead (UtopiaCon 2015)
#Nerd: Top 50 Summer Reads (Buzzfeed.com 2015)
The Hashtag Series: Best Contemporary Series of 2016 (UtopiaCon 2016)
#Nerd Book Trailer: Best Book Trailer of 2016 (UtopiaCon 2016)
#Nerd Book Trailer: Top 50 Most Cinematic Book Trailers of All Time (film-14.com)
#Nerd: Book Most Wanted to be Adapted to Screen: (2018)
Amnesia: Mystery Book of the Year (2018)

Cambria Hebert owns and operates Cambria Hebert Books, LLC.
You can find out more about Cambria and her titles by visiting her website:
http://www.cambriahebert.com

CPSIA information can be obtained
at www.ICGtesting.com
Printed in the USA
BVHW070149220122
626772BV00001B/30

9 781946 836366